The children looked up into the broad, leafy
boughs of the tree. They felt tremendously
excited. The Faraway Tree in the Enchanted
Wood! Oh, what magic there seemed to be in
the very names!

They picked up their basket and went home,
all of them thinking the same thought:

'We must go up the Faraway Tree and see
what is at the top!'

Also by Enid Blyton in Egmont

Enid Blyton™

The Faraway Tree Stories

The Enchanted Wood
The Magic Faraway Tree
The Folk of the Faraway Tree

 EGMONT

First published in Great Britain as three separate volumes:

The Enchanted Wood
First published by Newnes 1939
Text copyright © 1939 Enid Blyton Limited
Illustration copyright © 2001 Jill Newton

The Magic Faraway Tree
First published by Newnes 1943
Text copyright © 1943 Enid Blyton Limited
Illustration copyright © 2001 Jill Newton

The Folk of the Faraway Tree
First published by Newnes 1946
Text copyright © 1946 Enid Blyton Limited
Illustration copyright © 2001 Jill Newton

The omnibus edition first published 1994
This edition published 2002
by Egmont Books Limited
239 Kensington High Street
London W8 6SA

ISBN 1 4052 0171 1

10 9 8 7 6 5 4 3

A CIP catalogue record for this title is available from
the British Library

Typeset by Dorchester Typesetting Group Ltd, Dorset
Printed and bound in Great Britain
by Cox & Wyman Ltd, Reading, Berkshire

The Enchanted Wood

CONTENTS

CONTENTS continued

I. HOW THEY FOUND
THE MAGIC WOOD

There were once three children, called Joe, Beth and
Frannie. All their lives they had lived in a town, but
now their father had a job in the country, so they were
all to move as soon as they possibly could.

'What fun to be in the country!' said Joe. 'I shall
learn all about animals and birds!'

'And I shall pick as many flowers as I want to,' said
Beth.

'And I shall have a garden of my own,' said Frannie.

When the day came for the move all the children
were excited. A small van came to their door and two
men helped their father and mother to pile everything
into it. When it was full the van drove away, and the
children put on their coats and hats to go with their
mother to catch a train to the station.

'Now we're off!' cried Joe.

'The country, the country!' sang Beth.

'We might see fairies there!' said Frannie.

The train whistled, and chuffed out of the station.
The children pressed their noses to the window and
watched the dirty houses and the chimneys race by.
How they hated the town! How lovely it would be to
be in the clean country, with flowers growing
everywhere, and birds singing in the hedges!

'We might have adventures in the country,' said Joe.
'There will be streams and hillsides, big fields and

1

dark woods. Oooh, it will be lovely!'

'You won't have any more adventures in the country than you will have in the town,' said their father. 'I dare say you will find it all very dull.'

But that's where he was quite wrong. My goodness, the things that happened to those three children!

They arrived at last at the tiny station where they were to get out. A sleepy-looking porter put their two bags on a trolley, and said he would bring them along later. Off they all went down the winding country lane, chattering loudly.

'I wonder if we've got a garden?' said Frannie.

But before they reached their new home they were tired out and could not bother to say a word more to each other. Their cottage was five miles from the station, and as the children's father could not afford to do anything but walk there, it seemed a very long way indeed. There was no bus to take them, so the tired children dragged their feet along, wishing for a glass of warm milk and a cosy bed.

At last they got there – and dear me, it was worth all the walk, for the cottage was sweet. Roses hung from the walls – red and white and pink – and honeysuckle was all round the front door. It was lovely!

The van was at the door, and the two men were moving all the furniture into the little house. Father helped, whilst Mother went to light the kitchen stove to make them all a hot drink.

They were so tired that they could do nothing but drink hot milk, eat some toast and tumble into their roughly-made beds. Joe looked out of the window but he was too sleepy to see properly. In one minute the two girls in their small room were asleep, and Joe too, in his even tinier room.

What fun it was to wake up in the morning and see the sun shining in at strange windows! It didn't take Joe, Beth and Frannie very long to dress. Then they were out in the little garden, running through the grass that had grown so long, and smelling the roses that grew all around.

Mother had cooked eggs for them, and they ate their breakfast hungrily.

'It's lovely to be in the country!' said Joe, looking out of the window to the far-away hills.

'We can grow vegetables in the garden,' said Beth.

'There will be glorious walks all round,' said Frannie.

That day everyone helped to get the little house straight and tidy. Father was going to work the next

day. Mother hoped there would be someone to give her washing to do, then she would make enough money to buy a few hens. That would be lovely!

'I shall collect the eggs each morning and evening,' said Frannie happily.

'Let's go out and see what the country round about is like,' said Joe. 'Can you spare us for an hour, Mother?'

'Yes, run along,' said Mother. So off the three children went, out of the tiny white front gate and into the lane.

They explored all round about. They ran across a field where pink clover was full of bees. They paddled in a small brown stream that chattered away to itself under the willow trees in the sunshine.

And then they suddenly came to the wood. It was not far from their cottage, at the back. It looked quite an ordinary wood, except that the trees were a darker green than usual. A narrow ditch separated the wood from the overgrown lane.

'A wood!' said Beth, in delight. 'We shall be able to have picnics here!'

'It's rather a mysterious sort of wood,' said Joe thoughtfully. 'Don't you think so, Beth?'

'Well, the trees are rather thick, but they seem about the same as any others,' said Beth.

'They don't quite,' said Frannie. 'The noise the leaves make is different. Listen!'

They listened – and Frannie was right. The leaves of the trees in the wood did not rustle in quite the same way as other trees nearby did.

'It's almost as if they were really talking to one

another,' said Beth. 'Whispering secrets – real secrets, that we just can't understand.'

'It's a magic wood!' said Frannie suddenly.

Nobody said anything. They stood and listened. 'Wisha-wisha-wisha-wisha-wisha!' said the trees in the wood, and bent towards one another in a friendly way.

'There might be fairy-folk in there,' said Beth. 'Shall we jump over the ditch and go in?'

'No,' said Joe. 'We might get lost. Let's find our way around before we go into big woods like this.'

'Joe! Beth! Frannie!' suddenly came their mother's voice from the cottage not far off. 'It's time for lunch, time for lunch!'

The children felt hungry all at once. They forgot the strange wood and ran back to their new home. Mother had new bread with strawberry jam for them, and they ate a whole loaf between them.

Father came in as they were finishing. He had been shopping for Mother in the village three miles away and he was hungry and tired.

'We've been exploring everywhere, Father!' said Beth, pouring him out a big cup of tea.

'We've found a lovely wood,' said Joe. 'The trees really seem to be talking to one another, Father.'

'That must be the wood I've heard about this afternoon,' said Father. 'It has a strange name, children.'

'What is it called?' asked Joe.

'It's called the Enchanted Wood,' said their father. 'People don't go there if they can help it. It's funny to hear things like this nowadays, and I don't expect there is really anything strange about the wood. But just be careful not to go too far into it, in case you get lost.'

The children looked in excitement at one another. The Enchanted Wood! What a lovely name!

And each child secretly thought the same thought – 'I shall go and explore the Enchanted Wood as soon as ever I can!'

Their father set them to work in the overgrown garden once they had finished their meal. Joe had to pull up the tough thistles and the two girls had to weed the untidy vegetable bed. They spoke to one another in joyful voices.

'The Enchanted Wood! We knew there was something magical about it!'

'I guessed there were fairies there!' said Frannie.

'We'll do some more exploring as soon as we can!' cried Beth. 'We'll find out what those whispering trees are saying! We'll know all the secrets of the wood before many weeks are past!'

And that night, at bedtime, all three stood at the window, looking out on the dark, whispering wood behind the cottage. What would they find in the Enchanted Wood?

II. FIRST VISIT TO THE WOOD

The three children had no chance to visit the Enchanted Wood until the next week, because they had to help their mother and father all they could. There was the garden to get tidy, clothes and kitchen things to be unpacked and put away, and a great deal of cleaning to be done.

Sometimes Joe was free and could have gone by himself. Sometimes the girls were sent out for a walk, but Joe was busy. None of them wanted to go without the others, so they had to wait. And then at last their chance came.

'You can have your lunch outdoors today,' said Mother. 'You've worked well, all of you, and you deserve a picnic. I'll cut you some sandwiches, and you can take along some nice fresh milk.'

'We'll go to the Wood!' whispered Beth to the others, and with excited faces and beating hearts they helped their mother to pack their picnic into a big basket.

They set off. There was a small gate at the bottom of their back garden that led into the overgrown lane running by the wood. They unlatched the gate and stood in the lane. They could see the trees in the wood, and hear them talking their strange tree-talk: 'Wisha-wisha-wisha-wisha!'

'I feel as if there are adventures about,' said Joe.

'Come on! Over the ditch we go – and into the Enchanted Wood!'

One by one the children jumped over the narrow ditch. They stood beneath the trees and peered about. Small freckles of sunshine lay here and there on the ground, but not very many, for the trees were so thick. It was dim and green there, and a small bird nearby sang an odd little song over and over again.

'It really *is* magic!' said Frannie suddenly. 'I can feel magic about somewhere, can't you, Beth? Can't you, Joe?'

'Yes,' said the others, and their eyes shone with excitement. 'Come on!'

They went down a little green path that looked as if it had been made for rabbits, it was so small and narrow.

'Don't let's go too far,' said Joe. 'We had better wait till we know the paths a bit better before we go deep into the wood. Look about for a place to sit down and have our sandwiches, girls.'

'I can see some wild strawberries!' cried Beth, and she knelt down and pressed back some pretty leaves, showing the others deep red strawberries below.

'Let's pick some and have them with our picnic too,' said Frannie. So they picked hard, and soon had enough to make a fine meal.

'Let's sit down under that old oak tree over there,' said Joe. 'It's all soft moss beneath. It will be like sitting on a green velvet cushion.'

So they sat down, and unpacked their sandwiches. Soon they were munching away happily, listening to the dark green leaves overhead saying 'Wisha-wisha' all the time.

And it was whilst they were in the middle of their picnic that they saw a very peculiar thing. Frannie noticed it first.

Not far off was a clear piece of soft grass. As Frannie looked at it she noticed bumps appearing on it. She stared in surprise. The bumps grew. The earth rose up and broke in about six places.

'Look!' said Frannie, in a low voice, pointing to the piece of grass. 'What's happening over there?'

All three of them watched in silence. And then they saw what it was. Six big toadstools were growing quickly up from the ground, pushing their way through, and rising up steadily!

'I've never seen *that* happen before!' said Joe, in astonishment.

'Shh!' said Beth. 'Don't make a noise. I can hear footsteps.'

The others listened. Sure enough they heard the sound of pattering feet and little high voices.

'Let's get behind a bush – quickly,' said Beth suddenly. 'Whoever it is that is coming will be frightened if they see us. There's magic happening here, and we want to see it!'

They scrambled up and crept quietly behind a thick bush, taking their basket with them. They hid just in time, for even as Beth settled down and parted the leaves of the bush to peep through, there came a troop of small men with long beards almost reaching the ground!

'Elves!' whispered Joe.

The elves went to the toadstools and sat down on

them. They were holding a meeting. One of them had a bag with him which he put down behind his toadstool. The children could not hear what was being said, but they heard the sound of the chattering voices, and caught one or two words.

Suddenly Joe nudged Beth and Frannie. He had seen something else. The girls saw it too. An ugly, gnome-like fellow was creeping up silently behind the meeting on the toadstools. None of the elves saw him or heard him.

'He's after that bag!' whispered Joe. And so he was! He reached out a long arm. His bony fingers closed on the bag. He began to draw it away under a bush.

Joe jumped up. He was not going to watch people being robbed without saying something! He shouted loudly:

'Stop thief! Hey, look at that gnome behind you!'

In a fright the elves all leapt up. The gnome jumped to his feet and sped off with the bag. The elves stared after him in dismay, not one of them following him. The robber ran towards the children's bush. He didn't know they were there.

As quick as lightning Joe put out his foot and tripped up the running gnome. Down he went, crash! The bag flew from his hand and Beth picked it up and threw it to the astonished elves, who were still standing by the toadstools. Joe tried to grab the gnome – but he was up and off like a bird.

The children tore after him. In between the trees they went, dodging here and there – and at last they saw the gnome leap up to the low branches of a great tree, and pull himself into the leaves. The children sank down at the bottom, out of breath.

'We've got him now!' said Joe. 'He can't get down without being caught!'

'Here are the elves coming,' said Beth, wiping her hot forehead. The little bearded men ran up and bowed.

'You are very good to us,' said the biggest one. 'Thank you for saving our bag. We have valuable papers in there.'

'We've got the gnome for you too,' said Joe, as he pointed up into the tree. 'He went up there. If you surround the tree and wait, you will be able to catch him as he comes down.'

But the elves would not come too near the tree. They looked half-frightened of it.

'He will not come down until he wants to,' said the biggest elf. 'That is the oldest and most magic tree in the world. It is the Faraway Tree.'

'The Faraway Tree!' said Beth, in wonder. 'What an odd name! Why do you call it that?'

'It's a very strange tree,' said another elf. 'Its top

reaches the far-away places in a way we don't understand. Sometimes its top branches may be in Witchland, sometimes in lovely countries, sometimes in peculiar places that no one has ever heard of. We never climb it because we never know what might be at the top!'

'How very strange!' said the children.

'The gnome has got into whatever place there is at the top of the tree today,' said the biggest elf. 'He may live there for months and never come down again. It's no good waiting for him – and it's certainly no good going after him. His name is Creepy, because he is for ever creeping about quietly.'

The children looked up into the broad, leafy boughs of the tree. They felt tremendously excited. The Faraway Tree in the Enchanted Wood! Oh, what magic there seemed to be in the very names!

'If only we could climb up!' said Joe longingly.

'You must never do that,' said the elves at once. 'It's dangerous. We must go now – but we do thank you for your help. If ever you want us to help *you*, just come into the Enchanted Wood and whistle seven times under the oak tree not far from our toadstools.'

'Thank you,' said the children, and stared after the six small elves as they ran off between the trees. Joe thought it was time to go home, so they followed the little men down the narrow green path until they came to the part of the wood they knew. They picked up their basket and went home, all of them thinking the same thought:

'We *must* go up the Faraway Tree and see what is at the top!'

III. UP THE FARAWAY TREE

The children did not tell their father and mother about the happenings in the Enchanted Wood, for they were so afraid that they might be forbidden to go there. But when they were alone they talked about nothing else.

'When do you suppose we could go up the Faraway Tree?' Frannie kept asking. 'Oh, do let's go, Joe.'

Joe wanted to go very badly – but he was a little afraid of what might happen, and he knew that he ought to look after his two sisters and see that no harm came to them. Just suppose they all went up the Faraway Tree and never came back!

Then he had an idea. 'Listen,' he said. 'I know what we'll do. We'll climb up the tree and just *see* what is at the top! We don't need to go there – we can just look. We'll wait until we have a whole day to ourselves, then we'll go.'

The girls were so excited. They worked hard in the house hoping that their mother would say they could have the whole day to themselves. Joe worked hard in the garden, too, clearing away all the weeds. Their parents were very pleased.

'Would you like to go to the nearest town and have a day there?' asked Mother, at last.

'No, thank you,' said Joe, at once. 'We've had enough of towns, Mother! What we'd really like is to go and have a whole-day picnic in the wood!'

'Very well,' said Mother. 'You can go tomorrow. Father is going off for the day to buy some things we need. And I have things to do here in the cottage. So, as I'll be close by you can take your lunch and dinner and go off by yourselves, if it is fine and sunny.'

How the children hoped the day would be fine! They woke early and jumped out of bed. They pulled their curtains open and looked out. The sky was as blue as cornflowers. The sun shone between the trees, and the shadows lay long and dewy on the grass. The Enchanted Wood stood dark and mysterious behind their garden.

They all had breakfast, then Mother cut sandwiches, and put them in a bag along with three cakes each. She sent Joe to pick some plums from the garden, and told Beth to take two bottles of lemonade. The children were most excited.

Father set off to town, and the children waved goodbye to him from the gate. Then they tore off indoors to get the bag in which their food had been put. They said goodbye to their mother and slammed the cottage door. Ah, adventures were in the air that morning!

> *Up the Faraway Tree,*
> *Joe, Beth and Me!*

sang Frannie loudly.

'Hush!' said Joe. 'We are not far from the Enchanted Wood. We don't want anyone to know what we're going to do.'

14

They ran down the back garden and
out of the little gate at the end. They stood
still in the overgrown, narrow lane and
looked at one another. It was the first big adventure of
their lives! What were they going to see? What were
they going to do?

They jumped over the ditch and into the wood. At
once they felt different. Magic was all around them.
The birds' songs sounded different. The trees once
again whispered secretly to one another: 'Wisha-
wisha-wisha-wisha!'

'Ooooh!' said Frannie, shivering with delight.

'Come on,' said Joe, going down the green path.
'Let's find the Faraway Tree.'

They followed him. He went on until he came to
the oak tree under which they had sat before. There
were the six toadstools too, on which the elves had
held their meeting, though the toadstools looked
rather brown and old now.

'Which is the way now?' said Beth, stopping. None
of them knew. They set off down a little path, but they
soon stopped, for they came to a strange place where
the trees stood so close together that they could go no
farther. They went back to the oak tree.

'Let's go this other way,' said Beth, so they set off in
a different direction. But this time they came to a
curious pond, whose waters were pale yellow, and
shone like butter. Beth didn't like the look of the pond
at all, and the three of them went back once more to
the oak tree.

'This is too bad,' said Frannie,
almost crying. 'Just when we've

15

got a whole day to ourselves we can't find the tree!'

'I'll tell you what we'll do,' said Joe suddenly. 'We'll call those elves. Don't you remember how they said they would help us whenever we wanted them?'

'Of course!' said Frannie. 'We had to stand under this oak tree and whistle seven times!'

'Go on, Joe, whistle,' said Beth. So Joe stood beneath the thick green leaves of the old oak and whistled loudly, seven times, 'Phooee, phooee, phooee, phooee, phooee, phooee, phooee!'

The children waited. In about half a minute a rabbit popped its head out of a nearby rabbit-hole and stared at them.

'Who do you want?' said the rabbit, in a furry sort of voice.

The children stared in surprise. They had never heard an animal speak before. The rabbit put his ears up and down and spoke again, rather crossly.

'Are you deaf? Who do you WANT? I said.'

'We want one of the elves,' said Joe, finding his tongue at last.

The rabbit turned and called down his hole, 'Mr Whiskers! Mr Whiskers! There's someone wanting you!'

There came a voice shouting something in answer, and then one of the six elves squeezed out of the rabbit-hole and stared at the children.

'Sorry to be so long,' he said. 'One of the rabbit's children has the measles, and I was down seeing to it.'

'I didn't think rabbits got the measles,' said Beth, astonished.

'They more often get the weasels,' said Mr

Whiskers. 'Weasels are even more catching than measles, as far as rabbits are concerned!'

He grinned as if he had made a huge joke, but as the children had no idea that weasels were savage little animals that caught rabbits, they didn't laugh.

'We wanted to ask you the way to the Faraway Tree,' said Beth. 'We've forgotten it.'

'I'll take you,' said Mr Whiskers, whose name was really a very good one, for his beard reached his toes. Sometimes he trod on it, and this jerked his head downwards suddenly. Beth kept wanting to laugh but she thought she had better not. She wondered why he didn't tie it round his waist out of the way of his feet.

Mr Whiskers led the way between the dark trees. At last he reached the trunk of the enormous Faraway Tree. 'Here you are!' he said. 'Are you expecting someone down it today?'

'Well, no,' said Joe. 'We rather wanted to go up it by ourselves.'

'Go up it by yourselves!' said Mr Whiskers, in horror. 'Don't be silly. It's dangerous. You don't know what might be at the top. There's a different place almost every day!'

'Well, we're going,' said Joe firmly, and he set his foot against the trunk of the tremendous tree and took hold of a branch above his head. 'Come on, girls!'

'I shall fetch my brothers and get you down,' said Mr Whiskers, in a fright, and he scuttled off, crying. 'It's so dangerous! It's so dangerous!'

'Do you suppose it *is* all right to go?' asked Beth, who was usually the sensible one.

'Come on, Beth!' said Joe impatiently. 'We're only

going to *see* what's at the top! Don't be a baby!'

'I'm not,' said Beth, and she and Frannie hauled themselves up beside Joe. 'It doesn't look *very* difficult to climb. We'll soon be at the top.'

But it wasn't as easy as they thought, as you will see!

IV. THE FOLK IN THE FARAWAY TREE

Before very long the children were hidden in the branches as they climbed upwards. When Mr Whiskers came back with five other elves, not a child could be seen!

'Hey, come down!' yelled the elves, dancing round the tree. 'You'll be captured or lost. This tree is dangerous!'

Joe laughed and peered down. The Faraway Tree seemed to be growing acorns just where he was, so he picked one and threw it down. It hit Mr Whiskers on the hat and he rushed away, shouting, 'Oh, something's hit me! Something's hit me!'

Then there was silence. 'They've gone,' said Joe, laughing again. 'I expect they don't much like when it rains acorns, funny little things! Come on, girls!'

'This must be an oak tree if it grows acorns,' said Beth, as she climbed. But just as she said that she stared in surprise at something nearby. It was a prickly chestnut case, with hard nuts inside!

'Good gracious!' she said. 'It's growing horse chestnuts just here! What a very peculiar tree!'

'Well, let's hope it will grow apples and pears higher up,' said Frannie, with a giggle. 'It's a most extraordinary tree!'

Soon they were quite high up. When Joe parted the leaves and tried to see out of the tree he was amazed to find that he was far higher than the tallest tree in the wood. He and the girls looked down on the top of all the other trees, which looked like a broad green carpet below.

Joe was higher up than the girls. Suddenly he gave a shout. 'I say, girls! Come up here by me, quickly! I've found something odd!'

Beth and Frannie climbed quickly up.

'Why, it's a window in the tree!' said Beth, in astonishment. They all peered inside, and suddenly the window was flung open and an angry little face looked out, with a nightcap on.

'Rude creatures!' shouted the angry little man, who looked like a pixie. 'Everybody that climbs the tree peeps in at me! It doesn't matter what I'm doing, there's always someone peeping!'

The children were too astonished to do anything but stare. The pixie disappeared and came back with a jug of water. He flung it at Beth and soaked her. She gave a scream.

'Perhaps you won't peep into other people's houses next time,' said the pixie with a grin, and he slammed his window shut again and drew the curtain.

'Well!' said Beth, trying to wipe herself dry with her handkerchief. 'What a rude little man!'

'We'd better not look in at any windows we pass,' said Joe. 'But I was so surprised to *see* a window in the tree!'

Beth soon got dry. They climbed up again, and soon had another surprise. They came to a broad branch that led to a yellow door set neatly in the big trunk of the Faraway Tree. It had a little door-knocker and a brightly-polished bell. The children stared at the door.

'I wonder who lives there?' said Frannie.

'Shall we knock and see?' said Joe.

'Well, I don't want water all over me again,' said Beth.

'We'll ring the bell and then hide behind this branch,' said Joe. 'If anyone thinks he is going to throw water at us he won't find us.'

So Joe rang the bell and then they all hid carefully behind a big branch. A voice came from the inside of the door.

'I'm washing my hair! If that's the butcher, please leave a pound of sausages!'

The children stared at one another and laughed. It was odd to hear of butchers coming up the Faraway Tree. The voice shouted again:

'If it's the oil man, I don't want anything. If it's the red dragon, he must call again next week!'

'Good gracious!' said Beth, looking rather frightened. 'The red dragon! I don't like the sound of that!'

At that moment the yellow door opened and a small fairy looked out. Her hair was fluffed out round her shoulders, drying, and she was rubbing it with a towel. She stared at the peeping children.

'Did *you* ring my bell?' she asked. 'What do you want?'

'We just wanted to see who lived in the funny little tree-house,' said Joe, peering in at the dark room inside the tree. The fairy smiled. She had a very sweet face.

'Come in for a moment,' she said. 'My name is Silky, because of my silky hair. Where are you off to?'

'We are climbing the Faraway Tree to see what is at the top,' said Joe.

'Be careful you don't find something horrid,' said Silky, giving them each a chair in her dark little tree-room. 'Sometimes there are delightful places at the top of the tree – but sometimes there are strange lands too. Last week there was the land of Hippety-Hop, which was dreadful. As soon as you got there, you had to hop on one leg, and everything went hippety-hop, even the trees. Nothing ever kept still. It was most tiring.'

'It does sound exciting,' said Beth. 'Where's our food, Joe? Let's ask Silky to have some.'

Silky was pleased. She sat there brushing her beautiful golden hair and ate sandwiches with them. She brought out a tin of Pop Cakes, which were lovely. As soon as you bit into them they went pop! and you suddenly found your mouth filled with new honey from the middle of the little cakes. Frannie took seven, one after another, for she was rather greedy. Beth stopped her.

'*You'll* go pop if you eat any more!' she said.

'Do a lot of people live in this tree?' asked Joe.

'Yes, lots,' said Silky. 'They move in and out, you know. But I'm always here, and so is the Angry Pixie, down below.'

'Yes, we've seen *him*!' said Beth. 'Who else is there?'

'There's a Mister Watzisname above me,' said Silky. 'Nobody knows his name, and he doesn't know it himself, so he's called Mister Watzisname. Don't wake him if he's asleep. He might chase you. Then there's Dame Washalot. She's always washing, and as she pours her water away down the tree, you've got to look out for waterfalls!'

'This is such an interesting and exciting tree,' said Beth, finishing her cake. 'Joe, I think we ought to go now, or we'll never get to the top. Goodbye, Silky. We'll come and see you again one day.'

'Do,' said Silky. 'I'd like to be friends.'

They all left the dear little round room in the tree and began to climb once more. Not long after they heard a peculiar noise. It sounded like an aeroplane throbbing and roaring.

'But there can't be an aeroplane in this tree!' said Joe. He peered all round – and then he saw what was making the noise. A funny old gnome sat in a deckchair on a broad branch, his mouth wide open, his eyes fast shut – snoring hard!

'It's Mister Watzisname!' said Beth. 'What a noise he makes! Mind we don't wake him!'

'Shall I put a cherry in his mouth and see what happens?' asked Joe, who was always ready for a bit of mischief. The Faraway Tree was now growing cherries all around for a change, and there were plenty to pick.

'No, Joe, no!' said Beth. 'You know what Silky said – he might chase us. *I* don't want to fall out of the Faraway Tree and bump down from bough to bough, if *you* do!'

So they all crept past old Mister Watzisname, and went on climbing up and up. For a long time nothing happened except that the wind blew in the tree. The children did not pass any more houses or windows in the tree – and then they heard another noise – rather a peculiar one.

They listened. It sounded like a waterfall – and suddenly Joe guessed what it was.

'It's Dame Washalot throwing out her dirty water!' he yelled. 'Look out, Beth! Look out, Frannie!'

Down the trunk of the tree poured a lot of blue, soapy water. Joe dodged it. Frannie slipped under a broad branch. But poor old Beth got splashed from head to foot. How she shouted!

Joe and Frannie had to lend her their handkerchiefs. 'I'm so unlucky!' sighed Beth. 'That's twice I've been soaked today.'

Up they went again, passing more little doors and windows, but seeing no one else – and at last they saw above them a vast white cloud.

'Look!' said Joe, in amazement. 'This cloud has a hole in it – and the branches go up – and I believe we're at the very top of the tree! Shall we creep through the cloud-hole and see what land is above?'

'Let's!' cried Beth and Frannie – so up they went.

V. THE ROUNDABOUT LAND

One big broad branch slanted upwards at the top of the Faraway Tree. Joe climbed on to it and looked down – but he could see nothing, for a white mist swirled around and about. Above him the enormous thick white cloud stretched, with a purple hole in it through which the topmost branch of the Faraway Tree disappeared.

The children felt tremendously excited. At last they were at the very top. Joe carefully pulled himself up the final branch. He disappeared into the purple hole. Beth and Frannie followed him.

The branch came to an end and a little ladder ran through the cloud. Up the children went – and before they knew what had happened, they were out in the sunshine, in a new and very strange land.

They stood on green grass. Above them was a blue sky. A tune was playing somewhere, going on and on and on.

'It's the sort of tune a carousel or a roundabout plays, Joe,' said Beth. 'Isn't it?'

It was – and then, suddenly, without any warning at all, the whole land began to swing round! The children almost fell over, with the swing-round beginning so suddenly.

'What's happening?' said Beth, frightened. The children felt terribly dizzy, for trees, distant houses, hills, and bushes began to move round. They too felt themselves moving, for the grass was going round as well. They looked for the hole in the cloud – but it had disappeared.

'The whole land is going round and round like a roundabout!' cried Joe, shutting his eyes with dizziness. 'We've passed over the hole in the clouds – we don't know where the topmost branch of the Faraway Tree is now – it's somewhere beneath this land, but goodness knows where!'

'Joe! But how can we get back home again?' cried Frannie, in a fright.

'We'll have to ask someone for help,' said Joe.

The three began to walk away from the patch of green field in which they were standing. Beth noticed that they had been standing on a ring of grass that seemed darker than the grass around. She wondered why it was. But she had no time to say anything, for really it was dreadfully difficult to walk properly in a land that was going round and round like a proper carousel all the time!

The music went on and on too, hurdy-gurdy, hurdy-gurdy. Joe wondered where it came from, and where the machinery was that worked the strange Roundabout Land.

Soon they met a tall man singing loudly from a book. Joe stopped him, but he went on singing. It was annoying.

'Hey-diddle, ho-diddle, round and round and round!' shouted the man, whilst Joe tried to make himself heard.

'How can we get away from this land?' Joe shouted.

'Don't interrupt me, hey-diddle, ho-diddle!' sang the man, and he beat time with his finger. Joe caught hold of the bony finger and shouted again.

'Which is the way out of this land, and what land is it?'

'Now you've made me lose my time,' said the tall man crossly. 'I shall have to begin my song again.'

'What is this land, please?' asked Frannie.

'It's Roundabout Land,' said the tall man. 'I should have thought anyone would have guessed that. You can't get away from it. It goes round and round always, and only stops once in a blue moon.'

'There must have been a blue moon when *we* climbed into it!' groaned Joe. 'It had certainly stopped then.'

The man went off, singing loudly. 'Hey-diddle, ho-diddle, round and round and round.'

'Silly old round-and-round!' said Frannie. 'Really, we do seem to meet the most peculiar people!'

'What I'm worried about is getting home,' said Beth. 'Mother will be anxious if we are not back before long. What shall we do, Joe?'

'Let's sit down under this tree and have a bit more to eat,' said Joe. So they sat down, and munched solemnly, hearing roundabout music going on all the time, and watching the distant hills and trees swinging round against the sky. It was all very strange.

Presently a pair of rabbits lolloped up and looked at the children. Frannie loved animals and she threw a bit of cake to them. To her surprise one of the rabbits picked up the cake in its paw and nibbled it like a monkey!

'Thanks!' said the rabbit. 'It's a change from grass! Where do you come from? We haven't seen you before, and we thought we knew everyone here. Nobody new ever comes to Roundabout Land.'

'And nobody ever gets away,' said the other rabbit, smiling at Frannie, and holding out its paw for a bit of cake too.

'Really?' said Beth, in alarm. 'Well, we are new to it, for we only came about an hour ago. We came up the Faraway Tree.'

'What!' cried both rabbits at once, flopping up their long ears in amazement. 'Up the *Faraway* Tree, did you say? Goodness, you don't mean to say that's touching this land?'

'Yes, it is,' said Beth. 'But I expect as this land is swinging round and round, that the topmost branch might be almost anywhere underneath it – there's no way of finding out.'

'Oh yes, there is!' said the first rabbit excitedly. 'If we burrow down a little way, and make a hole, we can see whereabouts the Faraway Tree is underneath, and we can wait for it to come round again, when the Land swings above it.'

'Well, we came up from the tree just where the grass was darker than the rest,' said Beth. 'I noticed that. Do you suppose that as the Roundabout Land swings round, it will come back to the same place again, and we could slip down the topmost branch?'

'Of course!' said the rabbits. 'We can easily burrow down that green patch of grass, and wait for the Land to turn around just over the tree again. Come on, quickly, there's no time to lose!'

All of them jumped up and sped off. Beth knew the way and so did the rabbits. Soon they were back in the field where the ring of dark grass stood. There was no opening now, leading through a cloud down to the tree. It had gone.

The rabbits began to dig quickly. Soon they found the ladder that led upwards. Then they made such a big hole that the children could see down it to a large white cloud that swirled below the Roundabout Land.

'Nothing there yet,' said the first rabbit, getting out a handkerchief and wiping his dirty front paws. 'We must wait a bit. I only hope the Land hasn't swung on and passed the Faraway Tree altogether!'

The roundabout music went on and on, then suddenly it began to slow down. One of the rabbits peeped out of the hole below and gave a shout.

'The Land has stopped going round – and the Faraway Tree is just nearby – but we can't reach it!'

The children peered through the cloud below the ladder and saw quite clearly that the Faraway Tree was very near – but not near enough to jump on. Whatever were they to do?

'Now don't try to jump,' warned the rabbits, 'or you'll fall right through the cloud.'

'But what shall we *do*?' asked Beth, in despair. 'We *must* get on the tree before we swing away again!'

'I've got a rope,' said one of the rabbits suddenly, and he put his hand into a big pocket and pulled out a yellow rope. He made a loop in one end and then threw it carefully at the topmost branch of a nearby tree. It caught and held! Good!

'Frannie, slip down the rope first,' said Joe. 'I'll hold this end.'

So Frannie, rather afraid, slid down the yellow rope to the tree – and then, just as she got there, the Roundabout music began to play very loudly and quickly, and the Roundabout Land began to move!

'Quick! Quick!' shouted Frannie, as the land swung nearer to the Faraway Tree. 'Jump! Jump!'

They jumped – and the rabbits jumped after them. The Roundabout Land swung off. The big white cloud covered everything. The children and the rabbits clung to the topmost branch and looked at one another.

'We look like monkeys on a stick,' said Joe, and they all began to giggle. 'My goodness, what an adventure! I vote we don't come up here again.'

But, as you may guess, they did!

VI. MOON-FACE AND
THE SLIPPERY-SLIP

The children clung to the top branches of the Faraway
Tree, whilst the rabbits slid down a bit lower. They
could still hear the enchanting music of the
Roundabout Land as it swung round overhead.

'We'd better get home,' said Joe, in rather a quiet
voice. 'It's been just a bit too exciting.'

'Come on then,' said Beth, beginning to climb
down. 'It will be easier to get down than it was to
climb up!'

But Frannie was very tired. She began to cry as she
clung to her branch. She was the youngest, and not so
strong as Joe and Beth.

'I shall fall,' she wept. 'I know I shall fall.'

Joe and Beth looked at one another in alarm. This
would never do. There was such a long way to fall!

'Dear Frannie, you simply *must* try!' said Joe,
gently. 'We've got to get home safely.'

But Frannie clung to her branch and wept great
tears. The two rabbits looked at her, most upset. One
put his paw into her hand. 'I'll help you,' he said.

But Frannie wouldn't be helped. She was tired out
and afraid of everything now. She wept so loudly that
two birds nearly flew off in fright.

Just as the others were really in despair, a small
door flew open in the trunk of the tree not far below,
and a round moon-like face looked out.

'Hey there! What's the matter?' shouted the moon-faced person. 'A fellow can't get any sleep at all with that awful noise going on!'

Frannie stopped crying and looked at Moon-Face in surprise. 'I'm crying because I'm frightened of climbing down the tree,' she said. 'I'm sorry I woke you up.'

Moon-Face beamed at her. 'Have you got any toffee?' he asked. (He liked chewy sweet things to eat.)

'Toffee!' said everyone in surprise. 'What do you want toffee for?'

'To eat, of course,' said Moon-Face. 'I just thought if you had any toffee to give me I'd let you slide down my slippery-slip – you get down to the bottom very quickly that way, you know.'

'A slide all the way down the Faraway Tree!' cried Joe, hardly believing his ears. 'Good gracious! Who ever would have thought of that!'

'*I* thought of it!' said Moon-Face, beaming again just like a full moon. 'I let people use it if they pay me toffee.'

'Oh!' said the three children, and looked at one another in dismay, for none of them had any toffee. Then Joe shook his head.

'We've no toffee,' he said. 'But I've a bar of chocolate, a bit squishy, but quite nice.'

'Won't do,' said Moon-Face. 'I don't like chocolate. What about the rabbits? Haven't they got any toffee either?'

The rabbits turned out their pockets. They had a very curious collection of things, but no toffee.

'Sorry,' said Moon-Face, and slammed his door

shut. Frannie began to cry again.

Joe climbed down to the door and banged on it. 'Hey, old Moon-Face!' he shouted. 'I'll bring you some lovely home-made toffee next time I'm up the tree if you'll let us use your slippery-slip.'

The door flew open again, and Moon-Face beamed out. 'Why didn't you say so before?' he asked. 'Come in.'

One by one the rabbits and the children climbed down to the door and went in. Moon-Face's house in the tree was very peculiar. It was one round room, and in the middle of it was the beginning of the slippery-slip that ran down the whole trunk of the tree, winding round and round like a spiral staircase.

Round the top of the slide was a curved bed, a curved table, and two curved chairs, made to fit the roundness of the tree-trunk. The children were astonished, and wished they had time to stay for a while. But Moon-Face pushed them towards the slide.

'You want a cushion each,' he said. 'Hey you, rabbit, take the top one and go first.'

One of the rabbits took an orange cushion and set it at the top of the slide. He sat down on it, looking a little nervous. 'Go on, hurry up!' said Moon-Face. 'You don't want to stay all night, do you?' He gave the rabbit a hard push, and the rabbit slid down the slippery-slip at a tremendous pace, his whiskers and ears blown backwards. Joe thought it looked a lovely thing to do. He went next.

He took a blue cushion, sat on it at the top of the slide and pushed off. Down he went on his cushion, his hair streaming backwards. Round and round and round went the slippery-slip inside the enormous trunk of the old tree. It was quite dark and silent, and lasted a very long time, for the Faraway Tree was tremendously tall. Joe enjoyed every second.

When he came to the bottom his feet touched a sort of trap door in the trunk at the foot of the tree and the trap flew open. Joe shot out and landed on a big tuft of green moss which was grown there to make a soft landing-place. He sat there, out of breath – then he got up quickly, for he didn't want Beth or Frannie landing on top of him.

Beth went next. She flew down on a fat pink cushion, gasping for breath, for she went so fast. Then Frannie went on a green cushion, and then the other rabbit. One by one they shot out of the little trap door, which closed itself tightly as soon as the slider had gone through.

They all sat on the ground, getting their breath and laughing, for it really was funny to shoot down inside a tree on a cushion.

The rabbits stood up first. 'We'd better be going,' they said. 'So pleased to have met you!'

They disappeared down the nearest burrow, and the children waved goodbye. Then Joe stood up.

'Come on,' he said, 'we really must get home. Goodness knows what the time is!'

'Oh, what a lovely way of getting down the Faraway Tree that was!' said Beth, jumping to her feet. 'It was so quick!'

'I loved it,' said Frannie. 'I'd like to climb up the tree every single day just so that I could slide down that super slippery-slip. But – what do we do with the cushions?'

At that moment a red squirrel, dressed in an old jumper, came out of a hole in the trunk.

'Cushions, please!' he said. The children gathered them up and handed them to the squirrel one by one. They were getting quite used to hearing animals talk to them now.

'Are you going to carry all these cushions up the tree to Moon-Face?' asked Frannie, in wonder.

The squirrel laughed. 'Of course not!' he said. 'Moon-Face lets down a rope for them. Look – here it comes!'

A rope came slipping down between the branches. The squirrel caught the end of it and tied the bundle of cushions firmly on to the rope. He gave three tugs, and the rope swung upwards again, taking the cushions with it.

'Good idea!' said Joe, and then they all turned to go home, thinking, as they walked, of the strange and exciting things that had happened that day.

They came to the ditch and jumped across. They went down the little lane and through their little back gate. By the time they reached the cottage they were ready to drop with tiredness. Their mother was still busy in the garden, and their father was not yet home.

So, sleepily, Beth made them all some hot milk, which they took up to their rooms to drink while sitting in bed.

'I'm not going up the Faraway Tree again,' said

Frannie, lying down.

'Well, *I* am!' said Joe. 'Don't forget we promised old Moon-Face some home-made toffee! We can climb up to his house, give him the toffee, and slide down that slippery-slip again. We don't need to go into any land at the top of the tree.'

But Beth and Frannie were fast asleep. And very soon Joe was too – dreaming of the strange Faraway Tree, and the curious folk who lived in its enormous trunk!

VII. BETH MAKES SOME TOFFEE
FOR MOON-FACE

The children talked about nothing else but the Faraway Tree and its strange folk for days after their adventure. Beth said they must certainly keep their promise to take toffee to Moon-Face.

'Promises must never be broken,' she said. 'I will make some toffee if Mother will let me have the sugar, syrup and milk. Then when it's done you can take it to Moon-Face, Joe.'

Mother said they could make toffee on Wednesday, after she had been to the shops. So on Wednesday Beth set to work making the best, sweetest, chewiest toffee she could.

She set it in a pan on the stove. It cooked beautifully. When it had cooled and was set nice and hard, Beth broke it up into small pieces. She put them into a paper bag, gave one piece each to the others, and popped one into her own mouth.

'I'll have to go at night, I think,' said Joe. 'I shan't get any time off this week, I know. We're so busy with the garden now.'

So that night, when the moon was shining brightly in the sky overhead, Joe slipped out of bed. Beth and Frannie woke up and heard him. They hadn't meant to go with him, but when they saw the moonlight shining everywhere and thought of that exciting Faraway Tree, they felt that they simply *couldn't* stay behind! Wouldn't you have felt that too?

They dressed quickly and whispered through Joe's door. 'We're coming too, Joe. Wait for us!'

Joe waited. Then they all three slipped down the creaky stairs and out into the moonlit garden. The shadows were very black indeed, just like ink. There was no colour anywhere, only just the pale, cold moonlight.

They were soon in the Enchanted Wood. But, dear me, it was quite, quite different now! It was simply alive with people and animals! In the very dark parts of the wood little lanterns were hung in rows. In the moonlit parts there were no lanterns, and a great deal of chattering was going on.

Nobody took any notice of the children at all. Nobody seemed surprised to see them. But the children were most astonished at everything!

'There's a market over there!' whispered Joe to Beth. 'Look! There are necklaces made of painted acorns and brooches made of wild roses!'

But Beth was looking at something else – a dance going on in the moonlit dell, with fairies and pixies chattering and laughing together. Sometimes, when they were tired of dancing on their feet, partners would fly in the air and dance there in the moonlight.

Frannie was watching some elves growing toadstools. As fast as the toadstool grew, an elf laid a cloth on it and put glasses of lemonade and tiny cakes there. It was all like a strange dream.

'Oh, I *am* glad we came!' said Beth, in delight. 'Who would have thought that the Enchanted Wood would be like this at night?'

They wasted a great deal of time looking at everything, but at last they got to the Faraway Tree. And even here there was a great difference! The whole tree was hung with strings of tiny lights and glittered softly from branch to branch, rather like a very enormous Christmas Tree.

Joe saw something else. It was a stout rope going from branch to branch, for people to hold on to when they wished to go up the tree.

'Look at that!' he said. 'It will be much easier to go up tonight. All we'll have to do is just to hold on to the rope and pull ourselves up by it! Come on!'

Other folk, and some animals too, were going up the tree. Not to the land at the top, but to visit their friends who lived in the trunk of the enormous old tree. All the doors and windows were open now, and there was a great deal of laughing and talking going on.

The children climbed up and up. When they came to the window of the pixie who had been so angry with them last week because they had peeped in, they found that he was in a very good temper now, sitting smiling at his open window, talking to three owls. But Joe didn't think they had better stop, in case the pixie remembered them and threw water over them again.

So on they went holding on to the thick rope, climbing very easily. They came to Silky's house, and called her. She was at her stove, baking something.

'Hallo!' she said, looking up and smiling.

'So here you are again – just in time, too, because I'm baking Pop Cakes, and they are most delicious hot!'

Her silky golden hair stood out round her tiny face, which was red with baking. Joe took out his bag of toffee.

'We're really taking them to Moon-Face,' he said, 'but do have one!'

Silky took one and then gave them three hot Pop Cakes each. My goodness, how lovely they were, especially when they went pop in the children's mouths!

'We mustn't stop, Silky dear,' said Beth. 'We've still a long way to go up the tree.'

'Well, look out for Dame Washalot's washing water, then,' said Silky. 'She's dreadful at night. She knows there are a lot of people up and down the tree, and she just loves to soak them with her dirty water!'

The children went on up. They passed Mister Watzisname, still fast asleep and snoring in his chair, and dodged Dame Washalot's water sloshing down. Nobody even got splashed this time! Frannie laughed.

'This really is the funniest tree I ever knew,' she said. 'You simply never know what's going to happen!'

They pulled themselves up and up by the rope and came at last to the top. They knocked on Moon-Face's yellow door. 'Come in!' yelled a voice, and in they went.

Moon-Face was sitting on his curved bed, mending one of his cushions. 'Hallo!' he said. 'Did you bring me that toffee you owe me?'

'Yes,' said Joe, handing him the bag. 'There's a lot there, Moon-Face – half to pay you for last week's slippery-slide, and half to pay you if you'll let us go down again tonight.'

'Oh my!' said Moon-Face, looking with great delight into the bag. 'What lovely toffee!'

He crammed four large pieces into his mouth and sucked with joy.

'Is it nice?' said Beth.

'Ooble-ooble-ooble-ooble!' answered Moon-Face, quite unable to speak properly, for his teeth were all stuck together with the toffee! The children laughed.

'Is the Roundabout Land at the top of the Faraway Tree?' asked Joe.

Moon-Face shook his head. 'Oooble!' he said.

'What land is there now?' asked Frannie.

Moon-Face made a face, and screwed up his nose. 'Oooble-oooble-oooble-oooble-oooble!' he said very earnestly.

'Oh dear, we shan't be able to get anything out of him at all whilst he's eating toffee,' said Beth. 'He'll just ooble away. What a pity! I *would* have liked to know what strange land was there tonight.'

'I'll just go and peep!' said Joe, jumping up. Moon-Face looked alarmed. He shook his head, and caught hold of Joe. 'Oooble-oooble-oooble-oooble!' he cried.

'It's all right, Moon-Face, I'm only going to peep,' said Joe. 'I shan't go into the land.'

'OOBLE-OOBLE-OOBLE-OOBLE!' cried Moon-Face in a fright, trying his best to swallow all the toffee so that he could speak properly. 'Oooble!'

Joe didn't listen. He went out of the door with the girls, and climbed up the last branch of the Faraway Tree. What strange land was above it this time? Joe peered up through the dark hole in the cloud, through which a beam of moonlight shone down.

He came to the little ladder that ran up the hole in the cloud. He climbed up it. His head poked out into the land at the top. He gave a shout.

'Beth! Frannie! It's a kind of ice and snow! There are big white bears everywhere! Oh, do come and look!'

But then a dreadful thing happened! Something lifted Joe right off the ladder – and he disappeared into the land of ice and snow above the cloud.

'Come back! Joe, come back!' yelled Moon-Face, swallowing all his toffee in fright. 'You mustn't even look, or the Snowman will get you!'

But Joe was gone. Beth looked at Moon-Face in dismay. 'What *shall* we do?' she said.

VIII. JOE AND THE MAGIC SNOWMAN

Moon-Face was most upset to see Joe disappear. 'I told him not to – I told him!' he groaned.

'You didn't,' sobbed Frannie. 'Your mouth was full of toffee and all you could say was 'Oooble-ooble-ooble!' And how could we know what that meant?'

'Where's Joe now?' asked Beth, quite pale with shock.

Yes, indeed – where *was* Joe? Someone had lifted him right off the ladder, up into the Land of Ice and Snow! And there, strangely enough, the moon and the sun were in the sky at the same time, one at one side and the other opposite, both shining with a pale light.

Joe shivered, for it was very cold. He looked up to see what had lifted him off the ladder, and he saw in front of him a big strange creature – a snowman! He was just like the snowmen Joe had so often made in the wintertime – round and fat and white, with an old hat stuck on his head and a carrot for a nose.

'This is luck!' said the Snowman, in a soft, snowy sort of voice. 'I've been standing by that hole for days, waiting for a seal to come up – and *you* came!'

'Oh,' said Joe, remembering that seals came up to breathe through holes in the ice. 'That wasn't a water-hole – that was the hole that led down the Faraway Tree. I want to go back, please.'

'The hole has closed up,' said the Snowman. Joe

43

looked – and to his great dismay he saw that a thick layer of ice had formed over the hole – so thick that he knew perfectly well he could never break through it.

'Whatever shall I do now?' he said.

'Just what I tell you,' said the Snowman, with a grin. 'This is splendid! In this dull and silent land there is nothing but polar bears and seals and penguins. I have often wanted someone to talk to.'

'How did you get here?' asked Joe, wrapping his coat firmly round him, for he was bitterly cold.

'Ah,' said the Snowman, 'that's a long story! I was made by some children long ago – and when they had finished me, they laughed at me and threw stones at me to break me up. So that night I crept away here – and made myself King, but what's the good of being King if you've only bears and things to talk to? What I want is a really good servant who can talk my language. And now *you've* come!'

'But I don't want to be your servant,' said Joe indignantly.

'Nonsense!' said the Snowman, and he gave Joe a push that nearly sent him over. Then, on big, flat snow-feet he moved forward to where there was a low wall of snow.

'Make me a good house,' he said.

'I don't know how to!' said Joe.

'Oh, just cut blocks of this stiff icy snow and build them up one on top of another,' said the Snowman. 'When you've finished I'll give you a warm coat to wear. Then you won't shiver so much.'

Joe didn't see that he could do anything but obey. So he picked up a shovel that was lying by the wall and began to cut big bricks of the frozen snow. When he had cut about twenty he stopped and placed them one on top of another till one side of the round house was made. Then he began to cut snow-bricks again, wondering all the time how in the world he would ever be able to escape from this strange land.

Joe had often built little snow-houses of soft snow in his garden at home during the winter. Now had made a big one, with proper snow-blocks, as hard as bricks. He quite enjoyed it, though he did wish the girls were there too. When he had finished it, and made a nice rounded roof, the Snowman came shuffling up.

'Very nice,' he said, 'very nice indeed. I can just get in, I think.'

He squeezed his big snow-body inside, and threw out a thick coat for Joe, made of wool as soft and as white as the snow all around. Joe put it on very thankfully. Then he tried to squeeze in after the Snowman, for he wanted to be out of the cold, icy wind.

But he was so squashed between the Snowman and the walls of the snow-house that he couldn't breathe.

'Don't push so,' said the Snowman disagreeably. 'Move up.'

'I can't!' gasped poor Joe. He felt quite certain that he would be pushed right out of the snow-hut through a hole in the wall!

Just then there came a curious grunt at the doorway. The Snowman called out at once.

'Is that you, Furry? Take this boy to your home under the ice. He's a nuisance here. He keeps squashing me!'

45

Joe looked up to see who Furry was – and he saw a great white bear looking in. The bear had a stupid but kind look on his face.

'Ooomph!' said the bear, and pulled Joe out into the open air. Joe knew it was no use to struggle. Nobody could get away from a bear as big as that! But the bear was certainly very kindly.

'Oooomph?' he said to Joe, with a loud grunting noise.

'I don't know what you mean,' said Joe.

The bear said no more. He just took Joe along with him, half carrying the little boy, for Joe found the way very slippery indeed.

They came to a hole that led under the ice and snow. The bear pushed Joe down it – and to Joe's enormous surprise he found there was a big room underneath, with five bears there, big and little! It was quite warm there too – Joe was astonished, for there was no heater, of course.

'Ooomph,' said all the bears politely.

'Ooomph!' said Joe. That pleased the bears very much indeed. They came and shook paws with Joe very solemnly and oomphed all over him.

Joe liked the look of the bears much more than he liked the look of the Snowman. He thought perhaps they might help him to escape from this silly land of ice and snow.

'Could you tell me the way back to the Faraway Tree?' he asked the bears politely and clearly.

The bears looked at one another and then ooomphed at Joe. It was quite clear that they didn't understand a word he said.

'Never mind,' said Joe, with a sigh, and made up his mind to put up with things till he could see a way to escape.

The Snowman was a great nuisance. No sooner did Joe settle himself down for a nap, leaning his head against the big warm body of a bear, than there came a call from the snow-house.

'Hey, boy! Come here and play dominoes with me!'

So Joe had to go and play dominoes, and as the Snowman wouldn't let him come into the house because he said he was squashed, Joe had to sit at the doorway and play, and he nearly froze to bits.

Then another time, just as he was eating a nice bit of fried fish that one of the bears had kindly cooked for him, the Snowman shouted to him to come and make him a window in his house. And Joe had to hurry off and cut a sheet of clear ice to fit into one side of the snow-house for a window! Really, that Snowman was a perfect nuisance!

I wish to goodness I'd never stepped into this silly land, thought Joe a hundred times. It's a good thing the bears are so nice to me. I only wish they could say something else besides 'Ooomph.'

Joe wondered what Beth and Frannie were doing. Were they very upset when he didn't come back? Would they go home and tell their father and mother what had happened?

Beth and Frannie *were* upset! It had been dreadful to see poor Joe disappear through the cloud like that.

Moon-Face looked very solemn too. He could speak quite well now that he had swallowed all his toffee.

'We must rescue him,' he said, his face shining like the full moon.

'How?' asked the girls.

'I must think,' said Moon-Face, and he shut his eyes. His head swelled up with his thinking. He opened his eyes and nodded his head.

'We'll go to Goldilocks and the Three Bears,' he said. 'Her bears know the Land of Ice and Snow. She might be able to help Joe that way.'

'But where does Goldilocks live?' asked Beth, in wonder. 'I thought she was just a fairy tale.'

'Good gracious, no!' said Moon-Face. 'Come on – we'll have to catch the train.'

'What train?' asked Frannie, in astonishment.

'Oh, wait and see!' said Moon-Face. 'Hurry now – go down the slippery-slip and wait for me at the bottom!'

IX. THE HOUSE OF THE
THREE BEARS

Beth took a cushion, put it at the top of the slide, and pushed off. Down she went, whizzzzzzz! She shot to the bottom, flew out of the trap door and landed on the cushion of moss. She had hardly got up before Frannie flew out of the trap door too.

'You know, that slippery-slip is the greatest fun!' said Beth. 'I'd like to do that all day long!'

'Yes, if only we didn't have to climb all the way up the tree first,' said Frannie.

The trap door flew open and out shot Moon-Face on a yellow cushion. He put the three cushions together, whistled to the red squirrel who looked after them, and threw them to him. Then he turned to the waiting girls.

'There's a train at midnight,' he said. 'We shall have to hurry.'

The wood was still bright with moonlight. The three of them hurried between the trees. Suddenly Beth heard the chuffing of a train, and she and Frannie stopped in surprise. They saw a small train winding in and out of the trees, looking for all the world like a old-fashioned clockwork toy train made big! The engine even had a key in its side – as if to wind it up!

There was a small station nearby. Moon-Face caught hold of the girls' hands and ran to it. The train was standing quite still there.

The carriages had tin doors and windows which didn't open, just like those of a clockwork train. Beth tried her hardest to open a door, but it was no use. The train whistled. It was anxious to be off.

'Don't you know how to get into this train?' asked Moon-Face, with a laugh. 'You *are* sillies! You just slide the roof off!'

As he spoke he pushed at the roof – and it slid off like the roof of a toy train's carriage.

'I think this is just a toy clockwork train made big,' said Frannie, climbing over the side of the carriage and getting in at the roof. 'I never saw such a funny train in my life!'

They all got in. Moon-Face couldn't seem to slide the roof on again properly, so he stood up inside the carriage, and when the train went off, Beth and Frannie, who couldn't possibly see out of the tin windows, stood up and looked out of the roof instead. They did look funny!

At the next station, which was called Dolls' Station, three dolls got into the carriage and stared at them very hard. One was so like Beth's own doll at home that she couldn't help staring back.

The second station was called Crosspatch Station, and standing next to the railway tracks were three of the crossest-looking old women that the girls had ever seen. One of them got into their carriage, and the three dolls at once got out, and climbed into the next one.

'Move up!' said the Crosspatch angrily to

Moon-Face. He moved up.

The Crosspatch was an uncomfortable person to travel with. She grumbled all the time, and her basket, which was full of prickly bunches of roses, kept bumping into poor Frannie.

'Here we are, here we are!' sang out Moon-Face, when they got to the next station, and the three of them got out gladly, leaving the Crosspatch grumbling away all to herself.

The station was called Bears Station, and there were a great many teddy-bears about, some brown, some pink, some blue, and some white. When they wanted to talk to one another they kept pressing themselves in the middle, where the button that made them talk was, and then they could talk quite well. Frannie wanted to giggle when she saw them doing this. It did look so funny.

'Please could you tell me the way to the Three Bears' House?' Moon-Face asked a blue teddy-bear politely.

The bear pressed himself in the middle and answered in a nice growly voice, 'Up the lane and down the lane and around the lane.'

'Thank you,' said Moon-Face.

'It sounds a bit funny to me,' said Beth doubtfully.

'Not at all,' said Moon-Face, leading them up a little lane through the honeysuckle. 'Here we are, going *up* a lane – and now you see it goes downhill – so we're going down – and presently we'll turn a corner and go *around* the lane!'

He was right. They went up and then down and then around – and there in front of them, tucked into a woody corner, was the dearest, prettiest little house the girls had ever seen! It was covered with pink roses from top to bottom, and its tiny windows winked in the moonlight as if they had eyes.

Moon-Face knocked at the door. A sleepy voice cried, 'Come in!' Moon-Face opened the door and they all went in. There was a table in front of them, and on it were three steaming bowls of what some people call porridge, and some call oatmeal, and round it were three chairs, one big, one middle-sized, and one tiny.

'It's the House of the Three Bears all right!' whispered Beth excitedly. It was just like seeing a fairy story come true!

'We're here!' said the voice from another room. Moon-Face went in with Beth and Frannie. The other room was a small bedroom, with a big bed in it, a middle-sized bed, and in the cot was a most adorable baby bear with the bluest eyes the girls had ever seen.

'Where's Goldilocks?' asked Moon-Face.

'Gone shopping,' said the father bear.

'Where does she sleep when she's here?' asked Beth, looking round. 'And does she always live with you now?'

'Always,' said the father bear, putting his big nightcap straight. 'She looks after us very well. There's a market on tonight in the Enchanted Wood and she's gone to see if she can buy some porridge cheap. As for where she sleeps, well, she just chooses any of our beds, you know, and we cuddle up together then. But she likes the baby bear's bed best, because it's so soft and warm.'

'She did in the story,' said Frannie.

'What story?' asked the mother bear.

'Well – the story of the three bears,' said Frannie.

'Never heard of it,' said the three bears, all together, which really seemed rather extraordinary to Beth and Frannie. They didn't like to ask any more questions after that.

'Here's Goldilocks now!' said the mother bear. The sound of a little high voice could be heard coming nearer and nearer. The baby bear sprang out of his cot and ran to the door in delight.

A pretty little girl with long, curling golden hair picked him up and hugged him. 'Hallo, dearest!' she said. 'Have you been a good bear?'

Then she saw Beth, Frannie and Moon-Face, and stared at them in surprise. 'Who are you?' she said.

Moon-Face explained about Joe, and how he had gone to the Land of Ice and Snow, where the big white bears lived.

'I'm afraid the Magic Snowman will make him a prisoner there,' said Moon-Face. 'And he'll have to live with the white bears. Could you get your three bears to come with us and ask the white bears to let Joe go free, Goldilocks?'

'But I don't know the way,' said Goldilocks.

'*We* do!' said the father bear suddenly. 'The white bears are cousins of ours. Moon-Face, if you can help us with a little bit of magic, we can visit the Land of Ice and Snow in a few minutes!'

'Good gracious!' said Beth, most astonished. 'But it's ever so far away, right at the top of the Faraway Tree!'

'That doesn't matter,' said the father bear. He took down a large jar from the mantelpiece and filled it with water. He put into it a yellow powder and stirred it with a big black crow's feather.

Moon-Face put his hands into the water and began to sing a string of such strange words that Beth and Frannie felt quite trembly. The water bubbled. It rose up to the top of the jar. It overflowed and ran on to the floor. It turned to ice beneath their feet! A cold wind filled the little house and everyone shivered.

Then Beth looked out of the window – and what she saw there filled her with such amazement that she couldn't say a word, but just pointed.

Frannie looked too – and whatever do you think? Outside lay nothing but ice and snow – they were in the same land as Joe! Though how this land happened neither Beth nor Frannie could make out.

'We're there,' said Moon-Face, taking his hands out of the jar and drying them on his red handkerchief. 'Can you lend us any coats, bears? We shall be cold here.'

The mother bear handed them thick coats out of a cupboard. They put them on. The bears already had thick fur and did not need anything extra.

'Now to go and find Joe!' said Moon-Face. 'Come on, bears – you've got to help!'

X. THE BATTLE OF THE BEARS

Goldilocks, the Three Bears, the girls, and Moon-Face all went out of the little cottage. How strange it seemed to see roses blossoming over the walls, when ice and snow lay all around!

'The thing is – *where* do we go to find the polar bears?' said Goldilocks.

'Over there, towards the sun,' said the father bear. Beth and Frannie were surprised to see both the moon and the sun shining in the sky. They followed the father bear, slipping and sliding, and holding on to one another. It was very cold, and their noses and toes felt as if they were freezing.

Suddenly they saw the little snow-house that Joe had built for the Magic Snowman.

'Look!' said the father bear. 'We'd better make for that.'

But before they got there a big white figure squeezed itself out of the snow-house and saw them. It was the Magic Snowman! As soon as he saw the Three Bears and the others, he began to shout loudly in a windy, snowy voice:

'Enemies! Enemies! Hey, bears, come and send off the enemies!'

'We're not enemies,' yelled Moon-Face, and Goldilocks ran forward to show the Snowman that she was a little girl. But Moon-Face pulled her back. He didn't trust that old Snowman!

The Snowman bent his big fat body down and picked up great handfuls of snow. He threw one at Goldilocks. She ducked down, and it passed over her and hit the baby bear.

'Oooooch!' he said, and sat down in a hurry. Then everything happened at once. A crowd of white polar bears hurried out of their underground home to help the Snowman, and soon the air was full of flying snowballs. The snow was hard, and the balls hurt when they hit anyone. It wasn't a bit of good the girls shouting that they were friends, not enemies. Nobody heard them, and soon there was a fierce battle going on!

'Oh dear!' gasped Beth, trying her best to throw straight. 'This is dreadful! We shall never rescue Joe by behaving like this!'

But there really didn't seem anything else to be done! After all, if people are fighting you, you can't do much but defend yourself, and the Three Bears, and the girls, and Moon-Face felt very angry at having hard snowballs thrown at them.

Smack! Thud! Biff! Squish! The snowballs burst as they hit, and soon there was a great noise of angry 'Ooomphs' from the white bears, and 'Oooches' from the teddy-bears, and yells from the children, and screeches from Moon-Face, who acted as if he was mad, hopping about and yelling and kicking up the snow as well as throwing it! His big round face was a fine target for snowballs, and he was hit more than anybody else. Poor Moon-Face!

Now whilst this fierce battle was going on, where do

you suppose Joe was? As soon as he heard the cry of 'Enemies! Enemies!' he had hidden in a corner, for he didn't want to be mixed up in any fight. When he saw the white bears going out, and he was left all alone, he began at once to think of escaping.

He crept to the hole that led above-ground. The battle was some way off, so Joe did not see that the enemies were really his own friends! If he had he would have gone to join them at once.

What a terrible noise they are all making! he thought. It sounds like a battle between gorillas and bears to me! I'm not going near them – I'd be eaten up or something! I shall just run hard the opposite way and hope I'll meet someone to help me.

So Joe, dressed in his big white woolly coat, and looking just like a little white bear himself, crept off over the ice and snow, not seen by anyone. He ran as soon as he thought he was out of sight. He ran and he ran and he ran.

But he met nobody. Not a soul was to be seen. Only a lonely seal lay on a shelf of ice, but even he dived below as soon as he saw Joe.

And then Joe stopped in the greatest astonishment and stared as if his eyes would fall out of his head. He had come to the cottage of the Three Bears, standing all alone in the middle of the ice and snow – and, of course, its roses were still blooming round it, scenting the air.

'I'm dreaming!' said Joe. 'I simply *must* be dreaming! A cottage – with roses – here in the middle of the snow! Well – I shall go and see who lives there.

Perhaps they would give me something to eat and let me rest, for I'm very hungry and tired.'

He knocked at the door. There was no answer. He opened the door and went in. How he stared! There was no one to be seen at all, but on the table stood three bowls of steaming porridge, one big, one middle-sized, and one small. It was rather dark, so Joe lighted a big candle on the table.

Then he sank down into the biggest chair – but it was far too big and he got up again. He sat down in the next sized chair – but that was too piled up with cushions, and he got up to sit in the smallest chair. That was just right, and Joe settled down comfortably – but alas, his weight was too much for it, and the chair broke to bits beneath him!

He looked at the delicious porridge. He tasted the porridge in the biggest bowl – it was much too hot and burnt his tongue. He tasted the next bowl – but that was far too sweet. But when he tasted the porridge in the little bowl, it was just right.

So Joe ate it all up! Then he felt so sleepy that he thought he really must rest. So he went into the bedroom and lay down on the biggest bed. But it was far too big, so he tried the middle-sized one. That was too soft and went down in the middle, so Joe lay down on the cot. And that was so small and warm and comfortable that he fell fast asleep!

All this time the snowball battle was going on. The Snowman was so big and the polar bears were so fierce that very soon the Three Bears, the children, and Moon-Face were driven backwards.

Then a snowstorm blew up, and the snow fell so

thickly that it was quite impossible to see anything. Moon-Face called out in alarm:

'Bears! Goldilocks! Beth! Frannie! Take hold of each other's hands at once and don't let go. One of us might easily be lost in the storm!'

Everyone at once took hands. The snow blew into their faces and they could see nothing. Bending forwards they began to walk carefully away from the white bears, who had stopped fighting now and were trying to find out where their enemies were.

'Don't shout or anything,' said Moon-Face. 'We don't want the white bears to hear us, in case they take us prisoners. They might not listen to the Three Bears. Move off, and we'll look for some sort of shelter till this storm is over.'

They were all very miserable. They were cold, rather frightened, and quite lost. They stumbled over the snow, keeping hold of one another's hands firmly. They went on and on, and suddenly Goldilocks shook off Moon-Face's hand and pointed in front of them.

'A light!' she said in astonishment. Everyone stopped.

'I say! I SAY! It's our cottage!' shrieked the baby bear, in surprise and delight. 'But who's inside? *Someone* must have lighted the candle!'

They all stared at the lighted window. Who was inside the cottage? Could the Magic Snowman have found it? Or the polar bears? Was it an enemy inside – or a friend?

'Wheeeeew!' blew the wind, and the snowflakes fell thickly on everyone as they stood there, wondering.

'Ooooh!' shivered Moon-Face. 'We shall get

dreadful colds standing out here in the snow. Let's go in, and find out who's there.'

So the father bear opened the door, and one by one they all trooped in, looking round the empty room, half afraid.

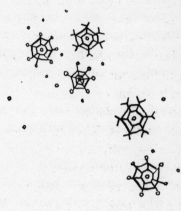

XI. MORE AND MORE SURPRISES

'There doesn't *seem* to be anyone here!' said Beth, cautiously looking around.

'Well, WHO lighted that candle?' asked Moon-Face, his big round face looking anxious. '*We* didn't leave it burning!'

Suddenly the father bear gave an angry growl, and pointed to his chair. 'Who's been sitting in *my* chair?' he said.

'And who's been sitting in *my* chair?' said the mother bear, pointing to hers.

'And who's been sitting in *my* chair and broken it all to bits?' squeaked the baby bear, in tears.

Beth giggled. 'This sounds like the story of the Three Bears coming true!' she said to Frannie. 'They'll talk about porridge next.'

They did.

'Who's been eating *my* porridge?' said the father bear angrily.

'And who's been eating *my* porridge?' said the mother bear.

'And who's been eating mine, and gobbled it all UP?' wept the baby bear, scraping his spoon round the empty plate.

'It's all very mysterious,' said Moon-Face. '*Somebody* lighted the candle – *somebody* sat in the chairs – *somebody* ate the porridge. But who?'

'Not me this time,' said Goldilocks. 'I was with you all the time we were snowballing, wasn't I, Bears?'

'You certainly were,' growled the father bear softly, patting the little girl on the back. He was very fond of her.

'I wish we had found poor Joe,' said Beth. 'Whatever will he be doing in this horrid cold land?'

'Do you suppose we ought to go out and look for him again?' said Frannie, shivering as she thought of the ice-cold wind outside.

'No,' said Moon-Face decidedly. 'No one is going out of this cottage again till we're safely in the wood at home. I'm afraid we can't possibly rescue Joe now.'

'What's that noise?' said Goldilocks suddenly. Everybody listened. *Someone* was snoring softly in the next room!

'We never thought of looking there,' said Moon-Face. 'Who can it be?'

'Shh!' said Goldilocks. 'If we can catch him asleep, we can hold him tight and he won't be able to get away. But if he wakes up he might be fierce.'

They tiptoed to the door of the bedroom. One by one they squeezed through.

'Who's been lying on *my* bed?' said the father bear, in a growly voice.

'Shh!' said Moon-Face crossly.

'Who's been lying on *my* bed?' said the mother bear.

'Shh!' said everyone.

'And who's been lying on *my* bed and is fast asleep there still?' said the baby bear.

Everyone stared at the cot. Yes – there was someone

there – someone covered in white. Was it a polar bear?

'It's a white bear!' said Moon-Face, half frightened.

'Let's lock him in before he wakes,' said the father bear. 'He might still think we are enemies!'

They all rushed out of the little room and slammed the door shut with a loud bang, locking it behind them.

'He's caught!' said Moon-Face joyfully.

Joe awoke with a jump. Who had locked him in? Had the Magic Snowman caught him again? He began to shout and bang on the door. And then Beth and Frannie recognised his voice and yelled out loudly:

'Moon-Face! It's Joe! It's Joe! It's Joe! Oh, it's Joe!'

They rushed to the door and unlocked it, and flung their arms around Joe. The boy was too astonished to speak. He hugged his sisters.

'How did you get here?' he asked.

'How did *you* get here?' cried Beth and Frannie.

'Come into the kitchen and we'll all have some hot porridge and milk,' said Goldilocks. 'We can talk then and get warm.'

So Joe went with the others, all chattering loudly about everything. Goldilocks ladled out porridge into blue bowls, and made some hot chocolate. Soon everyone was putting sugar on porridge and drinking the hot chocolate. Joe poured some milk over his porridge and smiled joyfully at everybody.

'What an adventure this has been!' he said. 'Shall I tell my tale first, or will you tell yours?'

He told his – and then Beth told how Moon-Face had gone to the Three Bears for their help, and all about the fierce snowball battle.

'It's a pity about the battle,' said the father bear mournfully. 'The white bears are cousins of ours, and have always been friendly – now they seem to be enemies.'

'Let's hope they don't discover our cottage,' said Goldilocks, eating her hot porridge. 'Moon-Face, hadn't we better make some magic and get back to the wood?'

'Plenty of time, plenty of time,' said Moon-Face, pouring himself another cup of hot chocolate.

But, you know, there *wasn't* plenty of time. For just at that moment Goldilocks gave a scream and pointed to the window.

'Someone looked in!' she said.

'Don't be silly!' said Moon-Face.

'I'm not,' said Goldilocks. 'I tell you, *somebody* looked in! Who could it be?'

'The handle of the door is moving!' yelled Moon-Face, and he leapt to the door. In a flash he had locked it and bolted it.

The father bear got up and went to the window. He looked out into the snowstorm.

'I can't see anything,' he said; and then he growled loudly. 'Yes, I can – I can see the white bears! They have surrounded our cottage! *Now* what shall we do?'

'Well, they can't get in at the door, and they *certainly* shan't get in at the window,' said Moon-Face, looking fierce. The door shook, but it held well. Someone battered on it.

'We shan't let you in!' yelled Joe.

'If anyone tries to open the window or break it, I'll throw this kettle at him!' shouted Moon-Face, who

65

was dancing about waving the kettle in the air.

'Moon-Face, that kettle has got hot water in it,' said Frannie. 'Do be careful. You nearly dropped some on me.'

'I'll drop it on to any bear that dares to come in here!' yelled Moon-Face, spattering the room with steaming drops.

'Oh dear!' said Beth. 'Hide behind the bed, Frannie. It seems to me that Moon-Face is almost as dangerous as the bears.' Moon-Face soon realised that they were right, and that waving a hot kettle around was a foolish and dangerous thing to do. So he put it down again, gently.

Then the father bear had an idea, and dragged the big table across the room to block the door. Things were getting exciting. Joe and the girls were frightened, but they couldn't help feeling terribly thrilled too. Whatever was going to happen next?

'Oooomph! Ooooomph!' boomed the big bears outside, but they couldn't get in at the door or window.

But they found another way! The chimney was wide and big, for the fireplace was one of the large, old-fashioned kind and needed a wide chimney. One of the bears climbed up on to the roof, followed by three more. The first one slipped into the big chimney. Down he went, whooosh! Down went another – and the third – and the fourth.

They landed with a crash on to the big hearth, and hurriedly jumped away from the flames of the fire.

'Surrender!' they cried to the startled children and bears. 'Surrender! The Magic Snowman is outside! Let him in!'

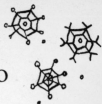

XII. WHAT HAPPENED TO THE SNOWMAN

Everyone stared at the big white bears in horror. No one had thought of the chimney. What a pity they hadn't stopped it up!

'I am going to let the Magic Snowman in,' said the first white bear.

Then the father bear spoke up, in a very sorrowful voice.

'Cousin, why are we enemies? We have always been good friends up till now.'

The four white bears looked at him and at the mother bear in sudden amazement. They rushed at them with loud ooomphy noises.

Joe thought they were going to fight the Three Bears. But no, the white bears were not going to fight – they were hugging the Three Bears as tightly as they could, and to the children's amazement tears were pouring down their furry faces!

'We didn't know it was you!' said the white bears. 'Why, cousins, we would never have fought you if only we had known you were the Three Bears we love so much!'

'There, there!' said the mother bear, wiping the tears of a white bear off her fur. 'It's all right. But for goodness' sake tell the other bears we're friends. We don't want the front door battered down.'

Moon-Face opened the door and yelled out of it,

'Bears, it's all right! This is the cottage of your cousins, the Three Bears! We're friends!'

But the white bears didn't answer or come in – instead a big white shape came up and squeezed through the door – the Magic Snowman!

A chill fell over the little room. The white bears were frightened of him, for he was their master. He shut the door and glared at everyone out of his stone eyes.

'So even my own bears have gone over to the enemy!' he said. 'Oho! What will you say if I turn you into ice and snow, everyone?'

Nobody said anything. But, to Beth's surprise, Moon-Face shut the door, and then went to the fire. He piled on three great logs and winked at Beth.

The Snowman took up a white bear by the scruff of his neck and shook him.

'So you found your voices, did you?' he said. 'Didn't I tell you that you were only to say 'Ooomph' and not speak a word to anyone? I won't have bears that talk!'

He picked up another white bear and shook him. 'So you are friends with my enemies, are you?' he said.

The room became very hot. Joe took off his coat. So did the others. Moon-Face slyly put on another log. The fire crackled and shot great flames up the chimney. Frannie wished she could take off everything, she was so hot.

Whatever does Moon-Face think he is doing, making the room so hot? she thought crossly. But just as she was about to tell him what she was thinking, he

68

winked at her, and she said
nothing. Moon-Face had some
strange plan that he was
carrying out.

The Snowman went on
and on, grumbling and
threatening. Everyone
listened and said nothing.
Moon-Face raked the fire
and it blazed up higher.

'Now this is what I'm
going to do,' said the Magic
Snowman. 'I'm going to take
this nice little cottage for my own

– and I shall live here. All of you others can live in a
snow-house and freeze, for all I care. You will all wait
on me and do whatever I say.'

'Yes,' said everybody. They all knew now what
Moon-Face's plan was. He meant to make the room
so hot that the Magic Snowman would melt. Clever
old Moon-Face! A little trickle of water began to run
from the Snowman's broad white back, which was
near the fire. Moon-Face pointed to it secretly and
grinned.

Frannie thought Moon-Face's beaming face looked
so funny that she began to giggle. She really couldn't
help it. Goldilocks giggled too, and stuffed her
handkerchief into her small mouth. The baby bear
gave a high squeak of a giggle.

'How dare you laugh!' shouted the Snowman angrily.
'Outside, all of you! Outside! This is my cottage now,
and not one of you shall stay here.'

They all crowded outside except Moon-Face, who crouched behind a big chair, determined not to leave the fire in case it burnt low.

Outside it was bitterly cold. The white bears quickly dug up the snow and made a high wall to shelter the others from the wind. They crouched there, cuddling close to one another for warmth. The big white bears wrapped their furry arms round the children and warmed them beautifully. Joe thought they were very kind indeed.

They waited and they waited. They could see smoke pouring from the chimney of the cottage and they knew that Moon-Face must be keeping up the fire. The bears ooomphed every now and again, and the children whispered to one another.

Then suddenly the door of the cottage was flung open and Moon-Face stood there, his big face beaming like a full moon.

'You can come back now!' he shouted. 'It's quite safe!'

They all crowded back to the cottage. Joe looked for the Snowman – but he was gone! There was nothing to show that he had been there, except for a very large puddle of water.

'He melted very quickly,' said Moon-Face. 'He may have been very magic and very powerful – but he was just made of snow after all. So he melted like a real snowman on a sunny morning.'

The polar bears ooomphed with delight. They had hated being servants to the Snowman.

'We'll all say goodbye to you now,' they said to the Three Bears. 'This cottage is cosy but it's too hot for us. Come and see us again whenever you like. Goodbye!'

Everyone hugged them goodbye, and Joe felt quite sad to see them go. Moon-Face shut the door after them.

'Now we'll get back home,' he said. 'I'm a bit tired of this land. Come on, Bears, help me to get the cottage back safely!'

He didn't do the same magic as before. He drew a circle on the floor in blue chalk and the Three Bears stood inside, holding paws. Moon-Face danced around them, singing strings of odd magic words. A wind rose up, and the cottage rocked. Darkness came down, and for a moment no one could see anything at all.

Then gradually the darkness went and the wind blew no more. The sun shone warmly in at the window. Beth gave a shout.

'I say! We're back in the little woody corner where we first saw the cottage! And it's daytime now, not night-time!'

'Well, we've been having this adventure all night long!' said Moon-Face, with a laugh. 'It's sunrise now – the night has gone. You'd better hurry off home, children, or you'll be scolded for leaving your beds at night.'

They hugged Goldilocks, and shook hands with the Three Bears. 'We'll come back and see you sometime,' said Frannie. 'Thank you so much for all your help!'

Goldilocks and the bears stood at the door and waved goodbye as Moon-Face hurried the three children away down the lane to catch the train back to the Enchanted Wood. It wasn't long before they had got to the station, waited for a train, slid off the roof and settled down in a carriage.

When they got to the Enchanted Wood they said goodbye to Moon-Face, and Frannie gave him a kiss for being such a help. He was so pleased that he went red all over his enormous face, and Beth laughed.

'You look like the setting sun now,' she said. 'You really ought to be called Sun-Face!'

'Goodbye, and see you soon, I hope!' called Moon-Face. Off went the children home, and got into bed just about an hour before their mother called them to get up. My goodness, they *were* sleepy all that day!

XIII. MOON-FACE GETS
INTO TROUBLE

The children didn't really feel that they wanted to go to any of the lands at the top of the Faraway Tree for a little while. It was a bit too exciting to climb through the clouds and see what was above them!

But they did want to see their friends in the Tree, especially dear old Moon-Face.

So the very next time they had a day to themselves they set off through the Enchanted Wood to the Faraway Tree. There was no rope to guide them this time. It was only at night that the rope was swung through the boughs to help the woodland-folk up and down.

The children began to climb up. Every door and window in the tree seemed shut today, and not a soul was about. It was quite dull climbing up the tree. Even when they reached Silky's house, that was shut too, and they couldn't hear Silky singing or anything. They knocked, but there was no answer.

So on they went up to Moon-Face's, keeping a good lookout for Dame Washalot's dirty water to come swishing down on them. But not even her water appeared that day! It all seemed very quiet and peaceful.

They reached Moon-Face's house at the top of the tree and knocked at his door. Nobody opened it.

But inside they could quite well hear somebody crying. It was very mysterious.

'It doesn't sound like Moon-Face,' said Frannie, puzzled. 'Let's go in and see who it is.'

So they opened the door and went in. And it was Silky, sitting in a corner crying bitterly!

'Whatever's the matter?' cried Joe.

'And where's old Moon-Face?' asked Frannie.

'Oh dear!' sobbed Silky. 'Moon-Face has been thrown into some dreadfully strange land at the top of the Faraway Tree because he was rude to Mister Watzisname down below.'

'What! That old man who's always sitting in a chair and snoring?' said Beth, remembering that they hadn't seen him that day. 'Whatever did Moon-Face do?'

'Oh, he was very naughty,' wept Silky. 'So was I. You see, we heard Mister Watzisname snoring as usual, and we crept up to him and saw that his mouth was wide open. And, oh dear, we popped a handful of acorns into it, and when he woke up he spluttered and popped, and then he caught sight of us hiding behind a big branch.'

'Goodness! Did you really dare to do such a naughty thing?' cried Beth. 'No wonder he was angry!'

'Moon-Face is dreadfully bad sometimes,' said Silky, wiping her eyes. 'He makes me naughty too. Well, we ran away up the tree to Moon-Face's house. I got in safely – but Moon-Face didn't. And Mister Watzisname caught hold of him and threw him right through the hole in the clouds into the land that is there today.'

'Good gracious! Well, can't he get back?' said Frannie, in alarm. 'He can climb down the ladder, surely, back into the Tree?'

'Yes, he could,' said Silky, 'but, you see, Mister Watzisname is sitting on the ladder ready to catch him and throw him back. So what's the use of that?'

'What land is up there today?' asked Joe.

'The Land of the Old Saucepan Man,' said Silky. 'He lives there in his cottage with his pots and pans, and is quite harmless. But, you see, Mister Watzisname will sit on the ladder till the land swings round and another one comes. Then Moon-Face won't be able to get back, and he may be lost forever!'

'Oh dear!' said Joe in dismay, and the girls stared at Silky in despair, for they were very fond of old Moon-Face now.

'Isn't there anything we can do?' asked Joe at last.

'Well, there's just one hope,' said Silky, fluffing out her lovely golden hair. 'The Old Saucepan Man is a great friend of Mister Watzisname's. If he knew his land was at the top of the Faraway Tree today he might come along and have a cup of tea with Mister Watzisname, and then Moon-Face could slip down the ladder back here!'

'Oh,' said the children, and looked at one another. They could quite well see that this meant one or all of them going up the ladder again and getting into another peculiar land.

'I'll go,' said Beth. 'After all, Moon-Face helped us last time. We must help him now.'

'We'll all three go,' said Joe. So they set off up the topmost branch to the little ladder. There they found Mister Watzisname sitting reading his newspaper and brewing a pot of tea that sent swirls of steam up through the hole in the clouds.

'Please can we pass?' asked Beth timidly.

'No, you can't,' said Mister Watzisname rudely.

'Well, we've got to,' said Joe. 'So if we tread on your feet you must excuse us.'

Mister Watzisname simply wouldn't move. He really was a very cross old man. He grumbled and growled at each of the children as they squeezed past him, and they were very glad when they had climbed through the hole and were in the land above.

'So this is the Land of the Saucepan Man,' said Frannie, when they were standing on the grass safely. 'What a funny little land!'

It was. It was an island floating in what seemed a sea of white. It wasn't really much bigger than a large field. Beth went to the edge and looked over.

'Goodness!' she said in alarm. 'It's like a cliff – and the sea is a big white cloud. Don't go too near the edge, anybody. It wouldn't be nice to fall off!'

'Hey! Hey!' suddenly yelled an excited voice. They turned around – and saw Moon-Face waving to them, and running hard towards them. 'Hey! How did you get here?'

'Hallo! We came to see what we could do for you,' said Joe. 'We heard what had happened. Old Mister Watzisname is sitting on the ladder still, waiting for you. But Silky says this is the land of the Saucepan Man, who is a great friend of Mister Watzisname's – so we've come to see him and ask him if he'll go and have tea with his friend. Then you can slip down safely and go home.'

'Ooooh, good!' said Moon-Face joyfully. 'I didn't know what land this was, and goodness me, I was quite afraid of falling off it, it's so small. Where do you suppose the Old Saucepan Man lives?'

'I can't imagine!' said Joe, looking round. All he could see was a very large stretch of grass, with no house and nobody at all in sight. Where in the world could the Saucepan Man live?

'We'll have to go carefully all round this funny little land,' said Beth. 'His house must be somewhere. But we'd better hurry, for you never know when the land will swing away from the Faraway Tree – and we don't want to live in this odd little place for ever!'

They began to walk round the land. Presently they came to a cliff that was not quite so steep as the others. They peered over it. Joe pointed to some things stuck in the cliff.

'Whatever are those?' he said.

'They look like some sort of steps down the cliffside,' said Beth.

'They're *saucepans*!' said Frannie suddenly. 'Yes – *saucepans* – with their handles stuck firmly into the cliff, and the pan part to tread on. How strange!'

'Well, this must be the way down to the Saucepan Man's house,' said Joe, excited. 'Come on. Be careful, girls, or you may fall and roll right over the edge of this land.'

So, very carefully, they began to climb down the cliff, treading on the saucepans stuck into the earth. It was really rather funny!

They got down at last. And then they heard a very curious noise indeed! It was a sound of crashings and bangings and clatterings and clangings! The children were quite alarmed.

'The noise is coming from just round the corner,' said Joe.

They crept very cautiously to the corner and peeped round.

There they saw a crooked little house with a saucepan for a chimney. The noise came from inside the house. The children crept to the window and looked in.

And inside they saw the strangest little man they had ever seen, dancing the strangest little dance! He had saucepans and kettles hung all over him, he wore a saucepan for a hat, and he crashed two saucepans together as he danced!

'Do you think he's dangerous?' said Joe, in a whisper.

XIV. THE FUNNY OLD
SAUCEPAN MAN

'I don't think he's at all dangerous,' said Frannie. 'He has quite a kind face.'

'Let's tap at the window,' said Beth. So she tapped. But the Saucepan Man took no notice. He just went on dancing away, crashing his saucepans together.

Joe tapped loudly. The Saucepan Man caught sight of him at the window and looked most astonished. He stopped dancing and went to the door.

'Come in and dance,' he said.

'Oh no, thank you,' said Joe. 'We've just come to ask you to tea.'

'Ask me for a bee?' said the Saucepan Man, looking surprised. 'I'm so sorry, but I don't keep bees, only saucepans.'

'Not bees,' said Joe. 'To ask you out to TEA.'

'But I don't want to go to the sea,' said the Saucepan Man. 'I don't like the water at all. Never did. Very kind of you, I'm sure, but I hate the sea.'

'Not the sea, but TEA, TEA, TEA!' cried Joe.

'Oh, tea,' said the Saucepan Man. 'Well, why didn't you say that before? Then I would have understood.'

'I *did* say that before,' said poor Joe.

'What? Shut the door?' said the Saucepan Man. 'Certainly, if you want to. Give it a push.'

'He can't hear very well,' said Frannie. 'He must be deaf.'

'No, I'm not,' said the Saucepan Man, hearing perfectly all of a sudden. 'Not a bit deaf. Only sometimes when my saucepans have been crashing round me rather a lot I get noises in my ears afterwards. But I'm not deaf.'

'I'm glad of that,' said Joe politely.

'Cat? No, I haven't got a cat,' said the Saucepan Man, looking all round. 'Did you see one?'

'I didn't say anything about a cat,' said Joe patiently.

'You did. I heard you,' said the Saucepan Man, vexed. 'I don't encourage cats. I keep mice instead. I shall look for that cat.'

And then, with his saucepans clanging round him he began to look for a cat that certainly wasn't there. 'Puss, Puss, Puss!' he called. 'Puss, Puss, Puss!'

'There's no cat in your house!' shouted Moon-Face.

'Mouse? Where did you see you a mouse?' said the old man, alarmed. 'I wouldn't like one of my mice to be caught by your cat.'

'I tell you we haven't GOT a cat!' cried Joe, feeling quite cross. 'We've come to tell you about your friend, Mister Watzisname.'

For once the Saucepan Man seemed to hear Joe, and at once he stopped looking for the cat. 'Mister Watzisname!' he cried. 'Where is he? He's a great friend of mine.'

'Well, wouldn't you like to go and have tea with him then?' said Joe.

'Yes, certainly I would,' said the Saucepan Man. 'Please tell me where he is.'

'He's sitting on the ladder leading from the Faraway Tree to your land,' shouted Joe. 'He's waiting there.'

'Yes – for me!' said Moon-Face in a whisper.

'Ssh!' said Frannie. The Saucepan Man gave a yell of joy when he heard where his old friend was, and he set off for the cliff, shouting in delight.

'Hurrah! I've come to the Faraway Tree! And I can see my friends again! And Mister Watzisname is waiting for me to have tea with him! Come on! Come on!'

Up the cliff he went, treading on the saucepan steps, his own saucepans and kettles rattling and banging all round him. The children and Moon-Face followed. The Saucepan Man ran helter-skelter to the hole that led down to the topmost branch of the Faraway Tree, dropping a few saucepans on the way.

When he got there he peered down and saw Mister Watzisname sitting on the ladder, watching for Moon-Face. But the Saucepan Man didn't know that, of course! He thought that his friend was waiting for *him*!

'Hey, hey, hey!' he yelled, dropping a saucepan on top of Mister Watzisname in his excitement. 'Hey, old friend!'

Mister Watzisname watched the saucepan bouncing off his foot, down the branch of the Faraway Tree, and wondered who it would hit. He looked up in amazement when he heard his friend's shouts.

'Saucepan!' he yelled. 'Dear old Saucepan! Fancy seeing *you*!'

'Glue?' said the Saucepan Man, suddenly hearing all wrong again. 'Glue? – No – I've not got glue with me. But I can soon make some for you.'

'Still the same silly old Saucepan Man, aren't you!' cried Mister Watzisname. 'Come down here. I didn't say anything about glue. Come and have a cup of tea with me. The kettle's boiling.'

'I don't want oiling,' said the Saucepan Man, though he really sounded as if he did, he was so full of clangs and clatters! 'I'll come and have tea and a talk with you. Hurrah!'

He put his foot on the ladder, but unfortunately he stepped on a kettle that had got round his leg, and down he went, clatter, bang, crash, smash, clang! Mister Watzisname caught at him as he went past, and down he went too, rolling off the ladder, down the branch, past Moon-Face's door and down the Tree!

'There they go!' said Moon-Face, in delight. 'All mixed up with kettles and saucepans. What a joke! They'll give old Dame Washalot a fright if they fall into her wash-tub!'

The children laughed till they cried. The Old Saucepan Man was really so funny, and they couldn't *imagine* what people in the Tree would think as he rolled down with such a clanging and banging.

'It's quite safe to go down now,' said Joe, peering down the ladder. 'They've disappeared. I shouldn't wonder if they're at the bottom of the Tree by now. Come on, Moon-Face.'

So down the ladder they all went, slid down the topmost branch, and opened Moon-Face's door. Silky was still there, looking scared out of her life. She gave a scream of joy when she saw them.

'Why are you looking so frightened?' asked Moon-Face, giving her a hug.

'Oh, goodness, a thunderbolt or something fell out of the sky just now and rolled crashing down the Tree!' said Silky.

'That was only the Saucepan Man and Mister Watzisname,' said Joe, laughing, and he told her the whole story. Silky laughed till her sides ached. She ran out of the door and peeped down the Tree.

'Look!' she said, pointing. 'Can you see far down there, between the branches?'

They all looked – and they saw Mister Watzisname and the Old Saucepan Man climbing painfully up to Mister Watzisname's home, both talking together at the top of their voices.

'They've forgotten all about us,' said Joe joyfully. 'Now for goodness' sake, Moon-Face, don't go putting acorns into Mister Watzisname's mouth again. Let's have something to eat, and then we must go home down your slippery-slip.'

So they all five sat round Moon-Face's funny room and ate some Pop Cakes that Silky fetched, and drank acornade, which was made of acorns and was most delicious. Then it was time for the children to go, and they chose cushions, sat at the top of the big tree-slide, pushed off and flew down the inside of the tree, sliding round and round and round till they shot out of the trapdoor at the bottom on to the cushion of moss. Then they ran home as fast as they could, for they were late.

'I expect the Old Saucepan Man's gone back to his odd little land by now,' said Joe, as they turned in at their gate.

But he hadn't. He came to see them the very next

day, his saucepans clanging so loudly that Mother looked quite alarmed.

'Whoever in the world is that?' she said, as the Saucepan Man came in at the gate.

XV. THE SAUCEPAN MAN GOES TO
THE WRONG LAND!

Mother and the children stared at the strange Old
Saucepan Man as he came in at the gate. He wore an
extra-large-sized saucepan for a hat, and, as he came,
he knocked two pans together, and sang an odd
nonsense song that went like this:

> *Two beans for a pudding,*
> *Two cherries for a pie,*
> *Two legs for a table,*
> *With a hi-diddle-hi!*

At the last 'hi' he banged on the door with a
saucepan. Mother opened it.

'Don't make such a noise,' she said.

'No, I haven't seen any boys,' said the Saucepan
Man, and he clashed his pans together so loudly that
Mother jumped. Then he caught sight of the children
and waved to them eagerly. 'Oh, there you are! Moon-
Face told me where you lived.'

'Whoever is he?' said Mother, in wonder. 'Children,
is this strange old man all right?'

'Oh yes,' said Joe, hoping that Mother wouldn't ask
them too many questions. 'Can we take him into the
garden, Mother? He makes such a noise indoors.'

'Very well,' said Mother, who wanted to get on with
her washing. 'Take him along.'

'A song?' said the Saucepan Man obligingly. 'Did you say you wanted a song, Madam?' He began to sing again, and crashed his pans in time to his song:

Two pigs for the pigsty,
Two shoes for the horse,
Two hats for the tigers,
Pink ones, of course.

The children bustled him out into the back-garden. 'That's a very, very silly song of yours,' said Beth loudly, right in his ear. 'What's it called?'

'It hasn't got a name,' said the Saucepan Man. 'I make it up as I go along. It's quite easy. Every line but the last one begins with the word 'two'. I'm sorry you think it's silly.' He looked rather offended. Then suddenly he smiled again and said, 'I've come to ask you all to tea in my cottage.'

'Will Mister Watzisname be there?' asked Joe, who wasn't at all keen to meet him again.

'Yes, you'd better brush your hair,' said the Saucepan Man, looking at Joe's untidy hair.

'I said "Will Mister Watzisname be there?"' said Joe, loudly.

'Something in the air?' said the Saucepan Man, and he looked up anxiously. 'Not a thunderstorm, I hope?'

'No, I certainly don't mean a thunderstorm,' said Joe, with a groan. 'Yes – we'll come. We must ask Mother first.'

Mother said they could go, though she still thought that Old Saucepan Man was very loud and annoying.

'Good day,' she said to him, as he and the children went off.

He really was a most peculiar sight, but he had such a twinkly sort of face that the three children couldn't help liking him and trusting him.

They soon came to the Faraway Tree, and saw that Moon-Face had thought of a marvellous idea. He had borrowed Dame Washalot's biggest washing basket and let it down on a rope. Then, as soon as they were all safely in it, he and Silky meant to haul them up, to save them the long, long climb!

'That's a really good idea!' said Joe, delighted. They all climbed in. It was a bit difficult to get the Saucepan Man in too, but they managed at last, though he seemed to find it most uncomfortable to sit on his saucepans.

'Up we go!' shouted Joe as the basket swung upwards through the branches. It ran very smoothly, and the children enjoyed the strange ride. At last they came to a big branch and stepped out on it. It was quite near Moon-Face's house at the top. Moon-Face was there, winding up the rope, a grin on his big, shining face.

'How did you like *that*?' he asked. The Saucepan Man looked at him anxiously.

'Cat?' he said. 'Another cat? Dear me! I hope it won't escape into my land. I've got my mice there.'

'Now he'll go looking for cats again,' said Beth. And sure enough the Saucepan Man began to peer here and there, calling, 'Puss, Puss, Puss!'

'Never mind him,' said Moon-Face. 'Go on up the ladder. He wants you to go to tea with him in his funny saucepanny house!'

'Come on, Saucepan Man!' called Joe. 'If you want us to come to tea, we'd better go!'

The Saucepan Man heard. He stopped looking for cats and ran up the ladder. With a bound he was through the hole in the cloud, and right above.

And no sooner had he gone out of sight than he began to yell:

'Ooooh! Oooohowww! Wowooo!'

The children listened in alarm. 'Whatever's the matter with him?' said Joe.

Crash! Bang! Clang! Smash!

'He sounds as if he's rolling about on all his kettles and saucepans!' said Beth. 'What can he be doing?'

'Ooooohooow!' shouted the Saucepan Man above them. 'Stop it! Ow! Stop it!'

'Somebody must be attacking him!' cried Joe. He leapt up the ladder. 'Come on, everyone! We'll soon send any enemies off!'

He shot up the ladder, followed by Beth, Frannie, and Moon-Face. They all clambered through the hole in the clouds and stood in the land above.

But oh, my goodness me! It was no longer the Land of the Saucepan Man, that tiny, little, cloud-edged country! It was another land altogether!

'My land's gone!' shrieked the Saucepan Man. 'I didn't know it had! This is somewhere else! Oooooh!'

No wonder he said 'Ooooh!' The bit of flat field he was standing on suddenly gave a shiver like a jelly, and then just as suddenly tipped itself up so that it made a hill! The Saucepan Man rolled down it at top speed, all his pans clattering like cymbals!

'This is Rocking Land,' said Moon-Face, in dismay. 'Quick! Come back to the ladder and get down the hole before we have forgotten where it is! Hey, Saucepan Man, come over here to us!'

'Bus, did you say?' shouted back the Saucepan Man, picking himself up and looking round. 'I can't see a bus. I'd like to catch one.'

'Come here to US, to US, to US!' shouted Joe, in despair. 'The hole through the clouds is here. We must get back again quickly!'

The Saucepan Man began to run downhill to them, but the ground all round suddenly tipped backwards, and he and the children and Moon-Face found themselves running downhill away from the hole in the clouds, where the precious ladder was! They tried to stop. They tried to walk back up the sudden hill – but the land tipped up all the more and in the end they couldn't stand up, but had to lie down.

Then they began to roll downhill. How they rolled!

Over and over and over and over, with the Saucepan Man making a dreadful clatter with all his pans.

'Oooooh! Ow! Oooooh!' cried everyone.

'We've lost the hole!' shouted Joe. But before he could say any more he bumped into a bush that knocked all the breath out of him! Soon everyone lay in a heap at the bottom of the hill, and tried to get back their breath.

'Now we're in a fix,' said Beth, dusting herself. 'What a very tiresome land to have got into. Does it do this sort of thing all the time, Moon-Face?'

'Oh, yes,' said Moon-Face. 'It never stops. It heaves up here and sinks down there, and rocks to and fro and gives sudden little jumps. People do say there's a giant just underneath, trying to throw the land off his back.'

XVI. WHAT HAPPENED IN
THE ROCKING LAND

The Rocking Land was really most annoying. No sooner did the children stand up very carefully and try to walk a few steps, than the earth beneath them either fell away or tipped up or slanted sideways in a very alarming manner.

Then down they all went, rolling over and over! The Saucepan Man made a tremendous noise and almost cried when he saw how battered his saucepans and kettles were getting.

'Moon-Face!' yelled Joe. 'How can we get out of here? Don't you know?'

'We can only get out by going down the ladder that leads to the Faraway Tree!' shouted back Moon-Face, who was busy rolling down a little hill that had suddenly appeared. 'Look for it all the time, or we'll never get away from here. As soon as the Rocking Land leaves the place where the Faraway Tree is, we've no way of escape!'

That gave the others a shock. The thought of living in a land of bumps and jolts was not at all pleasant! They all began to look about for the hole through which they had come into the Rocking Land.

Soon the earth began to do something very different. It heaved up and down very quickly as if it were breathing fast! When it heaved up it threw the children and the others into the air. When it breathed downwards they rolled into holes and stayed there. It was all dreadfully uncomfortable.

'I'm getting awfully bruised!' shouted Beth. 'For goodness' sake let's find a place on this land where it's not quite so fidgety. I think we must be on the worst bit.'

As soon as the earth stopped heaving about they all ran hard to where a wood grew. And there, just inside the wood, they saw a shop!

It was such a surprising thing to see in the Rocking Land that they all stopped and stared.

'What does it sell?' said Joe.

'You don't feel *well*?' said the Saucepan Man, quite deaf for a time. 'I don't either. I feel as if I've been on a ship in a very rough sea!'

'I said, "What does the shop *sell*?"' said Joe.

'No, I didn't hear a bell,' said the Saucepan Man, looking round as if he expected to see an enormous bell somewhere.

Joe gave up. He looked hard at the shop. It was just a wide stall, with a tiny house behind it. No one seemed to be there, but smoke rose from the chimney, so someone must live there, Joe thought.

'Come on,' he said to the others. 'Take hold of each others' hands, so that we keep together. We'll go and see this funny shop and see if we can get help.'

They walked up to it. The stall was piled high with cushions of all colours, each one with a rope tied to it.

'How funny!' said Beth, in astonishment. 'Cushions with ropes! Now who in the world would want to buy cushions here?'

'Well, I would, for one!' said Moon-Face at once. 'My goodness, if I had a fine fat cushion tied on the front of me, and another tied at the back, I wouldn't mind being bumped around nearly so much!'

'Oh, of course – that's what the cushions and ropes are for,' said Beth joyfully. 'Let's buy some – then we shan't get bruised any more.'

Just then a sharp-nosed little woman, with cushions tied all round her, came out of the tiny house and looked at the children. She even had a small cushion tied on her head, and she did look funny.

Frannie giggled. She was a dreadful giggler. The woman looked cross and glared at Frannie.

'Do you want to buy my cushions?' she asked.

'Yes please,' said Moon-Face, and he reached into his pocket. 'How much are they?'

'Five silver pieces of money each,' said the woman, her little green eyes shining as she saw Moon-Face putting his hand into his pocket for the money. Moon-Face looked at her in dismay.

'That's much too high a price!' he said. 'I've only got one silver piece. Have you got any money, Saucepan Man?'

'No, I don't sell honey,' said the Saucepan Man.

'MONEY, MONEY, MONEY!' shouted Moon-Face, showing the Saucepan Man his one silver piece.

'Oh, money,' he said, taking out a round leather bag from one of his kettles. 'Yes, I've plenty in here.'

But the round leather bag was empty! The Saucepan Man stared at it in dismay.

'All my money must have fallen out when I rolled about,' he said. 'There's nothing left!'

The children had no money at all. The sharp-nosed little woman shook her head when Moon-Face begged her to lend them some cushions in return for his silver piece.

'I don't lend anything,' she said, and went back to her house, banging the door loudly.

'It's too bad,' said Moon-Face, taking hold of Joe's hand and walking off gloomily. 'Mean old thing! Oh, look – there are some more people – all wearing cushions!'

Sure enough they met plenty of odd-looking folk, well-padded with cushions of all colours, sizes and shapes, walking carefully about the paths. One man wore a big quilt all round him, which Beth thought was a fine idea.

'The Rocking Land is quite peaceful for a change,' she said to Frannie. But she spoke too soon – for even as she said these words the earth began to heave up, first one way and then another!

Over went the children and everybody else and rolled here and there and up and down as the land jumped up first in one place and then in another.

'Ooooooh!' groaned the children.

'Wish I had a few cushions!' cried Moon-Face, who had rolled on his nose and bent it sideways.

Crash! Clank! Bang! went the Saucepan Man, rolling on his kettles and pans very noisily.

'Oooh, look!' shrieked Beth suddenly, in delight, and pointed back towards the little wood where the shop was. The earth there had risen steeply upwards, and all the cushions were rolling down towards the children.

'Grab them!' shouted Joe. So they all caught the cushions, and began to tie them firmly round them. My goodness, it did make a difference when they rolled about!

'It serves that mean old woman right!' said the Saucepan Man as he tried his hardest to put cushions round himself and his saucepans.

Suddenly one of the people of the Rocking Land gave a frightened shout and clutched hold of a nearby tree. A strange wind blew with a low, musical sound.

'Now what's going to happen?' cried Moon-Face.

'Get hold of a tree! Get hold of a tree!' shouted the people round about. 'When the wind makes that sound it means the whole of the land is going to tip up sideways and try to roll everyone off. Your only hope is to catch hold of a tree!'

Sure enough, the land was tipping up – not in bits and pieces as it had done before, but the whole of it! It was extraordinary. Moon-Face was frightened. He tried to get to a tree, and he shouted to the others.

'Catch hold of a tree! Hurry up!'

But not one of them could, for they had left the wood behind them and were in a field. Slowly and surely the land tipped sideways, and the children and Moon-Face and the old Saucepan Man began to roll downhill on their cushions. They were not bruised, but they were very much frightened. What would happen to them if they rolled right off the land?

Down they went and down, nearer and nearer to the edge of the Rocking Land – and then, quite suddenly, Moon-Face disappeared! One moment he was there – the next he was gone! It was most peculiar.

But in half a minute they heard his voice, lifted up in the greatest excitement. 'I say, I say, everyone! I've fallen down the hole to the ladder that leads to the Faraway Tree, quite by accident. I'll throw my cushions up through the hole so you'll know where it is. Roll to it if you can! But hurry!'

Then the children and the Saucepan Man saw two cushions appear, and they knew where the hole was. They did their best to roll to it, and one by one they got nearer and nearer.

Beth rolled right down it, plop, and caught hold of the ladder as she fell. Joe rolled down next, missed the ladder and landed with a bump on the top branch of the Faraway Tree.

The Saucepan Man rolled to it next, but he got stuck in the hole, for he was now so fat with cushions as well as kettles and saucepans that he could hardly get through.

'Oh, quick, quick, quick!' shouted Joe. 'Get in, Saucepan Man, get in! Poor Frannie will roll right past the hole if you don't hurry up!'

The Saucepan Man saw Frannie was rolling past. Poor Frannie! Once she rolled past the hole she couldn't possibly roll back again, for it would be all uphill. Quick as lightning the Saucepan Man reached out his hand and caught hold of one of the ropes that tied Frannie's cushion to her back. She stopped with a jerk.

One of the Saucepan Man's kettles gave way and he fell through the hole to the ladder, making a tremendous noise. Moon-Face caught him – and then the Saucepan Man gave a tug at Frannie's rope and

she came down the hole too, landing softly on the top
branch of the Faraway Tree, for she was well-padded
with her cushions!

'Well, thank goodness you found the hole, Moon-
Face!' said everyone, still looking rather scared. '*What
an adventure!*'

XVII. AN INVITATION FROM
MOON-FACE AND SILKY

Nobody had really enjoyed their visit to the Rocking Land, which had been a mistake, anyhow. They sat in Moon-Face's house, untying their cushions from their backs and fronts, and looking at all the bruises they had got.

'What shall we do with these cushions?' said Beth.

'Moon-Face could do with them, I expect,' said Frannie. 'He uses such a lot for his slippery-slip, don't you, Moon-Face?'

'Yes, they'd do very well,' said Moon-Face, his big face beaming joyfully. 'Some of mine are getting very old and worn. We can't possibly give them back to that cross old woman in the Rocking Land, so we might as well put them to some use here.'

'Right,' said Joe, and he handed Moon-Face his two cushions. Everyone else did the same. Moon-Face was pleased. He poured lemonade for everyone, then handed round a little box full of what looked like all sorts of toffee.

'I don't feel as if I ever want to see what land is at the top of the Faraway Tree again,' said Joe, as he munched a peculiar piece of toffee which seemed to get bigger in his mouth instead of smaller.

'Neither do I,' said Beth.

'I certainly never will!' said Frannie. 'It seems as if there are never any lands there worth visiting. They are all most uncomfortable.'

'Except *my* little land,' said the Saucepan Man, rather mournfully. 'I was always very comfortable there.'

Joe's toffee was now so big that he couldn't say a word. Then it suddenly exploded in his mouth, went to nothing, and left him feeling most astonished.

'Oh dear – did you take a Toffee Shock?' said Moon-Face, noticing Joe's surprised face. 'I'm so sorry. Take a different one.'

'No, thank you,' said Joe, feeling that one Toffee Shock was quite enough. 'I think we'd really better be going. It must be getting late.'

'What's going to happen to the old Saucepan Man now that he's lost his land?' asked Beth, picking up a yellow cushion, ready to slide down the tree.

'Oh, he'll live with Mister Watzisname,' said Moon-Face. 'Hallo – he's taken a Toffee Shock by mistake. Oh, *do* watch him!'

They all watched. The Saucepan Man's Toffee Shock had got enormous, and was about to explode. It did – and went back down to nothing again in his mouth. The Saucepan Man blinked his eyes and looked so astonished that everyone shouted with laughter.

'That was a Toffee Shock you were eating!' said Moon-Face.

'A Coffee Clock?' said the Saucepan Man, even more surprised. 'Dear me!'

'Come on!' said Beth, giggling. 'It's time we went. See you another day, Moon-Face! Goodbye, Saucepan Man!'

She shot off down the slide, round and round and out of the trapdoor at the bottom. Then Frannie slid off, and then Joe.

'Goodbye,' he called. 'Goodbye!'

Mother was astonished to see their bruises. 'Whatever have you been doing?' she said. 'I shan't let you play with the Saucepan Man again if you come home like this. And how dirty your clothes are!'

Joe longed to tell Mother about the Rocking Land and their adventure there, but he felt sure she would think he was making it all up. So he said nothing and went off to change his dirty clothes.

Things did not go very well the next week. Father lost some money one night, and Mother could not get very much washing to do. So money was very scarce, and the children did not have as much to eat as they would have liked.

'If only we could have a few hens!' sighed Mother. 'They would at least give us eggs to eat. And a little goat would give us milk.'

'And what I want is a new garden shovel,' said Father. 'Mine broke yesterday and I can't get on with the garden. It's very important that we should grow as many vegetables as possible, for we can't afford to buy them!'

To make things worse their father was very cross with them for having spoilt their clothes the day that they had gone off with the Saucepan Man.

'If that's the way you treat the only nice clothes you have, you will just have to stay at home and not go out at all!' he scolded.

The children did not like being scolded, and Beth mended their clothes as nicely as she could. Two weeks went by, and the children had not even had two hours to themselves to go and see Moon-Face.

'He'll be wondering what has happened to us,' said Frannie.

Moon-Face certainly *was* wondering. He had waited each day and each night to see the children, and he and Silky wondered what was the matter.

'We'll send the Barn Owl with a note to tell the children to come quickly,' said Silky at last. So she slipped down the Faraway Tree to the hole where the Barn Owl lived. She knocked at his door, and he pecked it open.

'What is it?' he asked in a hoarse voice.

'Oh, Barny dear, will you take this note to the children at that little cottage over by the wood?' asked Silky, in her sweetest voice. 'You're going out hunting tonight, aren't you?'

'Yes,' said the Barn Owl, and he took the note in one of his great clawed feet. 'I'll take it.'

He slammed the door shut behind him and rose into the air on great creamy wings, as silent as the wind. He flew to the children's cottage. They were in bed, asleep.

Barny sat on the tree outside and screeched loudly. The children awoke with a jump.

'Whatever's that?' said Beth.

Joe came into the room. 'Did you hear that?' he asked. 'Whatever could it be?'

The Barn Owl screeched again. He certainly had a

dreadful voice. The children jumped. Joe went bravely to the window and looked out. 'Is anyone being hurt?' he called.

'Meeeeeeee!' screeched the owl again, and Joe nearly fell out of the window with fright! The Barn Owl spread his great soft wings and flew to Joe. He dropped the note on to the window-sill, screeched again, and flew off into the night to look for mice and rats.

'It was a Barn Owl!' said Joe. 'It left a note! Quick, turn on your bedside lamp and let's see what the letter says!'

They turned the lamp on and crowded round the note. This is what it said:

> *Dear Joe, Beth and Frannie,*
> *Why don't you come to see us? Are you upset?*
> *Please come soon, because there is a wonderful*
> *land at the top of the Tree now. It is the Land of*
> *Take-What-You-Want. If you want anything, you*
> *can usually get it there for nothing. Do come, and*
> *we'll all go together.*
> *Love from,*
> *Moon-face and Silky*

'Ooooh!' said Frannie, excited. 'The Land of Take-What-You-Want! Well, *I'd* like to get a few hens.'

'And *I'd* like a goat!' said Beth.

'And *I'd* like a new shovel for Father!' said Joe.

But then he frowned. 'I'd quite made up my mind not to go up to any more of those strange lands,' he said. 'You just never know what might happen there. We'd better not go.'

'Oh, *Joe*!' cried Beth. 'Please let's go! After all, if there *is* a nice land we might as well visit it.'

'Sssh! You'll wake up Mother!' said Joe. 'We'll see tomorrow what happens. If we can get some time to ourselves we'll go and ask Moon-Face if the land is really *safe* to go to. Now we'd better go to bed and sleep.'

But they didn't sleep much! No – they were all wondering what the Land of Take-What-You-Want was like, and if they were really going to visit it tomorrow!

XVIII. THE LAND OF
TAKE-WHAT-YOU-WANT

The next day was very fine. The children helped their mother to clean the whole house, and Joe proudly brought in some fine green beans and lettuces from the garden, which he had grown himself. Mother was pleased.

'You can go off and play after lunch if you like,' she said. 'You have been very good today.'

The children looked at one another in glee. Just what they had hoped for! Good!

'Come on!' said Joe, after lunch. 'We won't waste any time!'

'What about something to drink?' said Beth. 'Shouldn't we take some lemonade with us?'

'I should think we can get lemonade all right from the Land of Take-What-You-Want!' said Joe, with a grin.

So they all ran off, waving to Mother as they went. They were soon in the Enchanted Wood, hearing the trees whispering secretly to one-another, 'Wisha-wisha-wisha!'

They ran through the bushes and trees to the Faraway Tree, and up they went. When they passed the window of the Angry Pixie, Joe peeped in, just for fun. But he was sorry he did, for the Angry Pixie was there, and he threw a bowl of cold soup all over poor Joe!

'Oh!' said Joe in dismay, as he saw his shirt all splashed with soup. 'You wicked pixie!'

The Angry Pixie went off into peals of delighted laughter, and banged his window shut.

'Pooh! You do smell of onions now, Joe!' said Beth, wrinkling up her nose. 'I hope the smell soon wears off.'

Joe wiped himself down with his handkerchief. He said to himself that one day he would pay the Angry Pixie back!

'Come on,' said Frannie impatiently. 'We'll never get there!'

They passed the Barn Owl's door and saw him sitting inside, fast asleep. They came to Silky's little yellow door too, but she wasn't in. There was a note pinned on her door which said, 'OUT. BACK SOON.'

'She must be with Moon-Face,' said Joe. 'Now just look out for Dame Washalot's water, everyone.'

It was a good thing he reminded them, for not long after that a fine waterfall of soapy suds came pouring down. Frannie screamed and dodged, so did Beth. Joe got some on his shirt and he was very cross.

'Never mind!' said Frannie, with a giggle. 'It will wash off some of the onion soup, Joe!'

They went on up, and came to Mister Watzisname's. He was, as usual, sitting in a deckchair, fast asleep, with his mouth open. And beside him, also fast asleep, was the Old Saucepan Man, looking most uncomfortable, draped round as usual with saucepans and kettles.

'Don't wake them,' whispered Joe. 'We'd better not stop and talk.' So they crept by them – but just as they

105

had got to the next branch the Saucepan Man woke up.

He sniffed hard, and jabbed Mister Watzisname. 'What's the matter, what's the matter?' said his friend.

'Can you smell onions?' asked the Saucepan Man. 'I distinctly smell them. Do you suppose the Faraway Tree is growing onions anywhere near us today? I love onion soup.'

Joe and the girls laughed till they cried. 'It's the onion soup on your shirt that the Saucepan Man smelt,' said Beth. 'My goodness! They'll spend all the afternoon looking for onions growing on the Faraway Tree!'

They left the two funny old men and went climbing up – and they got nicely caught by Dame Washalot's second lot of water. She was doing a great deal of washing that day, and she emptied a big wash-tub down just as the three children were nearly underneath.

Slishy-sloshy-slishy-sloshy! The water came pouring down and soaked all the children. They gasped and shook themselves like dogs. 'Quick!' said Joe. 'We will go as fast as we can to Moon-Face's house and borrow some towels from him. This is dreadful!'

They arrived at Moon-Face's at last. Old Moon-Face and Silky rushed out to hug them – but when they saw how dripping wet the children were, they stopped in surprise.

'Is it raining?' said Moon-Face.

'Have you had a bath in your clothes?' asked Silky.

'No. It's just Dame Washalot's water as usual,' said Joe crossly. 'We dodged the first lot, but didn't manage to dodge the second lot. Can you lend us towels?'

Moon-Face grinned and pulled some towels out of his curved cupboard. As the children rubbed themselves down, Moon-Face told them all about the Land of Take-What-You-Want.

'It's a marvellous land,' he said. 'You are allowed to wander all over it and take whatever you want for yourselves without paying a penny. Everyone goes there if they can. Do come and visit it with me and Silky.'

'Is it quite, quite safe?' asked Joe, rubbing his hair dry.

'Oh yes,' said Silky. 'The only thing is we must be careful not to stay there too long, in case it leaves the Faraway Tree and we can't get down. But Moon-Face says he will sit by the ladder and give a loud whistle if he sees any sign of the Land moving away.'

'Good,' said Joe. 'Well, there are plenty of things we want. So let's go now, shall we?'

They all climbed up the topmost branch to the great white cloud. The ladder led through the hole as usual to the land above. One by one they climbed it and stood in the strange country above the magic cloud.

It was indeed strange! It was simply crowded with things and people! It was quite difficult to move about. Animals of all kinds wandered here and there; sacks of all sorts of things, from gold to potatoes, stood about; stalls of the most wonderful vegetables and fruit were everywhere; and even such things as chairs and tables were to be found waiting for anyone to take them!

'Good gracious!' said Joe. 'Can we really take

anything we want?'

'Anything!' said Moon-Face, settling himself down by the ladder in the cloud. 'Look at those gnomes over there! They mean to take all the gold they can find!'

The children looked where Moon-Face was pointing. Sure enough there were four gnomes, hauling at all the sacks of gold in sight. One by one they staggered off to the ladder with them and disappeared down to the Faraway Tree. Other fairy folk hunted for the different things they wanted – dresses, coats, shoes, singing birds, pictures, all kinds of things! As soon as they had found what they were looking for, they rushed off to the ladder in glee and slipped down it. Moon-Face found it fun to watch them.

The others wandered off, looking at everything in surprise.

'Do you want a nice fat lion, Joe?' asked Silky, as a large lion wandered by and licked Silky's hand.

'No, thank you,' said Joe, at once.

'Well, what about a giraffe?' said Silky. 'I believe they make fine pets.'

'You believe wrong then,' said Beth, as a tall giraffe galloped past like a giant rocking horse. 'Nobody in their senses would want to keep a giraffe for a pet.'

'Oh look,' cried Frannie, as she came to a shop in which stood a great many large and beautiful clocks. 'Do let's take a clock back home!'

'No, thank you,' said Joe. 'We know what we want and we'll take that and nothing else.'

'I think *I* should like a clock,' said Silky, and she picked up a small clock with a very nice smiley face. It had two feet underneath, which wiggled hard as Silky picked up the clock.

'It wants to walk!' said Beth with a scream of laughter. 'Oh, do let it, Silky. I've never seen a clock walk before!'

Silky put the clock down and it trotted beside them on its big flat feet. The children thought it was the funniest thing they had ever seen. Silky was very pleased with her new clock. It was the kind that chimed every hour, on the hour, and sometimes in between too. And it had to be wound up with a key every night, to keep it ticking.

'Just what I've always wanted,' she said. 'I shall keep it at the back of my room.'

'You don't suppose it will stay there, do you, Silky?' asked Beth. 'It will wander round and about and poke its nose into everything you're doing. And if it doesn't like you it will run away!'

'Ding-dong-ding-dong!' said the clock suddenly, in a clear voice, making them all jump. It stopped walking when it chimed, but it ran after the children and Silky again at once. It was really a most extraordinary clock!

'Now we really must look for what *we* want,' said Joe. 'Are those hens over there, Beth?'

'Yes, they are!' said Beth. 'Good! Come along and we'll get them. Oh, this is really a lovely land! I *am* glad we came! What fun it will be getting everything we want. I do wonder what Mother will say when we get home!'

XIX. MOON-FACE GETS INTO A FIX

The children went over to the hens that Joe had seen.
They were lovely ones, but a very peculiar colour, for
their wings were pale green and the rest of their
feathers were buttercup yellow. They had funny high
voices, and were very friendly indeed, for they came to
press themselves round the children's legs like cats!

'Do you suppose Mother would like hens this
colour?' asked Joe, doubtfully.

'I don't see why not,' said Beth. 'I think they are
very pretty. The thing is – do they lay good eggs?'

One of the hens at once laid an egg. It was large
and quite an ordinary colour. Beth was pleased.

'There you are!' she said. 'If they lay eggs as big as
this one, Mother will be *very* pleased. How many hens
are there – one, two, three, four, five, six, seven! I
wonder how we could take them all.'

'Oh, they'll follow you,' said Silky. 'Just like my
clock follows me! Tell them you want them
and they'll come.'

'We want you to come with us,
hens,' said Joe at once, and the seven
green-winged birds came over to
him and lined up
in a row to follow
the children. It was
really very funny.

'Well, that's our hens found!' said Beth, pleased. 'Now for the goat and the shovel.'

They wandered along, looking at everything. It didn't matter what anyone wanted, they were sure to find it sooner or later! There were boats there, all kinds of dogs, shopping-baskets, rings, toys, work-baskets, and even such small things as thimbles!

'It's the strangest land I ever saw!' said Joe.

'We look pretty strange too!' said Frannie, giggling, as she looked round and saw the seven hens and the big clock padding along behind them. 'Oh, look – there's the dearest, prettiest white goat I ever saw! Do let's take her!'

Sure enough, not far off was a lovely white nanny-goat, with soft brown eyes and perky ears. She looked quite ordinary except for two blue spots by her tail.

'Little white goat, come with us!' cried Frannie, and the goat trotted up at once. It took its place behind the hens, but it didn't seem to like the clock, which bumped into it every now and again, just to tease it.

'Don't do that, clock,' said Silky.

'I hope your clock won't be a nuisance,' said Beth. 'I think it likes acting silly!'

'Now for the garden shovel,' said Joe, as he suddenly saw a fine strong shovel standing up against a fence with some other garden tools. 'What about this one, girls? This looks strong enough for Father, doesn't it?'

He took a hold of it and jabbed it into the ground. It was just the sight sort. Joe put it over his shoulder, and the four of them grinned happily at each other.

'We've got everything we want,' said Joe. 'Come on.

We'll go back to old Moon-Face and then we'll take some cakes to eat at home.'

So, followed by the seven hens, the white goat, and the clock, the four of them made their way back to where they had left Moon-Face. But he wasn't sitting where they had left him. He was pulling at a lovely rug, which was hanging from a tree. It was perfectly round, with a hole in the middle.

'Hallo, hallo!' yelled Moon-Face, as he saw them. 'Look what I've got! Just what I've always wanted for my round tree room – a round rug with a hole in the middle where the slippery-slip begins! Wonderful!'

'But, Moon-Face, you said you'd watch to see that the Land of Take-What-You-Want kept by the Faraway Tree alright, didn't you?' said Silky anxiously. 'Where is the hole that leads down to the tree?'

'Oh, it's somewhere over there,' said Moon-Face, draping the rug round him and staggering off. 'Come on. We're sure to find it.'

But they didn't! It had gone – for the Land of Take-What-You-Want had moved away from the Faraway Tree.

'Moon-Face! That's very bad of you!' said Joe anxiously. 'You did promise.'

Moon-Face looked worried and pale. He hunted about for the hole – but there was no hole to be seen. He began to shake with fright.

'I've g-g-g-got you all into a t-t-terrible fix!' he said, in a trembling voice. 'Here we are – stuck in a l-l-land where there's everything we w-w-want and the only thing we w-w-w-want is to get away!'

Everyone looked upset. This was just too bad!

'I feel cross with you, Moon-Face,' said Joe, in a stern voice. 'You said you'd keep guard and you didn't. I don't think you are much of a friend.'

'And I am ashamed of you too, Moon-Face,' said Silky, who had tears in her eyes.

'We'll find someone to help us,' said Moon-Face gloomily, and they all set off, followed by their hens, their goat, and the clock, which kept striking four o'clock, nobody knew why.

But now they found a very curious thing. There didn't seem to be anyone at all in the Land of Take-What-You-Want! All the gnomes, the pixies and the elves had gone.

'They must have known the land was going to move off,' said Moon-Face with a groan. 'And they all slipped down the ladder in time. Oh, why did I leave it?'

They wandered all over the land, which was not really very large, but was more crowded with things and animals than anywhere they had ever seen.

'I can't think what to *do*!' said Silky. 'It's true that there is everything here we want – we shan't starve – but it isn't the sort of place we want to live in for ever!'

They walked here and there – and then suddenly they came to something they hadn't noticed before. It was a large and shining aeroplane! The kind that was open-topped, so that you could see all round when you sat inside.

'Ooooh!' said Joe, his eyes gleaming. 'Look at that! How I wish I could fly an aeroplane! Can you fly one, Moon-Face?'

Moon-Face shook his head. Silky shook hers too. 'That's no good then,' said Joe, with a sigh. 'I thought we might fly away from this land in the airplane.'

He climbed into the aeroplane and had a good look at it. There were five handles there. One had a label on it that said UP. Another had a label that said DOWN. A third had one that said STRAIGHT ON, and a fourth and fifth said TO THE RIGHT and TO THE LEFT.

Joe stared at the handles in excitement. 'I believe I could fly this aeroplane,' he said. 'I do believe I could! It looks quite easy.'

'No, Joe, don't,' said Beth, in alarm. But Joe had pressed the handle labelled UP and before anyone could say another word the shining aeroplane had risen upwards with Joe, leaving the others staring open-mouthed on the ground below.

'Now Joe's gone!' said Frannie, and burst into tears.

The aeroplane rose up and up. It circled round when Joe pressed the handle labelled TO THE RIGHT It flew straight on when he pressed the third handle. And it flew down when he pressed the DOWN handle. It was just as easy as that!

Joe flew neatly down to the ground and landed not far away from the others. They rushed to him, shouting and laughing.

'Joe! Joe! Did you really fly it yourself?'

'Well, you saw me,' said Joe, beaming at everyone and feeling tremendously proud. 'It's quite easy. Get in, everyone, and we'll fly off. Maybe we'll come to somewhere that Moon-Face knows, if we fly long enough!'

They all got in. Beth packed the seven squawking hens at the back, and sat the white goat on her knee. The shovel went on the floor. The clock made a nuisance of itself because it wouldn't stay where it was put, but kept climbing over everybody's feet to look out of the window. Silky began to wish she hadn't brought it.

'Ready?' asked Joe, pressing the handle marked UP. And up they went! What a lovely feeling it was! They really couldn't help feeling excited.

Silky's clock got terribly excited too. It chimed twenty-nine without stopping.

'I shan't wind you up tonight if you don't keep quiet,' said Silky suddenly. And that finished the clock! It lay down in a corner and didn't say another ding or another dong!

'Where are we off to, I wonder?' said Beth.

But nobody knew!

XX. OFF TO DAME SNAP'S SCHOOL

Joe flew the aeroplane very well indeed. As soon as he was high enough, he pressed the STRAIGHT ON handle, and the shining airplane flew forward.

The children leaned over the side to see what they were flying over. They had soon passed the Land of Take-What-You-Want, and came to a strange desolate country where no trees or grass grew, and not a house was to be seen.

'That's the Country of Loneliness,' said Moon-Face, peering over. 'Don't land there, Joe. Fly on.'

Joe flew on. Once he came to an enormous hill, and he had to quickly press the handle marked UP or the aeroplane would have flown straight into it. But otherwise it really was great fun. Joe had no idea that it was so easy to fly.

The little white goat on Beth's knee was as good as gold. It licked Beth's cheek every now and then just as if it were a dog! The hens were good and quiet, and the clock lay perfectly still.

The aeroplane flew over a land of great towers and castles. 'Giantland!' said Silky, looking in wonder at the enormous buildings. 'I hope we don't land here!'

'Rather not!' said Joe, and he pressed the STRAIGHT ON handle down still further, so that the aeroplane flew forward like a bird, faster and faster.

The children's hair streamed backwards, and as for

Silky's mop of golden hair, it looked like a field of buttercups blown in the wind! Over the Land of Lollipop they went, and over the Country of Flop. And then the airplane began to make a funny noise!

'Hallo!' said Joe. 'What's wrong?'

'I believe the aeroplane's tired,' said Moon-Face. 'It sounds out of breath.'

'Don't be silly, Moon-Face,' said Joe. 'Airplanes don't get out of breath.'

'This kind does,' said Moon-Face. 'Can't you hear it panting?'

It certainly seemed as if the aeroplane *was* panting! 'Er-her – er-her – er-her!' it went.

'Had we better go down and give it a rest?' said Joe. 'Yes,' said Moon-Face, peering over the side. 'It seems safe enough. I don't know what land this is, but it looks quite ordinary. There's a big green house down below with an enormous garden. Perhaps you could land on that long smooth lawn, Joe. It shouldn't get too bumpy then.'

'Right,' said Joe, and pressed the handle marked DOWN. And down they went, gliding smoothly. Bump! They reached the grass and ran along on the airplane's big wheels. It stopped, and everyone got out, glad to stretch their legs.

'Ten minutes' rest, and the aeroplane will be ready to go off again,' said Moon-Face, patting it.

'I wonder where we are,' said Silky, looking round. Moon-Face gazed at the big green house in the distance – and then he frowned.

'Oh my!' he groaned. 'I know whose house that is! It's a school and it belongs to old Dame Snap! All the naughty pixies and gnomes and fairies are sent there to learn to behave better! Let's hope Dame Snap doesn't catch sight of *us*!'

Everyone looked about nervously – suddenly down a path came a tall old woman, with large spectacles on her long nose and a big white bonnet on her head. Moon-Face ran to the airplane.

'Quick!' he said. 'It's Dame Snap!'

But the old lady was up to them before they could escape. 'Aha!' she said. 'So here is another lot of naughty folk sent to me to be cured! Come this way, please.'

'We *haven't* been sent to you,' said Joe. 'We landed here to give our aeroplane a rest. We are on our way home.'

'Naughty boy, to tell stories like that!' said Dame Snap, suddenly, in such a loud and frightening voice that it made him jump. 'Come with me, all of you.'

There didn't seem to be anything else they could do. Joe, Beth, Frannie, Moon-Face, Silky, the white goat, and the seven hens followed Dame Snap, looking very miserable. The clock wouldn't walk, so Silky had to carry it.

Everyone felt very hungry. Joe pulled Dame Snap's sleeve timidly. 'Could we please have something to eat?' he asked.

'A meal will be ready in a few

119

minutes,' said Dame Snap, 'Heads up, everyone! Don't stoop, little girl!' snapped the old woman. The little girl she meant was poor Frannie, who got such a fright that she stood up straight. Really, Dame Snap was not at all a nice person. It was very bad luck to have landed in her garden.

But everybody cheered up a little at the thought of a meal. They were taken into a large hall, full of pixies and other fairy folk. They were all sitting down in rows at wooden tables, but they stood up when Dame Snap came into the room.

'Sit over there,' said Dame Snap, pointing to an empty table. The children, Moon-Face, Silky, the goat, and the hens all took their places. The clock was stood at the end, and looked very sulky. The children looked down the tables. Oooh! What lovely cakes! What big jugs of lemonade!

Dame Snap ran her eyes over the little folk standing at the tables. She frowned. 'Twinkle, come here!' she snapped. A small pixie walked up to her.

'Haven't I told you to brush your hair properly for meal-times?' shouted Dame Snap so loudly into Twinkle's ear, that he burst into tears.

'And there's Doodle over there with a torn shirt!' said Dame Snap. 'Come here Doodle.'

Doodle came and was shouted at very loudly indeed. Beth and Frannie felt nervous, and hoped their hair and hands and dresses were clean and tidy.

'Sit!' said Dame Snap, and everyone sat. 'Have a cake?' said Joe, and passed Beth and Frannie a plate of delicious-looking cakes, with cherries in the middle.

But what a shock for them! As soon as the cakes

touched their plates they turned into round hard pieces of stale bread! The children didn't dare to say a word. They saw that the same thing happened to everyone in the room except Dame Snap, who had a marvellous meal of cakes, lemonade and sandwiches.

The lemonade turned into water as soon as it was poured into the children's glasses. It was all dreadfully disappointing. In the middle of the meal a gnome-servant came in to say that someone wanted to speak to Dame Snap, and she went out of the room.

And then, dear me, the children found that the pixies and fairies in the room were really very naughty indeed! They crowded round them and jabbed at them and pinched them, and made such rude remarks that Frannie began to cry.

They made such a noise that nobody heard Dame Snap coming back again! My goodness, wasn't she angry! She clapped her hands together and made everyone jump nearly out of their skin!

'What's all this?' she snapped loudly, in a very fierce voice. 'Form up in a line! March past me at once!'

To the children's dismay the cross old lady shouted right in everyone's ear as they passed – but when *they* passed her she didn't shout at them, for she knew that they had been teased by the others. So they were very glad indeed, and felt a little more cheerful.

'Go to the schoolroom,' said Dame Snap, when the last of the line had gone by. So to the schoolroom they all went and took their places, even the little green-winged hens.

'Now, please, answer the questions written on the blackboard,' said Dame Snap. 'You have each got paper and pencil. Anyone putting down the wrong answers will be very sorry indeed.'

Joe looked at the questions on the board. He read them out to the others, in great astonishment.

'If you take away three caterpillars from one bush, how many berries will there be left?'

'Add a pint of milk to a pound of peas and say what will be left over.'

'If a train runs at six miles an hour and has to pass under four tunnels, say what the driver's mother is likely to have for dinner on Sundays.'

Everybody gazed at the board in despair. Whatever did the questions mean? They seemed to be nonsense.

'I can't do any,' said Moon-Face, in a loud voice, and he threw down his pencil.

'It's all silly nonsense!' said Joe, and he threw down his pencil too. The girls did the same, and Silky tore her paper in half! All the pixie and fairy-folk stared at them in the greatest astonishment and horror.

'*In*deed!' said Dame Snap, suddenly looking twice as big as usual. 'If that's how you feel, come with me!'

Nobody wanted to go with her – but they found that they had to, for their legs walked them after Dame Snap without them even trying to. It was most extraordinary. Dame Snap led them to a small room and pushed them all in. Then she shut the door with a slam and turned the key in the lock.

'You will stay there for three hours, and then I will come and see if you are sorry,' she snapped.

'This is awful,' said Joe gloomily. 'She's no right to keep us here. We don't belong to her silly school. We haven't been naughty. It was just an accident that we came here.'

'Well, what are we to do now?' said Silky, pushing back her golden hair. 'It seems as if we'll have to stay here for three hours, and then say we're sorry and be shouted at again! I don't like it at all.'

Nobody liked it. They all sat on the floor and looked angry and miserable. If only they could escape from Dame Snap's silly old school!

XXI. SILKY'S CLOCK IS VERY CLEVER

Joe sat hunched up near to Moon-Face. Silky and Beth and Frannie talked together. The white goat sat on Beth's knee and slept. The seven hens tried to scratch the hard floor, and clucked softly.

'Where's my clock?' said Silky suddenly.

Everyone looked round the room for it. It wasn't there.

'It must have been left behind in the school-room,' said Joe. 'Never mind, Silky. You may get it back, if we get out of here in three hours' time.'

'I hope so,' said Silky. 'It was a nice clock, and I liked it having feet to walk about on.'

'It's lucky not to be locked up like us,' said Joe gloomily. 'If there was a window in this silly round room, we might break it and escape through that. But there isn't even a small window.'

'And there isn't a fireplace either,' said Moon-Face. 'If there was we might squeeze up the chimney. Listen!' he said suddenly. 'There's someone knocking at the door!'

They listened. Certainly there *was* someone outside, knocking gently.

'Come in, if you can!' said Moon-Face. 'Unlock the door if the key's left in.'

But the key wasn't left in! No, Dame Snap had taken that away, you may be sure!

'Who's there?' asked Silky.

'Ding-dong-ding-dong!' said a voice softly.

'It's my clock!' cried Silky excitedly. 'It's come to join us!'

'Oooh!' said Moon-Face, his big face going red with joy. 'Tell your clock to go and get the key from somewhere and let us out, Silky.'

'That's no good,' said Silky. 'I noticed that Dame Snap wore all her keys on a string that hung from her waist. The clock could never get our key from her.'

'Oh,' said Moon-Face sadly. Everybody thought hard.

'Ding-dong-ding-dong!' said the clock outside, and knocked again.

'Look here, clock, it isn't any good your dinging and donging and knocking to get in!' called Joe. 'We are locked into this room, and we haven't got a key to get us out!'

'Dong!' said the clock dolefully. And then it gave an excited 'ding!' and began to dance about on its big feet, up and down, with the little door in its back wide open.

'Whatever is that clock doing?' said Silky, in astonishment.

'Warming its feet up, I think,' said Frannie, with a giggle.

But it wasn't. For it was an old clock that had to be wound up with its own key. And it was jumping about trying to jolt its own key off the little hook inside it! At last it managed to do it. Clang! The key fell to the ground.

'What*ever* is your clock doing?' said Joe to Silky. 'It must have gone mad.'

It hadn't. It was being very sensible. It kicked at the key with one of its feet – and the key slid under the door and into the room where the children were.

'Oooh, look!' said Moon-Face, in astonishment. 'Your clock has jiggled its key off the hook – and kicked it under the door, Silky. Really, it's a most peculiar clock!'

Joe snatched up the key. 'It might fit the door!' he said. He tried it in the lock. It almost turned but not quite. He was dreadfully disappointed.

But Moon-Face grinned. He took the key and rubbed it with a little magic powder that he kept in a box in his pocket.

'Now try it,' he said. So Joe slipped it into the lock once more – and it turned right round and unlocked the door!

They crowded quietly out of the room, Joe taking the clock's key with him. Silky gave the clock a hug and it said ding-dong quite loudly with joy!

'Ssh!' said Silky. 'Don't make a sound!'

'We'll try and find our aeroplane,' said Joe. 'Let's try to get out of a door into the garden. We shall soon find it then.'

They tiptoed down a long passage – but just as they got to the end, who should they see coming along but old Dame Snap herself!

'Quick! Hide behind these curtains!' said Joe. They slipped behind them – but Dame Snap had heard something and came up to the curtains. She was going to pull them apart when Silky's clock walked out,

126

shouted 'Ding-dong!' in her ear, and trod on her toes! Dame Snap gave a shout of rage and she kicked out at the clock. But she missed and it ran away down the passage, with Dame Snap running after it.

'Good old clock!' said Silky joyfully. 'It just walked out and ding-donged in time. Another minute and we would all have been found.'

'Come on,' said Moon-Face, peeping out of the curtains. 'We'd better do our best to get into the garden now, whilst the old dame is out of the way.'

They tiptoed down a long room and came to a door leading into the garden. Just as Joe was going to open it he pushed them all quickly back into the room.

'Dame Snap is coming in here!' he whispered. 'Quick! Hide behind the furniture!'

So, quick as lightning, everyone crouched down behind the sofas and chairs, whilst Dame Snap opened the door and came in, grumbling, 'Wait till I get that clock!'

And at that very moment the clock came running in on its flat feet and ding-donged very rudely at her! Dame Snap picked up her long skirts and tore down the long room and up the passage after it! The children and Moon-Face and Silky, the hens and the goats, rushed to the garden door, opened it and crowded out into the garden.

'Find the aeroplane, quick!' cried Joe. They ran down the path and looked for the shining airplane.

'There it is!' shouted Moon-Face, pointing to the plane standing waiting on the smooth grass. They all ran to it, and squeezed in.

'I don't like leaving my clock behind,' said Silky. 'It

has been so clever. I wonder where it is.'

'Look! There it is, with old Dame Snap after it!' cried Joe. Sure enough they saw the clock come waddling out from behind a bush, chiming hard – and Dame Snap was after it, panting, and very red in the face.

The clock dodged neatly round a bush. Dame Snap tripped over a stone and fell down. The clock shot away to the aeroplane, and Silky helped it in. It sank down into a corner, and chimed sixty-three times without stopping.

But this time nobody minded. They thought the clock was really quite a hero!

Dame Snap picked herself up and ran towards the aeroplane. Joe pressed the UP handle. The engine started to whirr and hum. The airplane quivered and shook. It rose gently into the air, and left Dame Snap below looking very angry indeed.

'Answer this question!' shouted Moon-Face, leaning overboard. 'If five people, seven hens, one white goat, and a clock go up in an airplane, write down how many times Dame Snap will have shouted at them by the time they get home!'

Everyone giggled.

'Do be careful where we land next time,' said Beth. 'We really must get home soon.'

'I think I know where we are now,' said Moon-Face as they flew over a curious land where the trees were yellow and the grass was pink. 'If you can fly straight on till you come to a silver tower – then fly right till you come to the Land of Seagulls – then to the left over the Three Bears' Wood – we shall soon be home!'

'Right!' said Joe. He watched out for the silver tower, and when he saw it, tall and gleaming, he pressed the handle marked TO THE RIGHT and flew on till he came to the Land of Seagulls. This was quite easy to know, for all round and about, flying on snow-white wings, were hundreds of magnificent gulls. The airplane had to go slowly through the crowds of lovely birds. Joe flew to the left, and soon they were over the Three Bears' Wood, and saw the rose-covered cottage where Goldilocks lived with the bears.

'Good! Now it won't be long before we're home!' said Joe. He flew on till he came over the Enchanted Wood, and then landed in a field not far from it. Everyone jumped out.

'That was a most exciting adventure,' said Frannie. 'But I hope we never see Dame Snap again!'

'Oh quick, catch the clock!' said Beth. 'It's trying to climb out of the plane and it will fall!'

'Dong, dong, dong, dong!' said the clock, and it slid to the ground.

'We'll have to rush home now,' said Joe, picking up his shovel. 'Goodbye Silky; goodbye Moon-Face. See you soon! Beth, bring the goat, and Frannie and I will shoo the hens in front of us.'

They left the aeroplane for Moon-Face and Silky to do what they liked with, and set off home.

And, dear me, *how* astonished

129

their mother was to see the green-winged hens, the snow-white goat, and the fine garden shovel!

'You must have been to the Enchanted Wood,' she said.

'We've been *much* farther than that!' said Joe. And they certainly had, hadn't they?

XXII. UP TO THE LAND OF TOYS

KNOCKITY-KNOCK-KNOCK

Bang-bang-BANG!

Rat-a-tarra-TAT!

'Good gracious! It sounds as if somebody's at the door!' said Joe. 'I'll go and open it, Mother.'

He went to open the door – and outside, looking very impatient, stood the old Saucepan Man. He was hung about with pots and pans and kettles as usual, and had a saucepan for a hat.

'Hello,' said the Saucepan Man, 'didn't you hear me knock? I've come to tell you that we must go to the top of the Faraway Tree tomorrow. There's a very nice land coming there.'

'What is it?' asked Joe.

'Toyland,' said Saucepan. 'You could bring a bag with you and collect quite a lot in time for Christmas.'

'Oh what a good idea!' said Joe. He called to his two sisters. 'Beth! Frannie! Did you hear what the Saucepan Man said?'

'Yes!' they cried running to the door. 'Oh, Saucepan, we really must come. Can we help ourselves to toys, do you think?'

'Well, I've an aunt there,' said Saucepan, 'and if I tell her you're my friends, you can have what you want. Can you meet me at the top of the Faraway Tree tomorrow morning?'

'Oh, yes – and will Moon-Face and Silky be coming too?' asked Beth, happily. 'We haven't seen them for ages.'

'We'll have *fun*!' said Frannie.

'Yes, please,' said Saucepan unexpectedly. 'I'd like one very much.'

'Like what?' said Beth, astonished.

'What you just offered me – a bun,' said Saucepan, looking round for it.

'Oh – you suddenly went deaf,' said Beth. 'Frannie just said, we'll have FUN.'

'Oh! All the same I'd like a bun,' said Saucepan.

Joe got him a bun out of the cake-tin. He went off, munching happily, his pans rattling and clanging round him. 'See you tomorrow!' he called.

The next day the three children set off to the Faraway Tree. Into the dark Enchanted Wood they went, and followed the winding path they knew so well. The trees whispered round them as they went. They always seemed to have secrets to tell one another. 'Wisha-wisha-wisha,' they whispered.

They came to the Faraway Tree in the middle of the wood. It looked even more enormous than usual. It towered up into the clouds, and the children couldn't even see the top of it. Its trunk was so big that it was quite a walk to go all the way round it!

'Great! The tree's growing blackberries today,' said Joe, picking some big ripe ones.

'Well, it shouldn't then,' said Beth. 'Blackberries grow

on bushes, not on trees. The
Faraway Tree's made a mistake!'

They began to climb the tree. A
little way up it stopped growing
blackberries and grew pine-cones!

'Not so good,' said Joe. 'We can't eat
pine-cones, Faraway Tree.'

'It's a very *exciting* tree, this,' said Frannie. 'Always
growing different things all the way up – and having
people living in it too – and a slippery-slip all the way
inside from the top to the bottom. I'm glad we live
near a tree like this. We're lucky.'

'Yes. I bet a lot of children wish they lived near it
too,' said Joe, helping Beth over a steep bit. 'My
goodness, the adventures we've had!'

'Look out – I can hear Dame Washalot's dirty water
coming down!' yelled Frannie suddenly.

And, sure enough, down came a cascade of soapy
water, running down the trunk, splashing on the
boughs, and soaking a little pixie who was sitting
nearby.

'Bother!' she said. 'And I brought an umbrella with
me, too, in case I didn't hear the water coming!'

Joe laughed. 'I should put on a swim-suit next time
and not bother about an umbrella,' he said. 'Anyway,
the sun will soon dry you!'

They went up, passing little windows in the
Faraway Tree, and came to Silky's small yellow door.
They knocked, but there was no answer.

'She's gone up to the top of the tree, I expect,' said
Joe. 'Come on – we don't want to keep the others
waiting.'

They climbed right up to Moon-Face's little door. From inside came the sound of chattering, and the noise of jangling and clanging.

'The Saucepan Man's there all right,' said Joe. 'And the others, too, I should think.' He banged on the door. Moon-Face opened it, beaming all over his big round face. 'Oh, come in,' he said. 'We're just having a snack before we go.'

'What sort of snack?' asked Beth, going in with the others. 'Pop Cakes? I love those.'

'No – something Saucepan bought when he was in the Land of Surprises,' said Moon-Face. 'Well-I-Never Rolls.'

'What a peculiar name,' said Joe, looking at the dish of nice crusty little rolls. 'What do they taste of?'

'Try one,' said Moon-Face. 'And tell us!'

Joe took a roll and bit into it. 'Tastes of cheese,' he said. 'No – well I never, it tastes of ginger now. No, it doesn't – it's chocolate! And now it tastes of coconut – and it's got bits of coconut in it – no, they've gone – it's treacly now. Well I never!'

'Yes. Most peculiar, isn't it?' said Moon-Face. 'No wonder they're called Well-I-Never Rolls. You just simply never know what they'll taste of next. Every chew you have tastes of something different.'

'Jolly good,' said Joe. 'I'll have another. My – this tastes of pickled onions – no, it doesn't – it's custard – lovely!'

'Mustard,' said Saucepan in disgust. 'I'd hate one to taste of mustard.'

'I said CUSTARD,' said Joe, and then made a face. 'Oh my goodness, it *is* mustard now. Horrible!'

'Just what I said. Mustard,' said Saucepan. He bit into his. 'Ah – mint! Delicious! Why, it's mint sauce, I can taste the tiny bits of mint.'

'You'll find you've got roast lamb next,' said Silky.

Saucepan looked surprised. 'No – it isn't ham,' he said.

'I said LAMB!' shouted Silky.

'No, it's not jam,' said Saucepan. 'Well I never, it's lamb! Lamb and mint sauce – how clever! Really these rolls are remarkable.'

So they were. The six of them finished up the whole dish of them. 'I wish I'd brought heaps more,' said Saucepan, getting up. 'Well, aren't we going up to Toyland? Do hurry up.'

They were all ready. They went out of Moon-Face's little round room and climbed up the topmost branch into a cloud. They came to the little ladder that led upwards through the last bit of cloud. Toyland should be at the top!

Saucepan went first. He climbed off the top rung of the ladder, and called down to the others.

'Yes, it's here. Come on!'

Up they all went, and at last stood in Toyland. But there seemed to be no toys about at all. Saucepan pointed to a town not far off. Flags flying brightly from little houses.

'There's the Village of Toys,' he said. 'Now we'll go and find my aunt.'

They set off to the village. But when they got there, Saucepan stopped and looked puzzled.

'Dear me,' he said, 'this isn't the land I hoped. The toys are all alive – look, isn't that a teddy bear walking about?'

'Yes,' said Beth. 'Goodness – we can't take toys like these away to play with at home! They're as big as we are!'

'I'll find my aunt,' said Saucepan, and they all walked down the village street, meeting three or four sailor dolls, a curious man who had no legs but just wobbled along, and some beautifully dressed dolls.

Saucepan's aunt was nowhere to be found. She kept a toyshop, and, of course, there was no toyshop there, because the toys lived in little houses made of coloured wooden bricks.

'Your aunt lives in the other land, you silly,' said Silky. 'This must be the Land of Toys, not Toyland.'

'Oh, well – let's enjoy ourselves, anyway,' said Saucepan. 'Here comes another wobbly man. Let's try and push him over.'

The wobbly man was astonished and annoyed when Saucepan gave him a push. He wobbled over backwards and then came forwards again, only to get another push, this time from Moon-Face.

'How dare you?' cried the wobbly man in a rage. 'That's not the way for visitors to behave! I'll report you to the Captain of the Toy Soldiers!'

He wobbled off at a remarkable speed. The three children and Silky felt a bit scared.

'You shouldn't go round pushing people, Saucepan,' said Joe. 'Not even to see them wobble. I do hope we don't get into trouble.'

Saucepan suddenly went deaf and didn't hear. He hardly ever did hear when somebody scolded him. 'Look, there's a clockwork mouse running along!' he said, pointing. 'Run, mouse, run! Meeow! MEEOW!'

The clockwork mouse was very frightened when it heard Saucepan mewing. It turned and ran off at top speed, almost bumping into a toy soldier.

'Look – there's the Captain of the Soldiers,' said Beth, afraid. 'And the Wobbly Man is with him. He's complained about us, as he said he would. We'd better run away.'

'No,' said Joe. 'We can easily explain, and Saucepan must say he's sorry.'

Up marched the toy soldier, as smart as could be. He saluted – click!

'You must come with me,' said the Captain, in a commanding voice. 'You are not toys, and should not be here. Also, your behaviour must be looked into. Follow me, quick MARCH!'

'We'd better follow,' said Joe. 'He can't do anything to us; he's only a toy, even if he *is* alive. And I must say I'd rather like to see what that toy fort is like inside.'

So they all followed the toy soldier and the wobbly man. Whatever was going to happen?

XXIII. THEY GET INTO TROUBLE

The Captain took them through the village and up to
the wooden fort. It was very like a toy fort that Joe had
once had. It even had a wooden drawbridge that could
be pulled up or let down.

It was let down for them to walk over. Toy cannons
stood here and there. Joe went up to one. 'Funny old
cannon!' he said. 'Look there's a knob to pull back
and then let go, just like the toy cannon I had in my
little fort at home.'

He pulled back the knob, let it go and then BANG!
The cannon went off with a loud noise! The wobbly
man was so shocked that he almost fell over, and it
took a lot of wobbles for him to stand upright again.

The toys in the village below were so frightened
when the cannon went BANG that they rushed out of
their little houses and ran for their lives! The Captain
was very angry indeed.

'Now see what you've done!' he said to Joe. 'Let off
the cannon, and scared everybody! You must be mad.'

'I'm very sorry,' said Joe. 'I never thought the
cannon would go off like that.'

'Well, what did you think it would do?' said the
Captain, angrily. 'Whistle a tune or dance a jig?'

Nobody dared to laugh. The Captain led them on
again, and soon they came to a door that led into a
wooden tower. They went in and found themselves in

a room with a table and a chair at one end, and nothing else. The Captain sat himself down in the chair.

'Stand up straight,' he said. Everyone stood up very straight, even Saucepan.

'Salute,' said the Captain, and everyone saluted, though Moon-Face used the wrong hand.

'Dismiss!' said the Captain, and everyone stared. What did he mean?

'No – that's wrong,' said the Captain. 'Don't dismiss. Stand at ease.'

They obeyed. The Captain rapped loudly on the table. 'You are accused of not being toys. You are accused of punching wobbly men. You are accused of setting off cannons. You –'

'Only *one* wobbly man, and *one* cannon,' said Joe. 'We're sorry and we won't do it again. We'll dismiss now!'

But before they could go they heard the noise of marching feet, and into the room came about fifty toy soldiers, all very wooden. They surrounded the children and the others.

'To the deepest dungeon with them!' shouted the Captain.

'NO!' shouted Joe, and he pushed the nearest soldier hard. The soldier fell against the soldier next to him and knocked him over. That one fell against the next one and he went down, too, knocking the soldier next to him – and before five seconds had passed every soldier was lying flat on the floor.

'It's like playing dominoes – knock the first over, and down goes the whole row!' said Frannie with a giggle.

The Captain looked alarmed. What was he to do with people like these? Goodness – one push, and all his soldiers were down! He banged on the table.

'Order! Order! Get up! Do you think you are skittles, men?'

The men got up, but none of them would go near the little group of six prisoners.

'Now listen,' said the Captain. 'Either you become toys, or you go to the deepest dungeon. You can choose.'

'All right – we'll be toys, then!' said Joe with a grin. 'I'll be a clockwork clown, and go head-over-heels all the time!'

He began to go head-over-heels all round the room, and knocked into one of the soldiers. Down they all went again, like a row of skittles!

'Right – you're a clockwork clown,' said the Captain. 'What will *you* be?' and he pointed at Moon-Face.

'A teddy bear,' grinned Moon-Face, 'with a growl in my middle.' And he pressed himself in the middle and pretended to growl.

'I'll be a doll,' said Silky, and began to walk about stiffly like a doll.

'And I'll be a furry grey rabbit!' said the Saucepan Man. 'I'll grow long floppy ears and grey fur!'

'We'll be dolls,' said Beth and Frannie together, and they walked about stiffly like Silky, giggling all the time.

'Right,' said the Captain thankfully. 'You are now toys, and can remain in the Land of Toys. Dis-MISS!'

The six of them went out laughing, Joe still turning

head-over-heels, just for fun. They went over the drawbridge and into the town. In the distance they saw an enormous Noah's Ark.

'Let's go and see the animals coming out two by two,' said Beth, and they set off.

Frannie was just going to say something to Saucepan, who was in front of her, when she stopped. She stared hard.

She saw something very peculiar. Saucepan wore a saucepan for a hat, as usual – but, goodness, he had suddenly grown two huge floppy ears! The saucepan sat on top, looking very odd.

'Saucepan,' said Frannie, astonished. 'Saucepan, what's wrong with you?'

Saucepan turned round, surprised, and everyone got a tremendous shock. His face was covered in grey fur and he had very long whiskers!

'He's a toy rabbit!' said Frannie, with a squeal. 'Saucepan – you're a toy rabbit! You said you would be, and now you are.'

They were all very surprised. They stared and stared at poor Saucepan. How peculiar to see his face all grey, topped with two floppy ears and long quivering whiskers!

Saucepan looked at himself in one of his bright pans, which he used as a mirror. He was shocked to see such a furry face looking back at him. He gazed round at the others, scared.

Then he gave a shout and pointed to Joe. 'Well! Look at *him*! He's a clockwork clown now, hat and all! Yes, and he's got a key in his back! Joe, you're a clown! No wonder you keep going head-over-heels!'

Joe turned another somersault at once. The others gazed at him. Yes, Joe was a clown, with a clown's hat and suit. His face was daubed in red and white like a clown's too.

Frannie looked at the others, and squealed again. 'Look at Moon-Face – he's a fat, round little teddy bear, with a round, teddy-bear face that's hardly like Moon-Face's at all! Oh, Moon-Face – is it really you?'

'Yes,' said Moon-Face, putting up his hand to feel his face. 'Oh dear – I've gone all furry. Where are my clothes? They've gone.'

Joe pressed him in the middle and an alarming growl came out – grrrrrrrrrr!

'Don't,' said Silky. 'You made me jump. Don't press him again, Joe. Oh, my goodness – this is dreadful. We're all toys. Look at *me*!'

'You're not so bad,' said Joe, looking at her. 'You are the prettiest doll I ever saw. And Beth and Frannie are dolls, too. Look at them walking about, as stiff as can be. Beth, can you sit down?'

'Not very easily,' said Beth, trying to sit on a nearby wall. 'I can't seem to bend. And I can't shut my eyes, either.'

'Perhaps they will shut when you lie down,' said Moon-Face, speaking in a funny growly voice.

So Beth lay down on some grass for a moment and at once her eyes shut!

'Yes, we're *really* toys,' said Frannie. 'It must have begun to happen when we said we'd be toys, and chose what we'd be. But we only said it for fun.'

'I know. But you never know what will happen in the Lands that come to the top of the Faraway Tree,' said Joe. 'Moon-Face, will we stop being toys when we get out of this Land?'

'No, I don't think so,' said the teddy bear. 'And anyway, how do you think you are going to head-over-heels down the Faraway Tree? We'll just have to hope this will all wear off.'

'I don't like being a toy rabbit,' said Saucepan sadly. 'I feel silly. Do you think my face will become my own again if I wash it?'

'No,' said Joe, turning head-over-heels for about the fiftieth time; 'toy rabbits always stay furry. It's your ears that look so funny with that saucepan stuck on top of them. Why don't you take it off?'

'Well, I might get a cold,' said Saucepan. 'I always wear a hat. I don't feel right without a saucepan for a hat.'

'You certainly don't *look* right now,' said Moon-Face, in his growly voice.

'Nor do you,' said Saucepan. 'I wish you'd look like Moon-Face again. I don't like you like that.'

'Oh, come on,' said Joe, going head-over-heels again. 'Let's explore the Village of Toys and hope all this wears off. If only I didn't have to go head-over-heels so often! I'm getting very tired of it.'

'So are we,' said Frannie, getting out of his way. 'Do keep over there, Joe – you'll knock me over.'

The little group went on through the Village of Toys. Nobody took much notice of them now because they looked exactly like toys. Wobbly men wobbled about, looking very busy, and teddy bears lazed around, fat and cheerful looking. Dolls of all kinds went here and there, and they saw the little clockwork mouse again.

143

'Meeow!' said Saucepan, and it fled.

'You're unkind to it,' said Frannie. 'It's a dear little thing. Oh, dear – I do feel funny, walking stiffly like this. I'm sure I couldn't run, even if I had to!'

'Look, here come the Noah's Ark animals,' said Joe, getting up from another somersault. 'Two by two, just as they should. Two lions, two bears, two rabbits . . .'

'Two ducks, two mice,' went on Frannie.

'MEEOW!' said Saucepan at once again. 'Meeow!'

But the Noah's Ark mice took no notice of him. However, somebody else did! Behind the mice were two cats, and one of them left the row of animals and came over to Saucepan, glaring at him.

'What did you say just then?' said the wooden cat.

'Meow,' said Saucepan, 'meow, meow, meow!'

'How dare you call me such rude names!' said the cat, and showed claws in her wooden paws. Saucepan backed away hurriedly.

'I didn't mean to call you names,' he said. 'I just said, "meow, meow, meow," to the mice.'

'Well, that means, "You're a very ugly cat with a crooked tail!"' said the cat angrily. 'My tail is *not* crooked. Don't use cat-language if you don't know what it means!'

'Get back into line, cat!' called Mr Noah, and the cat obeyed. Saucepan was very relieved. Goodness – to think those simple meows had meant all that in cat-language! He really must be careful.

'Let's go on,' he said to the others, who were as surprised as he was. 'Moon-Face might suddenly begin to growl, and goodness knows what that might mean in bear-language! We don't want those two white bears and the two brown ones to come after us.'

'Well, let's go another way,' said Joe, gloomily turning another somersault. 'Blow this head-over-heels business. I'm tired of it!'

They turned down another way. Oh, dear – was this strange spell wearing off yet? It didn't seem like it!

XXIV. MR OOM-BOOM-BOOM

They came to a little garage. A very furry rabbit was busy putting petrol into a car driven by another toy rabbit. They looked at Saucepan in surprise as he came along with the others.

'Hello!' said the garage rabbit. 'What's the idea of wearing a saucepan for a hat? I can't say I've ever seen a rabbit wearing a hat before.'

'Well, you've seen one now,' said Saucepan, not very politely. 'Bother these awful floppy ears. I hate them. They make me look like a toy rabbit.'

'Well, you *are* a toy rabbit, floppy ears and all,' said the rabbit, staring.

'That's where you're wrong,' said Saucepan. 'I'm not. I hate being one. Ugly creatures, with stupid long ears and quivering whiskers!'

'Stop it, Saucepan,' said Joe, in a warning voice. He turned to the surprised rabbit.

'You must excuse him,' he said, 'he's really a Saucepan Man, as you can see. And I'm not really a clockwork clown, I'm a boy. Oh – excuse me, I can feel another somersault coming on!'

He turned head-over-heels and then stood up straight again.

'I see,' said the rabbit. 'Well, I should just hate to be an ugly little Saucepan Man, so I know what he feels about being a rabbit – though rabbits are very handsome creatures – like myself. He should be pleased he's turned into one.'

'Well, we really like being ourselves best,' said Frannie. 'I'm a little girl, not a doll. And this teddy bear is really Moon-Face.'

'Never heard of him,' said the rabbit. 'Didn't know there were such things as Moon-Faces.'

Frannie giggled. Silky went up to the rabbit and smiled at him. 'Please do help us,' she said.

The rabbit stared at her. He thought she was the prettiest doll he had ever seen in the Village of Toys. The rabbit who was inside the car leaned out.

'Of course we'll help you,' he said. 'What do you want us to do?'

'Well, we did hope all this would wear off,' said Silky in a high doll's voice that was quite sweet. 'But it hasn't. And we wondered if you knew how we could get back into ourselves again.'

The two rabbits looked at one another. 'Difficult,' said one. 'Very,' said the other.

'What about the old Spell-Maker, Mr Oom-Boom-Boom?' said the first one. 'If he's in a good mood, he might do something for them.'

'Yes. But if he's in a bad mood, he might turn them into something worse,' said the second rabbit.

'Then we won't go there,' said Joe hurriedly, and turned another somersault.

'We could see if he's in a good or bad mood before we say anything,' said the rabbit. 'I'll take you there in my car, if you can all squeeze in.'

'Well, we could try,' said Moon-Face,

147

his little round teddy bear face looking worried.

The rabbit told Silky to sit next to him. He thought she was really beautiful, and very sweet. 'I am sure, if *you* went to ask Mr Oom-Boom-Boom a favour he would say "yes" at once,' he said. 'I never saw anyone as pretty as you.'

'Well you're a very handsome rabbit,' said Silky, and that pleased him very much. They all squeezed into the car somehow, waved to the friendly garage rabbit, and set off.

'I feel a somersault coming on,' said Joe suddenly. 'I'm so sorry – but will you please stop the car so that I can get out and turn head-over-heels?'

'You're going to be a bit of a nuisance,' said the rabbit driver. 'Can't you do about a dozen, and make those do for a while?'

'I'll try,' said poor Joe. So he got out and did nine, but no more would come, so he got back into the car. 'I do wish you didn't wear so many pans and kettles,' he said to Saucepan. 'Move that kettle, will you? It's sticking its spout into me.'

'Kettles don't have snouts,' said Saucepan.

'SPOUT, I said, not Snout,' said Joe crossly. 'Now there's something else sticking into me – a saucepan handle.'

'I haven't got any candles,' said Saucepan, mishearing again. 'You know I haven't. You're just making a fuss, with all your chatter about snouts and candles.'

'I said SHOUTS and PANDLES,' bawled Joe, losing his temper. 'No, I don't mean that – I mean, I mean . . .'

'Pouts and Scandles,' said Frannie with a squeal of

148

laughter. 'Be quiet, you two. Saucepan, dear, be sensible. He meant Spouts and Handles – look, they're sticking into him.'

'Well, why didn't he say so then,' grumbled Saucepan, moving the kettle and the saucepan and sticking them into Moon-Face instead. 'Goodness, Moon-Face, what are *you* growling about now?'

Moon-Face turned his teddy-bear face to Saucepan. 'You're not kind,' he said.

'No, I don't mind,' said Saucepan, whose hearing had gone quite wrong with the noise of the car and the jangling of his pans. 'Of course I don't mind. Why should I mind? Mind what, anyhow?'

'Stop talking,' said the rabbit at the wheel. 'I keep listening and it all sounds so mad that I'm sure I shall drive into a tree or something. Anyway, I want to talk to this dear doll here, Silky.'

Nobody talked after that except Silky and the toy rabbit. The car went on and on, and at last Joe wanted to get out and go head-over-heels again. 'Can you stop?' he called.

'Goodness, I've gone right past Mr Oom-Boom-Boom!' said the rabbit, putting on the brake so suddenly that the saucepan flew off Saucepan's head and rolled away down the road. 'Yes, get out and somersault for a bit while I turn the car round.'

So Joe turned about ten somersaults, while the toy rabbit turned the car round again. Then back they went to find Mr Oom-Boom-Boom.

'Don't start talking to Silky or you'll go right past again,' begged Frannie. But this time the rabbit kept an eye open for Mr Oom-Boom-Boom's house and

suddenly put on the brakes again.

'There goes another of my saucepans,' groaned Saucepan. 'Do we *have* to stop so suddenly?'

Nobody took any notice of him. They stared at a funny little door set in a grassy hill. On it was printed in bold black letters:

OOM-BOOM-BOOM. KNOCK SEVEN TIMES.

'Silky, you go,' said Frannie. 'Perhaps Oom-Boom-Boom will be nice to you. You really do look very sweet.'

'All right. I'll knock,' said Silky bravely, though she felt very scared. She got out of the car, and went up to the little door. She took hold of the knocker and knocked seven times – blam-blam-blam-blam-blam-blam-blam!

A loud voice came from inside. 'Stop knocking. Once is quite enough!'

'Oh dear – he's in a bad mood!' called the rabbit. 'Come back quickly, Silky, and we'll drive off.'

'I can't come,' wailed Silky. 'The knocker has got hold of my hand. It won't let go!'

Joe jumped out at once and went to help her. But Silky was quite right. The knocker had tight hold of her hand and wouldn't let it go.

Moon-Face went to help, too, and then the Saucepan Man, looking very worried. And just at that very moment the door opened, pulling poor Silky with it, and a voice boomed out loudly:

'WHAT'S ALL THIS? DISTURBING ME IN THE MIDDLE OF MY SPELLS!'

Everyone thought that Oom-Boom-Boom was a very good name for him, booming at them like that. But he wasn't a bit like his voice. He was an old pixie with a beard so long that it trailed behind him. He had big, pointed ears, and wore a funny little round hat with feelers on it like a butterfly's. His eyes were as green as grass and very bright indeed.

He frowned at them all – and then he saw Silky, still held by the knocker.

'Ah,' he said, and a smile broke over his face like the sun shining out suddenly. 'Ah! What a dear little doll! No wonder my knocker wouldn't let you go. Where did you come from? I've never seen a doll as pretty as you! Do you know where you ought to be?'

'No,' said Silky, with a gasp.

'You ought to be standing at the very top of the great big Christmas Tree that Santa Claus has in his castle!' said Oom-Boom-Boom in his booming voice. 'He's always looking for the prettiest doll in the world to put there, but he's never found one as pretty as you yet!'

'I'm not a doll,' said Silky. 'I'm a fairy. I've been turned into a doll today.'

'Let her go, knocker,' said the pixie. 'Come in, all of you. Why have you paid me this visit?'

'He seems in a very good mood now,' whispered Joe to Moon-Face. 'I think it's safe to go in.'

They all went in and the door shut with a bang that

151

made them jump. Inside there was a narrow, very winding passage that led into the hill. They followed the pixie down it, everybody stumbling over his very long beard that trailed out behind him. He didn't seem to mind.

He took them to a big room with a very low ceiling. A great fire burned in the middle, but the flames were green, not red, and no heat came from them.

'I was just making a few spells,' said Oom-Boom-Boom, his big voice echoing all round the room. 'I'm a spell-maker, you know.'

'Yes. That's why we came,' said Silky, feeling very nervous. 'Please, dear Mr Oom-Boom-Boom, will you use a spell to help us? We want to go back to our right selves. I'm a fairy, really, as I told you.'

'And we're really little girls,' said Beth and Frannie. 'And this clown is a boy, and the toy rabbit is old Saucepan Man . . .'

'And I'm Moon-Face,' said Moon-Face, his little teddy-bear face looking very earnest. 'Please do help us.'

'Ha,' said Oom-Boom-Boom, looking round at them and beaming, 'well, I don't mind doing that. That's easy. But I'll do it on one condition.'

'What's that?' asked Joe, his heart sinking.

'I'll turn five of you back to your own shapes – but I want this little doll here, the very pretty one, to stay with me so that I can sell her to Santa Claus to put on the top of his Christmas Tree! It will be such an honour for her. You'd love that, wouldn't you, my dear?' he said to Silky, turning to her.

Silky looked very frightened. 'Well – I'll stay and let

you sell me to Santa Claus,' she said, 'if you will use a spell on the others.'

'Oh, dear, darling Silky!' said Moon-Face, putting his furry arm round her, 'How sweet you are! But we wouldn't let you. We'd never leave you here alone.'

'Never,' said Joe. 'NEVER!'

'Never, never, never, never,' said Joe, Beth and Frannie.

'I'm going to stay,' said Silky, looking as if she was going to cry, but smiling at them all the same. 'It won't be so bad, going to Santa Claus, though it sounds very dull standing on the top of his Christmas Tree. But it's for you, you see, so I want to do it!'

'Of course she wants to do it,' said Oom-Boom-Boom. 'She's a sensible little doll.'

'Be quiet,' said Joe. 'I tell you we won't let her do it! We'd rather be toys all our lives than that!'

Then Mr Oom-Boom-Boom lost his temper. He rushed at Joe – but Joe did a very clever thing. He caught him by his very long beard, dragged him to a big table and tied him to it with his beard, making dozens of knots!

'Now, quick, let's go!' he cried. 'Sorry about tying you up, Oom-Boom-Boom, but you're not going to have Silky. Run everyone!'

They ran up the winding passage and came out on the hillside. And oh, thank goodness, there was the rabbit waiting in his car! What a wonderful sight!

XXV. IN SANTA CLAUS' CASTLE

Joe got to the car first. 'Quick!' he cried. 'I can hear Oom-Boom-Boom coming! He must have got free.'

So he had! He appeared at the door of his peculiar house, and they saw that he had freed himself by cutting his beard short. He did look strange.

The toy rabbit revved up his car and it shot off, almost before Saucepan was safely in. A kettle flew, clanging, down the road, and Saucepan groaned.

'Well, thank goodness that kettle's gone,' said Joe. 'It can't stick into me again. Oh, dear – I feel I want to turn head-over-heels.'

'Well, you can't,' said Moon-Face firmly. 'Unless you want to be caught by the Oom-Boom-Boom fellow. Here, Saucepan, hang on to Joe, and stop him turning head-over-heels in the car!'

It was difficult to stop him, but they managed it. After they had gone a good way the rabbit stopped the car for a talk, and Joe took the chance of turning about a dozen somersaults.

'You know, I think you should go to the Land of Santa Claus,' said the rabbit. 'I do really. Not to give him Silky, of course, that would never do – but to tell him you aren't toys and to ask him if he can stop you being what you're not.'

'That's a bit muddling,' said Moon-Face, trying to work it out. 'Yes – it seems a good idea. After all, he deals in toys, doesn't he? He must know them very well. He'll be able to tell we're not real toys, and *might* help us.'

'We know he's kind,' said Silky. 'He's so fond of children. Let's go to him. How can we get there, though? This Land may stay at the top of the Faraway Tree for some time – and the Land of Santa Claus may not be the next one to arrive.'

'That's true enough,' said the rabbit. 'Actually the next Land on the timetable is the Land of Squalls, which doesn't sound too good. But I'll tell you what I can do for you!'

'What!' asked Joe.

'I can drive you to the next station and put you on a train for the land of Santa Claus,' said the toy rabbit. 'I happened to notice that some trains there do go to his Land. What about it, friends?'

'A very good idea,' said everyone, and off they went. They came to a funny little station after a while, and they all got out.

'I wish you could stay in my Land for ever, Silky doll,' said the rabbit to Silky. 'You really are the prettiest thing I ever saw. But there – you'd be unhappy and I couldn't bear that.'

'I'll write to you,' said Silky.

'Will you really?' said the rabbit. 'Do you know, I've never had a letter in my life! It *would* make me feel important! Look, there's a train in!'

'Wow! This train's going to the Land of Santa Claus! What a bit of luck!' cried Moon-Face. 'Goodbye, rabbit. You really have been a good friend. I'll write to you.'

'My goodness – fancy me getting two letters!' said the delighted rabbit.

'We'll *all* write,' said Joe, shaking his furry hand warmly. 'Goodbye. It's been lovely meeting you.'

Silky gave him a kiss and he nearly cried for joy. 'I've never been kissed before,' he said. 'Never. A kiss – and letters – my goodness, I *am* a lucky rabbit!'

They all climbed into the train and waved goodbye.

'Nice fellow, that rabbit,' said Joe. 'Well, we're off again. I wonder how far it is.'

It was quite a long way, and they all fell asleep. A porter woke them up at last. 'Hey, you! Don't you want to get out here?' he said. 'This is where toys usually get out.'

They scrambled out because the station board said, 'Get out here for the Castle of Santa Claus!'

'Just in time,' said Joe, yawning. 'Oh – here I go, turning head-over-heels again!'

'There's the castle – look!' said Beth, pointing to a magnificent castle with many towers, rising high on a hill nearby. 'And, goodness – look at the snow! Anyone would think it was winter here.'

'Oh, it always is,' said the porter. 'It wouldn't be much good for sleighs, would it, if there wasn't snow? Is Santa Claus expecting you? His sleigh usually meets the train in case there are any visitors for him.'

'Is that it down there?' asked Moon-Face, pointing down into the snowy station yard. A sleigh was there, with four lovely reindeer, whose bells jingled as they moved restlessly. A small red pixie held the reins.

'Yes, that's the sleigh. Better go and get in,' said the porter. He stared hard at Silky. 'Goodness, isn't that a pretty doll? I bet Santa Claus will want her for his own Christmas Tree.'

They went to the sleigh and got into it. 'To Santa Claus, please,' said Joe, and off they went, gliding smoothly over the snow, drawn by the four eager reindeer.

They arrived at the castle. They felt rather nervous when they saw how big and grand it was. They stood at an enormous door, carved with all kinds of toys, and rang a great bell.

The door swung open. 'Please come in,' said a teddy bear, dressed like a footman. 'Santa Claus will see you in a few minutes.'

They went into a big hall and then into a great room, where many little pixies and goblins were at work. 'You might like to look round while you're waiting,' said the bear footman. 'You'll see the pixies painting the dolls' houses, and the goblins putting growls into us bears, and you'll see how the somersaults are put into the clockwork clowns.'

'I don't want to see that,' said Joe, feeling at once that he wanted to go head-over-heels. He turned a few and then stood up again. 'What are those pixies doing over there?' he said.

'Putting the hum into tops,' said the footman. 'But don't go too near. One of the hums might get into you by mistake, and that's *such* a nuisance, you know!'

They stood at a safe distance, watching. It was very interesting indeed. So many things were going on; there was so much to see and hear, that they almost forgot they were toys themselves.

'How's your growl, bear?' said a little pixie, running up to Moon-Face. He pressed him in the middle and Moon-Face growled deeply. 'Grrrrrr! Leave me alone! I don't like people doing that. Grrrrr!'

'Look – oh, look – isn't that Santa Claus himself?' cried Beth, suddenly, as a big man came into the room dressed in bright red. He wore a hood trimmed with white, and his jolly face had eyes that twinkled brightly.

'Yes. It's Santa Claus!' cried Joe. Santa Claus heard him and came over at once. He looked in surprise at Silky.

'Why!' he said. 'Where did you come from? *You* weren't made in my castle, by pixies and goblins. You are the loveliest doll I've ever seen. I've a good mind to keep you for myself and put you at the very top of my own big Christmas Tree.'

'No, no, please not!' said Silky. Santa Claus looked down at the others. He seemed puzzled.

'Where do you all come from?' he said. 'I am quite sure I have never had any toys made like you. The

158

rabbit, dressed up in kettles and saucepans, for instance – and this funny little bear. He doesn't seem like a proper teddy.'

'We're *not* proper toys!' said Beth. 'Santa Claus, we got turned into toys in the fort of the toy soldiers. I'm a little girl really.'

'And I'm Moon-Face, who lives at the top of the Faraway Tree,' said Moon-Face.

'What! The famous Moon-Face, who has a slippery-slip in his room, going down the tree from the top to the bottom!' cried Santa Claus. 'My goodness – I've often wanted to see that! Do you think I'm too fat to go down it?'

'No – no, I don't think so,' said Moon-Face, looking at him. 'I could give you *two* cushions to sit on instead of one. If you'd like to come now, you can go up and down the Faraway Tree as often as you like – we'll haul you up in the washing basket every time you arrive at the bottom, and you can slide down again from the top!'

'Let's go now,' said Santa Claus in delight. 'Well, well – to think I'm meeting the famous Moon-Face at last! And I suppose this lovely doll is Silky the fairy. And, of course – this is the old Saucepan Man!'

'But – how do you know us?' asked Moon-Face, astonished.

'Oh, I've heard about you from the children,' said Santa Claus. 'They keep asking me for books about you, to go into their Christmas stockings and they looked so exciting that I read them all. I *did* want to meet you!'

Well, wasn't that a bit of luck? Santa Claus called

159

his sleigh and they all got in. 'To the top of the Faraway Tree,' commanded Santa Claus, and away they went. It didn't take very long. In quite a little while the sleigh landed on a broad bough near the top of the tree, and they all got out.

'My room is just a bit higher up,' said Moon-Face, and led the way. They were soon in his little round room. He pointed to the curious hole in the middle of the floor.

'There you are,' he said. 'That's the slippery-slip – it goes round and round from top to bottom of the tree – and you fly out of the trap door at the bottom, and land on a soft cushion of moss.'

'Splendid!' said Santa Claus. 'Will somebody else go first, please? Goodness, it's exactly the same as I read about in the books!'

'Er – do you think you could just change us back to our ordinary selves?' asked Joe, afraid that in his excitement Santa Claus might forget to do what they so badly wanted. 'I feel as if I'm going to somersault again, and I don't want to turn head-over-heels all the way down the slippery-slip.'

'Change you back? Yes, of course; it's easy!' said Santa Claus. 'The slippery-slip is just the right place for a spell. Shut your eyes, please.'

They all shut their eyes. Santa Claus touched each one gently, chanting a curious little song:

> *Go in as you are,*
> *Come out as you were,*
> *Go in as you are,*
> *Come out as you were!*

They opened their eyes. Moon-Face got a cushion and pulled Beth on to it. He gave her a tremendous push and she shot down the slippery-slip at top speed – round and round – and then out she flew through the trap door at the bottom, and landed on a tuft of moss.

'Oh,' she said, breathless. 'Oh! I'm myself again. I'm not a stiff-jointed doll any longer – and I can shut and open my eyes properly!'

She got up – and out of the trap door flew Joe. 'Joe! You're all right again! You're you!' cried Beth in delight. 'And here comes Silky – she's not a doll any more – and here's Frannie – she's all right, too. Look out – here's the old Saucepan Man – yippee he's back to normal!'

'And he's lost his floppy ears,' said Silky. 'I'm rather sorry. I liked him with those long ears. Good old Saucepan.'

And then, WhooooOOOOOOSH! The trap door shot open with a bang and out sailed Santa Claus, his hood on the back of his head! Bump! He went on to the cushion of moss, and sat there, panting and full of delight.

'What a thrill! WHAT a thrill! Better than anything I've got in my castle.'

'Look out! Here comes Moon-Face!' cried Joe, and out came Moon-Face, no longer a fat teddy bear, but his own beaming self once more.

'I'd like to do that again,' said Santa Claus, standing up. 'How did you say we got back to the top of the tree? In a basket?'

'Yes,' said Joe, 'but if you don't mind, we won't come with the others. You see, our mother will be wondering about us. So we'd better say goodbye and thank you very much.'

'Goodbye. See you next Christmas,' said Santa Claus. 'I'll bring you something extra nice. Ah – here comes the basket, let down on a rope. Do we get in?'

The last thing that Joe, Beth and Frannie saw was Santa Claus in the big basket, being pulled slowly up by all the squirrels at the top of the tree. Moon-Face and Silky and Saucepan were with him, leaning over the edge of the basket, waving to them.

'Well – I suppose dear old Santa Claus will be going down that slippery-slip till it's dark,' said Joe. 'Oh dear – surely I'm not going to turn head-over-heels again! I feel just like it!'

'Oh, you'll soon get out of the habit,' said Beth. 'I still feel as if I want to walk stiffly like a doll. Goodness, wasn't that an adventure!'

'We'll never have a better one,' said Frannie.

Oh yes, you will, Frannie, Beth and Joe. You just wait and see!

XXVI. THE ARMY OF RED GOBLINS

One day Mother said that since she had to be out for the whole day, she would prefer if the children asked the Old Saucepan Man to come and stay with them, and bring any other two friends they had made.

'Good!' said Joe. 'We'll ask Moon-Face and Silky.'

Beth wrote a note, and gave it to the little white goat to take to Moon-Face.

The white goat was a wonderful creature. It gave the most delicious milk, it ran errands, and if any of the hens got out, it found them and drove them back. It was most useful.

The goat took the note in its mouth, and ran off to the Enchanted Wood. It came to the Faraway Tree and bleated to the red squirrel, who peeped out from his hole low down in the trunk.

The squirrel took the note and bounded up to Moon-Face with it. Moon-Face was delighted, and shouted down to Silky, who came up and read it.

'We'll ask the Old Saucepan Man as soon as Mister Watzisname is asleep,' said Moon-Face. 'The children haven't asked Watzisname – so Saucepan will have to creep down the tree with us, without telling him.'

They sent a note back by the little goat, saying that they would arrive at three o'clock that afternoon. The children were excited. Mother was preparing to leave, and the girls began to make the cottage look pretty with jars of flowers. Beth baked some chocolate cakes, and Frannie made some toffee. Joe made up some sandwiches.

'We'll have a wonderful time,' he said. 'I hope the Saucepan Man won't be too deaf this afternoon.'

By three o'clock everything was ready. The children were neat and clean. The table looked fine with its sandwiches, cakes, and toffee. Beth went to the gate to look for their visitors.

She couldn't see them coming down the lane. 'They *are* late!' she called to the others. 'I expect the Saucepan Man has got tangled up with his saucepans or something!'

Half-past three came and no visitors. The children were rather disappointed. 'Perhaps Moon-Face read my letter wrongly, and thought it was four o'clock,' said Beth.

But when four o'clock came and still no Moon-Face, Silky or Saucepan Man arrived, they got really worried.

'I do hope nothing has happened,' said Beth, feeling upset. 'There's all our nice food and nobody to eat it.'

'We'll wait a bit longer, then we'll eat our share,' said Joe. So, when five o'clock came, and nobody had arrived, the children sadly ate half of the food themselves.

'Something's happened,' said Joe gloomily.

'Oh dear! What do you think it is?' said Beth, alarmed. 'Could we go and see?'

'No,' said Joe. 'Not now, anyway. Mother will be back soon. We'd better go tonight. The rope is let down the

165

Tree then for us to pull ourselves up, and it won't take long to climb up.'

'We really must find out what's wrong,' said Beth, clearing the plates away. 'We'll take their share of the food with us.'

So, that night, when it was quite dark, the three children slipped out of bed, dressed, and crept out of the back door. They took a lantern that Joe had found, for there was no moon that night. Joe swung it in front of him and they could see where to walk.

Down the dark lane they went, over the ditch and into the Enchanted Wood. The trees were whispering very loudly together tonight. 'Wisha-wisha-wisha!' they said.

'Oh, how I wish I knew what they were saying!' said Frannie.

'Come on,' said Joe. 'We'd better not be too long, Frannie. We want to be back by daylight.'

They made their way through the dark wood. As there was no moon there were no fairy-folk about at all that night. The children soon came to the Faraway Tree, and looked for the rope.

But there was no rope at all this time – and they had to begin to climb up as usual, holding onto the boughs and branches carefully, for it was very difficult to see.

Before they had got farther than two branches up, a strange thing happened. Someone caught hold of Joe's shoulder and pushed him roughly down! Joe fell, caught hold of the lowest branch, and just saved himself in time.

'Who did that?' he cried angrily. He undid his

lantern from his belt, where he had put it whilst climbing, and flashed it up the Tree, calling to Beth and Frannie to go no farther.

And standing grinning in the lower branches of the tree were four red goblins, with pointed ears, wide mouths, and wicked little eyes!

'No one is allowed to come up the Tree now,' said one of the goblins. 'And no one is allowed to come down either.'

'But why not?' asked Joe, astonished.

'Because it's *our* Tree now!'

'*Your* Tree! What nonsense!' said Joe. 'We've come to see our friends who live in the Tree. Let us pass.'

'No!' said the goblins, and they grinned widely. 'You – can't – come – up!'

'It's no good,' said a tiny voice beside Joe. 'The goblins have taken everyone prisoner in the Tree. If you go up they'll only push you down, or take you prisoners too.'

Joe flashed his lantern downwards, and the children saw that it was the little red squirrel speaking – the one who looked after the cushions for Moon-Face.

'Hallo!' said Joe. 'Do tell me what's happened. I can't understand it!'

'Oh, it's easy enough to understand,' said the squirrel. 'The Land of the Red Goblins came to the top of the Faraway Tree. The goblins found a hole that leads down through the clouds, and poured down it! They took everyone prisoner. Moon-Face and everyone else are locked up in their houses in the tree-trunk. I can tell you Mister Watzisname and the Angry Pixie have nearly battered their doors down in rage!'

'But why have the goblins locked them up?' asked Beth, in surprise.

'Well, they want some magic spells that the Tree-dwellers know,' said the squirrel. 'They are going to keep them all locked up till they tell the spells. Isn't it dreadful?'

'Oh dear!' said Frannie. 'Whatever can we do to help them?'

'I don't know,' said the squirrel sadly. 'If only you could get up to them you might be able to make some plan. But the goblins won't let anyone up the Tree.'

'Wisha-wisha-wisha-wisha!' whispered the trees loudly.

'You know, I can't help feeling that the trees want to tell us something tonight,' said Beth suddenly. 'I always feel that they are whispering secrets to one another – but tonight I feel that they want to tell them to *us*!'

'I shouldn't be surprised,' said the squirrel. 'The Faraway Tree is King of the Wood, and now that trouble has come to it all the other trees are angry. Perhaps they want to help us.'

'Wisha-wisha-wisha-wisha,' said the trees loudly.

'Put your arms round a tree-trunk and press your left ear to the tree,' said the squirrel suddenly. 'I have heard it said that that is the only way to hear a tree's words.'

Each of the children found a small tree. They put their arms round the trunks and pressed their left ears to the trees. And then they could quite clearly hear what the trees were whispering.

'Help the Faraway Tree-dwellers!' the leaves whispered. 'Help them!'

'But how can we?' whispered back the children eagerly. 'Tell us!'

'Go up the slippery-slip,' said the trees, in their leafy voices. 'Go through the trap-door and up the slippery-slip!'

'Oh!' cried the children all at once. 'Of course! Why ever didn't we think of it ourselves?'

'Ssh!' said the squirrel, in alarm. 'Don't let the goblins hear you. What did the trees say?'

'They said we were to go through the trap-door and up the slippery-slip,' said Joe, in a low voice. 'We can get right up to Moon-Face's then. It's a wonderful idea.'

'Come on then!' said Beth, and the three of them ran to the Faraway Tree, and felt about for the little trap-door. Ooooh! Another adventure!

XXVII. A MOST EXCITING NIGHT

'If only we can creep up the slippery-slip that turns right round and round in the middle of the trunk, and get to Moon-Face's at the top, we shall be able to help him!' said Joe, feeling about for the trap-door.

'I wonder why Moon-Face didn't slip down it himself,' said Beth.

'Oh, he'd think that there would be plenty of red goblins at the bottom of the Tree, ready to catch him when he flew out of the trap-door,' said Joe. 'But I don't believe they know about this slide!'

He found the trap-door and swung it open. 'Hold it open for me whilst I climb in,' he said. Beth held it. Joe began to climb up.

But, dear me, it was most terribly slippery! He simply couldn't manage to get up the slippery-slip at all! As fast as he climbed up a little way he slid down again. He groaned.

'This is awful! We can never get up this way! I shall keep slipping down all the time.'

'Let *me* try!' said Beth eagerly. So Joe slid out of the trap-door and Beth crept in. But it was just the same for her as for Joe. The slide was far too steep and slippery to be climbed.

'Wisha-wisha-wisha!' said the trees nearby. Beth ran to one, put her arms around its trunk, and pressed her left ear to it. She listened.

'Tell the squirrel to go!' whispered the leaves. 'Tell the squirrel to go!'

'Red squirrel, *you* go up!' said Beth at once. 'Can you manage to, do you think?'

'Yes,' said the squirrel. 'I have claws on my feet to hold with, and I am used to climbing. But what's the use of me going? I am not clever enough to make plans with Moon-Face.'

'Wisha-wisha-wisha!' said the trees loudly. Joe pressed his ear to one. 'The squirrel can throw a rope down the slippery-slip!' whispered the tree.

'Of course,' said Joe, in delight. 'Why didn't I think of it?'

'Tell us,' said the girls. Joe told them. 'The squirrel must climb the slide to the top. He must ask Moon-Face for the rope that is let down for the cushions. But instead of letting it down through the branches of the tree, he must let it down through the slide inside. Then we can hang on and be pulled up!'

'Oooh! That's a really good idea,' said Beth.

'Ssh!' said Joe, as he heard a shout from a goblin up the tree. 'We don't want them to guess what we're doing.'

'The goblins are coming down!' whispered Frannie in alarm. 'I can hear them. What shall we do?'

'We'd better get inside the trap-door and sit at the bottom of the slippery-slip as quiet as mice,' whispered Joe. 'Go in first, squirrel, and climb up. You know what to do, don't you?'

'Yes,' said the squirrel, and disappeared up the slide, digging his sharp claws into it just as if he were climbing up the outside of a tree-trunk! Joe pushed

171

Beth inside and then Frannie. He climbed in himself and shut the trap-door just in time.

Three goblins jumped down to the foot of the tree and began hunting round about. 'I *know* I heard someone!' said one of them.

'Well, so long as we don't let them pass us up the tree, they can't do much!' said another with a laugh. 'I don't think you heard any one – it was just the trees whispering'

'Wisha-wisha-wisha!' said the trees at once.

'There! What did I tell you?' said the goblin. They jumped back into the boughs of the Faraway Tree, and the children hugged one another and chuckled.

'I wonder if the squirrel has got up to the top of the slide yet,' said Joe.

As he spoke a little sound came down the slide – a

soft, slinky sound – and something suddenly touched them!

'Oooh! A snake!' cried Beth in alarm.

'Don't be silly! It's the rope that the good little squirrel has sent down!' said Joe, feeling it. 'Now, we'd better go up one at a time, for Moon-Face will never be able to pull us all up at once.'

Frannie went first. She was hauled all the way up the slide. It was very strange, so dark and quiet. At last she reached the top. Moon-Face was there, red-faced from pulling the rope. A light burned in his funny round room. He was simply overjoyed to see Frannie. He hugged her, and then sent down the rope for Beth. She came up – and then Joe.

'Don't make too much noise,' said Moon-Face in a low voice, as he hugged them all. 'The goblins are outside everyone's door.'

'Oh, Moon-Face, we're so sorry you are captured like this,' said Joe. 'Couldn't you have slid down the slide and escaped? Or did you think there might be goblins at the bottom?'

'Well, I did,' said Moon-Face, 'but I also thought that if I slid down I'd be leaving all my friends behind in the tree, and that seemed a mean thing to do.'

'Yes, it would be rather mean,' said Joe, 'to save yourself and leave the others. Moon-Face, what can we do to help?'

'Well, I simply don't know,' said Moon-Face. 'I've thought and I've thought – but I can't think of anything really good at all.'

'It's a pity Silky isn't here,' said Joe. 'We could talk it all over with her then. She's clever.'

'We can't possibly get to *her*,' said Moon-Face. 'She's locked in, just as I am.'

'Joe! Moon-Face!' said Frannie suddenly, her face red with excitement. 'I've thought of a way to help.'

'What?' cried the others.

'Well – couldn't the red squirrel slip down the slide, out the trap-door, and take a note to the elves in the wood?' asked Frannie. 'Do you remember how we helped them when we first came to the wood – they said they would always be pleased to help us if we wanted them?'

'Yes – but how could *they* help?' asked Moon-Face doubtfully. Nobody quite knew. But Joe suddenly nodded his head and gave a squeal.

'Ssh!' said everyone at once.

'Sorry,' said Joe, 'but I really have got an idea at last. Listen! The red squirrel can tell the elves to come up here in crowds – we'll pull them up on the rope. Then Moon-Face can shout out to the goblins outside that he'll tell them the magic spells they want to know – and when they open the door the elves and all of us can pour out and overpower the goblins!'

'That's a *splendid* idea!' said Moon-Face, looking at Joe in admiration.

'Simply wonderful!' said the girls. Joe was pleased.

'And we'll unlock everyone's doors and they can all join in!' he said. 'My goodness, this is going to be exciting! Can you see how dreadfully angry the Angry Pixie will be – and Mister Watzisname? Those goblins had better watch out!'

Everyone chuckled. The red squirrel touched Joe's knee. 'Will you give me the note then?' he said. 'I know where Mister Whiskers lives, and I will take the letter to him, and let him call all the elves together.'

Joe took out his pencil and wrote a note on Moon-Face's paper. He folded it and gave it to the red squirrel, who folded it even smaller and tucked it inside his cheek.

'That's in case I'm caught by the goblins,' he said. 'They'll never think of looking for a note inside my cheek!' He sat on his bushy tail, gave himself a push, and set off down the slippery-slip at a tremendous pace.

Frannie giggled. 'His tail is his cushion,' she said. 'Isn't he a darling? I do hope he'll find Mister Whiskers all right.'

'Well, we'd better just sit quietly and wait,' said Moon-Face. 'I don't want the goblins opening my door and seeing you all here. They'll know we've got a plan then.'

'We brought you some of the meal you didn't eat this afternoon,' said Beth, and she unpacked the bag. 'Here are some sandwiches, some cakes, and some toffee.'

'We'll all have some,' said Moon-Face. 'And I've got some Pop Cakes too.'

So they sat round quietly on Moon-Face's curved sofa and bed and chairs, and ate and whispered, waiting for the squirrel to come back with Mister Whiskers and the elves. Whatever would happen then?

XXVIII. THE RED GOBLINS
GET A SHOCK

It seemed a long time before anything happened.
Then Moon-Face pricked up his ears and listened.
'Someone's coming up the slippery-slip,' he said. 'It
must be the little squirrel.'

'I hope it isn't a goblin!' said Frannie, looking
rather scared.

But it was the red squirrel. He hopped out of the
slippery-slip hole and nodded at everyone. 'It's all
right,' he said. 'The elves are coming. I found Mister
Whiskers and he has slipped out to fetch all his family.
There are fifty-one of them!'

'We'd better let the rope down then,' said Moon-
Face, and he let it slither down the slide. Someone
caught hold of it at the other end, and the rope
tightened.

'There's an elf there now!' said Moon-Face, and he
and Joe hauled on the rope. It was heavy. They pulled
and they pulled, panting hard.

'This elf is rather heavy!' said Joe. And no wonder –
for when they at last got the rope to the top, there was
not one elf – but five, hanging on to the rope! They
leapt into Moon-Face's tiny round room, and began
to whisper excitedly. Moon-Face told them all about
the goblins, and they grinned when they heard his
plan.

Down went the rope again, and this time six elves

came up on it. By this time the room was very crowded. But nobody minded.

'We'll have to sit on each other's knees,' said Joe, and giggled at the sight of so many people in Moon-Face's little tree-room.

The elves all looked exactly the same. They all had very long beards, though Mister Whiskers' beard was the longest. It reached right down to his toes.

The rope fetched up all the fifty-one little men, and by that time there was really no room to move! Everyone was excited, and there was such a lot of whispering that it sounded like a thousand leaves rustling at once!

'Now I'm going to bang on the inside of my door and tell the goblins I will let them know the magic spell they want!' said Moon-Face. 'As soon as they open the door you must all rush out and grab hold of them.'

'Wait! I've thought of such a good idea,' said Joe suddenly. 'Let's push them into this room of Moon-Face's – and send someone down the tree to bolt the trap-door – and when they slide down, thinking to escape, they'll all be nicely boxed up in the slide till *we* decide to open the trap-door!'

'That *is* a good idea,' said Mister Whiskers. 'Two elves had better go up the ladder that leads through the clouds, to stop any goblins trying to escape that way – and six of us had better slide down to the foot of the Tree to stop them escaping into the wood.'

Six of the elves at once took cushions and slid down the slippery-slip. They shot out of the trap-door, and bolted it on the outside. They surrounded the foot of the Tree, ready to prevent any naughty goblins from escaping.

The rest of them waited for Moon-Face to speak to the goblins outside. They were all tremendously excited.

Moon-Face banged on the inside of his door. A goblin outside shouted to him:

'Stop that noise!'

'Let me out!' yelled Moon-Face.

'Not till you tell us one of the magic spells you know!' said the goblin.

'I know a spell that will turn people into kings and queens!' shouted Moon-Face.

'Tell us it then,' said the goblin at once.

'Well, open my door,' said Moon-Face. There came the sound of a key turned in a padlock, and then Moon-Face's door was opened. At once the whole crowd of elves poured out like a stream of water! Joe, Beth, and Frannie went out with them, and when the goblins saw the crowd, they gave a yell and leapt down the tree to warn their friends.

Two elves leapt up to the ladder and sat there to prevent any goblins escaping to the land above. Joe, Moon-Face, Beth and Frannie climbed quickly down the tree to let out all the people locked into their homes. How glad everyone was!

Dame Washalot was very angry at being locked in. 'I'll teach those goblins to lock me in!' she shouted. And the old dame picked up her washtub and began to throw water over all the goblins climbing about the tree. What a shock for them! Joe

178

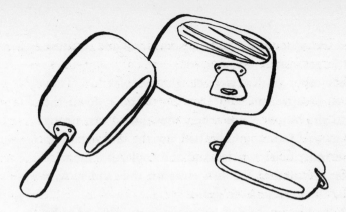

couldn't help laughing.

He unlocked Mister Watzisname's door, and out came Watzisname, shouting and raging, followed by the Saucepan Man. Watzisname chased hard after the terrified goblins!

The Saucepan Man acted in a surprising manner. He took off one saucepan after another, one kettle after another, and threw them after the escaping goblins. Crash! Bang! Clatter!

They let out the Barn Owl, and the three owls that lived together. They flew at the goblins, screeching and hooting. The Angry Pixie was so angry that he flew at Joe when he let him out, and Joe only just explained in time that it was the goblins who were to blame – not him!

Beth let Silky out, but Silky was frightened by all the noise and shouting. Still she managed to catch one goblin by throwing one of her curtains over him. Silky and Beth then took the goblin up the tree and pushed him into Moon-Face's room. When he found the slippery-slip he slid down it in delight, thinking he could escape. But, alas for him, he stopped at the bolted trap-door, and there he stayed, unable to climb up or to get out!

Many other goblins were caught that way too. They tried to escape from the elves by running down the tree to the wood – but when they found six strong elves at the foot they climbed up the tree again to escape into their own land at the top! And then, of course, they found the two elves on the ladder, who pushed them back down again.

So into Moon-Face's house they went, pushed in by Joe, who took great delight in doing so. One by one they tried to escape by sliding down the slippery-slip, and soon the slide was crowded with goblins, piled one on top of the other!

Dawn came, and the sun shone out, lighting up the great branches of the enormous Faraway Tree.

'Now we can see if any goblins are hiding anywhere,' called Moon-Face, who was thoroughly enjoying himself. So he and the elves and Watzisname looked into every hole and corner, behind every branch and tuft of leaves, and pulled out any goblins hidden there. They were marched up to Moon-Face's room, and down the slippery-slip they went. Soon there wasn't a single goblin left. They were all piled on top of one another in the slide, most uncomfortable and upset.

'There!' said Moon-Face at last, pleased with himself and everyone else. 'We've got them all safe. My word, I *am* hungry! What about having a good meal?'

'Look!' called Silky, waving to a lower part of the great tree. 'The Faraway Tree is growing ripe plums just down there! What about having a feast of those?'

'Good!' said Moon-Face. 'Squirrel, go down to the six elves at the foot of the tree and tell them they can come up now. Hey, you two elves on the ladder, you can come down. Silky, can you make us some hot chocolate to drink? Plums and hot chocolate would make a lovely meal.'

Just as they were sitting down to eat and drink, a strange figure came up the tree. He was thin and ragged and knobbly, but his face beamed as if he knew everybody.

'Who's that?' said Frannie at once.

'Don't know,' said Moon-Face, staring.

'I seem to have seen his face before,' said Beth.

'He's a funny-looking creature,' said Joe. 'He looks rather like a scarecrow to me!'

The ragged man came up, and sat down on a branch nearby. He held out his hand for a cup of hot chocolate.

'Who are you?' said Moon-Face.

'What's your name?' asked Silky.

'Play a game?' said the thin man, beaming. 'Yes, certainly – what game shall we play?'

And then everyone knew who it was! It was the Old Saucepan Man – without his kettles and saucepans! He had thrown them all after the goblins, and now he had none left to wear.

'Saucepan! You *do* look different!' said Watzisname, hugging him. 'I didn't know you! Come and have a plum.'

The Saucepan Man looked alarmed. 'Hurt your *thumb*?' he said. 'Oh, I *am* sorry!'

'No, I didn't say I'd hurt my thumb,' said

Watzisname, roaring with laughter, and clapping Saucepan on the back. 'I said, have a PLUM, a PLUM, a PLUM!'

'Thanks,' said the Saucepan Man, and put two large plums in his mouth at once.

'And now,' said Moon-Face, when everyone had finished, 'what about those goblins in the slippery-slip?'

XXIX. THE PUNISHMENT OF
THE RED GOBLINS

'It's certainly time we dealt with those red goblins,' said Mister Whiskers, the chief elf, wiping his long beard with a yellow handkerchief. He had dropped plum-juice all down it.

And just at that moment there came a great surprise. A deep voice behind them said 'Oho! Here's a nice little party! What about coming back with me into Wizard Land and doing a few jobs?'

Everyone turned in dismay. They saw a curious figure above them, leaning down from a big branch. It was a wizard, whose green eyes blinked lazily like a cat's.

'It's Mighty-One the Wizard!' said Moon-Face, and he got up to bow, for Mighty-One was as mighty as his name. Everyone did the same.

'Who is he?' whispered Frannie.

'He's the most powerful wizard in the whole world,' whispered back Silky. 'He's come down the ladder – so that means that the Land of Red Goblins has gone and the Land of the Wizards has come! They are always on the look-out for servants, and I suppose Mighty-One has come down to look for some.'

'Well, *I'm* not going to be a servant to a wizard,' said Frannie.

'You won't be,' said Silky. 'He's not a bad fellow. He won't take anyone who doesn't want to go. It's good training for a fairy who wants to learn magic.'

Mighty-One blinked his eyes slowly and looked at the little crowd on the branches before him. 'I need about a hundred servants to take back with me,' he said. 'Who will come?'

Nobody said a word. Moon-Face got up and bowed again.

'Your Highness,' he said, 'we none of us want to leave the Enchanted Wood, where we are very happy. You may perhaps find others who would like to go back with you. We beg you not to take any of us.'

'Well,' said the wizard, sliding his green eyes from one person to another, 'I haven't much time. My land will swing away from the Faraway Tree in about an hour. Can you get me the servants I want? If you can, I will not take you.'

Everybody looked worried. But Joe jumped up with a beaming face.

'Your Highness! Would red goblins do for your servants?'

'Excellently,' said Mighty-One. 'They are quick and obedient – but goblins would never agree to coming with me! They belong to their own land.'

Moon-Face, Watzisname, and the Saucepan Man all began to talk at once. Mighty-One lifted up his hand and they stopped. 'One at a time,' said the wizard.

So Moon-Face spoke. 'Sir,' he said, ' we have about a hundred goblins boxed up in the middle of this tree. For a while they held us as prisoners. It would be a very good if you took them away to teach them some discipline and some good manners.'

Mighty-One looked astonished. 'A hundred

goblins!' he said. 'That is very strange. Explain.'

So Moon-Face explained. Mighty-One was most interested to hear of their adventure.

'We'll all go down to the bottom of the tree and let the goblins out one by one,' said Joe, excited. 'Come on! What a shock for them when they see the wizard!'

So they all trooped down the tree in the bright rays of the rising sun. Really, it was all most exciting!

They came to the trap-door at the foot of the tree. Behind it they could hear a lot of shouting and quarelling and pushing.

'Don't push!'

'You're squashing me!'

Moon-Face unbolted the trap-door and opened it. Out shot a red goblin and fell on a green cushion of moss. He picked himself up, blinked in the bright sunlight, and then turned to run. But Mighty-One tapped him with his wand and he stood still. He couldn't move! He looked scared when he saw the wizard.

One by one the red goblins tumbled out of the trap-door, and were tapped by the wizard. Ten, twenty, thirty, forty, fifty, sixty – they came shooting out of the trap-door, surprised and frightened. sliding gradually down the slippery-slip, as one after another slid from the trap-door.

Frannie giggled. It was a funny sight to see.

'It's a very good punishment for those bad goblins,' she said to Silky. 'They came down the ladder to trap *you* and now someone else has trapped *them*, and is taking them back to his land!'

The red goblins stood in a sulky row, quite unable

to run away. 'Quick – MARCH!' said the wizard, when the last one had slid out of the trap-door – and up the tree went the sulky goblins. It was no use trying to escape. The wizard had put a spell on their legs, and they had to go up to the top of the tree, through the big white cloud and into Wizard Land.

'Just what they deserve,' said Joe. 'My goodness, what an exciting night we've had! I *did* enjoy it.'

'Isn't it cold!' said the Saucepan Man, shivering.

'Cold!' cried Beth and Frannie, who were feeling hot in the morning sun. 'Why, it's as warm as can be.'

'It's because he hasn't got his kettles and saucepans hung around him as usual,' said Watzisname. 'I expect they feel like a coat to him. Poor old Saucepan!'

'I don't like the look of him without his saucepans,' said Frannie. 'He doesn't look right. Can't we collect them for him? They're on the ground – and all about the tree.'

So they began to collect the Saucepan Man's belongings. He was very pleased. They hung his kettles on him, and put his saucepans all round him, with his special one for a hat. Some of them were dented and bent, but he didn't mind a bit.

'There!' said Frannie, pleased. 'You look like yourself now. You looked horrid without all your saucepans on – like a snail without its shell.'

'I never had a bell,' said the Saucepan Man.

'SHELL, I said,' said Frannie.

'Smell?' said the Saucepan Man, looking round. 'I can't smell anything at the moment.

186

What sort of smell – nice or nasty?'

'SHELL, not smell,' said Frannie impatiently.

'Oh, *SHELL*. What shell?' said the Saucepan Man. But Frannie had forgotten what she had said, and she shook her head and laughed. 'Never mind!' she shouted.

'We really must go,' said Joe. 'Mother will be awake now and wondering whatever has happened to us. Oh dear – I do feel sleepy! Come on, girls.'

They said goodbye to all the Tree-dwellers and set off through the Enchanted Wood. Silky went back to her house in the tree, wondering what had happened to her clock, which hadn't joined in the adventure at all. It had been fast asleep.

Moon-Face went back to the tree, yawning. Watzisname and the Saucepan Man climbed back, so tired that they fell fast asleep before they reached their hole, and had to be put safely in the corner of a broad branch by the Angry Pixie, in case they fell down.

Dame Washalot went back, making up her mind to do no washing *that* day. Soon there was peace in the tree, and only the snores of Watzisname could be heard.

Far away up in the tree in the Land of Wizards the red goblins were working hard. Ah – they had got just what they deserved, hadn't they? They wouldn't be in such a hurry to catch other people in future.

The three children got home, and their mother stared at them in surprise.

'You *are* up early this morning,' she said. 'I thought

you were still in bed and asleep. Fancy getting up and going out for a walk before breakfast like that.'

How sleepy the children were that day! And, dear me, didn't they go to bed early that night!

'No more wandering through the Enchanted Wood and up the Faraway Tree for me tonight,' said Joe, as he got into bed. 'I vote we don't go there for a long time. It's getting just a bit too exciting.'

But it wasn't long before they went again, as you will see!

XXX. A PLAN FOR BETH'S BIRTHDAY

A week later it was Beth's birthday. She was very excited, because Mother said she could have a small party.

'We'll ask all our friends in the Faraway Tree,' she said.

'Do you really think we should?' said Joe doubtfully. 'I don't think Mother would like Dame Washalot – or Mister Whiskers – or the Angry Pixie.'

'Well, we can't very well ask some and not others,' said Beth. 'The ones we left out would be very hurt indeed.'

'It's awkward,' said Frannie. 'We'd better go and tell Moon-Face and Silky, and ask them what to do.'

But Mother wouldn't let the two girls go off with Joe that day. She said there was a lot of work for them to do in tidying up their room.

'Oh bother!' said Frannie to Joe. 'You'll have to go alone, Joe, and ask Moon-Face and Silky what we ought to do about our party. Don't be too long, or we'll be worried about you. And please don't go climbing up into any strange land without us.'

'Don't worry!' said Joe. 'I'm not going to visit any more lands at the top of the Faraway Tree. I've had enough adventures to last me for the rest of my life!'

He set off. He ran through the Enchanted Wood and came to the Faraway Tree. It was a hot afternoon and not many of the little folk were around.

It seemed almost too hot to climb the tree. Joe whistled. The little red squirrel popped down from the tree and looked at him.

'Leap up to the top of the tree and ask old Moon-Face if he'll drop me down a rope with a cushion on the end, and haul me up, squirrel,' said Joe.

The squirrel bounded lightly up the tree. Soon a rope, with a cushion tied to it, came slipping down the tree. Joe caught hold of it. He sat astride the cushion and tugged the rope. It began to go up the tree, bumping into branches as it went.

It was a funny ride, but Joe enjoyed it. He waved to the Angry Pixie, who was sitting outside his house. He stared at Joe in surprise and then grinned when he saw who it was. The owls were all asleep in their homes. Mister Watzisname was awake for once, and fell out of his chair in alarm when he suddenly saw Joe swinging up through the air, bumping into branches!

When he saw it was Joe, he was so pleased that he fell off his branch on to the Saucepan Man, who was snoozing in a chair just below.

'Ooooouch!' said the Saucepan Man, startled. 'What's the matter? Why are you jumping on me?'

'I'm not,' said Watzisname. 'Look, there's Joe!'

'Go? I don't want to go,' said the Saucepan Man, settling down again. 'Don't be so restless.'

'I said, "There's JOE!"' roared Watzisname.

'Where?' said the Saucepan Man in surprise, looking all round. But by that time, of course, Joe was far away up the Tree, laughing over funny Watzisname and dear old Saucepan!

Watzisname climbed back to his chair and shut his eyes. Soon his snores reached Joe, who was far above, hoping that Silky would see him and go up to Moon-Face's to talk to him. He forgot to look out for Dame Washalot's water, but it missed him nicely, splashing down heavily on poor old Watzisname, making him dream that he was falling out of a boat and into the sea.

Silky did see him, and waved. She climbed the tree quickly to go up to Moon-Face's. By the time she got there Joe had just arrived and was getting off the cushion.

'Hallo!' said Moon-Face and Silky, pleased to see him. 'Where are Beth and Frannie?'

Joe told them. He told them about Beth's birthday too, and her difficulty about how many people she should ask.

'We'd like everyone,' said Joe. 'But Mother wouldn't like some of them, we're sure. What shall we do?'

'I know! I know!' said Silky, clapping her hands suddenly. 'Next week the Land of Birthdays comes to the top of the Faraway Tree – and anyone who has a birthday can go there and give the most wonderful party to all their friends. Oh, it would be lovely! Last time the Birthday Land came, nobody had a birthday, so we couldn't go. But this time we can, because Beth could ask us all!'

'It sounds good,' said Joe. 'But I didn't really want to go into any strange land again, you know. We always seem to get mixed up in odd adventures. So far we've always escaped all right – but we might not another time.'

'Oh, no harm can come to you in the Land of Birthdays!' said Moon-Face, at once. 'It's a wonderful land. You really *must* come! It's a chance you mustn't miss.'

'All right,' said Joe, beginning to feel excited. 'I'll tell the girls when I get back.'

'And we'll tell everyone in the Tree, and Mister Whiskers, and his elves too,' said Silky. 'Beth would like everyone to go, wouldn't she?'

'Oh yes!' said Joe. 'What happens, though? I mean, do we have to arrange for things to eat, or anything? And what about a birthday cake? Frannie was going to make one for Beth.'

'Tell her not to,' said Silky. 'She'll find everything she wants up in the Birthday Land. My word, we *are* lucky! Fancy someone really having a birthday just as the Birthday Land comes along!'

'Beth's birthday is on Wednesday,' said Joe. 'So we'll go up the tree then. I'd better go back and tell the girls now. I said I wouldn't be long.'

'Have a Toffee Shock?' said Moon-Face.

'No, thank you,' said Joe. 'I'd rather have a Pop Cake.'

So they sat and munched the lovely Pop Cakes, and talked about the exciting time they had had with the red goblins.

'Now I really must go,' said Joe, and he got up. He chose a red cushion, said goodbye to Silky and Moon-Face, and shot off down the slippery-slip.

Joe thought he really could do that all day, it was such a lovely feeling! He flew out of the trap-door at the bottom and landed on the moss. He got up and ran off home.

The girls were pleased to see him back so soon. When they heard about the Birthday Land they were tremendously excited.

'Ooooh!' said Beth, going red with joy. 'I am lucky! I wonder what will happen. Do you suppose there will be cake for me?'

'Certainly!' said Joe. 'And lots of other things too, I expect!'

'We shall have to tell Mother,' said Frannie. 'I wonder if she will let us go.'

Mother didn't seem to mind. 'I expect it's just some sort of birthday joke your friends in the wood are playing on you!' she said. 'Yes, you can go, if you like. Our cottage is really too small for a very large party.'

'I shall wear my best dress,' said Beth happily. 'The one Mother got me last week, with the blue ribbon!'

But Mother wouldn't let her!

'No,' she said firmly. 'You will all go in your old clothes. I remember quite well what you looked like when you went off to see that funny friend of yours, the Old Saucepan Man. I certainly shall not allow any of you to wear nice things next Wednesday.'

Beth was nearly in tears. 'But, Mother, I can't go to my own birthday party in old clothes,' she said.

But it was no good. Mother said they could wear old clothes or else not go. And that was it.

'I don't know what everyone will think of us, going

193

to the Birthday Land in our oldest things.' said Joe gloomily. 'I've a good mind not to go.'

But when Wednesday afternoon came, they all thought differently! Old clothes or not, they were going to go!

'Come on!' said Joe. 'It's time we went to the Land of Birthdays!'

XXXI. THE LAND OF BIRTHDAYS

The children set off once again to the Enchanted Wood. They knew the way to the Faraway Tree very well by now.

'Wisha-wisha-wisha!' whispered the trees, as the children ran between them. Beth put her arms round one, and pressed her left ear to the trunk. 'What secret are you saying today?' she asked.

'We wish you a happy birthday,' whispered the leaves. Beth laughed! It was fun to have a birthday!

When they came to the Faraway Tree, how marvellous it looked! The folk of the tree had bedecked it with lots of little brightly-coloured flags because it was Beth's birthday, and it looked simply lovely.

'Oooh!' said Beth, pleased. 'I do feel happy. The only thing I wish is that I had proper party clothes on, not my old ones.'

But that couldn't be helped. They were just about to climb the tree when Dame Washalot's big washing-basket came bumping down on the end of Moon-Face's rope for the children to get into.

'Good,' said Joe. 'Get in, girls.' They all got in and went up the tree at a tremendous rate. 'Moon-Face must have someone helping him to pull,' said Joe, astonished.

He had. Mister Whiskers was there, with Watzisname and the Old Saucepan Man, and they were all pulling like anything. No wonder the basket shot up the tree!

'Many happy returns of the day,' said everyone, kissing Beth.

'Oh, good! You're not in your best clothes,' said Moon-Face. 'We wondered if you would make it a fancy-dress party, Beth.'

'Oh, I'd love to!' said Beth. 'But we haven't got any fancy dress.'

'We can easily get that in the Birthday Land!' said Silky, clapping her hands for joy. 'Good, good, good! I do like a fancy-dress party!'

'Everybody is ready to go,' said Moon-Face. 'The elves are just below us. Where's Saucepan Man? Hey, Saucepan, where have you got to?'

'He stepped into your slippery-slip by mistake,' said an elf, appearing out of Moon-Face's house. 'He went down the slide with an awful noise. I expect he's at the bottom by now.'

'Good gracious! Just like silly old Saucepan!' said Moon-Face. 'We'd better let down the washing-basket for him, or he'll never get up to us!'

So down went the washing-basket again, and old Saucepan got into it and came up with a clatter of saucepans and kettles.

'Now are we really all ready?' said Moon-Face. 'Silky, Watzisname, Saucepan, the Angry Pixie, Dame Washalot, Mister Whiskers, the elves . . .'

'Goodness! What a lovely lot of people are coming!' said Beth, seeing all the elves and tree-folk on the branches below. 'Is that Dame Washalot? What a nice old woman!'

Dame Washalot was beaming happily. For once she

was going to leave her wash-tub. Going to the Land of Birthdays was not a treat to be missed!

'Come on, then,' said Moon-Face, and he led the way up the ladder. Up he went, popped his head above to make quite sure that the Land of Birthdays was there, and then jumped straight into it!

Everyone climbed up. 'That's all, I think,' said Moon-Face, peering down. 'Oh no – there's someone else. Whoever is it? I thought we were all here?'

'Goodness! It's my clock!' said Silky. 'The one I got in the Land of Take-What-You-Want!'

Sure enough, it was. 'Ding-dong-ding-dong!' it cried indignantly, as it climbed up on its flat feet.

'All right, all right, we'll wait for you!' said Silky. 'Go carefully up the ladder. You weren't really asked, you know.'

'Oh, I'd love your clock to come to my party,' said Beth at once. 'Come along, clock.'

'Ding-dong,' said the clock, pleased, and managed

to get up the ladder.

The Land of Birthdays was simply beautiful. To begin with, there was always birthday weather there – brilliant sunshine, blue sky, and a nice little breeze. The trees were always green, and there were always daisies and buttercups growing in the fields.

'Oh, it's lovely, it's lovely!' cried Beth, dancing around joyfully. 'Moon-Face, what about our fancy-dress? Where do we get that?'

'Oh, you'll find everything in that house over there,' said Moon-Face, pointing to a very pretty house. They all trooped over to it. As they went, small brown rabbits hopped out of holes, called 'A Happy Birthday!' to Beth, and popped back inside. It was all very exciting.

Everyone crowded into the pretty house. It was full of cupboards – and in the cupboards were the most thrilling costumes you can think of.

'Oh, look at this!' cried Joe, in delight, as he came across a sailor's outfit, with a smart hat that had blue, white and gold on it, just like the captain of a ship. 'Just the right size for me!'

He put it on. Beth chose a dress like a fairy's, and Frannie chose a clown's costume with a pointed hat. She looked just like the real thing.

Moon-Face dressed up as a pirate and Silky became a daffodil. Watzisname was a policeman, and as for the Old Saucepan Man, he simply could *not* find a costume to fit him, because he was so bumpy with kettles and saucepans!

Everyone else dressed up and, oh my, they did look convincing! Beth had wings with her dress, but she was disappointed because she couldn't fly with them. How she would have loved to spread her wings and fly, as the real fairies did!

'Now for balloons!' said Silky, and she danced into the sunshine and ran to an old balloon-seller who was sitting surrounded by a great cloud of coloured balloons. Everybody chose one, and what games they had!

Suddenly a bell rang, and Moon-Face gave a shout of joy.

'Birthday feast! Come on, everyone!'

He rushed to a long, long table set out in the field. Beth ran with the others, and took her place at the head of the table. But to her great surprise and disappointment there was no food on the table at all – just empty plates, cups, and glasses!

'Don't look so upset!' whispered Silky. 'You've got to *wish* your own birthday feast!'

Beth gave a squeak. *Wish* her own birthday feast! Oooh! That would be the best fun in the world!

'Don't wish for bread and butter!' called Moon-Face. 'Wish for an ice-cream sundae, I like those!'

'I wish for an ice-cream sundae!' said Beth at once. And immediately the biggest, tallest sundae you ever saw appeared on one of the empty plates. Moon-Face helped himself.

'Wish for strawberries and vanilla ice-cream!' cried Frannie, who simply loved that.

'I wish for strawberries and vanilla ice-cream!' said Beth, and an enormous dish of strawberries appeared, with a large tub of vanilla ice-cream beside it. 'And I wish for chocolate cake too – and lemonade – and – and – and . . .'

'Fruit salad!' yelled someone.

'Doughnuts!' cried Watzisname.

'Cheese sandwiches!' begged Mister Whiskers.

'Ding-dong-ding-dong!' said Silky's clock in the greatest excitement. Everyone laughed.

'Don't wish for ding-dongs!' said Joe. 'We've got plenty of those, as long as Silky's clock is here!'

The clock chimed fourteen without stopping. It wandered about, looking as happy as could be.

Everyone began to eat. My goodness, it was a wonderful feast! The strawberries and vanilla ice-cream and the sundae went almost at once, for Mister Whiskers and fifty elves decided that they liked those very much too! So Beth had to wish for some more.

'What about my birthday cake?' she asked Silky. 'Do I wish for that too?'

'No, it just comes,' said Silky. 'It will appear right in the middle of the table. You just watch.'

Beth watched. There was a wonderful silver dish in the middle of the table. Something seemed to be forming there. A curious sort of mist hung over it.

'The birthday cake is coming!' shouted Joe, and everyone watched the silver dish. Gradually a great cake shaped itself there – oh, a wonderful cake, with red, pink, white, and yellow decorations made from sugar, and shaped like little flowers. On the top were eight candles burning, for Beth was eight that day. Her name was written in big sugar letters on the top: BETH. A VERY HAPPY BIRTHDAY!

Beth felt very proud. She had to cut the cake, of course. It was quite a difficult job, for there were so many people to cut a slice for.

'This is a wishing-cake!' said Moon-Face, when everyone had a piece on their plate. 'So wish, wish, wish, when you eat it – and your wish will come true!'

The children stared at him in delight. What should they wish? Frannie was just holding her cake in her hand, thinking of a wish, when the Old Saucepan Man upset everything! Whatever do you think he did?

XXXII. THE LITTLE LOST ISLAND

'Wouldn't you like to wish?' said Moon-Face, turning to the Old Saucepan Man, who was just about to bite into his cake.

'Fish?' said the Saucepan Man, in delight. 'Yes, I'd love to fish! I wish we were all fishing for fine fat fishes in the middle of the sea.'

Well! What a wish to make, just as he was eating a wishing-cake, for he hadn't heard Moon-Face properly.

Anyway, the wish immediately came true. A wind blew down, and lifted up the whole crowd of guests at the table. Sitting on their chairs, clinging tightly, they flew through the air for miles!

Whatever was happening?

Down flew the chairs in the big wind. A shower of salt spray drenched everyone. Joe gasped and looked down. Bump! He and everyone else landed on soft sand, rolled off their chairs, and sat up, blinking in surprise.

The long-bearded elves looked frightened. Moon-Face kept opening and shutting his mouth like a fish, he was so astonished. Joe was cross, and so was the Angry Pixie.

'*Now* what's happened?' said Dame Washalot, in a most annoyed voice. 'Why have we come here?'

'Look at all those fishing-rods!' said Silky, pointing to a whole row of rods standing in the sand, with their fishing lines in the water.

'Waiting for *us*!' groaned Moon-Face. 'Silly old Saucepan Man didn't hear what I said about wishing – he thought I said *fishing* – and he wished us all here, fishing in the sea!'

'Goodness!' said Beth, alarmed. 'Where are we, then?'

'I think we're on the Little Lost Island,' said Silky, looking round. 'It's a funny little place, always floating about and getting lost. But there's always good fishing to be had from it.'

'Fishing!' said Joe, in disgust. 'Who wants to go fishing in the middle of a birthday party? Let's get back at once.'

'Ding-dong-ding-dong!' said Silky's clock, walking about at the edge of the sea and getting its feet wet in the waves.

'Come back, clock!' called Silky. 'You know you can't swim.'

The clock came back and wiped its feet on the grass that grew around. Beth thought it was a remarkably sensible clock, and she wished she had one like it.

'You know, we really must do something about getting back to the Land of Birthdays,' said Joe, getting up and looking around the little island. 'What can we do? Is there a boat here?'

There was nothing except the fishing-rods! Nobody even touched them, for they didn't feel in the least like fishing. The Little Lost Island was just a hilly stretch of green grass and nothing else whatsoever.

203

'I really don't know *what* to do!' said Moon-Face, frowning. 'Do you, Mister Whiskers?'

Mister Whiskers was dressed up like Santa Claus, and looked very fine indeed, with his long beard. He rubbed his nose thoughtfully and shook his head.

'The difficulty is,' he said, 'that none of us has any magic with him, because we're all in fancy-dress and our other clothes are in the Land of Birthdays. So the spells and magic we keep in our pockets are not here.'

'Well, we shan't starve,' said Watzisname. 'We can always fish.'

'Fancy eating fish and nothing but fish always!' said Joe, making a face. 'When I think of all those lovely things that Beth wished for – and nobody to eat them now! Really, I could cry!'

Frannie had something in her hand and she looked down to see what it was. It was a piece of the birthday cake. Good! She could eat that, at any rate. She lifted the delicious cake to her mouth and took a nibble.

'What are you eating?' asked Moon-Face, bending over to see.

'A bit of the birthday cake,' said Frannie, cramming all of it into her mouth.

'Don't eat it! Don't swallow it!' yelled Moon-Face suddenly, dancing round Frannie as if he had gone quite mad. 'Stop! Don't swallow!'

Frannie stared at him in astonishment. So did everyone else.

'What's gone wrong with Moon-Face?' asked Silky anxiously. Frannie stood still with her mouth full of birthday cake, looking with amazement at Moon-Face.

'What's the matter?' she asked with her mouth full.

'You've got a bit of the wishing-cake in your mouth, Frannie!' shouted Moon-Face, hopping first on one leg and then on the other. 'Wish, dear girl, wish!'

'What shall I wish?' said Frannie.

'Wish us back to the Land of Birthdays, of course!' yelled everyone in excitement.

'Oh,' said Frannie, 'I didn't think of that! I wish we were all back in the Land of Birthdays, enjoying our feast!'

Darkness fell round everyone very suddenly. No wind came this time. Moon-Face put out his hand and took Silky's. What was happening?

Then daylight came back again – and everyone gave a shout of surprise and delight. They were back in the Land of Birthdays! Yes – there was the table in front of them and more chairs to sit down on, and the same delicious food as before!

'Oh, good, good, good!' shouted everyone, and sat down at once. They beamed at one another, very thankful to be back from the Little Lost Island.

'What a strange little adventure!' said Joe, helping himself to a large piece of wishing-cake. 'Please be careful what you wish, everybody – we don't want any more adventures like that in the middle of a party!'

'I wish that my wings could fly!' said Beth, as she munched her cake. And at once her silver wings spread themselves out, and she rose into the air like a big butterfly, flying beautifully. Oh, it was the loveliest feeling in the world!

'Look at me – look at me!' she cried – and everyone looked. Frannie called out to her. 'Don't fly too far,

Beth. Don't fly too far!'

Beth soon flew down to the table again, her cheeks red with excitement and joy. This was the loveliest birthday party she had ever had!

Everybody wished their wishes except the Old Saucepan Man, who had already wasted his. Frannie, too, had wished her wish when she was on the Little Lost Island, but when she looked upset because she had lost her wish, Moon-Face whispered to her.

'Don't be upset. Tell me what you really wanted to wish and I'll wish it for you. I don't want a wish for myself.'

'Oh, Moon-Face, you *are* kind!' said Frannie. 'Well, if you really mean it, I did want a doll that could walk and talk.'

'Easy!' said Moon-Face at once. 'I wish that Frannie had a doll that walks and talks.'

And at that very moment Silky cried out in wonder and pointed behind her. Everyone looked. Coming along on small, plump legs was a doll, beautifully dressed in blue, with a bag in its hand. It walked to Frannie and looked up at her.

'Oh! You lovely, beautiful doll!' cried Frannie in the greatest delight, and she lifted the doll on to her knee. It cuddled up to her and said, 'I belong to you. I am your own doll. My name is Peronel.'

'What a sweet name!' said Frannie, hugging the doll. 'What have you got in that bag, Peronel?'

'All my other clothes,' said the doll, and opened her bag. Inside were nightdresses, a dressing-gown, an overcoat, a raincoat, overalls, dresses, and all kinds of other clothes. Frannie was simply delighted.

'What did you wish, Joe?' asked Beth. Joe was looking all round and about as if he expected something to arrive at any moment.

'I wished for a pony of my own,' said Joe. 'Oh! Look! Here it comes! What a beauty!'

A little black pony, with a white mark on its forehead and four white feet, came trotting up to the party. It went straight to Joe.

'My own little pony!' cried the little boy, in delight. 'Let me ride you! I shall call you Midnight Star – for the little white star on your black coat.'

He jumped on the pony's back and together they went galloping round the Land of Birthdays.

'Now let's play games!' cried Moon-Face, capering about. And as soon as he said that, the table vanished and music began to play.

'Musical chairs! Musical chairs!' shouted Silky, as the chairs suddenly put themselves together in a long row. 'Come on, everybody!'

XXXIII. SAFE BACK HOME AGAIN – AND GOOD-BYE!

The party went on and on. The game of musical chairs was fun, for instead of somebody taking a chair away each time the music stopped, the chair took itself away, walked neatly off, and stood watching.

Silky won that game. She was so quick and light on her feet. A big box of chocolates came flying down through the air to her, when she sat down on the very last chair and pushed Moon-Face away! She was delighted.

'Let's all have one!' she said, and opened the box at once. Whilst they were eating they saw a most astonishing sight.

'Look!' said Moon-Face, almost swallowing his chocolate in astonishment. 'What's this coming?'

Everyone looked. It seemed like a lot of little brightly coloured men, running very upright. What do you suppose they were?

'Birthday presents!' shouted Watzisname, jumping off his seat in delight. 'Presents – running to us – ready to be unwrapped!'

Really, those presents were the greatest fun! They were like little

gift-wrapped boxes on tiny legs, dodging away, trying not to be caught! Everyone ran after them, laughing and shouting. One by one the happy little boxes were caught, and then they were unwrapped and opened. My goodness, what special things there were inside!

'I've got a brooch in the shape of the Faraway Tree!' cried Frannie, pinning it on herself.

'I want one too,' said her doll.

'Well, you must catch a present then, Peronel,' said Frannie, and how she laughed to see her doll running about after a red birthday-present box! Peronel caught one at last and brought it back to Frannie. Inside there was a teddy-bear shaped brooch, which Peronel was simply delighted with!

Joe found a shining silver whistle inside his present. When he blew it sounded just like all the birds in the Enchanted Wood. He was very happy with it. Moon-Face found a special squeaker that sounded just like a cat mewing, and made the Old Saucepan Man go hunting for cats all the time! Naughty Moon-Face! He pressed his squeaker behind the Saucepan Man and laughed till he cried to hear him calling, 'Puss! Puss! Puss!' and looking under tables and chairs.

Silky's clock wanted a present too. So it ran after one, and trod on one to catch it. It held it with its foot and unwrapped it with Silky. What do you suppose was in it? A tiny can of oil!

'Just the thing to oil your clockwork wheels and springs with!' said Silky in delight. The clock was very pleased. It chimed twenty-two times without stopping, much to the walking doll's astonishment.

They played hide-and-seek, and immediately the most exciting bushes and trees sprang up everywhere to hide behind. Really, the Birthday Land was the most exciting country to be in!

Then they played pin-the-tail-on-the-donkey – and a giant toy donkey and a big fluffy tail appeared out of nowhere!

Then they thought they would have races – and, hey presto – they saw a crowd of small cars drive up, all ready to be raced! In got everyone, choosing the car they liked best. There was even a tiny one for Peronel the doll, and an extra one for Silky's clock, who joined in the fun and ding-donged merrily all the time.

The Old Saucepan Man won the race, though he dropped a few saucepans on the way. Moon-Face handed him a box of toffee that had appeared for the winner.

'You've won!' he said.

'Run?' said the Saucepan Man. 'All right, I'll run!' And he ran and ran, just to show how fast he could run when he wanted to. What a noise he made, with his kettles and saucepans clattering all round him!

'Supper-time, supper-time!' shouted Moon-Face

suddenly, and he pointed to a lovely sight. About a hundred toadstools had suddenly grown up, and appearing on them were jugs of all kinds of delicious drinks, and cakes and fruit. Smaller toadstools grew beside the big ones.

'They are for seats!' cried Silky, sitting down on one and helping herself to some acornade. 'I'm hungry! Come on, everyone!'

Beth flew down from the air. She *did* love flying. Frannie ran up with her doll, who followed her everywhere, talking in her little high voice. Joe galloped up on his pony. Everyone was very happy.

It began to get dark, but nobody minded, because big lanterns suddenly shone out everywhere in the trees and bushes. As they sat and ate, there came a loud bang-bang!

Peronel cuddled up to Frannie, frightened. Silky's clock tried to get on Silky's knee, scared, but she pushed it off.

'What's that?' said Joe, patting his frightened pony.

'Fireworks! Fireworks!' shouted the Angry Pixie in delight. 'Look! Look!'

And there, in front of them, were the fireworks, setting themselves off beautifully. Rockets flew high and sizzled down in coloured stars. Firework wheels whizzed round and round. Firecrackers popped and banged and jumped around. It was splendid to watch!

'This is the loveliest birthday party I've ever heard of,' said Beth happily, flapping her big wings, as she sat and watched the fireworks. 'Lovely things to eat – wishes that come true – exciting games – splendid presents – and now fireworks.'

'We have to go home at midnight,' said Moon-Face, pushing away Silky's clock, which was trying to sit on his toadstool with him.

'How shall we know when it's midnight?' asked Frannie, thinking that it really was time her doll went to bed.

They knew all right – because when midnight came Silky's clock stood up and chimed loudly, twelve times – Dong-dong-dong-dong-dong-dong-dong-dong-dong-dong-dong-dong!

'To the ladder! To the ladder!' cried Moon-Face, hurrying everyone there. 'The Birthday Land will soon be on the move!'

The ladder was there. Everyone climbed down it and called goodbye. The elves took cushions and slid off down the slippery-slip. Mister Whiskers got his beard caught round one of the legs of Moon-Face's sofa and nearly took that with him down the slide. Moon-Face just stopped it in time, and unwound his beard.

'What about my pony?' asked Joe anxiously. 'Do you suppose he will mind sliding down, Moon-Face?'

'Well, he can't climb down the tree, and he certainly wouldn't like going down in the washing-basket,' said Moon-Face. So they sat the surprised pony on a cushion and he slid down in the greatest astonishment, wondering what in the world was happening to him!

Frannie slid down with her sleepy doll on her knee. Beth carefully took off her wings and folded them up. She didn't want to have them spoilt. She wanted to use them every day. She was very proud of them.

The pony arrived on the cushion of moss quite safely. Joe mounted him. It was dark in the wood, but the moon was just rising, and they would be able to see their way home quite well.

'Goodbye!' called Moon-Face from the top of the tree. 'We've had a lovely time!'

'Goodbye!' called Silky. 'Ding-dong!' said her clock sleepily.

'Take care of yourselves!' shouted Watzisname.

Moon-Face pressed his squeaker loudly, and then giggled to hear the Saucepan Man call, 'Puss! Puss! Puss! Wherever *is* that cat!'

Slishy-sloshy-slishy-sloshy! Good gracious, was that Dame Washalot doing washing already? Joe dodged away on his pony and the girls ran from the tree. Mister Whiskers got the water all over him, for he was standing nearby, and he was most upset.

'Come on, girls!' said Joe, laughing. 'We really *must* go home! We shall never wake up in the morning!'

So they went home once more, through the Enchanted Wood, with the moon shining pale and cold between the trees.

'Wisha-wisha-wisha!' whispered the leaves.

Joe put his pony into the field outside the cottage. Frannie undressed Peronel and put her into her doll's bed. Beth put her wings carefully into a drawer. They all undressed and got sleepily into bed.

'Goodnight!' they said. 'What a lovely day it's been. We *are* lucky to live near the Enchanted Wood!'

They were, weren't they? Perhaps they will have more adventures one day; but now we must say goodbye to them, and leave them fast asleep, dreaming of the Land of Birthdays, and all the lovely things that happened there!

THE END

CONTENTS

I. RICK COMES TO STAY

Once upon a time there were three children, Joe, Beth and Frannie. They lived with their mother and father in a little cottage deep in the country. They had to help their parents both in the house and in the garden, as there was lots to do.

Now, one day their mother had a letter. She didn't very often have letters, so the children wondered what it was about.

'Listen!' she said. 'This is something quite exciting for you. Your cousin Rick is coming to stay with us!'

'Ooh!' said all the children, pleased. Rick was about the same age as Joe. He was a happy boy, rather naughty, and it would be such fun to have him.

'He can sleep with me in my little bedroom!' said Joe. 'Oh, Mother, what fun! When is he coming?'

'Tomorrow,' said Mother. 'You can put up a little bed for him, and you must make room for Rick's things in your cupboard. He is going to stay quite a long time, because his mother is ill and can't look after him.'

The three children flew upstairs to get Joe's room ready for Rick as well.

'Hey! What will Rick say when we tell him about the Enchanted Wood and the Faraway Tree?' cried Joe.

'And what will he say when we show him our friends there – Silky, and old Moon-Face, and the dear old deaf Saucepan Man, and everyone!' said Beth.

'He *will* get a surprise!' said Frannie.

They got everything ready for their cousin. They put up a little camp bed for him, and found some blankets. They made room in Joe's cupboard and bedside cabinet for Rick's clothes. Then they looked out of the window. It looked on to a dark, thick wood, whose trees waved in the wind, not far from the bottom of the garden.

'The Enchanted Wood!' said Beth softly. 'What marvellous adventures we have had there. Maybe Rick will have some, too.'

Rick arrived the next day. He had travelled in the delivery van from the village shop, with a small bag of clothes. He jumped down and hugged the children's mother.

'Hello, Aunt Polly!' he said. 'It's good of you to have me. Hello, Joe! I say, aren't Beth and Frannie big now? It's lovely to be with you all again.'

The children took him up to his room. They helped him to unpack his bag and put his things neatly away in the cupboard and the bedside cabinet. They showed him the bed he was to sleep on.

'I expect I shall find it rather dull here after living in the city,' said Rick, putting his washing on top of the bedside cabinet. 'It seems so quiet. I shall miss the noise of buses and cars.'

'You won't find it dull!' said Joe. 'My word, Rick, we've had more adventures since we've been here than we ever had when we lived in town.'

'What sort of adventures?' asked Rick in surprise. 'It seems such a quiet place that I shouldn't have thought there was even a small adventure to be found!'

The children took Rick to the window. 'Look, Rick,' said Joe. 'Do you see that thick, dark wood over there, backing on to the lane at the bottom of our garden?'

'Yes,' said Rick. 'It seems quite ordinary to me, except that the leaves of the trees seem a darker green than usual.'

'Well, listen, Rick – that's the *Enchanted Wood*!' said Beth.

Rick's eyes opened wide. He stared at the wood. 'You're making fun of me!' he said at last.

'No, we're not,' said Frannie. 'We mean what we say. Its name is the Enchanted Wood – and it *is* enchanted. And oh, Rick, in the middle of it is the most wonderful tree in the world!'

'What sort of tree?' asked Rick, feeling quite excited.

'It's a really enormous tree,' said Joe. 'Its top goes right up to the clouds – and oh, Rick, at the top of it is always some strange land. You can go there by climbing up the top branch of the Faraway Tree, going up a little ladder through a hole in the big cloud that always lies on the top of the tree – and there you are in some strange land!'

'I don't think I believe you,' said Rick. 'You're making it all up.'

'Rick! We'll take you there and show you what we mean,' said Beth. 'It's all quite true. We've had such exciting adventures at the top of the Faraway Tree. We've been to the Rocking Land, and the Birthday Land.'

'And the Land of Take-What-You-Want and the Land of the Snowman,' said Frannie. 'You just can't imagine how exciting it all is.'

'And, Rick, all kinds of odd folk live in the trunk of the Faraway Tree,' said Joe. 'We've lots of good friends there. We'll take you to them one day. There's a dear little fairy called Silky, because she has such a mop of silky golden hair.'

'And there's funny old Mister Watzisname,' said Frannie.

'What's his real name?' asked Rick in surprise.

'Nobody knows, not even himself,' said Joe. 'So everyone calls him Mister Watzisname. Oh, and there is the Old Saucepan Man. He's always covered with kettles and saucepans and things, and he's so deaf that he always hears everything wrong.'

222

Rick's eyes began to shine. 'Take me there,' he begged. 'Quick, take me! I can't wait to see all these exciting people.'

'We can't go till Mother says she doesn't need us in the house,' said Beth. 'But we *will* take you – of course we will.'

'And, Rick, there's a slippery slip, a slide that goes right down the inside of the tree from the top to the bottom,' said Frannie. 'It belongs to Moon-Face. He lends people cushions to slide down on.'

'I do want to go down that slide,' said Rick, getting terribly impatient. 'Why do you tell me all these things if you can't take me to see them now? I'll never be able to sleep tonight! Goodness! My head feels in a whirl already to think of the Faraway Tree and Moon-Face and Silky and the slippery-slip.'

'Rick, we'll take you as soon as we can,' promised Joe. 'There's no hurry. The Faraway Tree is always there. We never, never know what land is going to be at the top. We have to be very careful sometimes because there might be a dangerous land – one that we couldn't get away from!'

A voice came from downstairs. 'Children! Are you going to stay up there all day? I suppose you don't want anything to eat? What a pity – because I have made some new bread and put out some honey!'

Four children raced down the stairs. New bread and honey! Goodness, they weren't going to miss those. Good old Mother – she was always thinking of some nice little treat for them.

'Joe, Father wants you to dig up some potatoes for him later,' said Mother. 'Rick can help you. And, Beth and Frannie, I need your help, because I have to take some mended clothes to Mrs Harris, and she lives such a long way away.'

The children had been hoping to take Rick to the Enchanted Wood. They looked disappointed. But they said nothing, because they knew that in a family everyone had to help when they could.

Mother saw their disappointed faces and smiled. 'I suppose you want to take Rick to see those peculiar friends of yours,' she said. 'Well now, listen – if you are good children today, and do the jobs you have to do, I'll give you a whole day off tomorrow! Then you may take your lunch and dinner and go to visit any friends you like. How would you like that?'

'Oh, Mother, thank you!' cried the children in delight.

'A whole day!' said Beth. 'Why, Rick, we can show you everything!'

'And maybe let you peep into whatever land is at the top of the Faraway Tree,' whispered Frannie. 'Oh, what fun!'

So they did their work well that afternoon and looked forward to the next day. Rick dug hard, and Joe was pleased with him. It was going to be fun to have a cousin with them, able to work and play and enjoy everything, too!

When they went to bed that night they left the doors of their rooms open so that they might call to one another.

'Sleep well, Rick!' called Beth. 'I hope it's fine tomorrow! What fun we'll have!'

'Goodnight, Beth!' called back Rick. 'I can't tell

you how I'm longing for tomorrow. I know I shan't be able to sleep tonight!'

But he did – and so did all the others. When Mother came up at ten o'clock she peeped in at the children, and not one was awake.

Joe woke first next day. He sat up and looked out of the window. The sun streamed in, warm and bright. Joe's heart jumped for joy. He leaned over to Rick's bed and shook him.

'Wake up!' he said. 'It's tomorrow now – and we're going to the Enchanted Wood!'

II. OFF TO THE ENCHANTED WOOD

The children ate their breakfast quickly. Mother told them to make sandwiches for themselves and to take a small chocolate cake from the cupboard.

'You can take some doughnuts too,' she said, 'and there are apples in that dish over there. When you come home, I'll bake some potatoes in the oven, and you can eat them with butter and cheese.'

'Oooh, Mother – we *will* be hungry!' said Joe at once. 'Let's hurry up with the sandwiches. We want to start off as soon as possible.'

'Now be home by six o'clock, or I shall worry,' said Mother. 'Look after your cousin, Joe.'

'Yes, I will,' promised Joe.

At last everything was ready. Joe packed the food into a leather bag and slung it over his shoulder. Then the four of them set off to the Enchanted Wood.

It didn't take them long to get there. A narrow ditch was between the lane and the wood.

'You've got to jump over the ditch, Rick,' said Joe. They all jumped over. Rick stood still when he was in the wood.

'What a strange noise the leaves of the trees make,' he said. 'It's as if they were talking

226

to one another – telling secrets.'

'Wisha, wisha, wisha, wisha,' whispered the trees.

'They *are* telling secrets,' said Beth. 'And do you know, Rick – if the trees have any message for us, we can hear it by pressing our left ears to the trunks of the trees! Then we *really* hear what they say.'

'Wisha-wisha-wisha-wisha,' said the trees.

'Come on,' said Joe impatiently. 'Let's go to the Faraway Tree.'

They all went on – and soon came to the mysterious magic tree. Rick stared at it in great astonishment.

'Wow, it's simply ENORMOUS!' he said. 'I've never seen such a big tree in my life. And you can't possibly see the top. Goodness me! What kind of tree is it? It's got oak leaves, and yet it doesn't really seem like an oak.'

'It's a funny tree,' said Beth. 'It may grow acorns and oak leaves for a little way – and then suddenly you notice that it's growing plums. Then another day it may grow apples or pears. You just never know. But it's all very exciting.'

'How do you climb it?' asked Rick. 'In the ordinary way?'

'Well, we will today,' said Joe, 'because we want to show you our friends who live inside the tree. But sometimes there's a rope that is let down the tree, and we can go up easily with the help of that. Or sometimes Moon-Face lets down a cushion on the end of the rope and then pulls us up one by one.'

He swung himself up into the tree, and the others followed. After a bit Rick gave a shout. 'Wow! It's extraordinary! This tree is growing nuts now! Look!'

Sure enough it was. Rick picked some and cracked them. They were hazelnuts, ripe and sweet. Everyone had some and enjoyed them.

Now when they had all got very high up indeed, Rick was most surprised to see a little window in the trunk of the Faraway Tree.

'Goodness – does somebody live just here?' he called to the others. 'Look – there's a window here. I'm going to peep in.'

'You'd better not!' shouted Joe. 'The Angry Pixie lives there, and he hates people peeping in.'

But Rick felt so curious that he just *had* to peep in. The Angry Pixie was at home. He was filling his kettle with water, when he looked up and saw Rick's surprised face at his window. Nothing made the pixie more angry than to see people looking at him. He rushed to the window at once and flung it open.

'Peeping again!' he shouted. 'It's too bad! All day and night people come peeping. Take that!'

He emptied the kettle of cold water all over poor Rick. Then he slammed his window and drew the curtains across. Joe, Beth and Frannie couldn't help laughing.

'I told you not to peep in at the Angry Pixie,' said Joe, wiping Rick with his hanky. 'He's nearly always in a bad temper. Oh, and by the way, Rick, I must warn you about something else. There's an old woman who lives high up in the tree who is always washing. She empties the water down the tree, and it comes slish-sloshing down. You'll have to look out for that or you'll get wet.'

Rick looked up the tree as if he expected the water to come tumbling down at once.

'Come on,' said Beth. 'We'll come to where the Owl lives soon. He's a friend of Silky's, and sometimes brings us notes from her.'

The Owl was fast asleep. He usually only woke up at night-time. Rick peered in at his window and saw the big Owl asleep on a bed. He couldn't help laughing.

'I *am* enjoying all this,' he said to Frannie. 'It's quite an adventure.'

The children climbed higher, and came to a broad branch. 'There's a sweet little yellow door, with a knocker and a bell!' cried Rick in surprise, staring at the door set neatly in the trunk of the tree. 'Who lives there?'

'Our friend Silky,' said Joe. 'Ring the bell and she'll open the door.'

Rick rang the little bell and heard it go ting-a-ling inside. Footsteps pattered to the door. It opened, and a pretty little fairy looked out. Her hair hung round her face like a golden mist.

'Hello, Silky!' cried Joe. 'We've come to see you – and we've brought our cousin, Rick, who has come to live with us. He's having a lovely time exploring the Faraway Tree.'

'How do you do, Rick?' said Silky, holding out her small hand. Rick shook hands shyly. He thought Silky was the loveliest creature he had ever seen.

'I'll come with you if you are going to visit Moon-Face,' said Silky. 'I want to borrow some honey from him. I'll take some Pop Cakes with me, and we'll have them in Moon-Face's house.'

'Whatever are Pop Cakes?' asked Rick, in surprise.

'Wait and see!' said Joe with a grin.

They all went up the Tree again. Soon they heard a funny noise. 'That's old Mister Watzisname snoring,' said Joe. 'Look – there he is!'

Sure enough, there he was, sitting in a comfortable chair, his hands folded over his big tummy, and his mouth wide open.

'How I'd love to pop something into his open mouth!' said Rick at once.

'Yes, that's what everybody feels,' said Joe. 'Moon-Face and Silky once popped some acorns in – didn't you, Silky? And Watzisname was very angry. He threw Moon-Face up through the hole in the cloud, and put him into the strange land there.'

'Where's the Old Saucepan Man?' asked Beth. 'He is usually with his friend, Mister Watzisname.'

'I expect he has gone to see Moon-Face,' said Silky. 'Come on. We'll soon be there.'

As they went up the Tree, Silky suddenly stopped. 'Listen,' she said. They all listened. They heard a curious noise – 'slishy-sloshy-slishy-sloshy' – coming nearer and nearer.

'It's Dame Washalot's dirty water coming!' yelled Joe. 'Get under a branch, everyone.'

Rick wasn't as quick as the others. They all hid under big boughs – but poor old Rick wasn't quite under his when the water came pouring down the tree. It tumbled on to his head and went down his neck. Rick was very angry. The others were sorry, but they thought it was very funny, too.

230

'Next time I climb this tree I'll wear my swimsuit,' said Rick, trying to wipe himself dry. 'Really, I think somebody ought to stop Dame Washalot pouring her water away like that. How disgusting!'

'Oh, you'll soon get used to it, and dodge the water easily,' said Joe. On they all went up the tree again, and at last came almost to the top. There they saw a door in the trunk of the tree, and from behind the door came the sound of voices.

'That's Moon-Face and the Old Saucepan Man,' said Joe, and he banged on the door. It flew open and Moon-Face looked out. His big round face beamed with smiles when he saw who his visitors were.

'Hello, hello, hello,' he said. 'Come on in. The Saucepan Man is here.'

Everyone went into Moon-Face's curious round room. There was a large hole in the middle of it, which was the beginning of the slippery-slip, the wonderful slide that went round and round down the inside of the tree, right to the bottom. Moon-Face's furniture was arranged round the inside of the tree trunk, and it was all curved to fit the curve of the tree. His bed was curved, the chairs were curved, the sofa and the stove. It was very odd.

Rick stared at it all in great surprise. He really felt as if he must be in a dream. There was somebody very peculiar sitting on the sofa.

It was the Old Saucepan Man. He really was a very curious sight. He was covered with saucepans and kettles, and he wore a saucepan for a hat. You could hardly see anything of him except his face, hands and feet, because he was so covered with saucepans and things. He made a tremendous clatter whenever he moved.

'Who's that?' he said, looking at Rick.

'This is Rick,' said Joe, and Rick went forward to shake hands.

The Saucepan Man was very deaf, though he did sometimes hear quite well. But he nearly always heard everything wrong, and sometimes he was very funny.

'Chick?' he said. 'Well, that's a funny name for a boy.'

'Not Chick, but RICK!' shouted Moon-Face.

'Stick?' said the Saucepan Man, shaking hands. 'Good morning, Stick. I hope you are well.'

Rick giggled. Moon-Face got ready to shout again, but Silky quickly handed him her bag of Pop Cakes. 'Don't get angry with him,' she said. 'Look – let's all have some Pop Cakes. They are freshly made today. And, oh, Moon-Face, do tell us – what land is at the top of the Faraway Tree today?'

'The Land of Topsy-Turvy,' said Moon-Face. 'But I don't advise you to go there. It's very uncomfortable.'

'Oh, yes let's,' cried Rick. 'Can't we just *peep* at it?'

'We'll see,' said Joe, giving him a Pop Cake. 'Eat this, Rick.'

Pop Cakes were lovely. Rick put one in his mouth and bit into it. It went pop at once – and he found his mouth full of sweet honey from the middle of the cake.

'Delicious!' he said. 'I'll have another. Oh, Joe, PLEASE let's take our lunch up into the land of Topsy-Turvy. Oh, please, please, please!'

III. THE LAND OF TOPSY-TURVY

'What is Topsy-Turvy Land like?' asked Joe, taking another Pop Cake.

'Never been there,' said Moon-Face. 'But I should think it's quite safe, really. It's only just come there, so it should stay for a while. We could go up and see what it's like and come down again if we don't like it. Silky, Saucepan and I will come with you, if you like.'

Moon-Face turned to the Saucepan Man, who was enjoying his fifth Pop Cake.

'Saucepan, we're going up the ladder,' he said. 'Are you coming?'

'Humming?' said Saucepan, looking all round as if he thought there might be bees about. 'No, I didn't hear any humming.'

'I said, are you COMING?' said Moon-Face.

'Oh, *coming*!' said Saucepan. 'Of course I'm coming. Are we going to take our lunch?'

'Yes,' said Moon-Face, going to a curved door that opened on to a tiny cupboard. 'I'll see what I've got. Tomatoes. Plums. Ginger snaps. Lemonade. I'll bring them all.'

He put them into a basket. Then they all went out of the funny, curved room on to the big branch outside. Moon-Face shut his door.

Joe led the way up to the very top of the Faraway

Tree. Then suddenly Rick gave a shout of astonishment.

'Look!' he cried. 'There's an enormous white cloud above and around us. Isn't it mysterious!'

Sure enough, a huge white cloud floated above them – but just near by was a hole right through the cloud!

'That's where we go, up that hole,' said Joe. 'See that branch that goes up the hole? Come on!'

They all went up the last and topmost branch of the Faraway Tree. It went up and up through the purple hole in the cloud. At the very end of the branch was a little ladder.

Joe climbed the ladder – and suddenly his head poked out into the Land of Topsy-Turvy!

Then one by one all the others followed – and soon all seven of them stood in the curious land.

Rick was not as used to strange lands as the others were. He stood and stared, with his eyes so wide open that it really seemed as if they were going to drop out of his head!

And, indeed, it was a strange sight he saw. Every house was upside down, and stood on its chimneys. The trees were upside down, their heads buried in the ground and their roots in the air. And the people walked upside down, too!

'They are walking on their hands, with their legs in the air!' said Joe. 'Goodness, what a peculiar thing to do!'

Everyone stared at the folk of Topsy-Turvy Land. They got along very quickly on their hands, and often stopped to talk to one another, chattering busily.

Some of them had been shopping, and carried their baskets on one foot.

'Let's go and peep inside a house and see what it's like, all topsy-turvy,' said Joe. So they set off to the nearest house. It looked really peculiar standing on its chimneys. No smoke came out of them – but smoke came out of a window near the top.

'How do we get in?' said Beth. They watched a Topsy-Turvy man walk on his hands to another house. He jumped in at the nearest window, going up a ladder first.

The children looked for the ladder that entered the house they were near. They soon found it. They went up it to a window and peeped inside.

'Gosh!' said Joe. 'Everything really *is* upside down in it – the chairs and tables, and everything. How uncomfortable it must be!'

An old lady was inside the house. She was sitting upside down in an upside down chair and looked very uncomfortable. She was angry when she saw the children peeping in.

She clapped her hands, and a tall man, walking on his hands, came running in from the next room.

'Send those rude children away,' shouted the old woman. The tall man hurried to the window on his hands, and the children quickly slid down the ladder, because the man looked rather fierce.

'It's a silly land, I think,' said Joe. 'I vote we just have our lunch and then leave this place. I wonder why everything is topsy-turvy.'

'Oh, a spell was put on everything and everybody,' said Moon-Face, 'and in an instant everything was topsy-turvy. Look – wouldn't that be a good place to sit and eat our lunch?'

It was under a big oak tree whose roots stood high in the air. Joe and Moon-Face set out the lunch. It looked very good.

'There's plenty for everybody,' said Joe. 'Have a sandwich, Silky? Saucepan, have a plum?'

'Crumb?' said Saucepan, in surprise. 'Is that all you can spare for me – a crumb?'

'PLUM, PLUM, PLUM!' said Moon-Face, pushing a ripe one into the Saucepan Man's hands.

'Oh, *plum*,' said Saucepan. 'Well, why didn't you say so?'

Everybody giggled. They all tucked in to a good lunch. In the middle of it, Joe happened to look round, and he saw something surprising. It was a policeman coming, walking on his hands, of course.

'Look what's coming,' said Joe with a laugh. Everyone looked. Moon-Face went pale.

'I don't like the look of him,' he said. 'Suppose he's come to lock us up for something? We couldn't get away down the Faraway Tree before this land swung away from the top!'

The policeman came right up to the little crowd under the tree.

'Why aren't you Topsy-Turvy?' he asked in a stern voice. 'Don't you know that the rule in this land is that everything and everyone has to be upside down?'

'Yes, but we don't belong to this silly land,' said Joe. 'And if you were sensible, you'd make another rule, saying that everybody must be the right way up. You've just no idea how

236

silly you look, policeman, walking on your hands!'

The policeman went red with anger. He took a sort of wand from his belt and tapped Joe on the head with it.

'Topsy-Turvy!' he said. 'Topsy-Turvy!'

And to Joe's horror he had to turn himself upside down at once! The others stared at poor Joe, standing on his hands, his legs in the air.

'Oh, fiddlesticks!' cried Joe. 'I can't eat anything properly now because I need my hands to walk with. Policeman, put me right again.'

'You *are* right now,' said the policeman, and walked solemnly away on his hands.

'Put Joe the right way up,' said Rick. So everyone tried to turn him over so that he was the right way up again. But as soon as they got his legs down and his head up, he turned topsy-turvy again. He just couldn't help it, because he was under a spell.

A group of Topsy-Turvy people came to watch. They laughed loudly. 'Now he belongs to Topsy-Turvy Land!' they cried. 'He'll have to stay here with us. Never mind, young man – you'll soon get used to it!'

'Take me back to the Faraway Tree,' begged Joe, afraid that he really and truly *might* be made to stay in this peculiar land. 'Hurry!'

Everyone jumped to their feet. They helped Joe along to where the hole ran down through the cloud. He wasn't used to walking on his hands and he kept falling over. They tried their best to make him stand upright, but he couldn't.

The spell wouldn't let him.

'It will be difficult to get him down through the hole,' said Rick. 'Look – there it is. I'd better go down first and see if I can help him. You others push him through as carefully as you can. He'll have to go upside down, I'm afraid.'

It was very difficult to get Joe through the hole, because his hands and head had to go first. Moon-Face held his legs to guide him. Rick held his shoulders as he came down the ladder, so that he wouldn't fall.

At last all seven of them were through the hole in the clouds, and were on the broad branch outside Moon-Face's house. Joe held on to the branch with his hands, his legs were in the air.

'Moon-Face! Silky! Can't you possibly take this spell away?' he groaned. 'It's dreadful.'

'Silky, what land is coming to the top of the Faraway Tree next?' asked Moon-Face. 'Have you heard?'

'I think it's the Land of Spells,' said Silky. 'It should come tomorrow. But I'm not really sure.'

'Oh, well, if it's the Land of Spells, we could easily get a spell from there to put Joe right,' said Moon-Face, beaming. 'Joe, you must stay the night with me and wait for the Land of Spells tomorrow. The others can go home and tell what has happened.'

'All right,' said Joe. 'I can't possibly climb up the tree again if I'm upside down – so I'll just have to wait here. Mother will never believe it, though, when the others tell her why I don't go home. Still, it can't be helped.'

They all went into Moon-Face's house. Joe stood on a chair, upside down. The others sat about and talked. Rick was sorry for Joe, but he couldn't help feeling a bit excited. Goodness – if this was the sort of adventure that Joe, Beth and Frannie had, what fun things were going to be!

The others began telling him all the adventures they had had. Silky made some hot chocolate, and went down the tree to fetch some more Pop Cakes. When it was half past five Beth said they must go.

'Goodbye, Joe,' she said. 'Don't be too unhappy. Pretend you are a bat – they always sleep upside down, you know, and don't mind a bit! Come on, Rick – we're going down the slippery-slip!'

Rick *was* excited. He took the red cushion that Moon-Face gave him and sat himself at the top of the slide. Beth gave him a push.

And off he went, round and round the inside of the enormous Faraway Tree, sitting safely on his cushion. *What* a way to get down a tree!

IV. THE LAND OF SPELLS

Rick shot round and down the inside of the Faraway Tree on his cushion. He came to the bottom. He shot out of the trapdoor there, and landed on the soft green moss. He sat there for a moment, out of breath.

'That's the loveliest slide I've ever had!' he thought to himself. 'O-o-oh – wouldn't I like to do that again!'

He had just got up from the moss when the trapdoor at the bottom of the tree opened once again, and Frannie shot out on a yellow cushion. Then came Beth, giggling, for she always thought it was a huge joke to slide down inside the tree like that.

'What do we do with the cushions?' asked Rick. 'Does Moon-Face want them back?'

'Yes, he does,' said Frannie, picking them up. 'The red squirrel always collects them and sends them back to him.'

As she spoke, a red squirrel, dressed in a sweater, popped out of a hole in the trunk.

'Here are the cushions,' said Frannie, and the squirrel took them. He looked up into the tree, and a rope came swinging down.

'Moon-Face always lets it down for his cushions,' said Beth. Rick watched the squirrel tie the three cushions to the rope end. Then he gave three gentle tugs at the rope, and at once the rope was pulled up, and the cushions went swinging up the tree to Moon-Face.

'I wish Joe was with us,' said Rick, as they all went home. 'Do you think Aunt Polly will be worried about him?'

'Well, we'll have to tell Mother the truth,' said Frannie. 'She is sure to ask where he is.'

Mother did ask, of course, and the girls told her what had happened.

'I find all this very difficult to believe,' said Mother, astonished. 'I think Joe is just spending the night with Moon-Face for a treat. I'll trust Moon-Face to take care of him tonight, but he *must* come back tomorrow.'

Nobody said any more. The girls and Rick felt very tired, and after some hot chocolate and baked potatoes for dinner, they all went to bed. Beth wondered how Joe was getting on at Moon-Face's.

He was getting on all right, though he was very tired of being upside down. It didn't matter how hard he tried to stand the right way up, he always swung back topsy-turvy again. The policeman had put a very strong spell on him!

'You had better try to sleep in my bed,' said Moon-Face. 'I'll sleep on my sofa.'

'I suppose I'll have to stand on my head all night,' said poor Joe. And that's just what he did have to do. It was very uncomfortable.

Once he lost his balance when he was asleep, and tipped off the bed. He almost fell down the slippery-slip, but Moon-Face, who was awake, reached out a hand and caught his leg just in time.

'My goodness!' said Moon-Face. 'Don't go doing things like this in the middle of the night, Joe. It's so disturbing.'

'Well, how can I help it?' said Joe.

'I'll tie your feet to a nail on my wall,' said Moon-Face. 'Then you can't topple over when you are asleep.'

So he did that, and Joe didn't fall down any more. When morning came he was surprised to find himself upside down, because at first he didn't remember what had happened.

'I'll just peep up through the hole in the cloud and see if by any chance the Land of Spells is there yet,' said Moon-Face. 'If it is, we'll go up and see what we can do for you.'

So off he went up the little ladder and popped his head out of the hole in the cloud to see if the Land of Topsy-Turvy was still there, or if it had gone.

There was nothing there at all – only the big white cloud, moving about like a thick mist. Moon-Face slipped down the ladder again.

'Topsy-Turvy has gone, but the next land hasn't come yet,' he said. 'We'll have breakfast and then I'll look again. Hello – there's Silky. Stay and have breakfast, Silky dear.'

'I came up to see how Joe was,' said Silky. 'Yes, I'd love to have breakfast. It's funny to watch Joe eating upside down. Hasn't the Land of Spells come yet?'

'Not yet,' said Moon-Face, putting a kettle on his stove to boil. 'There's nothing there at all. But Topsy-Turvy is gone, thank goodness!'

They all had breakfast. Moon-Face cooked some porridge. 'What do you want on your porridge?' he asked Joe. 'Syrup – sugar – cream?'

Joe couldn't see any syrup, sugar or cream on the table. 'Syrup,' he said, 'please, Moon-Face.' Moon-Face handed him a small jug that seemed to be quite empty.

'Syrup!' he said to the jug in a firm voice. And syrup came pouring out as soon as Joe tipped up the jug. Silky wanted cream – and cream came out when Moon-Face said 'Cream!' to the jug. It was great fun.

Moon-Face went again to see if the Land of Spells had come. This time he came back excited.

'It's there!' he said. 'Come on! I'd better take some money with me, I think, in case we have to buy the spell we want.'

He took a small bag down from a shelf, and then he and Silky helped Joe to walk upside down up the branch that led through the hole in the cloud to the little ladder. Up he went with great difficulty, holding on tightly to the rungs of the ladder with his hands. At last he was up in the Land of Spells.

This land was like a big market-place. In it were all kinds of curious little shops and stalls. All kinds of people sold spells. In some of the shops sat tall wizards, famous for their magic. In some of them were green-eyed witches, making spells as fast as they could. Outside, in the market-place, sat all kinds of fairy folk at their stalls – pixies, gnomes, goblins, elves – all crying their wares at the tops of their high voices.

'Spell to make a crooked nose straight!' cried one pixie, rattling a yellow box in which were magic pills.

'Spell to grow blue daffodils!' cried a gnome, showing a bottle of blue juice.

'Spell to make cats sing!' cried another gnome. Joe could hardly believe his ears. How odd! Who would want to make cats sing?

'Now, we must just see if we can possibly find a spell to make you stand up straight again,' said Moon-Face, and he went into a little low shop where a strange goblin sat.

The goblin had blue, pointed ears, and his eyes sparkled as if they had fireworks in them.

'I want a spell,' said Moon-Face.

'What for?' asked the goblin. 'I've a spell for everything under the sun in my shop! Very powerful spells too, some of them. Would you like a spell to send you travelling straight off to the moon?'

'Oh, no, thank you,' said Moon-Face at once. 'I know I look like the man in the moon, with my big round face – but I'm nothing at all to do with the moon really.'

'Well, would you like a spell to make you as tall as a giant?' said the goblin, picking up a box and opening it. He showed Moon-Face a large blue pill inside. 'Now, take that pill, and you'll shoot up as high as a house! You'll feel fine. It only costs one piece of gold.'

'No, thank you,' said Moon-Face. 'If I grew as big as that I'd never get down the hole in the cloud back to the Faraway Tree. And if I did, I'd never be able to get in at the door of my tree house. I don't want silly spells like that.'

'Silly!' cried the goblin, in a rage. 'You call my marvellous spells silly! Another word from you, stupid old Round-Face, and I'll use a spell that will turn you into a big bouncing ball!'

Silky pulled Moon-Face out of the shop quickly. She was quite pale. 'Moon-Face, you know you shouldn't make these people angry,' she whispered. 'You might find yourself turned into a bouncing ball, or a black beetle, or something, if you are rude to them. For goodness' sake, let *me* ask for the spell we want. Look – here's a bigger shop – with a nice-looking witch inside.'

They all went in. The witch was knitting socks from the green smoke that came from her fire. It was marvellous to watch her. Joe wished he wasn't upside down so that he could see her properly.

'Good morning,' said the witch. 'Do you want a spell?'

'Yes, please,' said Silky in her most polite voice. 'We want to make our friend Joe stand the right way up again.'

'That's easy,' said the witch, her green eyes looking in a kindly way at poor Joe. 'I've only got to rub a Walking Spell on to the soles of his feet – and he will be all right. The Walking Spell will make his feet want to walk – and he will have to stand up the right way to walk on them – so he will be cured. Come here, young man!'

Joe walked over to the witch on his hands. She took down a jar from a shelf and opened it. It was full of purple ointment. The witch rubbed some on to the soles of Joe's shoes.

> *Rimminy-Romminy-Reet,*
> *Stand on your own two feet!*
> *Rimminy-Romminy-Ro,*
> *The right way up you must go!*

And, of course, you can guess what happened! Joe swung right over, stood on his two feet again, and there he was, as upright as Moon-Face and Silky. Wasn't he glad!

V. SAUCEPAN MAKES A MUDDLE

Joe, Silky and Moon-Face were very pleased that Joe
was the right way up again.

'It feels funny,' said Joe. 'I feel quite giddy the right
way up after standing upside down for so long. Thank
you, witch. How much is the spell?'

'One piece of gold,' said the witch. Moon-Face put
his hand into his money bag. He brought out a piece
of gold. The witch threw it into the fire, and at once
bright golden smoke came out. She took up her
knitting needles and began to knit the yellow smoke
into the socks she was making.

'I wanted a yellow pattern,' she said, pleased. 'Your
piece of gold came just at the right moment.'

'Gosh, this is a very magic land, isn't it?' said Joe, as
the three of them walked out of the extraordinary
shop. 'Fancy knitting socks out of smoke! Don't let's
go home yet, Moon-Face. I want to see a few more
things.'

'All right,' said Moon-Face, who wanted to explore
a bit too. 'Come on. Hey, look at the gnome who is
selling a spell to make cats sing! Somebody has
brought a cat to him – I wonder if the spell will really
work!'

A witch's assistant had brought along a big black
cat. He handed the gnome two silver pieces of money.
The gnome took the cat on his knee. He opened its

mouth and looked down it. Then he took a silver whistle and blew a tune softly down the cat's pink throat. The cat swallowed once or twice and then jumped off the gnome's knee.

'Will it sing now?' asked the witch's assistant. 'I won't go back to my witch unless it does.'

'It will sing whenever you stroke it,' said the gnome, turning to another customer.

The witch's assistant went off with the cat following behind. Joe took hold of Moon-Face's arm and whispered to him:

'I'm going to stroke the cat. I DO want to hear if it really will sing!'

Moon-Face and Silky wanted to as well. They giggled to see Joe running softly after the big black cat. He caught up with it. He gently stroked it.

And then, oh, what a peculiar thing! The cat stopped, lifted up its head, and sang in a very deep man's voice:

> *Oh, once my whiskers grew so long*
> *I had to have a shave!*
> *The barber said: 'It's not the way*
> *For whiskers to behave,*
> *If you're not careful, my dear cat,*
> *They'll grow into a beard,*
> *And then a billy-goat you'll be,*
> *Or something very weird!'*
>
> *Oh, once my tail became so short*
> *It hadn't got a wag,*
> *The baker said . . .*

But whatever the baker said about the cat's short tail nobody ever knew. The witch's assistant turned round in surprise when he heard the cat singing, because he knew that he hadn't stroked it. He saw Joe and the others grinning away nearby, and he was very angry.

'How dare you use up the cat's singing!' he cried. 'You wait till I tell the witch. She'll be after you. And *you* won't sing if she catches you!'

'Quick! Run!' said Moon-Face. 'If he does fetch the witch we'll get into trouble.'

So they ran away fast, and were soon out of sight of the cat and the assistant. They sank down under a tree, laughing.

'Oh, dear! That cat did sing a funny song!' said Joe, wiping his eyes. 'And what a lovely deep voice it had. Do you think its whiskers really did grow very long?'

Just then the three of them heard a loud noise coming along: 'Clankity-clank, rattle, bang, crash!'

'The Saucepan Man!' they all cried. 'He's come up here, too!'

And sure enough, it *was* Old Saucepan, grinning all over his face. He had so many kettles and saucepans on that day that nothing could be seen of him except his face and his feet.

'Hello, hello!' he said. 'I guessed you were up here. Been having fun?'

'Yes,' said Joe. 'I'm all right again – look! It's so nice to walk the proper way up again. And oh, Saucepan, we've just heard a cat sing!'

Saucepan actually heard what Joe said – but he couldn't believe that he had heard right, so he put his hand behind his ear and said, 'What did you say? I thought you said you'd heard a cat sing – but I heard wrong, I know.'

'No, you heard right,' said Moon-Face. 'We *did* hear a cat sing!'

'Let's go and explore a bit more,' said Joe. So they got up and went off.

A witch was selling a spell to make ordinary broomsticks fly through the air. The four of them watched in amazement as they saw her rubbing a pink ointment on to a broomhandle belonging to an elf.

'Now get on it, say "Whizz away!" and you can fly home,' said the witch. The elf sat astride the broomstick, a smile on her pretty face.

'Whizz away!' she said. And off whizzed the broomstick up into the air, with the elf clinging tightly to it!

'I'd like to buy that spell,' said Joe. 'I wonder how much it is.'

The witch heard him. 'Three silver pieces,' she said. Joe hadn't even got one. But Moon-Face had. He took them out of his money bag and gave them to the witch.

'Where's your broomstick?' she said.

'We haven't got one with us,' said Joe. 'But can't you give us the ointment instead, please?'

'Well, I'll give you just a little,' said the witch. She took a tiny pink jar and put a dab of the pink ointment into it. Joe took it and put it into his pocket. Now maybe his mother's broomstick would learn to fly!

At the next stall a goblin was selling a spell to make things big. The spell was in big cans, and looked like paint.

'Just think what a useful spell this is!' yelled the

goblin to the passers-by. 'Have you got visitors coming to dinner and only a small cake to offer them? A dab of this spell and the cake swells to twice its size! Have you got a suit you have grown out of? A dab of this spell and it will grow to the right size! Marvellous, wonderful, amazing and astonishing! Buy, buy, buy, while you've got the chance!'

Saucepan heard all that the goblin said, as he was shouting at the top of his voice. He began to look in all his kettles and saucepans.

'What do you want?' asked Joe.

'My money,' said the Saucepan Man. 'I always keep it in one of my kettles or saucepans – but I never remember which one. I simply *must* buy that spell. Think how useful it would be to me. Sometimes when I go round selling my goods a customer will say to me, "Oh, you haven't a big enough kettle!" But now I shall be able to make my kettles just as big as I like! And we can dab the Pop Cakes with the spell, too, and make them twice as big.'

He found his money at last and paid it to the goblin, who handed him a can of the spell. Saucepan was very pleased. He longed to try it out on something. He took the brush and dabbed a daisy nearby with the spell. The daisy at once grew to twice its size. Then Saucepan dabbed a bumble-bee and that grew enormous. It buzzed around Moon-Face and he waved it away.

'Saucepan, don't do any more bees,' he begged. 'I expect their

stings are twice as big, too. Look – let's go to that
store over there and buy some treats. It would be fun
to make them twice as big!'

They hurried to the shop – but on the way a
dreadful thing happened! Saucepan fell over one of his
kettles and upset the can which had the spell in it. It
splashed up – and drops of it fell on to Moon-Face,
Silky and Joe – and the old Saucepan Man, too! And
in a moment they all shot up to twice their size! Silky
grew to three times her size because more drops fell
on her.

They stared at one another. How small the Land of
Spells suddenly seemed. How little the witches and
goblins looked, how tiny the shops were!

'Saucepan! You really *are* careless!' cried Moon-
Face, angrily. 'Look what you've done to us. *Now*
what are we to do?'

Silky clutched hold of Moon-Face's arm. 'Moon-
Face!' she said. 'Oh, Moon-Face – do you think we
are too big to go down the hole through the cloud?'

Moon-Face turned pale. 'We'd better go and see,'
he said. 'Come on, everybody.'

Frightened and silent, all four of them hurried to
where the hole led down to the Faraway Tree. How
little it seemed to the four big people now! Moon-
Face tried to get down. He stuck. He couldn't slip
down at all.

'It's no use,' he said. 'We're too big to go down.
Whatever shall we do?'

VI. WHAT CAN THEY DO NOW?

Joe, Moon-Face, Silky and Saucepan sat down by the hole and thought hard. Silky began to cry.

The Saucepan Man looked most uncomfortable. He was very fond of Silky. 'Silky, please do forgive me for being so careless,' he said in a small voice. 'I didn't mean to do this. Don't cry. You make me feel dreadful.'

'It's all right,' sobbed Silky, borrowing Moon-Face's handkerchief. 'I know you didn't mean to. But I can't help feeling sad when I think I won't ever be able to see my dear little room in the Faraway Tree any more.'

The Saucepan Man began to cry, too. Tears dripped with a splash into his saucepans and kettles. He put his arm round Silky, and two or three kettle-spouts stuck into her.

'Don't!' she said. 'You're sticking into me. Moon-Face – Joe – can't you think of something to do? Can we possibly squeeze down if we hold our breath and make ourselves as small as we can?'

'Quite impossible,' said Moon-Face gloomily. 'Listen – there's somebody coming up the ladder.'

They heard voices – and soon a head popped up out of the hole in the cloud. It was Rick's! He stared in surprise at the four enormous people sitting by the hole.

He climbed up and stood beside them, looking

very, very small. Then up came Beth and Frannie. Their eyes nearly fell out of their heads when they saw how big Joe and his friends were.

'What's happened?' cried Rick. 'We got worried because you didn't come home, Joe – so we climbed up to see where you were. But why are you so ENORMOUS?'

Joe told them. Silky sobbed into Moon-Face's hanky. Beth put her arm round her. It was funny to feel Silky so very big. Beth's arm only went half way round Silky's waist!

'And now, you see, we can't get back down the hole,' said Joe.

'*I* know what you can do!' said Rick suddenly.

'What?' cried everyone hopefully.

'Well, rub the hole with the spell, and it will get bigger, of course!' said Rick. 'Then you'll be able to get down it.'

'Why ever didn't we think of that before!' cried Joe, jumping up. 'Saucepan, where's that can with the spell in?'

He picked up the can – but, oh! It was completely empty. Every single drop had been spilt when Saucepan had fallen over.

'Well, never mind!' said Moon-Face, cheering up. 'We can go and buy some more from that goblin. Come on!'

They all set off, Rick, Beth and Frannie looking very small indeed next to the others. They went up to the goblin who had sold them the spell.

'Please can we have another can of that spell you sold us just now?' asked Moon-Face, holding out the empty can.

'I don't have a drop left,' said the goblin. 'And I can't make any more till the full moon comes. It can only be made in the moonlight.'

Everyone looked so miserable that the goblin felt sorry for them. 'Why do you look so unhappy?' he said. 'What has happened?'

Joe told him everything. The goblin listened with interest. Then he smiled. 'Well, my dear,' he said, 'if you can't get a spell to make the hole big, why don't you buy a spell to make yourselves small? My brother, the green goblin over there, sells that kind of spell. Only be careful not to put too much on yourselves, or you may go smaller than you mean to!'

They went over to the green goblin. He was yelling at the top of his voice.

'Buy my wonderful and most amazing spell! It will make anything as small as you like! Do you have an enemy? Dab him with this and see him shrink to the size of a mouse! Is your nose too big? Dab it with this, and make it the right size! Oh, wonderful, astonishing, amazing . . .'

Everyone hurried up. Moon-Face took some money out of his money bag. 'I'll have the spell, please,' he said. The green goblin gave him a can. The spell in it looked rather like paint, just as the other had done.

'Now go slow,' said the goblin. 'You don't want to get too small. Try a little at a time.'

Moon-Face dabbed a little on Silky. She went a bit smaller at once. He dabbed again. She went smaller still.

'Is she the right size yet?' asked Moon-Face.

255

Everyone stared at Silky.

'Not *quite*,' said Beth. 'But she is almost, Moon-Face. So be careful with your next dab.'

Moon-Face was very careful. At the next dab of the spell Silky went to exactly her right size. She was so pleased.

'Now you, Joe,' said Moon-Face. So he dabbed Joe and got Joe back to his right size again, too. Then he tried dabbing the Saucepan Man, and soon got him right. His kettles and saucepans went right, too. It was funny to watch them.

'Now I'll do you, Moon-Face,' said Joe.

'No, thanks, I'll do myself,' said Moon-Face. He dabbed the spell on to himself and shrank smaller. He dabbed again and went smaller still. Then he stopped dabbing and put the brush down.

'You're not quite your ordinary size yet,' said Joe.

'I know,' said Moon-Face. 'But I always thought I was a bit on the short side. Now I'm just about right. I always wanted to be a bit taller. I shan't dab myself any more.'

Everyone laughed. It was funny to see Moon-Face a bit taller than usual. As they stood there and laughed, a curious cold wind began to blow. Moon-Face looked all round and then began to shout.

'Quick, quick! The Land of Spells is on the move! Hurry before we get left behind!'

Everyone got a shock. Wow! It would never do to be left behind, just as everyone had got small enough to go down the hole in the clouds.

They set off to the hole. The wind blew more and more strongly, and suddenly the sun went out. It was as if somebody had blown it out, Joe thought. At once darkness fell on the Land of Spells.

'Hold hands, hold hands!' cried Joe. 'We'll lose one another if we don't!'

They all took hold of one another's hands and called out their names to make sure everyone was there. They stumbled on through the darkness.

'Here's the hole!' cried Joe, at last, and down he went. He felt the ladder and climbed down that, too. The others followed one by one, pushing close behind in the dark, longing to get down to the Faraway Tree they knew so well. How lovely it would be to sit in Moon-Face's room and feel safe!

But down at the bottom of the ladder there was no Faraway Tree. Instead, to Joe's surprise, there was a narrow passage, lit by a swinging green lantern.

'Oh my goodness,' he said to the others, 'What's this? Where's the Faraway Tree?'

'We've come down the wrong hole,' groaned Moon-Face. 'Oh, goodness, what bad luck!'

'Well, where are we?' asked Rick in wonder.

'I don't know,' said Moon-Face. 'We'd better follow this passage and see where it leads to. It's no use climbing back and trying to find the right hole. We'd never find it in the dark – and anyway, I'm pretty sure the Land of Spells has moved on by now.'

Everyone felt very miserable. Joe led the way down the passage. It twisted and turned, went up and down steps, and was lit here and there by the green lanterns swinging from the roof.

At last they came to a big yellow door. On it was a blue knocker, a blue bell, a blue mail-box and a blue notice that said:

Mister Change-About. Knock once, ring twice, and rattle the mail-box.

Joe knocked once, very loudly. Then he rang twice, and everyone heard the bell going 'R-r-r-r-r-r-ring! R-r-r-r-r-ring!' Then he rattled the mail-box.

The door didn't open. It completely disappeared. It was so peculiar. One minute it was there – and the next it had gone, and there was nothing in front of them. They could see right into a big underground room.

At the end of it, by a roaring fire, sat a round, fat person. 'That must be Mister Change-About!' whispered Rick. 'Dare we go in?'

VII. MR CHANGE-ABOUT AND THE ENCHANTER

Everyone stared at Mr Change-About. At least, as he was the only person in the room, they thought that was who it must be. He got up and came towards them.

He was a fat, comfortable-looking person with a broad smile on his face. 'Hmm, what a lot of visitors!' he said. 'Do sit down.'

There was nowhere to sit except on the stone floor, which looked rather cold. So nobody sat down.

Something happened to Mr Change-About when nobody obeyed him. He grew tall and thin. His broad smile disappeared and a frown came all over his face. He looked a very unpleasant person.

'SIT DOWN!' he roared. And everybody sat down in a hurry!

Mr Change-About looked at the Saucepan Man, who had sat down with a tremendous clatter.

'Have you got a nice little kettle that would boil enough water to make two mugs of hot chocolate?' he asked.

The Saucepan Man didn't hear. So Joe shouted in his ear, and he beamed, got up, and undid a little kettle that he had on him.

'Just the thing!' he said, handing it to Mr Change-About. 'Try it and see!'

Mr Change-About changed again, and became

happy-looking with dancing eyes and a sweet smile. He took the kettle.

'Thank you,' he said. 'So kind of you. Just what I wanted. How much is it?'

'Nothing at all,' said the Saucepan Man. 'A present for you!'

'Well, allow me to hand round some chocolate to you all in return for such a nice present,' said Mr Change-About, and he fetched an enormous box of chocolates from a cupboard. Everybody was pleased.

Rick looked carefully into the box when his turn came. His hand stretched out for the very biggest chocolate of all. Mr Change-About at once changed again and flew into a rage.

He became thin and mean-looking, his nose shot out long, and his eyes grew small.

'Bad boy, greedy boy!' he shouted. 'You shan't have any of my chocolates now! Horrible, greedy children!'

And at once all the chocolates changed into little hard stones. Beth had hers in her mouth, and she spat it out at once. The others looked disgusted. The Old Saucepan Man gave a yell.

'I've swallowed mine – and now I suppose I've got a stone inside me. Oh, you nasty Mr Change-About! I'll show you what I think of your chocolates!'

And to everyone's surprise Saucepan rushed at Mr Change-About, knocked his box of chocolates all over the room, and began to shake him hard.

Rattle, rattle, shake, shake! Gosh, how the Old Saucepan Man shook Mr Change-About. And Mr Change-About tried to shake Saucepan back – but what was the good of that? Saucepan was so covered in pots and pans that nobody could possibly shake him about without hurting themselves!

Clang, clatter, clang, clatter, clash! The kettles and saucepans made an enormous noise, and everyone began to laugh, because really Saucepan looked too funny for words, dancing about on the floor, pushing and shaking Mr Change-About.

Mr Change-About suddenly got very big and fierce-looking, but old Saucepan didn't seem to mind at all. He just went on shaking and pushing at him, and shouted: 'The bigger you are, the more there is to punish!'

So then Mr Change-About got very small, as small as a mouse, and ran squealing across the floor in fright. Quick as lightning, Saucepan picked him up, popped him into a kettle, and put the lid on!

'Oh, Saucepan! Whatever will you do next?' said Joe, wiping tears of laughter from his eyes. 'I've never seen such a funny sight in my life. Be careful Mr

Change-About doesn't squeeze out of the spout.'

'I'll stuff it with paper,' said Saucepan, tearing some from the box of chocolates. 'Now he's secure. Well – what do we do next?'

'We'd better get out of here,' said Joe, standing up. He turned towards the doorway – but what was this! There was no doorway – and no door! Only a wall of rock that ran all round the underground room now.

'Oh no! How *do* we get out?' said Joe, puzzled. 'This is a very magic kind of place.'

'There's no window, of course, because we are underground,' said Rick. 'What are we going to do?'

'What about the chimney?' asked Frannie, running to the fire. 'It looks pretty big. Perhaps we could put the fire out and climb up.'

'Well, that looks like our only chance of getting out of here,' said Joe. He looked round for some water to put out the fire. He saw a water pump by the wall and went to it. He put a bucket underneath and pumped the handle up and down. The water was bright green, and soon filled the bucket. Joe threw it on the fire. It made a terrific sizzling noise and went out at once, puffing clouds of green smoke into the room.

Joe stepped on to the dead fire and looked up the chimney. 'There's an iron ladder going right up!' he called in excitement. 'Come on! We'll get dirty, but we can't help that. Hurry, before any more mysterious things happen!'

He went up the ladder. It was hot from the heat of the fire, but grew colder the higher he went.

'What a long chimney!' called back Joe. 'Is everyone coming?'

'Yes! Yes!' called six voices below him. Joe climbed steadily upwards. At last the ladder came to an end. Joe clambered over the top of it and found himself in a creepy place.

'This looks like some kind of cellar,' he said to the others, as they scrambled up beside him. 'Look at all those sacks piled up! What do think is in them?'

'Let's look,' said Rick, who was always curious about everything. He undid a sack – and, good heavens! – out poured a stream of bright gold pieces! Everyone looked at it in amazement.

'Somebody VERY rich must live here,' said Joe at last. 'I've never seen so much gold. I can't believe that *all* the sacks are full of it!'

He undid another sack – and out poured gold again. Just as everyone was running their fingers through it, marvelling at the gleam and shine of so much gold, they heard quick footsteps overhead.

A door above them opened, and a gleam of sunlight shone on to a flight of stone steps leading up from the cellar to the door. A tall man in a pointed hat looked down.

'Gosh! It's an enchanter!' whispered Moon-Face in a fright. 'We must still be in the Land of Spells. Oh, dear!'

'Robbers! Thieves! Burglars!' shouted the enchanter in a loud voice. 'Guards, come here! Capture these robbers! They are after my gold! See – they have undone two sacks already!'

'We don't want your gold!' cried Rick. 'We only wanted to know what was in all these sacks!'

'I don't believe you!' cried the enchanter, as about a dozen small elves came running past him down the

263

steps to the cellar. 'Capture them, guards, and lock them up!'

The little elves pulled everyone up the cellar steps into a big, sunlit room. Its ceiling was so high that nobody could see it. 'Now lock them up,' commanded the enchanter.

Moon-Face suddenly snatched a kettle from Saucepan and snapped the string that tied it to him. He went towards the enchanter fearlessly.

'Wait!' he cried, much to the surprise of all the others. 'Wait before you do this foolish thing! *I* am an enchanter, too – and in this kettle I have Mr Change-About! Yes – he is a prisoner there! And let me tell you this, that if you dare to lock me up, I'll put *you* into this kettle, too, with Mr Change-About!'

From the kettle came a small, squealing voice: 'Set me free, Enchanter, set me free! Oh, do set me free!'

The enchanter turned quite pale. He knew it was Mr Change-About's voice.

'Er – er – this is most peculiar,' he said. 'How did you capture Mr Change-About? He is a very powerful person, and a great friend of mine.'

'Oh, I'm not going to tell you what magic I used,' said Moon-Face boldly. 'Now – are you going to let us go – or shall I put you into this kettle, too?'

'I'll let you go,' said the enchanter, and he waved them all towards a door at the end of the room. 'You may leave at once.'

Everyone rushed to the door gladly. They all ran through it, expecting to come out into the sunshine.

But they didn't! The enchanter had played a trick on them! They found themselves going up many hundreds of stairs, up and up and up – and when they came to the top there was nothing but a round room with one small window! A bench stood at one end and a table at the other.

The enchanter's voice floated up to them.

'Ho! Ho! I've got you nicely! Now I'm going to get my friend, Wizard Wily, and he'll soon tell me how to deal with robbers like you!'

'We *are* in a trap!' groaned Joe. 'Moon-Face, you were very clever and very brave. But honestly, we are worse off than ever. I simply don't see any way out of this at all!'

VIII. HOW CAN THEY ESCAPE?

Moon-Face looked all round the room at the top of the tower. 'Well, we're in a nice fix now,' he said gloomily. 'It's no use going down the stairs again – we shall find the door at the bottom locked. And what's the good of a window that is half a mile from the ground!'

Joe looked out of the window. 'Gosh!' he said, 'the tower is *so* tall! I can hardly see the bottom of it. Hello – there's the enchanter going off in his carriage. I suppose he is going to fetch his friend, dear Wizard Wily.'

'I don't like the sound of Wizard Wily,' said Silky. 'Joe – Rick – Moon-Face – please, please think of some way to escape!'

But there really WASN'T any way. No one wanted to jump out of the window.

They all sat down. 'I'm *very* hungry,' said Beth. 'Has anyone got anything to eat?'

'I may have some Pop Cakes,' said Moon-Face, feeling in his pockets. But he hadn't. 'Feel in *your* pockets, then.'

They all felt inside their pockets, hoping to find a bit of toffee or chocolate. Rick brought out a collection of string, bits of paper, a pencil and a few marbles. Joe took out much the same kind of things – but with his bits came a pink jar, very small and heavy.

'What's in that jar?' asked Beth, who hadn't seen it before. 'Isn't it pretty!'

'Let me see – what can it be?' wondered Joe, as he unscrewed the lid. 'Oh – I know. We saw a witch selling whizz-away ointment for broomsticks in the Land of Spells – and I thought it *would* be fun to rub some on mother's broomstick and see it fly through the air. So we bought some. Smell it – it's delicious.'

Everyone smelt it. Moon-Face suddenly got very excited. 'I say –' he began. 'I say – oh, I say!'

'Well, say then!' said Joe. 'What's the matter?'

'Oh, I SAY!' said Moon-Face, stammering all the more. 'Listen! If only we could get a broomstick – we could rub this pink ointment on it – and fly away on it!'

'Moon-Face, that's a very good idea – if only we had a broomstick – but we haven't!' said Joe. 'Look at this room – a table and a bench – no sign of a broomstick at all!'

'Well, I'll run down the stairs and see if I can possibly get a broomstick,' said Moon-Face, getting all excited. 'I saw some standing in a corner of that room we were in. I'll do my best, anyway!'

'Good old Moon-Face!' said everyone, as they watched the round-faced little man scurry down the hundreds of steps. 'If only he gets a broomstick!'

Moon-Face hurried down and down. It seemed such a very long way. At last he came to the bottom of the stairs. An enormous wooden door was at the bottom, shut tight. Moon-Face tried to open it, but he couldn't. So he banged on the door loudly.

A surprised voice called out: 'Hey, there! What are you banging on the door for? What do you want?'

'A broomstick!' said Moon-Face loudly.

'A *broomstick*!' said the voice, more astonished than ever. 'Whatever for?'

'To sweep up some crumbs!' said Moon-Face, quite untruthfully.

'A dust-pan and brush will do for that!' cried the voice, and the door opened a crack. A dust-pan and brush shot out with a clatter and came to rest by Moon-Face's feet. Then the door shut with a bang and was bolted at the other side.

'A dust-pan and brush!' said Moon-Face in disgust. 'Now, who can ride away on those?' He banged on the door again.

'*Now* what's the matter?' yelled the voice angrily.

'These won't do,' said Moon-Face. 'I want a BROOMSTICK!'

'Well, go on wanting,' said the voice. 'You won't get one. I suppose you think you'll fly away on one if I give it to you. I'm not quite so silly as that. What do you suppose the enchanter would say to me when he came back if I'd given you one of his broomsticks to escape on?'

Moon-Face groaned. He knew it was no good asking again. He picked up the dust-pan and brush and climbed the stairs slowly, suddenly feeling very tired.

Everyone was waiting for him. 'Did you get it, Moon-Face?' they cried. But when they saw Moon-Face's gloomy face and the dust-pan and brush in his hand, they were very disappointed.

They all sat down to think. Joe looked up. 'Would it be any good to rub the whizz-away ointment on to

268

anything else?' he asked. 'Would it make anything but broomsticks fly away?'

'I shouldn't think so,' said Moon-Face. 'But we could try. What is there to try on, though? We haven't a stick of any sort.'

'No – but there's a table over there, and this bench,' said Joe, getting excited. 'Couldn't we try it on those? We could easily sit on them and fly off, if only the magic would work.'

'But it won't,' said Silky. 'I'm sure of that. It's only for broomsticks. But try it, Joe.'

Joe took off the lid of the jar again. He dabbed a finger into the pink ointment and rubbed some all over the top of the wooden bench, which was very like the ones at school. 'Now for the table,' said Joe. He turned it upside down, thinking that it would be more comfortable to sit on that way. They could hold the legs as they went!

He rubbed the ointment all over the underside of the table. As he was doing this everyone heard the sound of horses' hooves clip-clopping outside. Silky ran to the window.

'It's the enchanter come back again – and he's got the Wizard Wily with him!' she cried. 'Oh, Joe, be quick! They'll be up here in a minute.'

'Moon-Face, Silky and Saucepan, you sit on the bench,' said Joe. 'You girls and Rick and I will sit on the table. Hurry up!'

Everyone scrambled to take their seats. Silky was trembling with excitement. She could hear the footsteps of the enchanter and the wizard coming up the steps.

'Now, hold tight, in case we really do go off!' said

Joe. 'Ready, everyone? Then WHIZZ-AWAY HOME!'

And, wow, the bench and the table began to move! Yes, they really did! They moved slowly at first, because they were not used to whizzing away – but as the children squealed and squeaked in surprise and delight, the table rose up suddenly to the window and tried to get out!

It stuck. It couldn't get through. 'Oh, table, do your best!' cried Joe. 'The enchanter is nearly here!'

The table tipped itself up a little – and then it could just manage to squeeze through the opening. The children each clung tightly to a leg, afraid of being tipped off. Then at last the table was through the window, and, sailing away upside down, its four legs in the air, carrying the excited children safely, it whizzed off over the Land of Spells!

Joe looked back to see if the wooden bench was coming, too. It had had to wait until the table was through the window. Just as it was about to jerk upwards to the window, the enchanter and the Wizard Wily had come rushing into the room. What would have happened if the old Saucepan Man hadn't suddenly thrown a kettle at them, goodness knows!

It was the kettle with Mr Change-About in! The lid came off. Mr Change-About jumped out and turned himself almost into a giant! The enchanter fell over him, and Mr Change-About, not seeing who it was, began to shake his fists, crying: 'I'll teach you to put me into a kettle!'

Wily grabbed Mr Change-About, not knowing who he was, or where he had suddenly sprung from. And there was a marvellous quarrel going on, just as the wooden bench flew out of the window. The enchanter saw it going and tried to get hold of it – but just at that moment Mr Change-About put out his foot and tripped him over!

'Go for it, Change-About!' yelled Moon-Face. 'Hold him back!'

And out of the window sailed the bench, with Moon-Face, Silky and Saucepan clinging tightly to it. Far away in the distance was the upside down table.

The table whizzed steadily onwards, over hills and woods, and once over the sea. 'We've come a very long way from home since we've been in the Land of Spells,' said Joe. 'I hope the table knows its way to our home. I don't want to land in any more strange lands for now!'

The table knew its way all right. Joe gave a shout as it flew over a big dark wood. 'The Enchanted Wood!' he cried. 'We're nearly home!'

The table flew down to the garden of the children's home. Their mother was there, hanging out some clothes. She looked round in wonder when she saw them arrive on the flying table.

'Well, really!' she said. 'Whatever next! Do you usually fly around the country on an upside down table?'

'Oh, Mother! We've had such an adventure!' said Joe, scrambling off. He looked up in the air to see if the bench was following – but there was no sign of it.

'Where's the bench?' said Rick. 'Oh, I suppose it will go to the Faraway Tree, as that is where the

others live. Gosh – I feel all trembly. Joe – I am NOT going into any more lands at the top of the Faraway Tree again. It's just a bit too exciting!'

'Right,' said Joe. 'I feel the same. No more adventures for *me*!'

IX. THE LAND OF DREAMS

The children had had enough of adventures for some
time. Their mother set them to work in the garden,
and they did their best for her. Nobody suggested
going to the Enchanted Wood at all.

'I hope old Moon-Face, Silky and the Saucepan
Man got back to the Tree safely,' said Joe one day.

Moon-Face was wondering the same thing about
the children. He and Silky talked about it.

'We haven't seen the children for ages,' he said.
'Let's slip down the Tree, Silky, and make sure they
got back all right, shall we? After all, it would be
dreadful if they hadn't got back, and their mother was
worrying about them.'

So one afternoon, just after lunch, Silky and Moon-
Face walked up to the door of the cottage. Beth
opened it and shrieked with delight.

'Moon-Face! So you got back safely after all! Come
in! Come in, Silky dear. Saucepan, you'll have to take
off a kettle or two if you want to get through the door.'

The children's parents were out for a while. The
children and their friends sat and talked about their
last adventure.

'What land is at the top of the Tree now?' asked
Rick curiously.

'Don't know,' said Moon-Face. 'Like to come and
see?'

'No, thanks,' said Joe at once. 'We're not going up there any more.'

'Well, come back and have tea with us,' said Moon-Face. 'Silky's got some Pop Cakes – and I've made some Google Buns. I don't often make them – and I tell you they're a treat!'

'Google Buns!' said Beth in astonishment. 'Whatever are they?'

'You come and see,' said Moon-Face, grinning. 'They're better than Pop Cakes – aren't they, Silky?'

'Much,' said Silky.

'Well – Frannie and I have finished our jobs,' said Beth. 'What about you boys?'

'We've got about half and hour's more work to do, that's all,' said Joe. 'If everyone helps, it will only take ten minutes. We could leave a note for Mother and Father. I would love to try those Google Buns!'

Everyone went into the garden to dig up the carrots and put them into piles. It didn't take more than ten minutes because they all worked so hard. They put away their tools, washed their hands, left a note for their parents, and then set off for the Enchanted Wood.

The Saucepan Man sang one of his ridiculous songs on the way:

> *Two tails for a kitten,*
> *Two clouds for the sky,*
> *Two pigeons for Christmas*
> *To make a plum pie!*

Everyone laughed. Joe, Beth and Frannie had heard

the Saucepan Man's silly songs before, but Rick hadn't.

'Go on,' said Rick. 'This is the silliest song I've ever heard.'

The Saucepan Man clashed two kettles together as he sang:

> *Two roses for Beth,*
> *Two scoldings for Joe,*
> *Two ribbons for Frannie,*
> *With a ho-diddle-ho!*

'It's an easy song to make up as you go along,' said Beth, giggling. 'Every line but the last has to begin with the word "Two". Just think of any nonsense you like, and the song simply makes itself.'

Singing silly songs, they all reached the Faraway Tree. Saucepan yelled up it:

'Hey, Watzisname! Let down a rope, there's a good fellow! It's too hot to walk up today.'

The rope came down. They all went up one by one, pulled high by the strong arms of Mister Watzisname.

Frannie was unlucky. She got splashed by Dame Washalot's water on the way up. 'Next time I go up on the rope I shall take an umbrella with me,' she said angrily.

'Come on,' said Moon-Face. 'Come and eat a Google Bun and see what you think of it.'

Soon they were all sitting on the broad branches outside Moon-Face's house, eating Pop Cakes and Google Buns. The buns were very strange. They each had a very large raisin in the middle, and this was filled with sherbet. So when you got to the raisin and bit it the sherbet frothed out and filled your mouth with fine bubbles that tasted delicious. The children got a real surprise when they bit their raisins, and Moon-Face almost fell off the branch with laughing.

'Come and see some new cushions I've got,' he said to the children when they had eaten as many cakes and buns as they could manage. Joe, Beth and Frannie went into Moon-Face's funny round house.

Moon-Face looked round for Rick. But he wasn't there. 'Where's Rick?' he said.

'He's gone up the ladder to peep and see what land is at the top,' said Silky. 'I told him not to. But he's quite a naughty boy, I think.'

'Gosh, no!' said Joe, running out of the house. 'Rick, come back, you silly!'

Everyone began to shout, 'Rick, RICK!'

But no answer came down the ladder. The big white cloud swirled above silently, and nobody could imagine why Rick didn't come back.

'I'll go and see what he's doing,' said Moon-Face. So up he went. And he didn't come back either! Then the Old Saucepan Man went cautiously up, step by step. He disappeared through the hole – and *he* didn't come back!

'Whatever has happened to them?' said Joe in despair. 'Look here, girls – get a rope out of Moon-Face's house and tie yourselves and Silky to me. Then I'll go up the ladder – and if anyone tries to pull me into the land above, they won't be able to, because you three can pull me back. OK?'

'Right,' said Beth, and she knotted the rope round

her waist and Frannie's, and then round Silky's too. Joe tied the other end to himself. Then up the ladder he went.

And before the girls knew what had happened, Joe was lifted into the land above – and they were all dragged up, too, their feet scrambling somehow up the ladder and through the hole in the cloud!

There they all stood in a field of red poppies, with a tall man nearby, holding a sack over his shoulder!

'Is that the lot?' he asked. 'Good! Well, here's something to make you sleep!'

He put his hand in his sack and scattered a handful of the finest sand over the surprised group. In a moment they were rubbing their eyes and yawning.

'This is the Land of Dreams,' said Moon-Face sleepily. 'And that's the Sandman. Goodness, how sleepy I am!'

'Don't go to sleep! Don't go to sleep!' cried Silky, taking Moon-Face's arm and shaking him. 'If we do, we'll wake up and find that this land has moved away from the Faraway Tree. Come back down the hole, Moon-Face, and don't be silly.'

'I'm so – sleepy,' said Moon-Face, and lay down among the red poppies. In no time he was snoring loudly, fast asleep.

'Get him to the hole!' cried Silky. But Joe, Rick and the Saucepan Man were all yawning and rubbing their eyes, too sleepy to do a thing. Then Beth and Frannie slid down quietly into the poppies and fell asleep, too. At last only Silky was left. Not much of the sleepy sand had gone into her eyes, so she was wider awake than the rest.

She stared at everyone in dismay. 'Oh dear,' she said, 'I'll never get you down the hole by myself. I'll have to get help. I must go and fetch Watzisname and the Angry Pixie and Dame Washalot, too!'

She ran off to the hole, slipped down the ladder through the cloud and slid on to the broad branch below. 'Watzisname!' she called. 'Dame Washalot! Angry Pixie!'

After a minute or two Joe woke up. He rubbed his eyes and sat up. Not far off he saw something that pleased him. It was an ice-cream seller. The man was ringing his bell loudly.

'Hey, Moon-Face! Wake up!' cried Joe. 'There's an ice-cream man. Have you got any money?'

Everyone woke up. Moon-Face felt in his money bag and then stared in great surprise. It was full of marbles.

'Now who put marbles there?' he wondered.

The ice-cream man drove up. 'Marbles will do to pay for my ice-cream,' he said. So Moon-Face paid him six marbles.

The man gave them each a bag and drove off, ringing his bell. Moon-Face opened his bag, expecting to find a delicious ice-cream there – but inside there was a big whistle! It was really odd.

Everyone else had a whistle too. 'How extraordinary!' said Rick. 'This is the kind of thing that happens in dreams!'

'Well – after all – this *is* Dreamland!' said Beth. 'I wonder if these whistles blow!'

She blew hers. It was very loud indeed. The others blew theirs, too. And at once six policemen appeared near by, running for all they were worth. They rushed up to the children.

'What's the matter?' they cried. 'You are blowing police whistles! What has happened? Do you want help?'

'No,' said Rick with a giggle.

'Then you must come to the swimming pool,' said the policeman, and to everyone's surprise they were all led away.

'Why the *swimming* pool?' said Frannie. 'Listen, policeman – we haven't got swim-suits.'

'Oh, you naughty story-teller!' said the policeman nearest to her.

And to Beth's surprise she found that she had on a blue and white swim-suit – and all the others had swim-suits too.

They came to the swimming pool – but there was no water in it at all. 'Get in and swim,' said the policeman.

'There's no water,' said Rick. 'Don't be silly.'

And then, very suddenly, all the policemen began to cry – and in no time the swimming pool was full of their tears!

'This sort of thing makes me feel funny,' said Joe. 'I don't want to swim in tears. Quick, everyone – push the policemen into the pool!'

And in half a second all the policemen were kicking feebly in the pool of tears. As the children watched they changed into blue fishes and swam away, flicking their tails.

'I feel as if I'm in a dream,' said Rick.

'So do I,' said Joe. 'I wish I could get out of it. Oh,

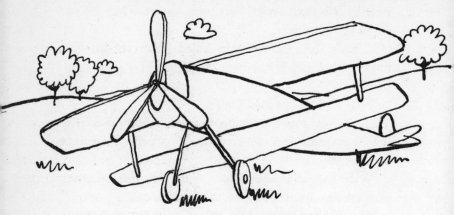

look – there's a 'plane coming down. Perhaps we could get into it and fly away!'

The 'plane, which was small and green, landed near by. There was nobody in it at all. The children ran to it and got in. Joe pushed down the handle marked UP.

'Off we go!' he said. And off they went!

X. A FEW MORE ADVENTURES

Everyone was very pleased to be in the 'plane, because they thought they could fly away from the Land of Dreams. After a second or two Beth leaned over the side of the 'plane to see how high they were from the ground. She gave a loud cry.

'What's the matter?' asked Joe.

'Joe! This isn't a 'plane after all!' said Beth in astonishment. 'It's a bus. It hasn't got wings any more. Only wheels. And we're sitting on seats at the top of the bus. Well! I *did* think it was a 'plane!'

'Gosh! Aren't we flying then?' said Joe.

'No – just running down a road,' said Frannie.

Everyone was silent. They were so disappointed. Then a curious noise was heard. Splishy-splash! Splash! Splash!

The children looked over the side of the bus – and they all gave a shout of amazement.

'Joe! Look! The bus is running on water! But it isn't a bus any more. Oh, look – it's got a sail!'

Everyone looked upwards – and there, billowing in the wind, was a great white sail. And Joe was now steering with a tiller instead of with a handle or a wheel. It was very confusing.

'This is definitely the Land of Dreams, no doubt about that,' groaned Joe, wondering whatever the ship would turn into next. 'The awful part is – we're awake

– and yet we have to have these dream-like things happening!'

An enormous wave splashed over everyone. Frannie gave a scream. The ship rocked backwards and forwards, to and fro, and everyone clung tightly to one another.

'Let's land somewhere, for goodness' sake!' cried Rick. 'Heaven knows what this ship will turn into next – a rocking-horse, I should think, by the way it's rocking itself backwards and forwards.'

And, guess what? No sooner had Rick said that than it did turn into a rocking-horse. Joe found himself holding on to its mane, and all the others clung together behind him. The water disappeared. The rocking-horse seemed to be rocking down a long road.

'Let's get off,' shouted Joe. 'I don't like the way this thing keeps changing. Slip off, Moon-Face, and help the others down.'

It wasn't long before they were all standing in the road, feeling rather confused. The rocking-horse went on rocking by itself down the road. As the children watched it, it changed into a large brown bear that scampered on its big paws.

'Ha!' said Joe. 'We got off just in time! Well – what are we going to do now?'

A man came down the road carrying a green-covered tray on his head. He rang a bell. 'Muffins! Fine muffins! He shouted. 'Muffins for sale!'

'Oooh! I really feel as if I could eat a muffin,' said Beth. 'Hey, muffin-man! We'll have six muffins please.'

The muffin-man stopped. He took down his tray

from his head and uncovered it. Underneath were not muffins, but small kittens!

The muffin-man seemed to think they were muffins. He handed one to each of the surprised children, and one to Moon-Face and Saucepan. Then he covered up his tray again and went down the road ringing his bell.

'Well, does he think we can eat kittens?' said Beth. 'Oh, but aren't they dear little things? What are we going to do with them?'

'They seem to be growing,' said Joe in surprise. And so they were. In a minute or two the kittens were too heavy to carry – they were big cats! They still went on growing, and soon they were as big as tigers. They played around the children, who were really rather afraid of them.

'Now listen,' said Joe to the enormous kittens. 'You belong to the muffin-man. You go after him and get on to his tray where you belong. Listen – you can still hear his bell! Go along now!'

To everyone's surprise and delight the great animals ran off down the road after the muffin-man.

'He *will* get a surprise,' said Rick with a giggle. 'Hey – don't let's buy anything from anyone else. It's a bit too risky.'

'What we really should do is try and find the hole that leads from this land to the Faraway Tree,' said Joe seriously. 'Surely you don't want to stay in this peculiar land for ever! Gosh, we never know what is happening from one minute to the next!'

'I feel very sleepy again,' said Moon-Face, yawning. 'I do wish I could go to bed.'

Just as he said that, there came a clippitty-cloppitty noise behind them. They all turned – and to their amazement saw a big white bed following them, trotting along on four fat legs.

'Gosh!' said Rick, stopping in surprise. 'Look at that bed! Where did it come from?'

The bed stopped just by them. Moon-Face yawned.

'I'd like to cuddle down in you and go to sleep,' he said to the bed. The bed creaked as if it was pleased.

Moon-Face climbed on to it. It was soft and cosy. Moon-Face put his head on the pillow and shut his eyes. He began to snore very gently.

This made everyone else feel tired and sleepy too. One by one they climbed into the big bed and lay down. The bed creaked in a very happy way. Then it went on its way again, clippitty-clopping on its four fat legs, taking the six sleepers with it.

Now what had happened to Silky? Well, she had found Dame Washalot, Mister Watzisname and the Angry Pixie, and had told them how the others had fallen asleep in the Land of Dreams.

'Oh, good heavens! They'll never get away from there!' said Watzisname anxiously. 'We must rescue them. Come along.'

Dame Washalot put a wash-tub of water on her head. The Angry Pixie picked up a kettle of water. Watzisname didn't take anything. They all went up to the ladder at the top of the tree.

'The Land of Dreams is still here,' said Silky when her head peeped over the top. 'I can't see that horrid Sandman anywhere. Now's a good chance to slip up and rescue the others. Come on!'

Up they all went. They stared round the field of poppies, but they couldn't see any of the others.

'We must hunt for them,' said Silky. 'Oh, look at that great brown bear rushing along! I wonder if he knows anything about the others.' She called out to him, but he didn't stop. He made a noise like a chicken and rushed on.

The four of them wandered on and on – and suddenly they saw something very puzzling coming towards them – something wide and white.

'What ever can it be?' said Silky in wonder. 'Goodness me – it's a BED!'

And so it was – the very bed in which the four children and Moon-Face and Saucepan were asleep!

'Oh, look!' squealed Silky. 'They're all here! Wake up, sillies! Wake up!'

But they wouldn't wake up. They just sighed a little and turned over. Nothing that Silky and the others could do would wake them up. And, in the middle of all this, there came footsteps behind them.

Silky turned round and gasped. 'Oh, it's the Sandman! Don't let him throw his sand into your eyes or you will go to sleep, too! Quick, do something!'

The Sandman was already dipping his hand into his big sack to throw sand into their eyes. But, quick as lightning, Dame Washalot picked up her wash-tub and threw all the water over the sack! It wetted the sand so that the Sandman couldn't throw it properly. Then the Angry Pixie emptied his kettle over the Sandman himself, and he began to choke and splutter.

Watzisname stared. He suddenly took out his small pocket scissors and cut a hole at the bottom of the sack. The sand was dry there. Watzisname took a handful of it and threw it at the spluttering Sandman's eyes.

'Now *you* go to sleep for a bit!' shouted Watzisname. And, of course, that's just what the big Sandman did! He sank down under a bush and shut his eyes. His sleepy sand acted on him as much as on anyone else!

'Now we've got a chance!' said Silky, pleased. 'Help me to wake everyone up!'

But, you know, they just would *not* wake up! It was impossible!

'Well, we can't possibly get the bed down the hole,' said Silky in despair. Then a bright idea came to her. She felt in Joe's pockets. She turned out the little pink jar of Whizz-Away ointment. 'There might be *just* a little left!' she said.

And there was – the very tiniest dab! 'I hope it's

enough!' said Silky. 'Get on the bed, Dame Washalot and you others. I'm going to try a little magic. Ready?'

She rubbed the dab of ointment on to the head of the bed. 'Whizz-Away Home, bed!' she said.

And, wow, that big white bed whizzed away. It whizzed away so fast that Silky nearly fell off. It rushed through the air, giving all the birds a dreadful scare.

After a long time it came to the end of the Land of Dreams. A big white cloud stretched out at the edge. The bed flew through it, down and down. Then it flew in another direction.

'It's going back to the Faraway Tree, I'm sure,' said Silky. And so it was! It arrived there and tried to get through the branches. It stuck on one and slid sideways. Everyone began to slide off.

'Wake up, wake up!' squealed Silky, shaking the children and Moon-Face and Saucepan. They woke up in a hurry, as they were no longer in Dreamland. They felt themselves falling and caught hold of branches and twigs.

'Where are we?' cried Rick. 'What has happened?'

'Oh, goodness, too many things to tell you all at once,' said Silky. 'Is everyone safe? Then for goodness' sake come into my house and sit down for a bit. I really feel quite out of breath!'

XI. UP THE TREE AGAIN

Everyone crowded into Silky's room inside the Tree. 'How did we get back to the tree?' asked Rick in amazement.

Silky told him. 'We found you all asleep on that big bed, and we rubbed some of the Whizz-Away ointment on it, the very last bit left. And it whizzed away here. Oh, and we wetted the Sandman's sand so that he couldn't throw sand into our eyes and make us go to sleep.'

'Watzisname was clever, too. He cut the bottom of the sack with his scissors, found a handful of dry sand there and threw it at the Sandman himself!' said the Angry Pixie. 'And he went right off to sleep and couldn't use his powers on us any more!'

'It was all Rick's fault,' said Joe. 'We said we wouldn't go to any more lands – and he went up there and got caught by the Sandman. So of course we had to go after him.'

'Sorry,' said Rick. 'Anyway, everything's all right now. I won't do it again.'

'We'd better go home,' said Beth. 'It must be getting late. Goodness knows when we'll come again, Silky. Goodbye everyone. Come and see us if we don't come to see you.'

They all slid down the slippery-slip at top speed. Then they walked home, talking about their latest adventure.

'It was so strange being awake and having dreams,' said Frannie. 'Do you remember the muffins that turned into kittens?'

'I wish a really *nice* land would come to the top of the tree,' said Joe. 'Like the Land of Take-What-You-Want. That was fun. I wonder if it will ever come again.'

For about a week the children did not even go into the Enchanted Wood. For one thing they were very busy helping their parents, and for another thing they felt that they didn't want any more adventures for a little while.

And then a note came from Silky and Moon-Face. This is what it said:

> *Dear Beth, Frannie, Joe and Rick,*
> *We know that you don't want any more adventures just yet, but you might like to know that there is a very exciting land at the top of the Faraway Tree just now. It is the Land of Do-As-You-Please, even nicer than the Land of Take-What-You-Want. We are going there tonight. If you want to come, come just before midnight and you can go with us. We will wait for you till then.*
> *Love from,*
> *Silky and Moon-face.*

The children read the note one after another. Their eyes began to shine.

'Shall we go?' said Frannie.

'Better not,' said Joe. 'Something silly is sure to happen to us. It always does.'

'Oh, Joe! Do let's go!' said Beth. 'You know how exciting the Enchanted Wood is at night, too, with all the fairy folk about – and the Faraway Tree lit with lanterns and things. Come on, Joe – say we'll go.'

'I really think we'd better not,' said Joe. 'Rick might do something silly again.'

'I would *not*!' said Rick in a temper. 'It's not fair of you to say that.'

'Don't quarrel,' said Beth. 'Well, listen – if you don't want to go, Joe, Frannie and I will go with Rick. He can look after us.'

'Pooh! Rick wants looking after himself,' said Joe.

Rick pulled a face at Joe, and Joe pulled a face back.

'Oh, don't!' said Beth. 'You're not in the Land of Do-As-You-Please now!'

That made everyone laugh. 'Sorry, Joe,' said Rick. 'Be a sport. Let's all go tonight. Or at any rate, let's go up the tree and hear what Silky and Moon-Face can tell us about this new land. If it sounds at all dangerous we won't go. OK?'

'All right,' said Joe, who really did want to go just as badly as the others, but felt that he shouldn't keep leading them into danger. 'All right. We'll go up and talk to Silky and Moon-Face. But remember – if I decide not to go with them, there's to be no grumbling.'

'We promise, Joe,' said Beth. And so it was settled. They would go to the Enchanted Wood that night and climb the Faraway Tree to see their friends.

It was exciting to slip out of bed at half-past eleven

and dress. It was very dark because there was no moon.

'We shall have to take a pocket light,' said Joe. 'Are you all ready? Now don't make a noise, or you'll wake Mother and Father.'

They all crept downstairs and out into the dark, silent garden. An owl hooted nearby, and something ran down the garden path. Beth nearly squealed.

'Sh! It's only a mouse or something,' said Joe. 'I'll switch on my light now. Keep close together and we'll see where we're going.'

In a bunch they went down the back garden and out into the little lane there. The Enchanted Wood loomed up big and dark. The trees spoke to one another softly. 'Wisha, wisha, wisha,' they said. 'Wisha, wisha, wisha!'

The children jumped over the ditch and walked through the wood, down the paths they knew so well. The wood was full of fairy folk going about their business. They took no notice of the children. Joe soon switched off his light. Lanterns shone everywhere and gave enough light to see by.

They soon came to the great dark trunk of the Faraway Tree. A rope swung down through the branches.

'Oh, good!' said Rick. 'Is Moon-Face going to pull us up?'

'No,' said Joe. 'We'll have to climb up – but we can use the rope to help us. It's always in the tree at night to help the many folk going up and down.'

And indeed there were a great

many people using the Faraway Tree that night. Strange pixies, goblins and gnomes swarmed up and down it, and elves climbed up, chattering hard.

'Where are they going?' asked Rick in surprise.

'Oh, up to the Land of Do-As-You-Please, I expect,' said Joe. 'And some of them are visiting their friends in the tree. Look – there's the Angry Pixie! He's got a party on tonight!'

The Angry Pixie had about eight little friends squashed into his tree-room, and looked as pleased as could be. 'Come and join us!' he called to Joe.

'We can't,' said Joe. 'Thanks all the same. We're going up to Moon-Face's.'

Everyone dodged Dame Washalot's washing water, laughed at old Watzisname sitting snoring as usual in his chair, and at last came to Moon-Face's house.

And there was nobody there! There was a note stuck on the door.

> *We waited till midnight and you didn't come. If you do come and we're not here, you'll find us in the Land of Do-As-You-Please.*
> *Love from,*
> *Silky and Moon-face.*
> *P.S. DO come. Just think of the things you want to do – you can do them all in the Land of Do-As-You-Please!*

'Gosh!' said Rick, longingly, 'what I'd like to do better than anything else is to ride six times on a roundabout without stopping!'

'And *I'd* like to eat six ice-creams without stopping!'

said Beth.

'And *I'd* like to ride an elephant,' said Frannie.

'And *I* would like to drive a train all by myself,' said Joe.

'Joe! *Let's* go up the ladder!' begged Frannie.

'Oh, please, please let's go! Why can't we go and visit a really nice land when one comes? It's so mean of you to say we can't.'

'Well,' said Joe. 'Well – I suppose we'd better! Come on!'

With shrieks of delight the girls and Rick raced up the ladder, through the cloud. A lantern hung at the top of the hole to give them light – but, lo and behold! as soon as they had got into the land above the cloud it was daytime! How magical!

The children stood and gazed round it. It seemed a very exciting land, rather like a huge amusement park. There were roundabouts going round and round in time to music. There were swings and see-saws. There was a train puffing along busily, and there were small 'planes flying everywhere, with elves, pixies and goblins having a fine time in them.

'Goodness! Doesn't it look exciting?' said Beth. 'I wonder where Moon-Face and Silky are.'

'There they are – over there – on that roundabout!' cried Joe. 'Look – Silky is riding a tiger that is going up and down all the time – and Moon-Face is on a giraffe! Let's get on, too!'

Off they all ran. As soon as Moon-Face and Silky saw the children, they screamed with joy and waved their hands. The roundabout stopped and the children got on. Beth chose a white rabbit. Frannie rode on a lion and felt very grand. Joe went on a bear and Rick chose a horse.

'So glad you came!' cried Silky. 'We waited and waited for you. Oh – we're off! Hold tight!'

The roundabout went round and round and round. The children shouted excitedly, because it went so fast. 'Let's have six rides without getting off!' cried Joe. So they did – and whoops, they *were* giddy when they did at last get off. They rolled about like drunken sailors!

'I feel like sitting down with six ice-creams,' said Beth. At once an ice-cream man drove up and handed them out thirty-six ice-creams. It did look a lot. When Joe had divided them all out equally there were six each. And how delicious they were! Everybody managed six quite easily.

'And now, what about me driving that train!' cried Joe, jumping up. 'I've always wanted to do that. Would you all like to be my passengers? Well, come on, then!'

And off they all raced to where the train was stopping at a little station. 'Hi there!' yelled Joe to the driver. 'I want to drive your train!'

'Come along up, then,' said the driver, jumping down. 'It's ready to go!'

XII. THE LAND OF
DO-AS-YOU-PLEASE

Joe jumped up into the engine of the train. A bright
fire was burning there, as it was a steam train. He
looked at all the shining handles and wheels.

'How shall I know which is which?' he asked the
driver.

'Well,' said the driver, pointing to the different
knobs and handles. 'That's the starting wheel – and
that's to make the whistle go – and that's to go
slow – and that's to go fast. You can't make a mistake.
Don't forget to stop at the stations, will you? And
oh – look out for the road crossing gates, in case they
are shut. It would be dangerous not to take care
there.'

Joe felt tremendously excited. Rick looked up
longingly. 'Joe! Could I come too?' he begged. 'Please
let me. Just to watch you.'

'All right,' said Joe. So Rick hopped up on to the
engine. Beth, Frannie, Moon-Face and Silky got into
a carriage just behind. The guard ran alongside
waving a flag and blowing his whistle.

'The signal's down!' yelled Rick. 'Go on, Joe! Start
her up!'

Joe twisted the starting wheel. The engine began to
chuff-chuff-chuff and moved out of the station.

'Joe's really driving the train!' cried Beth. 'Oh, isn't
he clever! He's always wanted to drive an engine!'

The engine began to go very fast – too fast. Joe pulled the 'Go Slow' handle, and it went more slowly. He was so interested in what he was doing that he didn't notice they were coming to a station. He shot right through it!

'Joe!' cried Rick, 'you've gone through a station. Gosh, the passengers waiting there did look cross – and oh, look, a lot of them in our train wanted to get out there!'

Sure enough quite a number of angry people were looking out of the carriage windows, yelling to Joe to stop.

Joe went red. He pulled the 'Stop' handle. The engine stopped. Then Joe pulled the 'Go Backwards' handle and the train moved slowly backwards to the station. It stopped there and Joe and Rick had the pleasure of seeing the passengers get out and in. The guard came rushing up.

'You passed the station, you passed the station!' he cried. 'Don't you dare to pass my station again without stopping!'

'All right, all right,' said Joe. 'Now then – off we go again!' And off they went.

'Keep a look-out for stations, signals, tunnels and road crossings, Rick,' said Joe. So Rick stuck his head out and watched.

'Road crossing!' he cried. 'The gates are shut! Slow down, Joe, slow down!'

But unluckily Joe pulled the 'Go Fast' handle instead of the 'Go Slow' and the train shot forward quickly. Just as the engine reached the gates, Joe pulled on the brakes. A little man rushed out of the cabin near by, just as the train came to a halt.

'You bad driver!' he shouted. 'You might have caused an accident!'

'That was a narrow escape,' said Joe. When the road crossing gates were open, Joe started off again.

'What's coming now, Rick?' Joe asked.

'A tunnel,' said Rick. 'Whistle as you go through in case anyone is working in it.'

So Joe made the engine whistle loudly. It really was fun. It raced through the dark tunnel and came out near a station.

'Stop! Station, Joe!' cried Rick. And Joe stopped. Then on went the train again, whistling loudly, rushing past signals that were down.

Then something happened. The 'Go Slow' and the 'Stop' handles wouldn't work! The train raced on and on past stations, big and small, through tunnels, past signals that were up, and behaved just as if it had gone mad.

'Hey!' said Rick in alarm, 'what's gone wrong, Joe?'

Joe didn't know. For miles and miles the train tore on, and all the passengers became alarmed. And then, as the train drew near a station, it gave a loud sigh, ran slowly and then stopped all by itself.

And it was the very same station it had started from! The driver of the train was there, waiting.

'So you're back again,' he said. 'My, you've been quick.'

'Well, the engine didn't behave itself very well,' said Joe, stepping down thankfully. 'It just ran away the last part of the journey. It wouldn't stop anywhere!'

'Oh, I dare say it wanted to get back to me,' said the driver, climbing into the engine. 'It's naughty sometimes. Come along and drive it again with me.'

'No, thank you,' said Joe. 'I think I've had enough. It was fun, though.'

Beth, Frannie, Moon-Face and Silky, got out of their carriages. They had been rather frightened the last part of the journey, but they thought Joe was very clever to drive the train by himself.

They all left the station. 'Now what shall we do?' said Moon-Face.

'I want to ride on an elephant,' said Frannie at once.

'There aren't any,' said Beth. But no sooner had she spoken than the children saw six big grey elephants walking solemnly up to them, swaying a little from side to side.

'Oh, look, look!' yelled Frannie, filled with excitement. 'There are my elephants. Six of them! We can all have a ride!'

Each elephant had a rope ladder going up its left side, leading to a little seat which was fixed around the elephant's back. The children, Moon-Face and Silky each climbed up the rope ladder and sat on a comfortable seat on an elephant's back. Then the big creatures set off, swaying through the crowds.

It was lovely. Frannie did enjoy herself. She called to the others. 'Wasn't this a good idea of mine, everybody? Aren't we high up? And isn't it fun?'

'It *is* fun,' said Moon-Face, who had never even seen an elephant before, and would certainly never have thought of riding one if he had. 'Oh, goodness – my rope ladder has slipped off my elephant! Now I shall never be able to get down! I'll have to ride on this elephant all my life!'

Everybody laughed – but Moon-Face was really alarmed. When the children had had enough of riding they all climbed down their rope ladders – but poor Moon-Face sat up on his elephant, looking very worried.

'I tell you I can't get down,' he kept saying. 'I'm up here for good!'

The elephant stood patiently for a little while. Then it swung its enormous trunk round, wound it gently round Moon-Face's waist, and lifted him down to the ground. Moon-Face was so surprised that he couldn't speak.

At last he found his tongue. 'What did the elephant lift me down with?' he asked. 'His nose!'

'No, his trunk,' said Joe, laughing. 'Didn't you know that elephants had trunks, Moon-Face?'

'No,' said Moon-Face, puzzled. 'I'm glad he didn't pack me away as baggage!'

The children laughed. They watched the big elephants walking off.

'What shall we do now?' said Joe. 'Rick, what do you want to do?'

'Well, I know I can't do it – but I would love to wade in the sea!' said Rick.

'Oooh, that *would* be nice!' said Frannie, who loved wading too. 'But there isn't any sea here.'

Just as she said that she noticed a sign-post near by. It pointed away from them and said, in big letters, 'TO THE SEA'.

'Wow, look at that!' said Frannie. 'Come on everyone!'

Off they all went, running the way the sign-post pointed. And, after going round two corners, there, sure enough, was the blue sea, lying bright and calm in the warm sunshine! Shining golden sands stretched to the little waves.

'Oh, good!' cried Rick, taking off his shoes and socks at once. 'Come on!'

Soon everyone was wading in the warm sea. Moon-

Face and Silky had never waded before, but they loved it just as much as the children did. Rick went out so far that he got his clothes soaking wet.

'Oh Rick! You're wet!' cried Beth. 'Come back!'

'This is the Land of Do-As-You-Please, isn't it?' shouted Rick, jumping about in the water and getting wetter. 'Well, I'll get as wet as I like, then!'

'Let's make a HUGE sandcastle!' cried Moon-Face. 'Then we can all sit on top when the sea comes up.'

'We can't,' said Silky, suddenly looking disappointed.

'Why not?' cried Joe. 'Isn't this the Land of Do-As-You-Please?'

'Yes,' said Silky. 'But it's time we went back to the Faraway Tree. This land will soon be on the move – and nice as it is, we don't want to live here for ever.'

'Gosh, no,' said Joe. 'Our parents couldn't do without us! Rick! Come back! We're going home!'

Rick didn't want to be left behind. He waded back at once, his clothes dripping wet. They all made their way to the hole that led down through the cloud to the Faraway Tree.

'We did have a lovely time,' sighed Joe, looking back longingly at the happy land he was leaving behind. 'It's one of the nicest lands that has ever been at the top of the Tree.'

They all felt tired as they crowded into Moon-Face's room. 'Don't fall asleep before you get home,' said Moon-Face. 'Take cushions, all of you.'

They went down the slippery-slip, yawning. They made their way home and fell into bed, tired out but happy. And in the morning their mother spoke to Rick.

'Rick, why are your clothes so wet this morning?'

'I waded too deep in the sea,' said Rick – and he couldn't understand why his Aunt Polly said he was a naughty little story-teller!

XIII. THE LAND OF TOYS

One afternoon Silky came to see the children as they were all working hard in the garden. She leaned over the gate and called to them.

'Hello! I've come to tell you something!'

'Oh, hello Silky!' cried everyone. 'Come in. We can't stop work because we've got to finish clearing this patch before dinner.'

Silky came in. She sat down on a bench. 'The Old Saucepan Man wants to give a party,' she said. 'And he says, will you come?'

'Is it his birthday?' asked Joe.

'Oh, no. He doesn't know when his birthday is,' said Silky. 'He says he hasn't got one. This is just a party. You see, the Land of Goodies is coming soon, and Saucepan thought it would be a good idea to go there with a large basket and collect as many good things to eat as he can find, and then give a party in Moon-Face's room, so we can eat all the lovely things.'

'That sounds great!' said Rick, who loved eating good things. 'When shall we come?'

'Tomorrow,' said Silky. 'About three o'clock. Will that be all right?'

'Oh, yes,' said Beth. 'Mother says we've been very good this week, so she's sure to let us come to the Saucepan Man's party tomorrow. We'll be there!

When is Saucepan going to get the goodies?'

'Tomorrow morning,' said Silky. 'He says that the Land of Goodies will be there then. Well, goodbye. I won't stay and talk today, as I said I'd make some Pop Cakes and Google Buns for tomorrow as well. I might make some Toffee Shocks, too.'

Silky went. The children talked excitedly about the party.

'I hope there will be Danish pastries,' said Rick.

'Danish pastries! At a party!' said Beth.

'Well, why not?' said Rick. 'They're delicious. I hope there will be pink and yellow ice-cream too.'

Everyone felt excited when the next afternoon came. Mother said they could go, but she wouldn't let them wear their best clothes.

'Not if you're going to climb trees,' she said. 'And, Rick, please don't get your clothes wet this time. If you do, you'll have to stay in all day while I dry them.'

The children ran to the Enchanted Wood. They had to climb up the Tree the ordinary way, because there was no rope that day. Up they went, shouting a greeting to the owl in his room, to the Angry Pixie and to Dame Washalot.

They reached Moon-Face's house. He and Silky were setting out cups and saucers and plates ready for all the goodies that Saucepan was going to bring back. Silky passed a bag around. 'Have a Toffee Shock?' she said.

All the children except Rick had had Toffee Shocks before, and, as long as you knew what the toffee did, it was all right. But if you didn't, it was a bit alarming.

A Toffee Shock gets bigger and bigger and bigger as you suck it, instead of smaller and smaller – and when it is so big that there's no more room for it in your mouth, it suddenly explodes – and goes to nothing. Joe, Beth and Frannie watched Rick as he sucked his Toffee Shock, nudging one another and giggling.

Rick took a big Toffee Shock, as he was rather a greedy boy. He popped it into his mouth and sucked hard. It tasted delicious. But it seemed to get bigger and bigger.

Rick tried to tell the others this, because it surprised him. But the Toffee Shock was now so big that he could hardly talk.

'Oooble, ooble, ooble!' he said.

'What language are you talking, Rick?' asked Moon-Face, with a giggle.

Rick looked really alarmed. His toffee was now so enormous that he could hardly find room in his mouth for it. And then suddenly it exploded – and his mouth was empty!

'Oooh!' said Rick, opening and shutting his mouth like a goldfish. 'Oooh!'

'Don't you like your toffee?' said Silky, trying not to giggle. 'Well, spit it out if you like, and have something else.'

'It's gone!' said Rick. Then he saw the others laughing, and he guessed that Toffee Shocks were not the usual kind of toffee. He began to laugh, too. 'Gosh, that did frighten me!' he said. 'I'd love to give my old school teacher a

Toffee Shock!'

Moon-Face looked at his clock. 'Old Saucepan is a long time,' he said. 'It's half-past three now, and he promised to be back really quick.'

'Hello – there's somebody coming now,' said Moon-Face, as he heard footsteps on the ladder that led up through the cloud. 'Perhaps it's old Saucepan. But I can't hear his kettles clanking.'

Down the ladder came a wooden soldier, wearing the red uniform of a guard, with a black helmet. He saluted as he went past.

'Hey!' shouted Moon-Face suddenly. 'Wait a minute! How is it that you live in the Land of Goodies?'

'I don't,' said the wooden soldier, in surprise. 'I live in the Land of Toys.'

'What! Is the Land of Toys up there now?' cried Moon-Face, standing up in amazement.

'Of course!' said the soldier. 'The Land of Goodies doesn't arrive until next week.'

'Oh,' groaned Moon-Face, as the soldier disappeared down the tree. 'Old Saucepan has made a mistake. He's gone to the Land of Toys instead of to the Land of Goodies. I expect he is hunting everywhere for nice things to bring down to us – he's such an old silly that he wouldn't know it wasn't the right land.'

'We'd better go and tell him,' said Silky. 'You children can stay here till we come back, and then we'll have a nice feast of Pop Cakes and Google Buns. Help yourself to Toffee Shocks while we're gone.'

'We'll come too,' said Beth, jumping up. 'The Land

of Toys sounds exciting. I wish I'd brought my doll. She would have loved to visit the Land of Toys.'

'Is it a dangerous land?' said Joe. 'Or just toys come to life?'

'Of course it's not dangerous,' said Silky.

They all went up the ladder. They were very anxious to see what the Land of Toys was like. It was exactly how they imagined it would be!

Dolls' houses, toy shops, toy stations stood about everywhere, but much bigger than real toys. Teddy bears, dolls of all kinds, stuffed animals and clockwork toys ran or walked about, talking and laughing.

'Wow! This is fun!' said Beth. 'Oh, look at those wooden soldiers all walking in a row!' They were just like the soldier who had come down the ladder at the top of the tree.

The children stared round, but Moon-Face beckoned them on.

'Come on,' he said. 'We've got to find out where the Old Saucepan Man has got to! I can't see him anywhere.'

The six of them wandered about the Land of Toys. Clockwork animals ran everywhere. A big Noah's Ark suddenly opened its lid and let out lots of wooden animals walking in twos. Noah came behind, singing.

The Saucepan Man was nowhere to be seen. 'I'd better ask someone if they've seen him,' said Moon-Face at last. So he stopped a big teddy bear and spoke to him.

'Have you seen a little man covered with kettles and saucepans?' he asked.

'Yes,' said the teddy bear at once. 'He's naughty. He

tried to steal some toffee out of the shop over there.'

'I'm sure Saucepan wouldn't steal a thing!' said Joe angrily.

'Well, he did,' said the teddy bear. 'I saw him.'

'I know what happened,' said Moon-Face, suddenly. 'Old Saucepan thought this was the Land of Goodies. He didn't know it was the Land of Toys. So when he saw the shop he thought he could take as many things as he liked. You can in the Land of Goodies, you know. And people must have thought he was stealing.'

'Oh, dear,' said Silky, in dismay. 'Teddy Bear, what happened to the Saucepan Man?'

'The policeman came up and took him off to jail,' said the teddy bear. 'There's the policeman over there. You can ask him all about it.'

The teddy bear went off. The children, Moon-Face and Silky went over to the policeman. He told them it was quite true what the teddy bear had said – Saucepan had tried to take toffee out of the shop, and he had been locked up.

'Oh, we must rescue him!' cried Joe at once. 'Where is he?'

'You must certainly not rescue him,' said the policeman, angrily. 'I shan't tell you where he is!'

And no matter how much the children begged him, he would NOT tell them where he had put poor Saucepan.

'Well, we must just go and look for him ourselves, that's all,' said Joe. And the six of them wandered off through the Land of Toys, calling loudly as they went.

'Saucepan! Dear old Saucepan! Where are you?'

XIV. AN EXCITING RESCUE

The children, Moon-Face and Silky went down the crooked streets of the Land of Toys, calling the Old Saucepan Man.

'Of course, Saucepan is very deaf,' said Joe. 'He might not hear us calling him, even if he was locked up somewhere near by.'

They went on again, shouting and calling. The toys hurrying by stared at them in surprise.

'Why do you keep calling "Saucepan, Saucepan"?' asked a well-dressed doll. 'Are you selling saucepans, or something?'

'No,' said Joe. 'We're looking for a friend.'

Just then Silky heard something. She clutched Joe's arm. 'Sh!' she said. 'Listen!'

Everyone stood still and listened. Then, floating on the air came a well-known voice, singing a silly song:

> *Two trees in a teapot,*
> *Two spoons in a pie,*
> *Two clocks up the chimney.*
> *Hi-tiddley-hie!*

'It's Saucepan!' cried Joe. 'Nobody but Saucepan sings those silly songs. Where is he?'

They looked all round. There was a toy soldier fort

not far off, but, of course, much bigger than an actual toy fort would be. The song seemed to come from there.

> *Two mice on a lamp-post,*
> *Two hums in a bee,*
> *Two shoes on a rabbit.*
> *Hi-tiddley-hee!*

Joe laughed loudly. 'I never knew such a stupid song,' he said. 'I can't imagine how old Saucepan can make it up. It's coming from that fort. That's where he is locked up.'

Everyone looked at the red-painted fort. Soldiers walked up and down it. A drawbridge was pulled up so that no one could go in or out. When a soldier wanted to go out the drawbridge was let down and the soldier stepped over it. Then it was pulled up again.

'Well, Saucepan is definitely in there,' said Moon-Face. 'And, by the way, don't call to him, any of you. We don't want the soldier guards to know that there are any friends of his here – or else they will guess that we want to rescue him.'

'Oh, do let's try and let him know we're here,' said Beth. 'He'd be very glad as he must feel so worried and unhappy.'

'I know a way of telling him we are here, without anyone guessing we are friends of his,' said Joe suddenly. 'Listen.'

He stood and thought for a moment. Then he raised his voice and sang a little song:

Two boys in the high road,
Two girls in the street,
Two friends feeling sorry.
Tweet-tweet-tweet-tweet-tweet!

Everyone roared with laughter. 'It's very clever, Joe,' said Rick. 'Two boys – Saucepan will know that's you and me – two girls – that's Beth and Frannie – two friends, Silky and Moon-Face! Saucepan will know we're all here!'

A terrible noise came from the fort – a clanging and a banging, a clanking and crashing. Everyone listened.

'That's old Saucepan dancing round to let us know he heard and understood,' said Joe. 'Now the thing is – how are we going to rescue him?'

They walked down the street, talking, trying to think of some good way to save poor Saucepan. They came to a clothes shop. In it were dolls' clothes of all sorts. In the window was a set of sailor's clothes, too. Joe stared at them.

'Now, I wonder,' he said. 'I just wonder if they've got any soldier's clothes. Moon-Face, lend me your money bag if it's got any money in it.'

Moon-Face put his money bag in Joe's hand. Joe disappeared into the shop. He came out with three sets of bright red soldier guard's uniforms, with big, black helmets.

'Come on,' he said in excitement. 'Come somewhere where we shan't be seen.'

They all hurried down the street and came to a field where some toy cows stood grazing.

They climbed over the gate and went behind the

bushes. 'Rick, see if this uniform will fit you,' said Joe. 'I'll put this one on.'

'But Joe – Joe – what are you going to do?' asked Beth in surprise.

'I thought you would have guessed,' said Joe, putting the uniform on quickly. 'We're going to see if we can march into the fort and get old Saucepan out! I should think they will let down the drawbridge for us if we are dressed like the other soldiers.'

'Is this third suit for me?' asked Moon-Face.

'No, Moon-Face,' said Joe. 'I didn't think you'd look a bit like a soldier, even if you were dressed like one. You must stay outside and look after Beth, Frannie and Silky. This third suit is for old Saucepan. The soldiers won't let us take him out of the fort covered in kettles and saucepans! They will know it's the prisoner and will stop him. He'll have to take off his kettles and things and wear this uniform. Then, maybe we can rescue him easily.'

'Joe, you really are very clever,' said Silky.

Joe felt very pleased. He buckled his belt, and put on his black helmet. He did look impressive! So did Rick.

'Now we're ready,' said Joe. 'Moon-Face, if by any chance Rick and I are caught, you must take the girls safely back to the Tree. OK?'

'OK,' said Moon-Face. 'Good luck, boys!'

Everyone went out of the field and walked back to the fort. When they got near it, Rick and Joe began to march very well indeed. Left, right, left, right, left, right!

They came to the fort. 'Soldier, let down the drawbridge!' yelled Joe, in his loudest and most

312

commanding voice. The guard peered over the wall of the fort. When he saw the two well dressed soldiers, he saluted at once, and began to let down the drawbridge. Crash! It fell flat to the ground, and Rick and Joe walked over it into the fort.

Creak, creeee-eak! The drawbridge was drawn up again. Joe and Rick marched right into the fort. Soldiers saluted at once.

'I wish to talk to the prisoner here,' said Joe.

'Yes, sir,' said a wooden soldier, saluting. He took a key from his belt and gave it to Joe. 'First door on the right, sir,' he said. 'Be careful. He might be dangerous.'

'Thanks. Good man.' said Joe, and marched to the first door on the right. He unlocked it and he and Rick went in and shut the door. Saucepan was there! When he saw the two soldiers, he fell on his knees.

'Set me free, set me free!' he begged. 'I didn't mean to steal the toffee. I thought this was the Land of Goodies.'

'Saucepan! It's us!' whispered Joe, taking off his helmet so that Saucepan could see him plainly. 'We've come to save you. Put on this uniform, quick!'

'But what about my kettles and saucepans?' said Saucepan. 'I can't leave them behind.'

'Don't be silly. You'll have to,' said Joe. 'Quick, Rick, help him off with them.'

The two boys stripped off every pan and made

Saucepan dress up in the red uniform. He trembled so much with excitement that they had to do up every button for him.

'Now march close to us and don't say a word,' said Joe, when Saucepan was ready. His kettles and saucepans lay in a heap on the floor. He fell over them as he scrambled across to Joe and Rick. Joe opened the door. All three marched out, keeping in step. Left, right, left, right, left, right!

The other soldiers in the fort looked up but saw nothing but three of their comrades – or so they thought. Joe shouted to the guard:

'Let down the drawbridge!'

'Very good, sir!' cried the guard, and let it down with a crash. Joe, Rick and Saucepan marched out at once. Left, right, left, right, left, right.

Moon-Face and the girls could hardly believe that the third soldier was old Saucepan. He did look different in his uniform, without his pans hung all round him. Silky flew to hug him.

And then the guard of the fort yelled out in a loud voice: 'I believe that's the prisoner! I believe he's escaped! Hey, after them!'

'Quick! Run! Run!' cried Joe. And they all ran. Fast! Soldiers poured out of the fort after them, teddy bears and dolls joined in the chase, and animals pattered behind on four feet.

'To the hole in the cloud!' shouted Joe. 'Run, Beth; run, Frannie! Oh, I hope we get there in time!'

XV. A SHOCK FOR THE TOYS

How the children and the others ran! They knew well that if they were caught they would be put into the toy fort – and then the Land of Toys would move away from the Faraway Tree, and goodness knows how long they might have to stay there!

So they ran at top speed. Frannie fell behind a little, and Joe took her hand to help her along. Panting and puffing, they raced down the streets of the Land of Toys, trying to remember where the hole was that led down through the cloud to the Faraway Tree.

Joe remembered the way. He led them all to the hole – and there was the ladder, thank goodness!

'Down you go!' cried Joe to Silky, Beth and Frannie. 'Hurry! Get into Moon-Face's room quickly.'

Down the girls went, and then Rick, Moon-Face, Saucepan and Joe. Joe only just got down in time, because a big teddy bear had almost caught them up – and as Joe went down he reached out and tried to catch Joe's shirt.

Joe jerked himself away. His shirt tore – and he half slid, half climbed down the ladder to safety. Soon he was in Moon-Face's house with the others – but what was this? The toys did not stay up in their land – they poured down the ladder after the children and their friends!

'They're coming in here!' yelled Moon-Face. 'Oh,

why didn't we shut the door?'

But it was too late then to shut the door. Wooden soldiers, teddy bears and dolls poured into Moon-Face's funny round room – and Moon-Face, quick as a flash, pushed them all towards the middle of his room.

The opening of the slippery-slip was there – and one by one all the surprised toys fell into the hole and found themselves sliding wildly down the inside of the tree!

As soon as Joe and the others saw what Moon-Face was doing, they did the same.

'Down you go!' said Joe to a big teddy bear, giving him a good push – and down he went.

'A push for you!' yelled Rick to a big rag doll – and down the slide went the doll.

Soon the children could do no more pushing, because they began to giggle. It was so funny to see the toys rushing in, then being pushed down the slide, shrieking and kicking. But after a while no more toys came, and Moon-Face shut his door. He flung himself on his curved bed, and laughed till the tears ran down his cheeks.

'What will the toys do?' asked Joe at last.

'Climb back up the Tree to the Land of Toys,' said Moon-Face, drying his eyes. 'We'll see them out of my window. They won't cause us any more trouble!'

After about an hour the toys began to come past Moon-Face's window, slowly, as if they were tired. Not one of them tried to open the door and get into Moon-Face's house.

'They're afraid that if they don't get back into their

land at once, it will move away!' said Silky. 'Let's sit here and watch them all – and have a few Google Buns and Pop Cakes.'

'I'm so sorry to have caused all this trouble,' said the Saucepan Man. 'And I didn't bring anything back to eat either. You see, I really thought, when I got into the Land of Toys, that it was the Land of Goodies, because one of the first things I saw was that shop selling toffee. And in the Land of Goodies you can just take anything you like without paying for it – so of course I went right into the shop and began to empty some toffees out of a box. That's why they put me into jail. It was dreadful. Oh, I *was* glad to hear Joe singing. I knew at once that you would try to rescue me.'

This was a very long speech for Saucepan to make. He looked so unhappy and sorry that everyone forgave him for making such a silly mistake.

'Cheer up, Saucepan,' said Moon-Face. 'The Land of Goodies will soon come along – and we'll ALL go and visit it, not just you – and we'll have the biggest feast we have ever had.'

'Oh, but do you think we should?' began Joe. 'Honestly, we seem to get into a fix every time we go up the ladder.'

'I'll make quite sure that the Land of Goodies is there,' said Moon-Face. 'Nothing can go wrong if we visit it. Don't be afraid. I must say, Joe, you and Rick and Saucepan look very grand in your soldier's uniforms. Are you always going to wear them?'

'Oh – I forgot we haven't got our proper clothes,' said Joe. 'Mother will be cross if we leave them in the

317

Land of Toys. We left them under a bush near the fort.'

'And I left my lovely kettles and saucepans in the fort,' said Saucepan in a sad voice. 'I feel funny without them. I don't like being a soldier. I want to be a Saucepan Man.'

'I'd like you to be our dear old Saucepan Man, too,' said Silky. 'It doesn't seem you, somehow, dressed like that. But I don't see how we are going to get anything back. Surely none of us is going back into the Land of Toys again!'

Just then three sailor dolls, last of all the toys, came climbing slowly up the Tree. They were crying. Their sailor clothes were torn and soaking wet.

Moon-Face opened his door. 'What's the matter?' he asked. 'What's happened to you?'

'Awful things,' said the first sailor. 'We were climbing up the Tree when we came to a window, and we all peeped in. And a very angry pixie flew out at us and pushed us off the branch. The Faraway Tree was growing thorns just there and they tore our clothes to bits. And then a whole lot of washing water came pouring down the Tree on top of us and soaked us. So we feel dreadful. If only we could get some new clothes!'

'Listen!' cried Joe suddenly. 'How would you like to have our soldier uniforms? They are quite new and very good.'

'Oooh!' said all the sailor dolls together. 'We'd love that. Would you really give us those? We'll get into trouble if we go back to the Land of Toys like this.'

'We'll give you them on one condition, sailor dolls,' said Joe. 'You must find our own things in the Land of

Toys and throw them down the ladder to us. We'll tell you where they are.'

'We can easily do that,' promised the sailors. So Joe, Rick and Saucepan stripped off their lovely uniforms and gave them to the sailor dolls who took off their torn blue clothes and dressed themselves in the red trousers, tunics and helmets. They looked very nice.

'Now, you *will* find our clothes for us, won't you?' said Joe. 'We are trusting you, you see.'

'We are very trustworthy,' said the dolls, and ran up the ladder after Joe had told them exactly where to find everything.

Joe, Rick and Saucepan sat in their underwear and shivered a little, because the uniforms had been warm. 'We'll look funny going home like this if those sailors don't keep their word!' said Rick. 'As a matter of fact, I'd have liked to keep that uniform. I like it much better than my clothes.'

'Look – something's coming down the ladder!' cried Moon-Face, and they all ran out to see. 'How quick the sailor dolls have been – or soldier dolls, as I suppose we should call them now.'

Two sets of clothes tumbled down the ladder and the children caught them. Then came a clatter and clanging as kettles and saucepans came down too. Saucepan was delighted. He put on a pair of ragged trousers and a funny old coat that came down with the pans – and then Silky helped him to string his kettles and saucepans round him as usual.

319

'Now you look like our dear old Saucepan again,' said Silky. The boys dressed too. Then Joe looked at Moon-Face's clock.

'We must go,' he said. 'Thanks for the Pop Cakes and everything. Now, Saucepan, don't get into any more trouble for a little while!'

'Smile?' said Saucepan, going suddenly deaf again. 'I *am* smiling. Look!'

'That's a grin, not a smile!' said Joe, as he saw Saucepan smiling from ear to ear. 'Now don't get into any more TROUBLE!'

'Bubble? Where's a bubble?' said Saucepan, looking all round. 'I didn't see anyone blowing bubbles.'

The children grinned. Saucepan was always very funny when he heard things wrong.

'Come on,' said Beth. 'Mother will be cross if we're home too late. Goodbye, Moon-Face. Goodbye, Silky. We'll see you again soon.'

'Well, don't forget to come to the Land of Goodies with us,' said Silky. 'That really will be fun. Nearly as much fun as the Land of Do-As-You-Please.'

'We'll come,' promised Beth. 'Don't go without us. Can I have a red cushion, Moon-Face? Thank you!'

One by one the four children slid swiftly down the slippery-slip to the bottom of the Tree. They shot out of the trap-door, gave the red squirrel the cushions and set off home.

'I'm looking forward to our next adventure,' said Rick. 'It makes my mouth water when I think of the Land of Goodies!'

XVI. THE LAND OF GOODIES

The four children were rather naughty over the next few days. Rick and Joe quarrelled, and they fell over when they began to wrestle with one another, and broke a little table.

Then Beth scorched a table cloth when she was ironing it – and Frannie tore a hole in her clothes when she went picking blackberries.

'Really, you are all very careless lately,' said their mother. 'Joe, you will mend that table as best you can. Rick, you must help him – and if I see you quarrelling like that again I shall send you both to bed at once. Frannie, why didn't you put on your old clothes when you went to pick blackberries, as I told you to? Now you will have to mend your clothes, and properly.'

Beth had to wash the table cloth carefully to try and get the scorch marks out of it.

'Oh my, it's a pity all these things have happened this week,' groaned Joe to Rick, as the two boys did their best to mend the table. 'I'm afraid the Land of Goodies will come and go before we get there! I daren't ask Mother or Father if we can go off to the Faraway Tree. We've been so careless that they are sure to say no.'

'Moon-Face and the others will be wondering why we don't go,' said Beth, almost in tears.

They were. The Land of Goodies had come, and a

delicious smell kept coming down the ladder. Moon-Face waited and waited for the children to come, but they didn't.

Then he heard that the Land of Goodies was going to move away the next afternoon, and he wondered what to do.

'We said we'd wait for the children – but we don't want to miss going ourselves,' he said to Silky. 'We had better send a note to them. Perhaps something has happened to stop them coming.'

So they wrote a note, and went down to ask the Owl to take it. But he was asleep. So they went to the woodpecker, who had a hole in the Tree for himself, and he said he would take it.

He flew off with it in his beak. He soon found the cottage and tapped on the window with his beak.

'A lovely woodpecker!' cried Joe, looking up. 'See the red on his head? He's got a note for us!'

He opened the window. Mother was there, in the same room as the children, and she looked surprised to see such an unexpected visitor.

Joe took the note. The bird stayed on the window sill, waiting for an answer. Joe read it and then showed it to the others. They all looked rather sad. It was dreadful to know that the lovely Land of Goodies had come and was going so soon – and they couldn't visit it.

'Tell Moon-Face we've been in trouble and can't come,' said Joe.

The bird spread its wings, but Mother looked up and spoke. 'Wait a minute!' she said to the bird. Then she turned to Joe. 'Read me the note,' she said.

Joe read it out loud:

> *Dear Joe, Beth, Frannie and Rick,*
> *The Land of Goodies is here and goes tomorrow.*
> *We have waited and waited for you to come. If you*
> *don't come tomorrow we shall have to go by*
> *ourselves. Can't you come?*
> *Love from,*
> *Silky, Saucepan and Moon-face.*

'The Land of Goodies!' said Mother in amazement.
'Well, I never did hear of such funny happenings! I
suppose there are lots of nice things to eat there, and
that's why you all want to go. Well – you have been in
trouble lately – but you've done your best to put
things right. You can go tomorrow morning!'

'Mother! Oh, Mother, thank you!' cried the
children. 'Thank you, Aunt Polly!' said Rick, hugging
her. 'Oh, how lovely!'

'Tell Moon-Face we'll come as soon as we can
tomorrow morning,' said Joe to the listening
woodpecker. He nodded his red-splashed head and
flew off. The children talked together, excited.

'I won't have any breakfast,' said Beth. 'It's not
much good going to the Land of Goodies unless we're
hungry!'

'That's a good idea,' said Rick. 'I think I won't have
any supper tonight either!'

So when the time came for the four children to set
off to the Enchanted Wood, they were all terribly
hungry! They ran to the Faraway Tree and climbed
up it in excitement.

'I hope there are doughnuts,' said Joe.

'I want chocolate mousse,' said Beth.

'I can't begin to say the things I'd like,' said greedy Rick.

'Well, don't,' said Joe. 'Save your breath and hurry. You're being left behind!'

They got to Moon-Face's, and shouted loudly to him. He came running out of his tree house in delight.

'Oh, good, good!' he cried. 'You *are* nice and early. Silky, they're here! Go down and call old Saucepan. He's with Mister Watzisname. I'm sure Saucepan would like to come too.'

It wasn't long before seven excited people were climbing up the ladder to the Land of Goodies. How they longed to see what it was like!

Well, it was much better than anyone imagined! It was a small place, set with little crooked houses and shops – and every house and shop was made from things to eat! The first house that the children saw was amazing.

'Look at that house!' cried Joe. 'Its walls are made of sugar – and the chimneys are chocolate – and the window sills are peppermint cream!'

'And look at that shop!' cried Rick. 'It's got walls made of chocolate, and the door is made of marzipan. And I'm sure the window sills are gingerbread!'

The Land of Goodies was really a very extraordinary place. Everything in it seemed to be eatable. And then the children caught sight of the trees and bushes and called out in surprise:

'Look! That tree is growing muffins!'

'And that one has got buds that are opening out

into cakes! It's a Cake Tree!'

'And look at this little tree here – it's growing big, flat, white flowers like plates – and the middle of the flowers is full of ice-cream. Let's taste it.'

They tasted it – and it *was* ice-cream! There was another small bush that grew clusters of a curious-looking fruit, like flat berries of all colours – and, will you believe it, when the children picked the fruit it was really little lollipops, all neatly growing together like a bunch of grapes.

'Ooh, lovely!' said Joe, who liked lollipops very much. 'Gosh, look at that white fence over there – surely it isn't made of marshmallow!'

It was. The children tore off pieces from the fence, and munched the marshmallow. It was the nicest they had ever tasted.

The shops were full of things to eat. You should have seen them! Joe felt as if he would like a hot dog and he went into a hot dog shop. The rolls were tumbling one by one out of a machine. The handle was being turned by an odd-looking person. He was flat and golden brown, and had raisin-like eyes.

'I think he is a gingerbread man!' whispered Joe to the others. 'He's just like the gingerbread people that Mother makes for us.'

The children chose a hot dog each and went out, munching. They wandered into the next shop. It had lovely big cakes, set out in rows. Some were yellow, some were pink, and some white.

'Your name, please?' asked the funny little woman there, looking at Beth, who had asked for a cake.

'Beth,' said the little girl in surprise. And there in

the middle of the cake her name appeared in pink sugar letters! Of course, all the others wanted cakes, too, then, just to see their names come!

'We shall never be able to eat all these,' said Moon-Face, looking at the seven cakes that had suddenly appeared. But, you know, they tasted so delicious that it wasn't very long before they all went!

Into shop after shop went the children and the others, tasting everything they could see. They had tomato soup, poached eggs, ginger buns, chocolate fingers, ice-creams, and goodness knows what else.

'Well, I just CAN'T eat anything more,' said Silky at last. 'I've been really greedy. I am sure I'll be ill if I eat anything else.'

'Oh, Silky!' said Rick. 'Don't stop. I can go on for quite a long time yet.'

'Rick, you're greedy, *really* greedy,' said Joe. 'You ought to stop.'

'Well, I'm not going to,' said Rick. The others looked at him.

'You're getting very fat,' said Joe suddenly. 'You won't be able to get down the hole! You be careful, Rick. You're not to go into any more shops.'

'All right,' said Rick, looking sulky. But although he did not go into the shops, can you guess what he did? He broke off some of a gingerbread window sill – and then he took a knocker from a door. It was made of peppermint, and Rick sucked it in delight. The others had not seen him do these things – but the man whose knocker Rick had pulled off *did* see him!

He opened his door and came running out. 'Hey, hey!' he cried angrily. 'Bring back my knocker at once! You bad, naughty boy!'

XVII. RICK GETS EVERYONE INTO TROUBLE

When Joe and the others heard the angry voice behind them, they turned in surprise. Nobody but Rick knew what the angry little man was talking about.

'Knocker?' said Joe, in amazement. 'What knocker? We haven't got your knocker.'

'That bad boy is eating my knocker!' cried the man, and he pointed to Rick. 'I had a beautiful one, made of lovely peppermint – and now that boy has nearly eaten it all up!'

They all stared at Rick. He went very red. What was left of the knocker was in his mouth.

'Did you really take his peppermint knocker?' said Joe, glaring at Rick. 'Whatever were you thinking of, Rick?'

'Well, I just never thought,' said Rick, swallowing the rest of the knocker in a hurry. 'I saw it there on the door – and it looked so nice. I'm very sorry.'

'That's all very well,' said the angry man. 'But being sorry won't bring back my knocker. You're a bad boy. You come and sit in my house till the others are ready to go. I won't have you going about in our land eating knockers and chimneys and window sills!'

'You'd better go, Rick,' said Joe. 'We'll call for you when we're ready to go home. We won't be long now. Anyway, you've eaten quite enough.'

So poor Rick had to go into the house with the

angry little man, who made him sit on a stool and keep still. The others wandered off again.

'We mustn't be here much longer,' said Moon-Face. 'It's almost time for this land to move on. Look! Strawberries and cream.'

The children stared at the strawberries and cream. They had never seen such a strange sight before. The strawberries grew by the hundred on strawberry plants – but each strawberry had its own big blob of cream growing on it, ready to be eaten.

'They are even sugared!' said Joe, picking one. 'Look – my strawberry is powdered with white sugar – and, oh, the cream is delicious!'

They enjoyed the strawberries and cream, and then Joe had a good idea.

'I know! What about taking some of these lovely goodies back with us?' he said. 'Watsizname would love a plum pie – and the Angry Pixie would like some of those ice-cream flowers – and Dame Washalot would like some strawberries.'

'And Mother would like lots of things, too,' said Beth happily.

So they began collecting puddings and pies and cakes. It was fun. The cherry pie had so many cherries that they dripped all down Moon-Face's leg.

'You'll have to take a bath, Moon-Face,' said Silky. 'You're very sticky.'

They nearly forgot to call for poor Rick. As they passed the house whose knocker he had eaten, he banged loudly on the window, and they all stopped.

'Gosh! We nearly forgot about Rick!' said Beth. 'Rick, Rick, come on! We're going!'

Rick came running out of the house. The little man called after him: 'Now, don't you eat anybody's knocker again!'

'Goodness! Why have you got all those things?' asked Rick in surprise, looking at the puddings and pies and cakes. 'Are they for our supper?'

'Rick! How can you think of supper after eating such a lot!' cried Joe. 'Well, I'm sure I couldn't even eat a piece of chocolate before tomorrow morning. No – these things are for Watzisname and Dame Washalot and Mother. Come on. Moon-Face says this land will soon be on the move.'

They all went to the hole that led down through the cloud. It didn't take long to climb down the ladder and on to the big branch outside Moon-Face's house.

Rick came last – and he suddenly missed his footing and fell right down the ladder on the top of the others below. And he knocked the puddings, pies and cakes right out of their hands! Down went all the goodies, bumping from branch to branch. The children and the others stared after them in dismay.

Then there came a very angry yell from below. 'Who's thrown a cherry pie at me? Wait till I get them. I've got cherries and syrup all over me. It burst on my head. Oh, oh!'

Then there came an angry shout from lower down still. 'Plum pie! Plum pie in my washtub! Hot dogs in my washtub! Peppermints down my neck! Oh, you rascals up there – I'm coming up after you, yes I am!'

And from still lower down came the voice of the Angry Pixie – and a very angry pixie he was indeed! 'Ice-cream on my nose! Ice-cream down my neck!

Ice-cream in my pockets! What next? Who's doing all this? Wait till I come up and tell them what I think!'

The children listened, half frightened and very amused. They began to giggle.

'Plum pie in Dame Washalot's tub!' giggled Joe.

'Ice-cream on the Angry Pixie's nose!' said Beth.

'Look out, I believe they really are coming up!' said Joe, in alarm. 'Look – isn't that Watzisname?'

They all peered down the Tree. Yes – it was Watzisname climbing up, looking very angry. The Saucepan Man leaned over a bit too far, and nearly fell. Rick just caught him in time – but one of his kettles came loose and fell down. It bounced from branch to branch and landed on poor old Watzisname's big head!

He gave a tremendous yell. 'What! Is it you, Saucepan, throwing all these things down the Tree? What you want is a good scolding. And you'll get it! And anybody else up there playing tricks will get a fine scolding, too!'

'A scolding!' said Dame Washalot's voice.

'A SCOLDING!' roared the Angry Pixie not far behind.

'Gosh!' said Joe in alarm. 'It looks as if the Land of Scoldings is about to arrive up here. I vote we go home. You'd better shut your door, Moon-Face, and you and Silky and Saucepan had better lie down on the sofa and the bed and pretend to be asleep. Then maybe those angry people will think it's somebody up in the Land of Goodies that has been throwing all those things down.'

'Rick ought to stay up there and get the scoldings,'

said Moon-Face gloomily. 'First he goes and eats somebody's door knocker and gets into trouble. Then he falls on top of us all and sends all the goodies down the Tree.'

'I'm going down the slippery-slip with the children,' said Silky, who was afraid of Mister Watzisname when he was in a temper. 'I can climb up to my house and lock myself in before all those angry people come down again. Saucepan, why don't you come too?'

Saucepan thought he would. So the children and Silky and Saucepan all slid down the slippery-slip. Just in time, too – for Mister Watzisname came shouting up to Moon-Face's door as Joe, who was last, slid down.

Moon-Face had shut his door. He was lying on his bed, pretending to be asleep. Watzisname banged hard on the door. Moon-Face didn't answer. Watzisname peeped in at the window.

'Moon-Face! Wake up! Wake up, I say!'

'What's the matter?' said Moon-Face, in a sleepy voice, sitting up and rubbing his eyes.

Dame Washalot and the Angry Pixie came up, too. The Pixie had ice-cream all over him, and Watzisname had cherry pie down him. They were all very angry.

They opened Moon-Face's door and went in. 'Who was it that threw all those things down on us?' asked Watzisname. 'Where's Saucepan? Did he throw that kettle? I'm going to scold him.'

'Whatever are you talking about?' said Moon-Face, pretending not to know. 'How sticky you are, Watzisname!'

'And so are you!' yelled Watzisname, suddenly,

seeing cherry syrup shining all down Moon-Face's legs. 'It was you who threw that pudding down on me! My, oh my, I'll give you such a scolding!'

Then all three of them went for poor Moon-Face, who got a terrible scolding. He rolled over to the slippery-slip, and slid down it in a fright.

He shot out of the trap-door just in time to see Silky and Saucepan saying goodbye to the children. They were very surprised when Moon-Face shot out beside them.

'I've had a scolding!' wept Moon-Face. 'They all scolded me because I was sticky, so they thought I'd thrown all the goodies at them. And now I'm afraid to go back because they will be waiting for me.'

'Poor Moon-Face,' said Joe. 'And it was all Rick's fault. Listen. Silky can climb back to her house; but you and Saucepan had better come back with us and stay the night. Rick and I will sleep downstairs on the sofa, and you can have our beds. Mother won't mind.

'All right,' said Moon-Face, wiping his eyes. 'That will be fun. Oh, what a pity we wasted all those lovely goodies! I really do think Rick is a clumsy boy!'

They all went home together, and poor Rick didn't say a word. But he did wish he could make up for all he had done!

XVIII. A SURPRISING VISITOR

The children's mother was astonished to see Moon-Face and Saucepan arriving at the cottage with the children.

'Mother, can they stay the night?' asked Joe.

'They've been so good to us in lots of ways – and they don't want to go back to the Tree tonight because somebody is waiting there to scold them.'

'Dear me!' said Mother, even more surprised. 'Well, yes, they can stay. You and Rick must sleep downstairs on the sofa. If they'd like to help in the garden for a day or two, they can stay longer.

'Ooooh!' said Moon-Face, pleased. 'That would be fine! I'm sure Watzisname will have forgotten about scolding us if we can stay away for a few days. Thank you very much. We will help all we can.'

'Would you like one of my very special kettles?' asked Saucepan gratefully. 'Or a big saucepan for cooking soup bones?'

'Thank you,' said Mother, smiling, for the Old Saucepan Man was a really funny sight, covered as usual with all his pans. 'I could do with a strong little kettle. But let me pay you.'

'Certainly not, madam,' said Saucepan, hearing quite well for a change. 'I shall be only too pleased to present you with anything you like in the way of kettles or saucepans.'

He gave Mother a little kettle and a good strong saucepan. She was very pleased. Moon-Face looked on, wondering what he could give her, too. He put his hand in his pocket and felt around a bit. Then he brought out a bag and offered it to the children's mother.

'Have a bit of toffee?' he asked. Mother took a piece. The children stared at her, knowing that it was a piece of Toffee Shock! Poor Mother!

The toffee grew bigger and bigger and bigger in her mouth as she sucked it, and she looked more and more surprised. At last, when she felt that it was just as big as her whole mouth, it exploded into nothing at all – and the children squealed with laughter.

'Mother, that was a Toffee Shock!' said Joe, giggling. 'Would you like to try a Pop Cake – or a Google Bun?'

'No, thank you,' said Mother at once. 'The Toffee Shock tasted delicious – but it *did* give me a shock!'

It *was* fun having Moon-Face and Saucepan staying with them in their cottage for a few days. The children loved it. Moon-Face was very, very good in the garden, because he dug and cleared away rubbish twice as fast as anyone else. The Old Saucepan Man wasn't so good because he suddenly went deaf again and didn't understand what was said to him. So he did rather peculiar things.

When Mother said: 'Saucepan, fetch me some carrots, will you?' he thought she had asked for sparrows, and he spent the whole morning trying to catch them.

Then he went into the kitchen looking very serious. 'I can't bring you any sparrows,' he said.

Mother stared at him. 'I don't want sparrows,' she said.

'But you asked me for some,' said Saucepan, in surprise.

'Indeed I didn't,' said Mother. 'What do you think I want sparrows for? To make porridge with?'

When Saucepan and Moon-Face had been at the children's cottage for two or three days, Silky came in a great state of anxiety.

She knocked at the door and Joe opened it. 'Oh, Joe! Have you still got Moon-Face and Saucepan here?' she asked. 'Well, tell them they must come back to the Tree at once.'

'Gosh! What's happened?' said Joe. Everyone crowded to the door to hear what Silky had to say.

'Well, you know the Old Woman Who Lives in a Shoe, don't you?' said Silky. '*Her* land has come to the top of the Tree! And the Old Woman came down the ladder through the cloud to see Dame Washalot, who is an old friend of hers. And when she saw that Moon-Face's house was empty, she said she was going to live there! She said she was tired of looking after a pack of naughty children.'

'Oh no!' said Moon-Face, looking very depressed. 'I don't like that Old Woman. She gives her children soup without any bread, and she punishes them and sends them to bed when they are only a little bit naughty. Couldn't you tell her that that house in the Tree is *mine* and I'm coming back to it?'

'I did tell her that, silly,' said Silky. 'But do you think she took any notice of me? Not a bit! She just said in a horrid kind of voice: "Little girls should be seen and not heard." And she went into your house, Moon-Face, and began to shake all the rugs.'

'Well!' said Moon-Face, his temper rising. 'Well! To think of somebody shaking *my* rugs! I hope she falls down the slippery-slip.'

'She won't,' said Silky. 'She peered down it and said: "Ha! A coal-hole, I suppose! How stupid! I shall have a board made and nail that up."'

'Well, I never!' cried Moon-Face, his big round face getting redder and redder. 'Nailing up my lovely slippery-slip! Just wait till I tell her a few things! I'm going this very minute!'

'I'll come with you,' said Saucepan. 'Are you coming, too, children?'

'Mother, Saucepan and Moon-Face have got to go back home,' called Joe. 'Can we go with them for a little while? We won't be long.'

'Very well,' said Mother. Moon-Face and Saucepan

337

went to say goodbye to her and thank her for having them. Then they and the four children and Silky sped off to the Enchanted Wood.

'I'll tell that Old Woman a few things!' cried Moon-Face. 'I'll teach her to shake my rugs! Does she think she is going to live in my dear little round house? Where does she think *I'm* going to live? In her Shoe, I suppose!'

The children couldn't help feeling rather excited as they ran to the Tree. They climbed up it quickly and at last came to Moon-Face's door. It was shut. Moon-Face banged on it so loudly that the door shook.

The door flew open and a cross-faced old woman glared out.

'Do you want to break my door down?' she cried.

''Tisn't your door!' shouted Moon-Face. 'It's mine.'

'Well, I've taken this house now,' said the Old Woman. 'I'm tired of all those naughty children, and I don't want to live in a shoe any more. I'm going to live by myself and have a good time. Dame Washalot is an old friend of mine and she and I will have lots of chats about old times.'

She slammed the door in their faces.

Moon-Face peered in at the window. He groaned. 'She's nailed up the slippery-slip,' he said. 'She's put my bed across the board she's nailed there. Whatever am I going to do?'

'*I'll* see if I can do something,' said the Old Saucepan Man unexpectedly. 'You're a good friend of mine, Moon-Face, and I'd like to do something for you.'

Saucepan began to clash his pans together and

make a dreadful noise. He
shouted at the top of his voice:
'Come out, you naughty Old
Woman! Come out and let Moon-
Face have his house! Your children are
hungry!'

Now he was making such a tremendous
noise that he didn't notice old Dame Washalot coming
up the Tree looking like thunder. She glared at the
little company outside Moon-Face's house. She was
short-sighted and she didn't see who they were. She
thought that they were seven of the Old Woman's
children who had come down from the Land above
and were making themselves a nuisance.

'I'll teach you to shout and scream like that!' said
Dame Washalot in a fierce voice – and before anyone
quite knew what was happening they were all picked
up one by one in Dame Washalot's strong arms and
flung right up through the hole in the cloud into the
Land of the Old Woman Who Lived in a Shoe!

And there they were, in a new and strange land
again, out of breath and very bewildered. They stared
round in surprise!

XIX. THE LAND OF THE OLD WOMAN

The children and the others were quite shocked at being thrown up the ladder, through the hole in the cloud and into such a funny land.

It was quite small, not much larger than a big garden. It had a high wall all round to prevent the children from falling off the edge of the Land. In the middle was a really peculiar thing.

'It's the Shoe!' said Joe. 'Gosh! I never imagined such a big one, did you?'

Everyone stared at the Shoe. It was as big as an ordinary house, and had been made very cleverly into a cottage. Windows were made in the side, and a door had been cut out. A roof had been put on, and chimneys smoked from it. A rose tree climbed around it, and honeysuckle covered one side.

'So that's the Shoe where those naughty children live?' said Beth, excitedly. 'I never thought it would be quite like that. How did the Old Woman get such a big one?'

'Well, it once belonged to a giant, you know,' said Silky. 'The Old Woman did him a good turn, and asked him for an old boot. She had so many children that she couldn't get an ordinary house. So the giant gave her one of his biggest boots, and she got her brother to make it into a house.'

'Look at all those children!' said Moon-Face.

'They're not very well behaved!'

About twenty boys and girls were playing round the house. They shouted and screamed, and they fought and wrestled one another.

'I'm not surprised the Old Woman wouldn't allow them bread with their soup, and punished them and sent them to bed,' said Silky. 'They deserved it!'

The children suddenly saw Joe and the others and ran up to them. They pulled Beth's hair. They tugged at Saucepan's kettles. They made fun of Moon-Face's round face. They trod on Joe's toes and bumped into Rick. They were very naughty and unkind.

'Now just you stop all this,' said Moon-Face, looking angry. 'If you don't, I'll fetch the Old Woman.'

'She isn't here, she isn't here!' shouted the naughty children, dancing round in delight. 'She says she's going to go away and leave us, and we're glad! Now we shall have bread with our soup – and we'll go to the cupboard and open cans of pineapple and jars of cherries! We'll sleep out of doors if we like, and we'll dress up in the Old Woman's clothes!'

'Whatever will she say to that?' said Beth in horror, thinking what her own mother would say if she stole her clothes!

'Oh, she would be FURIOUS!' cried the children. 'But she's gone, so she won't know. Oh, we'll have a great time now!'

One of the children in the Shoe called to the others. 'Hey, I've opened a can of pineapple! Come and taste it! It's lovely!'

With screams of delight the children rushed to the Shoe. Joe looked at the others. 'I've got an idea,' he

341

said. 'What about telling the Old Woman about the children dressing up in her best clothes? She might rush back here then to get her precious clothes, and we could slip down the ladder, go to Moon-Face's house and bolt the door on the inside.'

'That's a really good idea,' said Silky. 'Joe, you go down and tell her.'

Joe was rather nervous about it. Nobody really wanted to go and see the fierce old lady again. At last Rick said he would. He badly wanted to make up for all the silly things he had done a few days before.

'I'll go,' he said. And down the ladder he went. He banged hard on Moon-Face's door. The Old Woman opened it.

'Old Woman, do you want your best clothes?' began Rick. 'Because if . . .'

'My best clothes! I'd forgotten all about them!' cried the Old Woman. 'Those children will be messing about with them. Boy, go to my house, get out all my clothes and bring them down here. You can have a toffee if you do.'

'Well, I think . . .' began Rick. But the Old Woman wouldn't listen to him. She pushed him away and cried 'Go now! Don't stop to argue with me. Go at once!'

Rick ran up the ladder. He waited there a minute or two, his head sticking out into the Land above. He saw the naughty children coming out of the Shoe dressed up in the Old Woman's clothes, shrieking with laughter, and *how* funny they looked dressed up in long skirts and dresses, and hats! Rick grinned to himself and slipped down the ladder again. He banged

342

at Moon-Face's door.

'Well, have you brought my clothes?' asked the Old Woman, opening the door. 'You naughty boy, you haven't.'

'Please, Old Woman, I couldn't bring them,' said Rick in his most polite voice. 'You see, your children have taken them all and they're dancing about, wearing them – and they've opened your cans of pineapple – and they're going to take their beds out of doors and sleep there – and . . .'

'Oh! Oh! The bad, naughty creatures!' cried the Old Woman.

She gathered up her black skirts and climbed the ladder at top speed. She appeared in the land above and saw at once her naughty children dancing about in her best clothes. She rushed after the surprised children.

'So you thought you could do what you liked, did you?' she cried. 'You thought I would never come back? Well, here I am, and I'll soon show you how to be sorry!'

She was so angry that she rushed round like a whirlwind. The children took off the clothes in fright, and ran away like hares. The Old Woman ran after them, so angry that she didn't notice that Joe and the others were not her own children. They got whirled in to the Shoe with the others. There they all were, about twenty-five or -six of them.

There was a big saucepan simmering on the kitchen stove. 'Get the soup bowls,' ordered the Old Woman. 'No bread for any of you tonight! Mary! Jean! Tom! Serve out the bowls and then come to me one by one for your supper!'

Joe and the others had bowls given to them too. They didn't dare say anything. They went up for soup in their turn. The Old Woman ladled it out of the big saucepan. She stared at the Old Saucepan Man when he came up.

'You bad boy!' she said. 'You've played a game with my kettles and saucepans, I see! Wait till you've finished your soup and I'll punish you.'

Poor Old Saucepan Man trembled so much that his pans clashed together as loudly as thunder. He rushed back to his place at once, spilling his soup as he went.

'I want some bread,' wailed a little boy. But he didn't get any. Everyone ate their soup, which was really very good.

'And now you will all go to bed – but first you know what happens to naughty children,' said the Old Woman, and she shook her fist. All the children began to howl and cry:

'We're sorry we were naughty, Old Woman! We didn't mean to dress up in your clothes!'

'Oh, yes, you did,' said the Old Woman. She beckoned to Rick. 'Come here, you bad boy!'

Rick got up. He whispered to the others. 'Look, I'll let her punish me, and whilst she does you creep out and run to the ladder. Hurry! I'll join you as soon as I can.'

Rick went boldly up to the Old Woman.

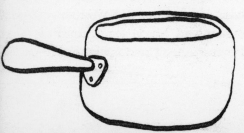

'Put your hands on your head and stand in the corner!' she said.

Poor Rick, he didn't

like it at all, because it made his arms ache. He began to howl as loudly as he could so that the others could creep away without being heard. One by one they slipped out of the door and rushed to the hole, looking for the ladder that led down to the Faraway Tree.

'Oh no! I believe this Land is just about to move!' said Moon-Face, looking round. A peculiar wind had got up and was blowing round them. Very often when the strange lands at the top of the Tree began to move away, this strange wind blew.

'Well, quick, let's get down the ladder!' cried Silky. 'We don't want to live in the Land of the Old Woman! I'd hate that!'

They all scrambled down the ladder, glad to be on the broad branch at the bottom. When they were safely there Beth began to cry.

'Poor Rick will be left behind,' she sobbed.

Everyone looked very sad. The land above the cloud began to make a strange noise.

'It's moving on,' said Moon-Face. 'We'll never see Rick again.'

But just then someone came slipping and sliding down the ladder – bump! Bump! BUMP! And, hey presto, there was Rick, in such a hurry to get down before the land moved right away that he had missed his footing and slid down the ladder from top to bottom!

'Rick! Rick! We're so glad to see you!' cried everyone. 'What happened?'

'Well, the Old Woman punished me, as you saw,' grinned Rick. 'And then when I went to take my place she saw you were all gone and sent me after you. I tore out – and she came, too. But I got to the ladder first, and now the land has moved on, so we're safe!'

Moon-Face went into his house, and they heard him banging about loudly. They went to see what he was doing.

'He's taking up the board that nailed up the slippery-slip,' giggled Joe. 'Good old Moon-Face! I'm glad he's got his house back again for himself. Come on – we'd better go home. We promised Mother we wouldn't be long. It's a good thing we can use the slippery-slip!'

And down it they went, their hair streaming out as they flew down on their cushions. What exciting times they have, don't they?

XX. THE LAND OF MAGIC MEDICINES

For a few days the children had no time even to think of going to their friends in the Faraway Tree. Their mother was in bed ill, and the doctor came each day.

'Just let her lie in bed and keep her warm,' he said to the children and their father. 'Give her what she likes to eat, and don't let her worry about anything.'

The children and Father were upset, but Father had to go out to work as usual. They all loved Mother, and it was strange to see her lying in bed.

'There's all that washing that I had to do for Mrs Jones,' she said. 'No, you children are not to try and do it. It's too much for you.'

Moon-Face and Silky came to visit the children one morning, and were very sorry to hear that the children's mother was ill.

'She worries about the washing,' said Beth. 'She won't let us do it. I don't know what to do about it!'

'Oh, we can manage *that* for you,' said Silky at once. 'Old Dame Washalot will do it for nothing. It's the joy of her life to wash, wash, wash! I believe if she's got nothing dirty to wash, she washes clean things. She even washes the leaves on the Faraway Tree if she's got nothing else to wash. Is that the basket over there? Moon-Face and I will take it up the tree now, and bring it back when it's finished.'

'Oh, thank you, Silky dear,' said Beth gratefully. 'Mother will be so pleased when I tell her. She'll stop worrying about that.'

Silky and Moon-Face went off with the basket. They took it to Dame Washalot, and how her face shone with joy when she saw such a lot of washing to be done!

'My, this is good of you!' she said, taking out the dirty things and throwing them into her enormous wash-tub of soapy water. 'Now this is what I really enjoy! I'll have them all washed and ironed by tonight.'

Silky was pleased. She knew how beautifully Dame Washalot washed and ironed. She went up to Moon-Face's house to have dinner with him.

'I do wish we could help make the children's mother better,' she said. 'She is such a lovely lady, isn't she? And the children love her so much. Moon-Face, can't you possibly think of anything?'

'Well, I don't think Toffee Shocks would be any good, do you?' said Moon-Face. 'I've got some of those.'

'Of course not, silly,' said Silky. 'It's medicine we want – pills or something – but as nobody is ill in the Faraway Tree there's nowhere to buy them from.'

That night they went to see if Dame Washalot had finished the washing. She had. It was washed and beautifully ironed and folded up in the basket, ready to be taken away.

'I've had a lovely time,' said the old dame, beaming at Silky. 'My, the water I've poured down the Tree today.'

'Yes, I've heard the Angry Pixie shouting like anything because he got soaked at least four times,' said Moon-Face with a grin. 'He's got plums growing on the tree just outside his house and he was picking them – and each time he went out to pick them he got soaked with your water. You be careful he doesn't come up and shout at you.'

'If he does I'll put him into my next wash-tub of dirty water and empty him down the tree with it,' said Dame Washalot.

'Oooh, I wish I could see you do that,' said Silky, tying a rope to the basket of washing, so that she could let it down the tree to the bottom. 'Well, Dame Washalot, thank you very much. The person who usually does this washing is ill in bed and can't seem to get better. It's such a pity. I wish I could make her well.'

'Why, Silky, the Land of Magic Medicines is coming tomorrow,' said the old dame. 'You could get any medicine you like there, and your friend would soon get better. Why don't you visit the land and get some?'

'That's a really good idea!' said Silky happily, letting down the basket bit by bit. Moon-Face had gone to the bottom of the tree to catch it. 'I'll tell Moon-Face, and maybe he and I could go and get some medicine.'

She slipped down the Tree and told Moon-Face what the old dame had said. Moon-Face put the basket of washing on his shoulder and beamed at Silky.

'That's good news for the children,' he said. 'Come on, we'll hurry and tell them.'

The children were delighted to have the washing back so quickly, all washed and ironed. Rick set off with it to Mrs Jones. Beth ran to tell her mother that she needn't worry any more about it.

Silky told Joe and Frannie about the Land of Magic Medicines coming the next day to the top of the Faraway Tree. They listened in surprise.

'Well, I vote we go there,' said Joe at once. 'I'd made up my mind none of us would go while Mother was ill – but if there's a chance of getting something to make her better, we'll certainly go! One of us must stay behind with Mother and the rest of us will go.'

So it was arranged that Joe, Rick and Beth should meet at Moon-Face's house early the next morning. Then they would go up to the strange land and see what they could find for their mother.

Frannie was quite willing to stay with her mother, though she felt a little bit left out. She said goodbye to Joe, Rick and Beth soon after breakfast the next day, and promised to wash up the breakfast things carefully, and to sit with her mother until the rest of them came back.

They set off and arrived outside Moon-Face's house at the top of the Tree very soon afterwards. Moon-Face and Silky were waiting for them. 'Is old Saucepan coming?' asked Joe.

'Hi, Saucepan, do you want to come?' shouted Moon-Face, leaning down the Tree.

Saucepan was with Watzisname. Amazingly, he heard what Moon-Face said and shouted back:

'Yes, I'll come, But where to?'

'Up the ladder!' yelled Moon-Face. 'Hurry!'

So Saucepan came with them and in a little while they all stood in the Land of Magic Medicines. It was just as peculiar as every land that came to the top of the Faraway Tree!

It didn't seem to be a land at all! When the children had climbed up the ladder to the top, they found themselves in what looked like a great big factory – a place where all kinds of pills, medicines, bandages and so on were made. Goblins and gnomes, pixies and fairies were as busy as could be, stirring great pots over curious green fires, pouring medicines into shining bottles, and counting out pills to put into coloured boxes.

In one corner a goblin was stirring a purple mixture in a yellow bowl. Beth looked at it.

'It's a kind of ointment,' she said to the others. 'I wonder what it's for.'

'It's to make bad legs strong again,' said the goblin,

stirring hard. 'Do you want some?'

'Well, I don't know anyone with bad legs,' said Beth. 'Thank you all the same. If I did I'd love to have some, because it would be marvellous to make somebody's bad legs better.'

A pixie near by was pouring some sparkling green medicine into bottles shaped like bubbles. The children and the others watched. It made a funny singing noise as it went in.

'What's that for?' asked Joe.

'Whoever takes this will always have shining eyes,' said the pixie. 'Shining, smiling eyes are the loveliest eyes in the world. Is it this medicine you have come for?'

'Well, no, not exactly,' said Joe. 'I'd like to have some, though.'

'Oh, your eyes *are* smiley eyes,' said the pixie, looking at him. 'This is for sad people, whose eyes have become dull. Come to me when you are an old man and your eyes cannot see very well. I will give you plenty then.'

'Oh,' said Joe. 'Well, I won't be here then! I've only just come on a short visit!'

Rick called to the others. 'Look!' he cried. 'Here's some really marvellous pills! Watch them being made!'

Everyone watched. It was most astonishing to see. First of all the pills were enormous – as large as footballs. A goblin blew on them with a pair of bellows out of which came green smoke, and they at once went down to the size of a cricket ball. He then splashed them with what looked like moonlight from a watering can. They went as small as marbles.

Then he blew on them gently – and they went as small as green peas, and each one jumped into a pill-box with a ping-ping-ping till the box was full.

'What are they for?' asked Rick.

'To make short people tall,' said the goblin. 'Some people hate being short. Well, these pills are made of big things – the shadow of a mountain – the height of a tree – the crash of a thunder storm – things like that – and they have the power to make anything or anyone grow.'

'Could I have some?' asked Rick eagerly.

'Take a boxful,' said the goblin. Rick took it. He read what was written on the lid.

'GROWING PILLS. ONE TO BE TAKEN THREE TIMES A DAY.'

Now Rick was not very tall for his age and he had always wanted to be big. He looked longingly at the pills. If he took three at once, maybe he would grow taller. That would be great!

He popped three of the pills into his mouth. He sucked them. They tasted so horrible that he swallowed them all in a hurry!

And goodness, WHAT a surprise when the others turned to speak to Rick. He was taller than their father! He was as tall as the ceiling in their cottage! He towered above them, looking down on them in alarm, for he hadn't expected to grow quite so much, or quite so quickly!

'Rick! You've been taking those Growing Pills!' cried Joe. 'Just the sort of stupid thing you *would* do! You're enormous! How in the world do you think you'll ever get down the hole in the cloud?'

'Oh, do something to help me!' begged Rick, who really was frightened to be so enormous. Everyone else looked so small. 'Joe, Moon-Face – what can I do? I'm still growing! I'll burst out of the roof in a minute!'

The goblins and pixies around suddenly noticed how fast Rick was growing. They began to shout and squeal.

'He'll break through the roof! He'll bring it down on top of us! Quick, stop him growing!'

XXI. SOME PECULIAR ADVENTURES

Rick was enormously tall. He had to bend down so that his head wouldn't touch the roof. The little people in the medicine factory rushed about, yelling and shouting.

'Fetch a ladder! Climb up it and give him some Go-Away Pills! Quick, quick!'

Somebody got a ladder and leaned it up against poor Rick.

A pixie ran up it on light feet. He carried a box of pills. He shouted to Rick:

'Open your mouth!'

Rick opened his mouth. The pixie meant to throw one pill inside, but in his excitement he threw the whole box. Rick swallowed it!

And at once he began to grow small again! Down he went and down and down. He got to his own size and grinned with delight. But he didn't stop there. He went smaller and smaller and smaller – and at last he couldn't be seen! It was a terrible shock to everyone.

'He's gone!' said Beth in horror. 'He's so small that he can't be seen! Rick! Rick! Where are you?'

A tiny squeak answered her from under a big chair. Beth bent down and looked there. She couldn't see a thing.

'Listen, Rick,' she said. 'I've got a pill bottle here. Come running over to me and put yourself in it. Then

we shall at least know where you are, even if we can't see you. And maybe we can get you right if only we've got you safely somewhere.'

A tiny squeaking sound came from the pill bottle after a minute, so Beth knew that Rick had done as he had been told and got into the bottle. But she couldn't see anyone there at all. She put on the lid, afraid that Rick might fall out.

She stood up and stared round at the wondering little folk there. 'What can we do for someone gone too small?' she asked. 'Haven't you any medicine for that?'

'It will have to be very specially made,' said a pixie. 'We can't give him the Grow-Fast Mixture because he's really too small for that. We'll have to prepare a special little bath of powerful medicine, and get him to go into it. Then maybe he will grow back to his own size. But he shouldn't have meddled with our magic medicine. It's dangerous.'

'Rick's so silly,' said Joe. 'He always seems to get himself and other people into trouble! I do hope you can make him right again. I wouldn't want him to live in a pill bottle all his life.'

'We'll do our best to get him right,' said the little folk, and they began to shout here and there, calling for the most peculiar things to make the bath for Rick.

'The whisk of a mouse's tail!' cried one.

'The sneeze of a frog!' cried another.

356

'The breath of a summer wind!' cried a third.

And as the children watched small goblins came running with little boxes and tins.

'What peculiar things their medicines are made of!' said Joe. 'Well, let's leave them to it, shall we? I'd like to wander round this big factory a bit more. Come on, Saucepan.'

Saucepan was very deaf because there was such a noise going on all the time. Fires were sizzling under big pots. Medicines were being poured into bottles with gurgles and splashes. Pans were being stirred with a clatter. Saucepan couldn't hear a word that was said – and it was because of that that he made his great mistake.

He stopped by a goblin who was pouring a beautiful blue liquid into a little jar. It shone so brightly that it caught Saucepan's eye at once.

'That's lovely,' he said to the goblin. 'What's it for?'

'To make a nose grow,' said the goblin.

'To make a rose grow!' said Saucepan in delight. 'Oh, I'd like some of that. If I had that I could make roses grow on the Faraway Tree all round Mister Watzisname's branch. He *would* like that!'

'I said to make a NOSE grow!' said the goblin.

'I heard you the first time,' said Saucepan. 'It would be lovely to be able to grow roses. Do I have to drink it?'

'Yes – if you want your nose to grow,' said the goblin, looking at Saucepan's nose.

Saucepan kept on hearing him wrong. He felt quite certain that the beautiful medicine was to make roses grow. He thought that if he drank it he would be able to make roses grow anywhere! That would be marvellous. So he took a jar of the medicine and drank it all up before the goblin could stop him.

'Now I'll make the roses grow out of my kettles and pans!' said Saucepan, pleased. 'Grow, roses, grow!'

But they didn't grow, of course. It was his poor old nose that grew! It suddenly shot out, long and pink, and Saucepan stared at it in surprise.

The others looked at him in amazement.

'Saucepan! What has happened to your nose?' cried Joe. 'It's as big as an elephant's trunk!'

'He *would* drink it!' said the goblin in dismay, showing the children the empty jar. 'I told him it was to make a nose grow – but he kept on saying it was to grow roses, not noses. He's quite mad.'

'No, he's just deaf,' said Joe. 'Oh, poor old Saucepan! He'll have to tie his nose round his waist soon. It's down to his feet already!'

'I can cure it,' said the goblin with a grin. 'I've got a disappearing medicine. I'll just rub his nose with it till it disappears back to the right size. I think you ought to watch him a bit, if he goes about hearing things all wrong goodness knows what may happen to him!'

Saucepan was crying tears that rolled down his funny long nose. The goblin took a box of blue ointment and began to rub the end of Saucepan's nose with it. It disappeared as soon as the ointment touched it. The goblin worked hard, rubbing gradually all up the long nose until there was nothing leftbut Saucepan's own pointed nose. Then he stopped rubbing.

'Cheer up!' he said. 'It's gone, and only your own

nose is left. My, you did look peculiar! I've never seen anyone drink a whole bottle of that nose medicine before!'

A shout came from behind the watching children. 'Where's that tiny boy in the pill bottle? We've got the bath ready for him now.'

Everyone rushed to where there was a tiny bath filled with steaming yellow water that smelt of cherries. Beth took the pill bottle from her pocket and opened it.

A squeaking came from the bottle at once. Rick was still there, too small to be seen! But, thank goodness, his voice hadn't quite disappeared, or the others would never have known if he was there or not!

'Get into this bath, Rick,' said Beth. 'You will soon be all right again, then.'

There came the tiniest splash in the yellow water. It changed at once to pink. A squeaking came from the bath and bubbles rose to the surface. Then suddenly the children could see Rick! At first it was a bit misty and cloudy – then gradually the mist thickened and took the shape of a very, very small boy.

'He's coming back, he's coming back!' cried Joe. 'Look, he's getting bigger!'

As Rick grew bigger, the bath grew, too. It was most astonishing to watch. Soon the bath was as big as an ordinary bath, and there stood Rick in it, his own size again, his clothes soaked with the pink water. He grinned at them through the steam.

'Just the same old cheerful Rick!' said Beth gladly. 'Oh, Rick, you gave us such a fright!'

'Step out of the bath, quick!' cried the pixie nearby.

'You're ready to be dried!'

Rick jumped out of the bath – just in time, too, for it suddenly folded itself up, grew a pair of wings, and disappeared out of a big window near by!

'Dry him!' cried the pixie, and threw some strange towels to the children and Moon-Face. They seemed to be alive and were very warm. They rubbed themselves all over Rick, squeezing his clothes as they rubbed, until in a few minutes he was perfectly dry. But his clothes were rather a curious pink colour.

'That can't be helped,' said the pixie. 'That always happens.'

'Well, I suppose I look a bit funny, but I don't mind,' said Rick. 'Goodness, that was a peculiar adventure.'

'A bit too peculiar for me!' said Joe. 'Now see you don't get into any more trouble, Rick, or I'll never bring you into any strange land again. I never knew anyone like you for doing things you shouldn't. Now, look here everyone – I vote we try and get some medicine for Mother, and then we'll go. Frannie is waiting patiently for us to go back, and I really think we'd better go before Rick or Saucepan do anything funny again.'

'What medicine do you want?' asked a goblin kindly. 'What is wrong with your mother?'

'Well, we really don't know,' said Rick. 'She just lies in bed and looks white and weak, and she worries dreadfully about everything.'

'Oh, well, I should just take a bottle of Get-Well Medicine,' said the goblin. 'That will be just the thing.'

'It sounds fine,' said Joe. The goblin poured a bubbling yellow liquid into a big bottle and gave it to Joe. He put it carefully into his pocket.

'Thank you,' he said. 'Now, come along everyone. We're going.'

'Oh, Joe – there's a medicine here for making teeth pearly,' said Saucepan, pulling at Joe's arm. 'Just let me take some.'

'Saucepan, that's for making hair CURLY!' said Joe. 'You've heard wrong again. Don't try it. Do you want curls growing down to your feet? Now take my arm and don't let go till we're safely back in the Tree. If I don't look after you, you'd have a nose like an elephant's, curly hair down to your toes, and goodness knows what else!'

They were not very far from the hole in the cloud, and they were soon climbing down the ladder, leaving behind them the Strange Land of Magic Medicines. Joe was very careful of the bottle in his pocket.

'Now we'll go straight home,' he said. 'I'm simply LONGING to give dear old Mother a dose of this magic medicine. It will be so lovely to see her looking well again and rushing round the house as she always did!'

XXII. WATZISNAME HAS SOME STRANGE NEWS

Frannie was delighted to see Joe, Beth and Rick back. 'Mother doesn't seem quite so well,' she said. 'She says she has such a bad headache. Did you get some medicine for her, Joe?'

'Yes, I did,' said Joe, showing Frannie the big bottle. 'It's a Get-Well medicine. Let's give Mother some now. It smells of plums, so it should be rather nice.'

They went into Mother's bedroom and Joe took a glass and poured out two teaspoonfuls of the strange medicine.

'Well, I hope it's all right, Joe dear,' said Mother, holding out her hand for it. 'I must say it smells most delicious – like plum pies cooking in the oven!'

It tasted simply lovely, too, Mother said. She lay back on her pillows and smiled at the children. 'Yes, I do believe I feel better already!' she said. 'My head isn't aching so badly.'

Well, that medicine was simply marvellous. By the time the evening came Mother was sitting up knitting. By the next morning she was eating a huge breakfast and laughing and joking with everyone. Father was very pleased.

'We'll soon have her up now!' he said. And he was right! By the time the bottle of Get-Well Medicine was only half-finished, Mother was up and about again, singing merrily as she washed and ironed. It was lovely to hear her.

'We'll put the rest of the bottle of magic medicine away,' he said. 'I don't need it any more – but it would be very useful if anyone else is ill.'

A whole week went by and the children heard nothing of their friends in the Faraway Tree. They were very busy helping their parents, and they wondered sometimes what land was at the top of the Tree now.

'If it was a very nice Land Silky and Moon-Face would be sure to let us know,' said Joe. 'So I don't expect it's anything exciting.'

One evening, when the children were in bed, they heard a little rattling sound against their windows. They sat up at once.

'It's Silky and Moon-Face!' whispered Joe.

'They've come to say there's a lovely Land at the top of the Tree,' said Rick, excited. The boys went into the girls' room to see if they were awake. They were looking out of the window.

'It isn't Silky or Moon-Face,' whispered Beth. 'I think it's old Watzisname!'

'Goodness! Whatever has *he* come for!' cried Joe.

'Sh!' said Frannie. 'You'll wake Mother. Whoever it is doesn't seem to want to come any nearer. Let's creep down and see if it *is* Watzisname.'

So they put on their dressing-gowns and crept downstairs. They went into the garden and whispered loudly: 'Who's there? What is it?'

'It's me, Watzisname,' said a voice, and Mister Watzisname

came nearer to them. He looked terribly worried.

'What's the matter?' asked Joe.

'Have you seen Silky, Moon-Face or Saucepan lately?' asked Watzisname.

'Not since we all went to the Land of Magic Medicines,' said Joe. 'Why? Aren't they in the Faraway Tree?'

'They've *disappeared*,' said Watzisname. 'I haven't seen them for days. They went – and never even said good-bye to me!'

'Oh, Watzisname! But what could have happened to them?' asked Beth. 'They must have gone up into some Land, that moved away from the top of the Tree – and that's why you haven't seen them.'

'No, that's not it,' said Watzisname. 'The same land has been there ever since the Land of Medicines moved away. It's the Land of Tempers. I'm quite sure that Moon-Face and the others wouldn't visit it, because it's well known that everyone there is always in a bad temper. No – they've gone – vanished – disappeared. And I DO so miss dear old Saucepan. It makes me very, very sad.'

'Oh, Watzisname, this is very worrying,' said Beth, feeling upset. 'Whatever can we do?'

'I suppose you wouldn't come back to the Faraway Tree with me, would you, and help me to look for them?' asked Watzisname. 'I feel so lonely there. And, you know, somebody else has taken Moon-Face's house and Silky's house, too. They have come from the Land of Tempers, and I'm so frightened of them that I just simply don't dare to go near them.'

'Good gracious! This is very bad news,' said Joe.

364

'Somebody else in Moon-Face's nice little house – and someone in Silky's house, too! Most extraordinary! I'm surprised you didn't hear anything, Watzisname. You know, I'm sure Moon-Face would have made a lot of fuss and bother if anyone had turned him out of his house. Are you sure you didn't hear anything?'

'Not a thing,' said Watzisname, gloomily. 'You know how I snore, don't you? I expect I was fast asleep as usual, and I shouldn't even have heard if they had called to me for help.'

'Well, listen, Watzisname, we can't possibly come tonight,' said Joe. 'Mother likes us to get the breakfast, and since she has been ill we make her have her breakfast in bed. But we will come just as soon as we can after breakfast. Will that do?'

'Oh yes,' said Watzisname, gratefully. 'That's marvellous. I shan't go back to the Tree tonight. It's too lonely without the others. May I sleep in that shed over there?'

'You can sleep on the sofa downstairs,' said Joe. 'Come in with us. I'll get you a rug. Then we can all start off together tomorrow morning.'

So that night old Watzisname slept on the sofa. He snored a lot, and Mother woke up once and wondered what in the wide world the noise was. But she thought it must be the cat, and soon went off to sleep again.

Next morning the children asked if they might go off with Watzisname. They explained what had happened.

'Well I don't know that I like you going off if something bad has happened,' said Mother. 'I don't want anything to happen to *you*.'

'I'll look after everyone,' said Joe. 'You can trust me, Mother; really you can. We'll be back soon.'

So Mother said they could go. They set off to the Enchanted Wood with Watzisname, feeling rather excited. Whatever *could* have happened to Silky and the others?

They climbed up the Faraway Tree. It was growing peaches that day, and they were really delicious. Rick ate far more than the others, of course, and nearly got left behind.

They came to Silky's house. The door was shut. From inside came a stamping and a roaring.

'That's one of the people from the Land of Tempers,' said Watzisname in a whisper. 'They're always losing their tempers, you know, whenever anything goes wrong. I just simply DAREN'T knock at the door and ask where Silky is.'

'Well, let's go on up to Moon-Face's,' said Joe, feeling that he didn't really want to go knocking at the door either.

So up they went, and at last came to Moon-Face's door. That was shut, too, and from inside came a banging and shouting.

'Gosh, they have got bad tempers, haven't they!' said Joe. 'I'm quite certain I shan't go visiting the Land of Tempers! Let's peep in at the window and see who's there.'

So they peeped in, and saw a round, fat little man, with large ears, a mop of dark hair, fierce eyes, and a very bad-tempered look on his face. He was looking for something on the floor.

'Where's it gone?' he shouted. 'You bad, wicked button! Where did you roll to? Don't you know that I want to put you on my coat again? I'll stamp you into a hundred bits when I find you!'

Joe giggled. 'If he does that it won't be much good trying to sew it on his coat!' he said.

Just then the little man looked up and saw the four children peering in at him. He got up in a rage, flew to the door and flung it open.

'How dare you pry and peep!' he yelled, stamping first one foot at them and then the other. 'How dare you look in at my window!'

'It isn't your window,' said Joe. 'This house belongs to a friend of ours, called Moon-Face. You'd better get out of it before he comes back, or he will be very angry.'

'Pooh! You don't know what you're talking about!' cried the bad-tempered man. 'I'm Sir Stamp-a-Lot,

and this is *my* house. My cousin, Lady Yell-Around, has taken the house a bit lower down. We've come to live in this tree.'

'But don't you belong to the Land of Tempers?' asked Joe. 'Are you allowed to leave your own land?'

'Mind your own business,' said Sir Stamp-a-Lot. 'MIND YOUR OWN BUSINESS!'

'Well, it *is* my business to find out what you are doing in my friend's house,' said Joe firmly. 'Now, you just tell me what has happened to Moon-Face – yes, and Silky and the old Saucepan Man, too.'

'Moon-Face said I could have his house whilst he went to live for a while in the Land of Tempers,' said Sir Stamp-a-Lot, doing a bit more stamping. 'And Silky said the same. The old Saucepan Man went with them.'

'Well, I just don't believe you,' said Watzisname suddenly. 'Moon-Face told me that the Land of Tempers had come, and he said nothing in the world would make him go there. So you are telling fibs.'

That sent Sir Stamp-a-Lot into such a rage that he nearly stamped the bark off the tree branch he stood on! 'How dare you talk to me like that?' he cried. 'I'll pull your hair! I'll pinch your noses! I'll scratch your ears!'

'What a nice, kind, pleasant person you are,' said Joe. 'What a beautiful nature you have! What a sweet, charming friend you would make!'

This made Sir Stamp-a-Lot so angry that he kicked hard at Joe, who dodged. Stamp-a-Lot lost his balance and fell. He fell down through the tree, yelling loudly.

'Quick!' said Joe. 'He'll be back in a minute; but we

might just have time to pop into Moon-Face's house and see if there is any message from him!'

They all crowded into the little round house and hunted hard. Wherever could their three friends be? It was too puzzling for words!

XXIII. THE LAND OF TEMPERS

The four children and Mister Watzisname hunted in every corner of Moon-Face's house, but there was no message anywhere from their friends.

'I say – that's old Stamp-a-Lot coming back,' said Frannie. 'I can hear him shouting. Let's get out, quick!'

'We can go down the slippery-slip,' said Joe. But he was wrong! The slippery-slip was stuffed up with all kinds of things – cushions, boughs, carpets, leaves – and nobody could possibly get down it. The children were all staring at it, puzzled, when Sir Stamp-a-Lot came back.

And, my goodness, what a rage he was in! He had bumped his head and his back in falling down the tree, and he had a tremendous bruise on his left cheek. He came in bellowing like a bull!

'How dare you go into my house!' he stormed. 'How dare you pry into my business! I'll throw you out! I'll throw you out!'

He tried to get hold of Frannie, but Joe and Rick stopped him. 'We're five to one,' said Joe. 'You might as well keep your temper, or we may do a bit of throwing out, too. We're going because we can only get fibs out of you, and it's quite plain that our friends are not here. But you'll feel very sorry for yourself when we do find our friends and we all come back to tell you what we think!'

Stamp-a-Lot was furious. He began to throw things after the children and Watzisname as soon as they had gone out of the house. Crash! That was the clock. Clatter! That was a picture. Bang! That was a chair!

'Oh dear! Poor Moon-Face won't find a single thing in his house when he gets home,' said Joe, dodging a soup plate that came flying past his head. 'Now, what shall we do next? Perhaps we had better go down to Silky's house and see if we can find anything from Lady Yell-Around or whatever her name is.'

Nobody really wanted to see Lady Yell-Around – but they saw her before they expected to. As they climbed down to where Dame Washalot lived, they heard a fierce quarrel going on.

'You emptied your dirty water down on me just as I was going shopping!' yelled an angry voice. 'You did, you did, you did!'

Then came Dame Washalot's voice. 'I did, I did, I did, did I? Well, I'm glad! If people can't look out for my washing water, it's their own fault!'

'Look how wet I am; look at me!' came the other voice.

'I don't want to look at you, you're a most unpleasant person,' said Dame Washalot. 'Now, look out – here comes some more water!'

There was a sound of splashing – and then squeals and screams as Lady Yell-Around got the whole lot on top of her. The children began to giggle. They climbed down to where Dame Washalot was standing by her empty tub, grinning as she looked down the tree. Lady Yell-Around was hurriedly climbing down, dripping wet, her shopping basket still in her hand.

'Dame Washalot – have you heard anything about Silky and the others?' asked Beth.

'Not a thing,' said the old dame. 'All I know is that that bad-tempered creature who calls herself Lady Yell-Around has taken Silky's house and says that Silky said she could have it, because she, Silky, wanted to go and live for a while in the Land of Tempers – a thing I don't believe at all, for a sweeter-tempered person than little Silky you could never find!'

'It's very funny,' said Joe, frowning. 'Silky, Moon-Face and Saucepan disappear – and these two horrible people take their places. There's only one thing to do. We'd better just pop up into the Land of Tempers to see if by any chance they *have* gone there.'

'Well, that's dangerous,' said Dame Washalot. 'Once you lose your temper up there you have to live there for always. And you might easily lose your temper with the cross lot of people who live there. I can't think how it is that these two have been able to leave.'

'It does sound dangerous,' said Joe. 'But I think we could all keep our tempers, you know, if we knew we had to. Anyway, I simply don't know what else to do. Perhaps it would be best if I just went by myself – then the others wouldn't have to risk getting into danger.'

But the others wouldn't hear of Joe going by himself. 'We share in this,' said Rick. 'If you can go to the Land of Tempers and keep your temper, we can, too. We need only go up and ask if Silky and the others are there. If they're not, we can come back straight away.'

'Well, then, we'd better go now,' said Joe.

So up the Tree they went, and then up the ladder through the hole in the cloud – and into the Land of Tempers.

Well, it *was* a funny Land! There was such a lot of shouting and quarrelling going on – such crashing noises made by people throwing things in a rage – such a stamping and yelling!

'Goodness! I vote we don't stay here long!' said Joe, dodging to miss a bag that someone had thrown. 'Look! Let's ask that man over there if he has seen Silky or the others.'

So he asked him. But he glared at them and answered rudely.

'Don't come bothering me with your silly questions! Can't you see I'm in a hurry?'

He pushed Joe roughly, and the little boy at once felt angry. He was just about to push the man roughly too when Frannie whispered to him:

'Joe! Don't lose your temper! Smile, quickly, smile!'

So Joe made himself smile, for he knew that no one can really lose his temper when he is smiling. The man glared at him and went away.

'Well, I can see that it would be jolly difficult to live here without getting angry almost every minute of the day,' said Joe. 'Hey there – do you know anything about our friends, Silky, Moon-Face and Saucepan?'

The boy he was calling to stopped and put out his tongue at Joe. 'Yah!' he said. 'Do you think I'm here to answer your questions, funny-face?'

'No, I don't,' said Joe. 'But I thought perhaps you might be polite enough to help me.'

373

The boy made a lot of rude faces at all of them and then pulled Frannie's hair very sharply before he ran off.

Rick and Joe felt angry, because they saw the tears come into Frannie's eyes. They began to run after the boy, shouting.

'Rick! Joe! Come back!' cried Watzisname. 'You are losing your tempers again.'

'So we are,' said the boys, and they stopped and made themselves look pleasant.

Watzisname went to meet them, and as he went two naughty little boys ran by. One put out his foot, and poor old Watzisname tripped over it, bang, on his nose. The boys stood and laughed till they cried.

Watzisname got up, his face one big frown. 'I'll teach you to trip me up!' he cried. 'I'll . . .'

'Smile, Watzisname, smile!' cried Beth. 'Don't look like that. You're losing your temper. Smile!'

And Watzisname had to smile, but it was very, very difficult. The two bad boys ran off. The children went walking on, telling themselves that they MUST remember, whatever happened, not to lose their tempers.

They met a very grand-looking fellow, wearing a gold chain about his shoulders. They thought he must be one of the head men of the Land of Tempers, and nobody liked to speak to him. But suddenly Frannie called to him.

'Do you know where Sir Stamp-a-Lot and Lady Yell-Around are?' she said. The haughty-looking man stopped in surprise.

'No, I don't,' he said. 'They have disappeared, and I am very angry about it.

Do *you* know where they are?'

'Yes, I do,' said Frannie boldly.

'Where are they, then?' asked the man.

'I'll tell you the answer to your question if you'll answer one of mine,' said Frannie.

'Very well,' said the man.

'Have our friends, Silky, Moon-Face and Saucepan come to live here for a while?' asked Frannie.

'Certainly not,' said the man. 'I've never heard of them. No one is allowed to live here unless they first lose their tempers and then get permission from me to take a house. And now – tell me where Stamp-a-Lot and Yell-Around are.'

'They have escaped from your Land and are living in the Faraway Tree,' said Frannie.

'But they are not allowed to do that!' cried the head man. 'How dare they? I didn't even know we were near the Faraway Tree. Wait till I catch them! I'll shake them till their teeth rattle. I'll scold them till they shiver like jellies.'

'Well, that would be very nice,' said Frannie. 'Goodbye. We're going.'

The others joined her as she ran towards the hole in the cloud. 'How brave and clever you are, Frannie!' said Joe. 'I should never have thought of all that! I'm quite, quite sure that Silky and the others aren't up here.'

'I was very afraid of that head man,' said Frannie. 'I just couldn't speak a word more to him. Hurry up – let's get back to the Tree. Silky isn't here. I can't imagine where they all are. There's something very, very mysterious about it.'

They all climbed down the ladder to the Tree, thankful to leave behind the horrible Land of Tempers. They went down to Silky's house and peeped in at the window. Lady Yell-Around wasn't there.

'I vote we go in and have a look round,' said Joe. But the door was locked and the key had been taken. Bother!

'Well, I'm sure I don't know WHAT to do,' said Joe. 'But we simply must do SOME-thing!'

XXIV. A MOST EXCITING TIME

As the children stood gloomily outside Silky's house, a voice called to them from further down.

'Is that you, Watzisname? Any news of our missing friends?'

'That's the Angry Pixie,' said Joe. 'Let's go down and talk to him.'

The Angry Pixie was looking very miserable.

'I can't understand all this mystery,' he said. 'I saw Silky and the others a few days ago – and then they suddenly disappear like smoke without a cry or a yell. It's funny.'

'We've just been up in the Land of Tempers,' said Frannie. 'But they're not there.'

'I thought of going up there to see,' said the Angry Pixie, 'but I was so afraid I'd lose my temper and have to stay there forever. You know what a temper I've got.'

'Yes,' said Joe. 'You certainly mustn't *dream* of going up there. You'd never come back.'

They sat there, looking at one another – and then they all pricked up their ears. They could hear a very peculiar noise.

Boom, boom, boom! Knock, knock, knock! Boom, boom, boom!

'Whatever's that?' said Frannie, looking all round. 'And where is it coming from?'

'I can't imagine,' said the Angry Pixie. 'I keep on hearing it. I heard it yesterday and last night and this morning. It just goes on and on.'

Everyone listened. The noise stopped and then went on again. Boom, boom, boom! Knock, knock, knock!

'Where *does* it come from?' said Beth.

'From the inside of the tree,' said Watzisname, listening hard. 'I'm sure of that!'

'Do you think – do you possibly think – that it might be Silky and the others – somewhere inside the tree?' said Frannie suddenly.

Boom, boom, boom! Knock, knock, knock! There it was again!

'I believe Frannie's right. I think Silky, Moon-Face and Saucepan are prisoners inside the slippery-slip. Stamp-a-Lot must have pushed them down there, and then stuffed up the hole with all those things,' said Watzisname.

'But they would have shot out of the trap-door at the bottom,' said Rick.

'We'll go down and open it and see if anything has been put there to stuff that up too,' said Joe. 'Come on, everyone.'

So they all went down to the tree to where the trap-door was at the bottom. Joe opened it. He looked inside and then gave a shout.

'This end is all stuffed up, too! These two horrible people from the Land of Tempers have got Silky and the others in there, I'm sure. Look – there's all kinds of things stuffed in here. The poor things can't get up or down. They're trapped!'

'Well, let's pull everything out and set them free!' said Rick, and he tugged at a great ball of moss. But it wouldn't move!

Everyone had a turn at tugging and pulling – but it was no use at all. Not a thing would move.

'They've stuffed everything in and then put a spell on it to make it stay where it is,' said Watzisname at last. 'It's no good. We'll never be able to move a thing. Look – there's Lady Yell-Around coming back from her shopping. We'll just see if we can make her do something about this!'

But that wasn't any good either. Lady Yell-Around pretended that she didn't know anything about the stopped-up hole.

'What's the good of shouting at me and asking me something I don't know anything about?' she said. 'You go and ask old Stamp-a-Lot. He'll tell you what you want to know.'

'No, he won't,' said Joe. 'He's just as big a fibber as you are.'

Anyway, no one wanted to see Stamp-a-Lot again. He was such a bad-tempered person. They all climbed back to the Angry Pixie's house, sat down, and looked gloomily at each other.

'*Can't* get in at the top of the slippery-slip, and *can't* get in at the bottom,' said Joe. 'How in the world can we rescue poor Silky and the others? It's simply dreadful.'

'They'll be starving!' said Frannie, beginning to cry. 'Oh, Joe, do think of something!'

But nobody could think of anything at all. It was only when the woodpecker flew by to go to his hole in

the tree that any idea came – and then Joe jumped up with his eyes shining.

'I know! I know!' he cried. 'Let's ask the woodpecker to help us.'

'But how could a bird help?' said Rick.

'Well, a woodpecker pecks holes in wood to make his nest,' said Joe. 'I've seen them pecking hard with their strong beaks. They make a kind of drumming noise, and can peck out quite a big hole in no time. If we asked him, I'm sure the woodpecker could peck a hole at the back of this room, right into the slippery-slip – and then we could pull Silky, Moon-Face and Saucepan through the hole.'

'Oh, that really does sound a marvellous idea!' said Frannie, beaming. 'Let's call him now.'

So they went outside on to a big branch of the Faraway Tree and called to the woodpecker.

'Woodpecker! Come here a minute!'

The woodpecker stared round in surprise. He was cleaning his wing feathers by running each one carefully through his beak. He was a lovely bird with his bright, red-splashed head. He spread his wings and flew down.

'What's the matter?' he asked.

Joe told him. The bird listened with his head on one

side and his bright eyes shining.

'Do you think you could possibly help us to rescue Silky and the others by pecking a hole at the back of the Angry Pixie's house?' said Joe, when he came to the end of his story. 'You have such a strong beak.'

'Yes, I know I have,' said the woodpecker. 'The only thing is I generally only peck rotten wood – that's easy to peck away, you know. It just falls to pieces. But good, growing wood like the trunk of the Faraway Tree – well, that's different. That's very hard, indeed. It would take me ages to peck a large hole through that.'

'Oh, dear!' sighed Joe. 'I'm so disappointed. We daren't let Silky and the others stay in the slippery-slip too long in case they starve. There's nothing to eat down there, you know. Whatever are we to do?'

Everybody thought hard. It was the woodpecker who had an idea first.

'I know!' he said. 'I could fetch my cousins who live in the Enchanted Wood in another tree – and maybe if there were three or four of us all pecking hard together we could make a good hole quite quickly. I know I couldn't make one by myself without taking two or three days – but a lot of us working together might do it easily.'

'Oh, good!' cried everyone. 'Go and get your cousins, there's a dear. Hurry!'

The woodpecker flew off. Everyone waited impatiently. They heard the noise from the

381

inside of the Tree again. Boom, boom, boom! Knock, knock, knock!

'Poor things!' said Beth, tears in her eyes. 'It must be so dreadful inside there in the dark, with nothing to eat or drink.'

After about ten minutes the woodpecker came back, and with him he brought *five* others! They were all woodpeckers, with bright, red-splashed heads, strong-looking birds with powerful beaks.

'Oh splendid!' cried Joe, and he took them all into the Angry Pixie's little house. 'Peck away at the back, here.'

The six birds stood in a row and began to peck as close to one another as they could. Peck, peck, peck! They pecked so hard and so very fast that they made a curious drumming noise that echoed through the little house. R-r-r-r-r-r-r-r-r-r-r-r-r-!

R-r-r-r-r-r-r-r-r-r-r-r-! R-r-r-r-r-r-r-r-r-r-r-r-!

They pecked hard for about an hour and then stopped for a rest. Joe pressed close to see how they were getting on. To his joy he saw that a small hole had been pecked right through into the slippery-slip. He asked the Angry Pixie for a torch and shone it through the hole. Yes – there was no doubt about it, the woodpeckers had got right through the tree trunk just there.

'Now you've only got to make the hole bigger!' cried Joe happily. 'Peck away, woodpeckers, peck away! You are doing marvellously!'

XXV. EVERYTHING COMES RIGHT

After a good rest the six woodpeckers set to work again at the hole they had made. R-r-r-r-r-r-r-r! went their strong beaks, drumming away at the wood. Everyone watched to see the hole getting bigger and bigger. Then a voice floated up, singing a mournful song:

> *Two kettles for Silky,*
> *Two saucepans for me,*
> *Two dishes for Moon-Face,*
> *We're sad as can be!*

'That's the old Saucepan Man!' said Joe in delight. 'Did you hear his silly song? That's to tell us they are all there. Move aside a bit, woodpeckers, and let me call to them.'

The woodpeckers made room for Joe by the hole. He stuck his head through it and yelled loudly: 'Silky! Moon-Face! Saucepan! We're going to rescue you. We'll pull you through a hole we've made at the back of the Angry Pixie's room.'

There was a squeal of delight from Silky, a shout from Moon-Face, and a clatter of pans from Saucepan.

'We're coming, we're coming!' yelled Moon-Face. 'We've got a rope to come up by. We shan't be long. Is the hole big enough to squeeze through?'

'Not yet,' shouted back Joe. 'But the woodpeckers are just going to set to work again, and they'll soon have made it bigger.'

'R-r-r-r-r-r-r-r-r! R-r-r-r-r-r-r-r-r! went the woodpeckers' strong beaks, and the hole grew larger and larger. At last it really was big enough for anyone to get through. Joe leaned through it, his torch shining into the slippery-slip. He saw a light gleaming a little way down, and noticed a rope shaking near by, as if someone was holding on to it.

'They're coming up,' he said to the others. 'They've got a light of some sort, too. Oh! – it's a candle. I can see Moon-Face now. He's the first. And he's helping Silky up. The old Saucepan Man is behind. They'll soon be here! Angry Pixie, put on a kettle to boil some water. I expect they would like some hot chocolate or something. And have you got anything to eat?'

'I've got Pop Cakes and Google Buns,' said the Angry Pixie, looking into a tin. 'They'll like those.'

Moon-Face at last hauled himself right up to the hole. His round face looked white and rather worried – but he gave Joe a grin as usual. 'Help Silky through first,' he said.

Joe and Rick pulled Silky through the hole. She looked pale, too, but how glad she was to see all her friends! She flung her arms round Beth and Frannie, and they all cried tears of joy down one another. Then Moon-Face squeezed through the hole, and last of all the old Saucepan Man, though he had to take off a few pans before he could get through!

'We never, never thought we'd be rescued!' said

Moon-Face. 'We'd quite given up hope. We kept knocking, and banging, hoping someone would hear us.'

'Yes, we did hear you,' said Joe. 'That's what made us think you might be trapped in the slippery-slip. But Moon-Face, how did you get there? What happened?'

'Wait a minute – let them have something to eat and drink first,' said Watzisname. 'They must be terribly hungry, not having had anything to eat and drink for so long.'

'Oh, we had plenty,' said Moon-Face, 'We didn't starve. But I'll tell you all about it.'

Everyone settled down to hear his story.

'You see, one morning this week, Silky, Saucepan and I were sitting up in my house talking,' began Moon-Face, 'and suddenly we saw two people from the Land of Tempers looking in at us.'

'Yes – Sir Stamp-a-Lot and Lady Yell-Around!' said Joe. '*We* know them!'

'Well, they looked very fiercely at us,' said Moon-Face, 'and they told us that they wanted to leave the Land of Tempers because the head-man was very angry with them about something. I think they had broken his windows in a temper. Well, they had escaped, and they meant to live in the Faraway Tree. They had found out by accident that their Land was over it, you see.'

'And they wanted your house!' cried Rick.

'Yes,' said Moon-Face. 'They had been down the Tree and seen that Silky's house was empty, because Silky was up here with me, and had taken that for themselves. At least Yell-Around meant to have it for herself. And Stamp-a-Lot meant to have mine.'

'And they said they had stopped up the trap-door at the bottom,' said Silky, 'and they meant to push us down the slippery-slip, and then stop up the hole in Moon-Face's room, so that we would be prisoners in the slide!'

'Well, you can guess how frightened we were!' said Moon-Face. 'Old Saucepan heard it all because Stamp-a-Lot shouted so loudly. And the clever old thing began to stuff his kettles and saucepans with food from my larder, and some candles, too, and matches – and a rope. I couldn't think what he was doing!'

'So, of course, when we were pushed into the slippery-slip we had plenty of food!' said Silky, putting her arm round Saucepan and hugging him. 'All because Saucepan was so clever.'

'He managed to tie the rope on to something so that we had that to climb up and down on if we wanted to,' said Moon-Face, 'and we found a little sort of cubby-hole halfway down where we could sit and eat and drink. We lit a candle, and then Silky thought of knocking and banging somewhere near to the Angry Pixie's house just in *case* you might be there and hear it.'

'Oh, we were so worried about you,' said Joe. 'We just simply didn't know WHAT to do! I'm so glad we thought of the woodpeckers. So you're really not very hungry or thirsty after all?'

'No, not very,' said Moon-Face. 'But some of the cake we brought got rather stale. Woodpeckers, would you like it?'

It was a treat for the woodpeckers and they pecked up the stale cake eagerly before they flew off. They had been very pleased to help.

'And now what are we going to do about turning Stamp-a-Lot and Yell-Around out of our houses?' said Silky. 'We can't all live with the Angry Pixie. His house is too small.'

Just as she said that there came the sound of shouting and yelling some way up the Tree. Everyone listened.

'That's Yell-Around, I'm sure,' said Silky. 'Let's go and see what's happening.'

Well, quite a lot was happening! About eight people from the Land of Tempers, with the head-man leading them, had come down the Tree to capture Stamp-a-Lot and Yell-Around! The head-man had remembered what Frannie had said, and had come to find the two escaped people. They had easily found Stamp-a-Lot, for he was asleep in Moon-Face's house, which was not far below the ladder leading up to the Land of Tempers.

But Yell-Around had not been so easily captured. She had seen the head-man climbing down the tree and had tried to escape. She had fallen, and had hung by one foot from a branch, yelling and squealing, because she was so afraid of falling. And the head-man picked her up by her foot and dragged her up the Tree like that.

Everyone watched in silence. Yell-Around was

squealing loudly in a terrible rage, but nobody took any notice.

'I won't go back to the Land of Tempers!' she yelled. 'I won't, I won't!'

But she had to! Up the ladder she was carried, upside down, and Stamp-a-Lot was pushed up, too.

'Serves them right,' said Moon-Face. 'Taking our houses from us and trapping us in the slippery-slip like that.'

They all went up. Moon-Face was sad to see his house so untidy and so many of his things broken. Everyone helped him to put it right. Then they all looked at the stuffed-up slippery-slip.

'The spell put on it will be gone now that those two horrible people have gone,' said Moon-Face. 'We can pull everything out.'

So it wasn't long before the hole was free of all the things that stuffed it up. Moon-Face shook out his cushions and grinned at the children.

'Well, everything's all right again,' he said. 'I'm so happy. It's lovely to have good friends like you.'

'We'd better get home now,' said Joe. 'We've been away a long time.'

'We can't slide down the slippery-slip because it's all stuffed up at the bottom,' said Frannie.

'Well, I'll send a message down to the red squirrel to clear it,' said Moon-Face. He whistled to a sparrow sitting on a nearby branch.

'Hey, little brown bird! Fly down to the red squirrel and tell him to open the trap-door at the bottom of the Tree, and clear the slide there, will you?' he asked. 'Tell him to do it at once.'

The sparrow flew off. Moon-Face handed round a tin of Toffee Shocks, and everyone took one. 'Just time to have one whilst the squirrel is clearing out the mess,' he said. 'Hark! I can hear the Land of Tempers moving off.'

Sure enough there came the noise of the Land moving away – the curious creaking, groaning noise that the strange lands always made when they went.

'What land will come next, I wonder?' said Joe.

'I know what it will be,' said Watzisname. 'I heard the head-man of the Land of Tempers say that the Land of Presents was due tomorrow.'

'Oooooh!' said Moon-Face, his eyes shining. 'We must all go to THAT! The Land of Presents! That's a marvellous land! We can all go and get as many presents as we like – just as if it was our birthday! Come tomorrow, will you? We'll all go! I can get some new carpets and things. Stamp-a-Lot spoilt so many of my belongings.'

'We'll come!' said Joe as he slid down the slippery-slip on a yellow cushion. 'We'll all come! RATHER!'

XXVI. THE LAND OF PRESENTS

Next day all the four children woke up feeling excited. It was so lovely when a really nice Land was at the top of the Faraway Tree. They had been to the Land of Birthdays before, and the Land of Take-What-You-Want. The Land of Goodies had been nice, and the Land of Do-As-You-Please. The Land of Presents sounded just as exciting!

'I wonder who gives the presents – and if you can choose them,' said Frannie. 'I'd like a necklace of blue beads.'

'And I'd like an enormous box of chocolates,' said Rick.

'You would!' said Joe. 'Anything to eat, and you're happy! I'd like a toy aeroplane that would fly from my hands and come back to them.'

'I shall bring something home for Mother,' said Beth. 'She wants a new purse. When can we start, Joe? I'm all ready.'

They set off about eleven o'clock, when they had done all their work. They were very excited. It was so lovely to think that Silky, Moon-Face and Saucepan were safe again and coming to enjoy the Land of Presents with them. Perhaps Watzisname, Saucepan and the Angry Pixie would come, too.

Well, everyone in the Faraway Tree had heard that the Land of Presents was at the top of the Tree that day; and, dear me, what a lot of people were steadily climbing up that morning! Brownies from the wood below, pixies and elves, even rabbits from their holes. The Angry Pixie's house was empty. He had gone already. The owl had gone, too, for he was not asleep in his little house as usual. Dame Washalot was gone, and no water came pouring down the Tree as the children climbed up.

'What a crowd there'll be!' said Joe happily. 'I hope we aren't too late. I hope there will be some presents left for us!'

'Oh, goodness! Let's hurry!' said Rick in alarm. He didn't want to lose the big box of chocolates he wanted!

Moon-Face, Silky and Saucepan were waiting most impatiently for them. 'Hurry, hurry!' cried Silky. 'The Land of Presents goes in an hour! It never stays long! Quick! Quick!'

Up the ladder they all went, talking and laughing in excitement. And, my goodness me, what a wonderful Land it was!

There were Christmas trees hung with presents of all kinds! There were lucky-dips full of exciting parcels. You had to dip in your hand for those. There were tables spread with the loveliest things. And, oh, the chattering and giggling that went on as people chose their presents and went off with them!

Rick marched up to a Christmas Tree because he saw hanging on it a most wonderful box of chocolates. A goblin was in charge of the Tree, and he smiled at Rick.

'I want that box of chocolates,' said Rick.

'Who is it for?' asked the goblin, getting out some scissors to cut down the box.

'For myself,' said Rick.

The goblin put away his scissors and shook his head gravely. 'This is the Land of Presents,' he said, 'Not the Land of Take-What-You-Want. You can only get things here to give to other people. I'm sorry. This isn't a selfish land at all.'

Rick looked very gloomy. He moved away. How stupid! He couldn't get anything for himself, then – and he had so much wanted the chocolates!

He saw a lovely blue necklace hanging on another tree, and he thought of Frannie. She had badly wanted a necklace of blue beads to go with her best blue frock. He went up to the goblin in charge of the tree.

'May I have that blue necklace to give to Frannie?' he asked.

'Where is she?' said the goblin, getting out his scissors. 'Call her.'

'Frannie, Frannie, come here!' cried Rick. 'I've got something for you!'

Frannie came running up. The goblin handed Rick the blue necklace and he gave it to Frannie.

'Put it round my neck for me and do up the clasp,' she said. 'Oh, Rick, thank you! It's lovely! Now – what present would you like me to get for *you*?'

'Oh, Frannie – I'd like that big box of chocolates,' said Rick, beaming all over his face. 'Would you like to get it for me?'

Frannie at once asked the goblin there for it and gave it to Rick. He undid the box and offered it to Frannie. 'Have a chocolate?' he said.

Well, as soon as the children knew how to set about getting the presents, they had a most wonderful time. All except dear old Saucepan, who would keep on getting the wrong presents for everyone, because he kept hearing things all wrong.

'What would you like for a present?' he asked Beth.

'Oh, Saucepan, I'd really like a frock!' said Beth.

Well, Saucepan thought she said 'clock', and off he went to find the biggest one in the Land. He managed to get one at last and put it on his back. It was a grandfather clock and so large that it quite bent him in two with its weight. Everyone stared in surprise as old Saucepan came up with it.

'Here you are, Beth dear – here's your clock,' said Saucepan, beaming at her.

'Saucepan, I said FROCK, not a *clock*,' said Beth, trying not to laugh. 'A FROCK!'

Poor Saucepan. He simply didn't know what to do with the clock after that, and in the end he left it in a field, striking all by itself very solemnly.

Then he asked Dame Washalot what *she* would like for a present.

'Well, I need a new iron,' said the old dame.

'I'll get you one,' said Saucepan. But, you know, he had heard quite wrong. He thought Dame Washalot said '*lion*', though if he had stopped to think one moment he would have known that she didn't want a lion – or a tiger or an elephant, either!

It was difficult to find a lion in the Land of Presents. But as the rule there was that whatever anyone wanted they must have, the goblins managed to produce one somehow.

He got a collar and a lead for it and took it back to
Dame Washalot and the others. They all stared at him
in amazement.

'What has Saucepan got a lion for?' said Joe.

'Dame Washalot, here is the lion you wanted,' said
Saucepan, beaming; and he put the lead in Dame
Washalot's hand. She dropped it at once and backed
away.

'Saucepan! Don't play this kind of joke on me. You
know I'm scared of lions.'

'Then why did you ask me to get you a lion?' asked
Saucepan, astonished.

'I said an IRON, not a LION,' said Dame Washalot
quite snappily.

'Well, then, wouldn't you like to put it into your
wash-tub and wash it clean?' said Saucepan.

But nothing would make Dame Washalot take the
lion, so in the end Saucepan had to take it into the

field where the clock was, and let it loose.

'Perhaps it will eat the grass and be happy,' said Saucepan.

'Oh, Saucepan, lions don't eat grass,' said Joe with a laugh. 'Now tell me – what do you want for a present?'

'Some more kettles and saucepans,' said the old Saucepan Man at once.

So Joe went to a lucky-dip and said what he wanted. He put in his hand and drew out four large, knobbly parcels – two shining kettles and two fine saucepans. The Saucepan Man was very pleased indeed. He put one of the new saucepans on for a hat.

Well, it was fun in the Land of Presents. Everyone went round getting something for the others. Rick got a toy sweet shop for Beth. She was delighted. She got a fine aeroplane for Joe that flew from his hand and cleverly came back to it each time it flew. Joe got a new hat for Watzisname with a yellow feather in it. Watzisname got a pair of silver shoes for Silky, and she put them on at once.

'Are we allowed to take anything home for our mother and father?' Joe asked Moon-Face.

'Of course, so long as you say it is for them and no one else,' said Moon-Face. So Joe went to where a Christmas Tree was hung with presents and got a beautiful boxed set of hankies for his father. And Beth got a large new purse for her mother.

Suddenly Joe looked at his watch. 'It's almost twelve o'clock,' he said. 'The Land of Presents will be moving off in a minute. We'd better go. Anyway, we really can't carry anything more! Goodness, what a lovely lot of things we've all got!'

So they left the lovely Land of Presents and went down the ladder to the Faraway Tree. They said goodbye to Moon-Face and the others, and sat carefully down on cushions, their presents on their knees so that they wouldn't break. And one by one they shot off down the slippery-slip and out of the front door.

They heard a curious roar as they landed on the moss outside the Tree. Joe looked up into the branches.

'Do you know, I believe that funny old lion followed us down the ladder!' he said. 'Whatever will Dame Washalot do with him if he won't leave her! I guess she will wash him every day in her wash-tub!'

'Well, he'll wish he hadn't left the Land of Presents then!' said Beth with a giggle. 'Come on – let's go home to Mother. What a lovely adventure! I hope it won't be the last.'

It won't, because the Faraway Tree is still there. But we must leave them now to have their adventures by themselves, for there is no time to tell you any more. There they all go through the Enchanted Wood, carrying their lovely presents – what a lucky lot of children they are, to be sure!

THE END

The Folk of the Faraway Tree

CONTENTS

I. CURIOUS CONNIE COMES TO STAY

One day Mother came to the three children, as they worked out in the garden, and spoke to them.

'Joe! Beth! Frannie! Listen to me for a minute. I've just had a letter from an old friend of mine, and I'm wondering what to do. I'll read it to you.'

Mother read the letter:

> *Dear Old Friend,*
> *Please will you do something for me? I have not been well for some time, and the doctor says I must go away on a long holiday. But, as you know, I have a little girl, Connie, and I cannot leave her by herself. So would you please let her stay with you until I come back? I will, of course, pay you well.*
>
> *Your three children are good and well behaved, and I feel that their friendship will be very good for my little Connie, who is, I am afraid, rather spoilt. Do let me know soon.*
> *Your old friend,*
> *Lizzie Haynes*

The three children listened in silence. Then Beth spoke.

'Oh, Mother! We've seen Connie once, and she was very selfish and spoilt – and so curious too, sticking her nose into everything! Have we *got* to have her?'

'No, of course not,' said Mother. 'But I could do with some extra money, you know – and I do think Connie would soon settle down and stop being spoilt if she lived with us. It would be good for her!'

'And I suppose we should help people if we can,' said Joe. 'All right, Mother – we'll have Connie, shall we, and just teach her not to be spoilt!'

'We'll be able to show her the Enchanted Wood and the Faraway Tree!' said Frannie.

'Yes – we used to have our cousin Rick, but now he's gone back home,' said Beth. 'We'll have Connie instead! If you put a little bed into the corner of Frannie's and my room, Mother, we can have her in there.'

Mother smiled at them and went indoors to write to her old friend, to say yes, she would have Connie. The children looked at one another.

'We'll soon tick Connie off if she starts any of her high-and-mighty ways here,' said Beth.

'And we'll stop her poking her nose into everything too!' said Frannie. 'Well – what about taking her up the Faraway Tree and letting her peep in at the Angry Pixie? He'll soon tick her off!'

The others giggled. They could see that they would have a bit of fun with Connie. She was always so curious and inquisitive about everything and everyone. Well – she would get a few shocks in the Enchanted Wood!

'It will be fun showing somebody else the Faraway Tree, and all the people there,' said Joe. 'I wonder what Curious Connie will think of the Saucepan Man, and Silky and Moon-Face!'

'And I wonder what they will think of *her*!' said Beth. 'What a lovely name for her, Joe – Curious Connie! I'll always think of her like that now!'

Curious Connie was to come the next week. Beth helped Mother put a little bed into the corner of the girls' bedroom. Connie wasn't very big. She was the same age as Frannie, but she was a fussy eater, and hadn't grown as big as Frannie. She was a pretty, dainty little thing, who liked wearing nice clothes.

'Brush that untidy hair, Frannie, before you meet Connie,' said Mother. Frannie's hair had grown rather long, and needed a trim.

The children went to meet the bus. 'There it is!' cried Joe. 'Coming round the corner. And there's Curious Connie on it, look – all dressed up as if she was going to a party!'

Connie jumped off the bus, carrying a bag. Joe politely took it from her, and gave her a welcoming kiss. The girls welcomed her too. Connie looked them up and down.

'Huh, you do look like country kids!' she said.

'Well, that's what we are,' said Beth. 'You'll look like us soon, too. I hope you'll be very happy here, Connie.'

'I saw Rick the other day,' said Connie, as she walked daintily along the lane with the others. 'He told me the most ridiculous stories!'

'*Rick* did! But he's not a story-teller!' said Joe, in surprise. 'What sort of stories did he tell you?'

'Well, he told me about a silly Enchanted Wood and a ridiculous Faraway Tree, and some stupid people

called Moon-Face and Dame Washalot and Mister Watzisname, and a crazy fellow called the Saucepan Man who was deaf,' said Connie.

'Oh! Do you think all those were silly and stupid?' said Joe at last.

'I didn't believe in any of it,' said Connie. 'I don't believe in things like that – fairies or elves or magic or anything. It's old fashioned.'

'Well, we must be *very* old fashioned then,' said Beth. 'Because we not only believe in the Enchanted Wood and the Faraway Tree and love our funny friends there, but we go to see them too – and we visit the lands at the top of the Tree as well! We did think of taking you too!'

'It wouldn't be much use,' said Connie. 'I won't believe in them at all.'

'What – not even if you saw them?' cried Frannie.

'I don't think so,' said Connie. 'I mean – it all

sounds quite impossible to me. Really it does.'

'Well, we'll see,' said Joe. 'It looks as if we'll have some fun with you, up the Faraway Tree, Connie! I would like to see the Angry Pixie's face if you tell him you don't believe in him!'

'Let's take her tomorrow!' said Beth, with a giggle.

'All right!' said Joe. 'But we'd better not let her go into any land at the top of the Tree. She'd never get down again!'

'What land? At the top of the *tree*? A land at the top of a tree!' said Connie, puzzled.

'Yes,' said Beth. 'You see, the Enchanted Wood is quite near here, Connie. And in the middle of it is the biggest, tallest tree in the world – very magic. It's called the Faraway Tree, because its top is so far away, and always sticks up into some strange magic land there – a different one every week.'

'I don't believe a word of it,' said Connie.

'All right. Don't then,' said Frannie, beginning to feel angry. 'Look – here we are, home – and there's Mother looking out for us!'

Soon Connie and the girls were unpacking Connie's bag and putting her things away into two empty drawers in the bedside cabinet. Beth saw that there were no really sensible country clothes at all. However could Connie climb the Faraway Tree in a flimsy dress? She should have some old clothes! Well, she and Frannie had plenty so they could lend her some.

'I suppose you are longing to show Connie the Enchanted Wood!' said Mother, when they went down to dinner.

'Oh – do *you* believe in it too?' said Connie,

surprised that a grown-up should do so.

'Well, I haven't seen the Tree, but I have seen some of the people that come down it,' said Mother.

'Look – here's one of them now!' said Joe, jumping up as he saw someone coming in at the front gate. It was Moon-Face, his round face beaming happily. He carried a note in his hand.

'Hello!' said Joe, opening the door. 'Come in and have some dinner, Moon-Face. We've got a little friend here – the girl I was telling you about – Connie.'

'Ah – how do you do?' said Moon-Face, going all polite as he saw the dainty, pretty Connie. 'I've come to ask you to dinner with me and Silky tomorrow, Connie. I hope you can come. Any friend of the children's is welcome up the Faraway Tree!'

Connie shook hands with the strange, round-faced little man. She hardly knew what to say. If she said she would go to dinner with him she was as good as saying that she believed in all this nonsense about the Faraway Tree – and she certainly didn't!

'Moon-Face, you have put poor Connie into a fix,' said Joe, grinning. 'She doesn't believe in you, you see – so how can she come to dinner with a person she doesn't believe in, at a place she thinks isn't there?'

'Quite easily,' said Moon-Face. 'Let her think it is a dream. Let her think *I'm* a dream.'

'All right,' said Connie, who really was longing to go to dinner with him, after all she had said. 'All right. I'll come. I'll think you're just a dream. You probably are, anyway.'

'And I'll think *you* are a dream too,' said Moon-

Face politely. 'Then it will be nice for both of us.'

'Well, I'm not a dream!' said Connie, rather indignantly. 'I should have thought you could see quite well I'm real, and not a dream.'

Moon-Face grinned. 'I hope you're a good dream, and not a bad one, if you *are* a dream,' he said. 'Well – see you all tomorrow. Four o'clock, in my house at the top of the Tree. Will you walk up, or shall I send down cushions on a rope for you?'

'We'll walk up,' said Joe. 'We really want Connie to meet the people who live in the Tree. She won't believe in any of them, but they'll believe in her all right – and it might be rather funny!'

'It certainly will!' said Moon-Face, and went off, grinning again, leaving Silky's polite invitation note in Connie's small hand.

'I'm not sure I like him very much,' said Connie, taking the last bun off the plate.

'What – not like *Moon-Face!*' cried Frannie, who really loved the strange little man. 'He's the dearest, kindest, funniest, nicest – '

'All right, all right,' said Connie. 'Don't go on for hours like that. I'll go tomorrow – but I still say it's all make-believe and pretence, and not really real!'

'You wait and see!' said Joe. 'Come on – we've time for a game before bed . . . and tomorrow, Connie, tomorrow, you will go up the Faraway Tree!'

II. UP THE FARAWAY TREE

The next day was bright and sunny. Connie woke up feeling rather excited. She was away from home, staying in the country – she had three playmates – and they had promised to take her up the Faraway Tree!

'Even if I don't believe in it, it will be fun to see what they think it is,' she said to herself. 'I hope we have a good time, and a nice dinner.'

The children usually had to do some kind of work in the mornings, even though it was holiday time. Beth and Frannie decided to help their mother, while Joe helped Father in the garden. There was a good deal to do there, because there had been some rain, and the weeds had come up by the hundred.

Connie didn't like having to help make the beds very much, but the children's mother was quite firm with her.

'You will do the same as the others,' she said. 'And don't pout like that, Connie. I don't like it. It makes you look ugly.'

Connie was not used to being spoken to like this. Her mother had always fussed round her and spoilt her, and she had been the one and only child in the house. Now she was one of four, and things were very different.

'Cheer up!' said Beth, seeing tears in Connie's eyes. 'Don't be a spoilt baby! Think of our treat this afternoon!'

Connie sniffed. 'Funny sort of treat!' she said, but all the same she did cheer up.

When three o'clock came Mother said the children could go. 'It will take you some time to get up the Tree, I am sure, if you are going to show Connie everything,' she said. 'And please don't let her get wet with Dame Washalot's water, will you?'

Connie looked up in surprise. 'Dame Washalot's water!' she said. 'Whatever do you mean?'

Beth giggled. 'There's an old woman who lives up the Tree, who is always washing,' she said. 'She just adores washing, and when she has finished she tips up her wash-tub, and the soapy water comes sloshing down the tree. You have to look out for it.'

'I don't believe a word of it!' said Connie, and she didn't. 'Doing washing up a tree! It sounds quite daft to me.'

'Let's go now,' said Beth, 'or we won't be at Moon-Face's by four o'clock.'

'I must go and change into a pretty dress,' said Connie.

'No, don't,' said Frannie. 'Go as you are. We don't change into nice clothes when we go up the Tree.'

'What – go out to dinner in ordinary clothes!' cried Connie. 'I just couldn't!' And off she went to put on a clean, white dress.

They all went to the edge of the Wood. There was a ditch there. 'Jump over this – and you're in the Enchanted Wood!' said Beth.

They all jumped, Connie too. As soon as she was across the ditch, and heard the trees whispering, 'wisha, wisha, wisha,' as they always did in the Enchanted Wood, Connie felt different. She felt excited and curious and happy. She felt as if there was magic about – although she didn't believe in magic! It was a really lovely feeling.

They went through the wood, and came to an enormous tree, with a tremendously thick and knotted trunk. Connie gazed up into the branches.

'Gosh!' she said. 'I've never seen such a tree before! Is this the Magic Faraway Tree? How marvellous!'

'Yes,' said Joe, enjoying Connie's surprise. 'And at the top, as we told you, there is a different land every week. I don't know what land is there now. We don't always go. Sometimes the lands aren't very nice. Once there was the Land of Bad Temper. That was horrid. And a little while ago there was the Land of Punishments. We didn't go there, you can guess! We asked our friends Silky and Moon-Face what it was like, and they said they didn't know either, but they could hear shouts and cries going on all the time!'

'Gosh!' said Connie, alarmed. 'I wouldn't like to go to a land like that. Although, of course,' she added quickly, 'I don't believe in such a thing.'

'Of course you don't,' said Joe, with a grin. 'You don't believe in the Faraway Tree either, do you? And yet you are going to climb it. Come on – up we go!'

They swung themselves up on the lower branches. It was a very easy tree to climb. The branches were broad and strong, and so many little folk walked up and down the Tree all day long that little paths had been worn on the broad boughs.

'What sort of tree is it?' said Connie.

410

'It looks like a cherry tree to me. Oh, look – there are some ripe cherries – just out of my reach, though. Never mind, I'll pick some further up.'

'Better pick them now, or you may find the Tree is growing walnuts a bit higher up,' said Beth, laughing. 'It's a magic Tree, you know. It grows all kinds of different things at any time!'

Sure enough, when Connie looked for ripe cherries a little way up, she found, to her surprise, that the Tree was now growing horse-chestnut leaves and had prickly covered horse chestnuts! She was surprised and disappointed – and very puzzled. Could it really be a magic tree, then?

Soon they met all kinds of little folk coming down the Tree. There were elves and pixies, a goblin or two, a few rabbits and one or two squirrels. It was odd to see a rabbit up a tree. Connie blinked her eyes to see if she really was looking at rabbits up a tree, but there was no doubt about it; she was. The funny thing was, they were dressed in clothes too. That was odder than ever.

'Do people live in this tree?' asked Connie, in wonder, as they came to a little window in the big trunk.

'Oh yes – lots of them,' said Joe. 'But don't go peeping into that window, now, Connie. The Angry Pixie lives inside the little house there, and he does hate people to peep in.'

411

'All right, I won't peep,' said Connie, who was very curious indeed to know what the little house looked like. She meant to peep, of course. She was far too inquisitive a little girl not to do a bit of prying, if she had the chance!

'My shoelace is undone,' she called to the others. 'You go on ahead, I'll follow.'

'I bet she wants to peep,' whispered Joe to Beth, with a grin. 'Come on! Let her!'

They went on to a higher branch. Connie pretended to fiddle about with her shoe, and then, when she saw that the others were a little way up, she climbed quickly over to the little window.

She peeped inside. Oh, what fun! Oh, how lovely! There was a proper little room inside the tree, with a bed and a chair and a table. Sitting writing at the table was the Angry Pixie, his glasses on his nose. He had an enormous inkpot full of ink, and a very small pen, and his fingers were stained with the purple ink.

Connie's shadow at the window made him look up. He saw the little girl there, peeping, and he flew into one of his tempers. He shot to his feet, picked up the enormous inkpot and rushed to his window. He opened it and yelled loudly:

'Peeping again! Everybody peeps in at my window, everybody! I won't have it! I really won't have it.'

He emptied the inkpot all over the alarmed Connie. The ink fell in big spots on her clothes, and on her cheek and hands. She was in a terrible mess.

'Oh! Oh! You wicked thing!' she cried. 'Look what you've done to me.'

'Well, you shouldn't peep,' cried the Angry Pixie,

still in a rage. 'Now I can't finish my letter. I've got no more ink! You bad girl! You horrid peeper!'

'Joe! Beth! Come and help me!' sobbed Connie, crying tears of anger and despair down her ink-smudged cheeks.

The Angry Pixie suddenly looked surprised and a little ashamed. 'Oh – are you a friend of Joe's?' he asked. 'Why didn't you say so? I would have shouted at you for peeping, but I wouldn't have thrown ink at you. Really, I wouldn't. Joe should have warned you not to peep.'

'I did,' said Joe, appearing at the window, too. 'It's her own fault. My, you do look a mess, Connie. Come on! We'll never be at Moon-Face's by four o'clock.'

Wiping away her tears, Connie followed the others up the Tree. They came to another window, and this time the three children looked in – but Connie wouldn't. 'No thank you,' she said: 'I'm not going to have things thrown at me again. I think the people who live here are horrid.'

'You needn't be afraid of peeping in at *this* window,' said Joe. 'The Owl lives here and he always sleeps in the day time, so he never sees people peeping in. He's a great friend of Silky the fairy. Look at him lying asleep on his bed. That red nightcap he's got on was knitted for him by Silky. Doesn't he look nice in it?'

But Connie wouldn't look in. She was angry and sulky. She went on up the Tree by herself. Joe suddenly heard a sound he knew very well, and he yelled loudly to Connie:

'Hey, Connie, Connie, look out! I can hear Dame Washalot's water coming down the tree. LOOK OUT!'

Connie was just about to answer that she didn't believe in Dame Washalot, *or* her silly water, when a cascade of dirty, soapy water came splashing down the Faraway Tree! It fell all over poor Connie, and soaked her from head to foot! Some of the suds stayed in her hair, and she looked a dreadful sight.

The others had all ducked under broad boughs as soon as they heard the water coming, and they didn't get a drop on them. Joe began to laugh when he saw Connie. The little girl burst into tears again.

'Let me go home, let me go home!' she wept. 'I hate your Faraway Tree. I hate all the people in it! Let me go home!'

A silvery voice called down the Tree. 'Who's in trouble? Come up and I'll help you!'

'It's dear Silky!' said Beth. 'Come on, Connie. She'll get you dry again!'

III. CONNIE MEETS A FEW PEOPLE

'I don't want to see any more of the horrid people who live in this tree,' wept poor Connie. But Joe took her firmly by the hand and pulled her up a broad bough to where a yellow door stood open in the Tree.

In the doorway stood the prettiest little fairy you ever saw. She had hair that stood out round her head like a golden mist, as fine as silk. She held out her hand to Connie.

'Poor child! Did you get caught in Dame Washalot's water! She has been washing such a lot today, and the water has been coming down all day long! Let me dry you.'

Connie couldn't help liking this pretty little fairy. How dainty she was in her shining dress, and what tiny feet and hands she had!

Silky drew her into her tidy little house. She took a towel from a peg and began to dry Connie. The others told her who she was.

'Yes, I know,' said Silky. 'We're going up to Moon-Face's house for dinner. He said he would ask Mister Watzisname too, but I don't expect he'll come, because I heard him snoring in his chair as usual a little while ago.'

'Mister who?' asked Connie.

'Mister Watzisname,' said Silky. 'He doesn't know his name nor does anyone else, so we call him

Watzisname. We've tried and tried to find out what his name is, but I don't expect we shall ever know now. Unless the Land of Know-All comes – then we might go up there and find out. You can find out anything in the Land of Know-All.'

'Oh!' said Joe, thinking of a whole lot of things he would love to know. 'We'll go there if it comes.'

Suddenly, there came a curious noise down the Tree – a clanking and jingling, crashing and banging. Connie looked scared. Whatever would happen next? It sounded as if a hundred saucepans, a few dozen kettles, and some odds and ends of dishes and pans were all falling down the Tree together!

Then a voice came floating down the Tree, and the children grinned.

> *Two books for a bookworm,*
> *Two butts for a goat,*
> *Two winks for a winkle*
> *Who can't sing a note!*

'What a very silly song!' said Connie.

'Yes, isn't it?' said Joe. 'It's the kind the Old Saucepan Man always sings. It's his 'Two' song. Every line but the last begins with the word 'Two'. Anyone can make up a song like that.'

'Well, I'm sure I don't want to,' said Connie, thinking that everyone in the Faraway Tree must be a bit crazy. 'Who's the Saucepan Man? And what's that awful crashing noise?'

'Only his saucepans and kettles and things,' said Beth. 'He carries them round with him. He's a dear.

416

Once we saw him without his saucepans and things round him, and we didn't know him. He looked funny – quite different.'

A very extraordinary person now came into Silky's tiny house, almost getting stuck in the door. He was covered from head to toe with saucepans, kettles and pans, which were tied round him with string. They jangled and crashed together, so everyone always knew when the Saucepan Man was coming.

Connie stared at him amazed. His hat was a very big saucepan, so big that it hid most of his face. Connie could see a wide grin, but that was about all.

'Who's this funny creature?' said Connie, in a loud and rather rude voice.

Now the Saucepan Man was deaf, and he didn't usually hear what was said – but this time he did, and he didn't like it. He tilted back his saucepan hat and stared at Connie.

'Who's this dirty little girl?' he said, in a voice just as loud as Connie's. Connie went red. She glared at the Saucepan Man.

'This is Connie,' said Joe. He turned to Connie. 'This is Saucepan, a great friend of ours,' he said. 'We've had lots of adventures together.'

'Why is she so dirty?' asked Saucepan, looking at Connie's ink-stained clothes and dirty face. 'Is she always like that? Why don't you clean her up?'

Connie was furious. She was always so clean and dainty and well dressed – how dare this horrid clanking little man talk about her like that!

'Go away!' she said, angrily.

'Yes, it's a very nice day,' said the Saucepan Man,

politely, going suddenly deaf.

'Don't stay here and STARE!' shouted Connie.

'I certainly should wash your hair,' said the Saucepan Man at once. 'It's full of soap suds.'

'I said, "Don't STARE!"' cried Connie.

'Mind that stair?' said the Saucepan Man, looking round. 'Can't see any. Didn't know there were any stairs in the Faraway Tree.'

Connie stared at him in rage. 'Is he crazy?' she said to Joe.

Joe and the others were laughing at this peculiar conversation. Joe shook his head. 'No, Saucepan isn't crazy. He's just deaf. His saucepans make such a clanking all the time that the noise gets into his ears, and he can't hear properly. So he keeps making mistakes.'

'That's right,' said the Saucepan Man, entering into the conversation suddenly. 'Cakes. Plenty of them. Waiting for us at Moon-Face's.'

'I said "Mistakes",' said Joe. 'Not cakes.'

'But Moon-Face's cakes aren't mistakes,' said Saucepan, earnestly.

Joe gave it up. 'We'd better go up to Moon-Face's,' he said. 'It's past four o'clock.'

'I hope that awful Saucepan Man isn't coming with us,' said Connie. Incredibly, Saucepan heard what she said. He looked angry.

'I hope this nasty little girl isn't coming with us,' he said, in his turn, and glared at Connie.

'Now, now, now,' said Silky, and patted the Saucepan Man on one of his kettles. 'Don't get angry. It only makes things worse.'

'Purse? Have you lost it?' said the Saucepan Man, anxiously.

'I said "worse" not "purse",' said Silky. 'Come on! Let's go. Connie's dry now, but I can't get the ink stains out of her dress.'

They all began to climb the Tree again, the Saucepan Man making an appalling noise. He began to sing his silly song.

> *Two bangs for a firework,*
> *Two...*

'Be quiet!' said Silky. 'You'll wake Mister Watzisname. He's fast asleep. He went to bed very late last night, so he'll be tired. We won't wake him. We'll be dreadfully squashed inside Moon-Face's house anyhow. Creep past his chair quietly. Saucepan, try not to make your kettles clang together.'

'Yes, lovely weather,' agreed Saucepan, mishearing again. They all crept past. Saucepan made a few clatters, but they didn't disturb Watzisname, who snored loudly and peacefully in his chair on the broad bough of the Tree outside his house. His mouth was wide open.

'You'd expect people would pop things in his mouth if he leaves it open like that,' whispered Connie.

'People do,' said Joe. 'Moon-Face put some acorns in once. Watzisname was very angry. He really was. It's a wonder he doesn't get soaked with Dame Washalot's water, but he doesn't seem to. He always puts his chair well under that big branch.'

They went on up the Tree. In the distance they saw

Dame Washalot, hanging out some clothes on boughs. 'They blow away if she doesn't get someone to sit on them,' said Silky to Connie. 'So she pays the baby squirrels to sit patiently on each bit of washing she does till it's dry and she can take it in and iron it.'

'They saw the line of baby squirrels in the distance. They looked sweet. Connie wanted to go nearer, but Joe said no, they really must go on; Moon-Face would be tired of waiting for them.

At last they came almost to the top of the Tree. Connie was amazed when she looked down. The Faraway Tree rose higher than any other tree in the Enchanted Wood. Far below them waved the tops of other trees. The Faraway Tree was really wonderful.

'Here we are, at Moon-Face's,' said Joe, and he banged on the door. It flew open and Moon-Face looked out, his big round face one large smile.

'I thought you were never coming!' he said. 'You *are* late!'

'We've brought this dirty little girl,' said Saucepan, and he pushed Connie forward.

Moon-Face looked at her.

'She does look a bit dirty,' he said, and smiled broadly. 'I suppose she got into trouble with the Angry Pixie – and got some of Dame Washalot's water on her too! Never mind! Come along in and we'll have a good meal. I've got some Hot-Cold Goodies!'

'Whatever are they?' said Connie, and even the others hadn't heard of them.

They all went into Moon-Face's exciting house. It was quite extraordinary. In the

420

very middle was a large hole, with a pile of coloured cushions by it. Round the hole was Moon-Face's furniture, all curved to fit the roundness of the tree trunk. There was a curious curved bed, a curved sofa, and a curved stove and chairs, all set round the trunk inside the Tree.

'It's very exciting,' said Connie, looking round. 'What's that hole in the middle?'

Nobody answered her. They were too busy looking at the lovely food that Moon-Face had put ready on the curved table. They wanted to know what the Hot-Cold Goodies were like. They knew Pop Cakes and Google Buns – but they didn't know Hot-Cold Goodies.

'What's this *hole*?' demanded Connie again, but no one bothered about her. She felt so curious that she went to the edge of the strange hole, and put her foot in it to see if there were steps down. She suddenly lost her balance, and stepped right into the hole! She sat down with a bump – and then, oh my goodness! She began to slide away at top speed down the hole that ran from the top of the Tree to the bottom!

'Where's Connie?' said Joe, suddenly, looking round.

'Not here. That's good!' said Saucepan.

'She must have fallen down the slippery-slip!' said Silky. 'Oh, poor Connie – she'll be at the bottom of the Tree by now! We'll have to go down and get her!'

IV. DINNER WITH MOON-FACE

Connie was frightened when she found herself slipping down the hole in the Tree. Usually people who used the slippery-slip had a cushion to sit on, but Connie hadn't. She slid down and down and round and round, faster and faster. She gasped, and her hair flew out behind her.

She came to the bottom of the Tree, and her feet touched a little trapdoor set in the side there. It flew open and Connie shot out, landing on a soft tuft of moss, which the little folk grew there specially, so that anyone using the tree slide would land softly.

Connie landed on the moss and sat there, gasping and scared. She was at the bottom of the tree! The others were all at the top! They would be having dinner together, laughing and joking. They wouldn't miss her. She would have to stay at the bottom of the tree till they came down again, and that might not be for ages.

'If I knew the way home I'd go,' thought Connie. 'But I don't. Oh – what's that?'

It was a red squirrel, dressed in an old sweater. He came out of a hole in the trunk, where he lived. He bounded over to Connie.

'Where's your cushion, please?' he said.

'What cushion?' said Connie.

'The one you slid down on,' said the squirrel.

'I didn't slide down on one,' said Connie.

'You must have,' said the red squirrel, looking all round for a cushion. 'People always do. Where have you put it? Don't be a naughty girl now. Let me have it. I always have to take them back to Moon-Face.'

'I tell you I didn't have a cushion,' said Connie, beginning to feel annoyed. 'I just slid down without one, and I got pretty warm.'

She stood up. The squirrel looked at the back of her. 'My! You've worn out the back of your dress, sliding down without a cushion,' he said. 'It's all in rags. Your underwear is showing.'

'Oh! This is a horrible afternoon!' said poor Connie. 'I've been splashed with ink and soaked with soapy water, and now I've worn out the back of my dress.'

The trapdoor suddenly shot open again and out flew Moon-Face on one of his cushions. He shouted to Connie.

'Well! Didn't you like my party? Why did you rush off so quickly?'

'I fell down that silly hole,' said Connie. 'Look at the back of my dress.'

'There's nothing to look at. You've worn it out, slipping down without a cushion,' said Moon-Face. 'Come on, I'll take you back. Look out – here comes a basket. It's one of Dame Washalot's biggest ones. I borrowed it from her to go back in. All right, red squirrel, don't take my cushion. I'll put it in the basket to sit on.'

The red squirrel said goodbye and popped back into his hole. Moon-Face caught the big basket that came swinging down on a stout rope and threw his yellow cushion into it. He helped Connie in, tugged at the rope, and then up they swung between the branches of the tree. Up and up and up – past the Angry Pixie's, past the Owl's home, past Mister Watzisname, still snoring, past Dame Washalot, and right up to Moon-Face's house.

'Here we are!' he called to Joe and the Saucepan Man, who were busy tugging at the rope, to bring up the basket. 'Thanks so much.'

Everyone was amused to see that the bottom part of poor Connie's dress was gone. 'She's ragged now as well as dirty,' said Saucepan, sounding quite pleased. He didn't like Connie. 'I wonder what will happen to her next.'

'Nothing, I hope,' said Connie, scowling at him.

'Soap? Yes, you do look as if you want a bit of soap,' said Saucepan, mis-hearing as usual. 'And a needle and thread too.'

'Now, stop it, Saucepan!' said Silky. 'I've never known you to be so quarrelsome. Come and eat the Hot-Cold Goodies. Nobody's had any yet.'

They went into Moon-Face's curved home, and sat down again. Connie tried not to go near the hole. She was very afraid of falling down it again. She took a Hot-Cold Goodie. It was like a very, very big chocolate.

Hot-Cold Goodies were mysterious. You put them into your mouth and sucked. As soon as you had sucked the chocolate part off, you came to what seemed like a layer of ice-cream.

'Oooh! Ice-cream!' said Joe, sucking hard. 'Cold as can be. Gosh, it's too cold to bear! It's getting colder and colder. Moon-Face, I'll have to spit out my goodie, it's too cold for me.'

But just as he said that the Hot-Cold Goodie stopped being cold and went hot. At first it was pleasantly warm, then it got very hot.

'It's almost burning me!' said Beth. 'Oh – now it's gone ice-cold again. Moon-Face, what extraordinary things. Wherever did you get them?'

'I bought them from a witch who popped down from the Land of Marvels today,' said Moon-Face, grinning. 'Funny, aren't they?'

'Yes – very exciting, and delicious to taste, once you get used to them changing from cold to hot, and hot to cold,' said Beth. 'I'll have another one.'

'What land did you say was at the top of the Tree today?' asked Silky. 'The Land of Marvels? Oh yes – I went there last year, I remember.'

'What was it like?' asked Frannie.

'Marvellous,' said Silky. 'All wonders and marvels. There's a ladder that hasn't any top – you go on and on climbing up it, and you never reach the top – and a tree that sings whenever the wind blows – a cat that tells your fortune – and a silver ball that takes you all round the world and back in the wink of an eye – well, I can't tell you all the marvels there are.'

'I'd like to go and see them,' said Joe.

'You can't,' said Silky. 'The land moves on today. It would be dangerous to go there now because it might move on at any moment. Then you'd be stuck in the Land of Marvels.'

'I don't believe a word of it,' said Connie.

'She doesn't believe in anything magic,' explained Joe, seeing that Silky looked rather surprised. 'Don't take any notice of her, Silky. She'll believe all right soon.'

'I will *not*,' said Connie. 'I'm beginning to think this is all a horrible dream.'

'Well, go home and go to bed and dream your dream there,' said Joe, getting tired of Connie.

'I will,' said Connie, getting up, offended. 'I'll climb down the Tree myself, and ask that kind red squirrel to see me home. This is a horrible party.'

The silly girl went to the door, opened it, went out and banged it shut. The others stared at one another.

'Is she always like that?' asked Moon-Face.

'Yes,' said Joe. 'She's a very spoilt child, you know. Wants her own way always, and turns up her nose at everything. I'd better fetch her back.'

'No, don't,' said Moon-Face. 'She can't come to any harm. Let her climb down the Tree if she wants

426

to. I only hope she peeps in at the Angry Pixie's again. When I went past in the basket he was writing a letter again, but with red ink this time.'

'Then Connie will probably get *red* spots on her dress now!' said Frannie.

But Connie hadn't gone down the Tree. She stood outside on a branch, sulking. She looked down the Tree and saw Dame Washalot busy washing again. Silly old woman! Connie didn't feel as if she wanted to go near her, in case she got water all over her again. She looked upwards.

She was nearly at the top of the Tree. She thought it would be fun to climb right up to the top, and look down on the Enchanted Wood. What a long way she would see!

She climbed upwards. She came to the top of the Tree – and to her great astonishment the last branch of all touched the clouds! Yes – it went straight up into a vast white cloud that hung, floating, over the top of the Tree.

'Strange,' said Connie, looking up into the purple hole made by the tree branch in the cloud. 'Shall I go up there – into the cloud? Yes – I will.'

She went up the last branch – and there was a little ladder leading through the thickness of the cloud from the branch. A ladder!

Connie was filled with curiosity. She could hardly bear waiting to see what was at the top of the ladder. She climbed it – and suddenly her head poked right through the cloud, and into a new and different land altogether!

'Well!' said Connie, in surprise. 'So the children

told the truth. There *is* a land at the top of the Faraway Tree – or am I really dreaming?'

She climbed up into the land. It was peculiar. There was a strange humming noise in the air. Strange people walked quickly past, some looking like witches, and some like goblins. They took no notice of Connie.

'The land is moving on!' cried one goblin to another. 'It's on the move again. Where shall we go to next?'

And then the Land of Marvels moved away from the top of the tree – and took poor Connie with it!

V. OFF TO JACK-AND-THE-BEANSTALK

Joe, Beth, Frannie and the others went on with their meal. They finished the Hot-Cold Goodies, then they started on some pink desserts that Moon-Face had made in the shape of animals. They were so nicely made that it seemed a pity to eat them.

'We'd better save some for Connie, hadn't we?' said Beth. 'Let's see if she's outside the door. I expect she's standing there, sulking.'

Moon-Face opened the door. There was no one there. He called loudly, 'Connie! Connie!'

There was no answer. 'She's gone down the Tree, I should think,' he said. 'I'll just call down to Dame Washalot and see if she saw her.'

So he shouted down to the old dame. But Dame Washalot shook her head. 'No,' she shouted back, 'no one has gone past since you came up in the basket, Moon-Face. No one at all.'

'Funny!' said Moon-Face, going to tell the others. 'Where's she gone, then?'

'Up through the cloud?' said Silky.

'No – surely she wouldn't have done that by herself,' said Joe, in alarm. 'Look, Moon-Face! There's the red squirrel who wants to speak to you.'

The red squirrel came in, trying to hide a hole in his old sweater. 'I heard you calling Connie, Moon-Face,' he said. 'Well, she's gone up the ladder through

429

the cloud. I expect she's in the Land of Marvels. I saw her go.'

'Good heavens!' cried Joe, jumping up in alarm. 'Why, the land is ready to leave here at any minute, didn't you say, Silky? What a silly she is! We'd better go and get her back at once.'

'I thought I heard the humming noise that means any land is moving on,' said Moon-Face, looking troubled. 'I don't believe we can save her. I'll run up the ladder and see.'

He climbed up the highest branch and went up the ladder. But there was nothing to be seen at all except swirling, misty cloud. He came down again.

'The Land of Marvels is gone,' he said. 'And the next land hasn't even come yet. I don't know what it will be, either. Well – Connie's gone with the Land of Marvels. She *would* do a silly thing like that!'

Beth went pale. 'But what can we do about it?' she said. 'Whatever can we do? We're in charge of her, you know. We really can't let her go like this. We must find her somehow.'

'How *can* we?' said Silky. 'You know that once a land has moved on, it doesn't come back for ages. Connie will have to stay there. It might do her good to be there for a while, anyway. She's not a very nice person.'

'Oh Silky, you don't understand!' said Joe. He looked very worried. 'She's our friend. And although she's silly and annoying at times, we're responsible and have to look after her and help her. How can we get to her?'

'You can't,' said Moon-Face.

Saucepan had been trying to follow what had been said, and he looked very concerned. He didn't like Connie, and he thought it was a very good thing she had gone off in the Land of Marvels. But he did know a way of getting there, and he badly wanted to tell the others.

But they all talked at once, and he couldn't get a word in! So, in despair he clashed his saucepans and kettles together so violently that everyone jumped and stared round at him.

'He wants to say something,' said Joe. 'Go on, out with it, Saucepan.'

Saucepan came out with it in a rush. '*I* know how to get to the Land of Marvels without waiting for it to arrive here again,' he said. 'You can get to it from the Land of Giants, which joins on to it.'

'Well, I don't see how that helps us,' said Moon-Face. 'We don't know how to get to the Land of Giants either, silly!'

'No, it's not hilly,' said Saucepan, going all deaf again. 'It's quite flat. The giants have made it flat by walking about on it with their enormous feet.'

'What *is* he talking about?' said Beth. 'Saucepan, stop talking about the geography of Giantland and tell us how to get there.'

'How to get there, did you say?' asked Saucepan, putting his hand behind his left ear.

'YES!' yelled everyone.

'Well, that's easy,' said Saucepan, beaming round. 'Same way as Jack-and-the-Bean-Stalk did, of course. Up the Bean-Stalk!'

Everyone stared at Saucepan in silence. They had

431

all heard of Jack-and-the-Bean-Stalk, of course, and how he climbed up the Bean-Stalk into Giantland.

'But where's the Bean-Stalk?' asked Joe at last.

'Where Jack lives,' said Saucepan, suddenly hearing well again. 'I know him quite well. Married a princess and lives in a castle.'

'I never knew that he was an old friend of yours,' said Moon-Face. 'How did you come to know him?'

'I sold him a lot of saucepans and kettles,' said the Saucepan Man. 'He was giving an enormous dinner party, and they didn't have enough things to cook everything in. So I came along just at the right moment and sold him everything I'd got. Very lucky for him.'

'And for you too,' grinned Moon-Face. 'Well, you'd better take us to your Jack, Saucepan. We'll go up the Bean-Stalk, and try and rescue that silly little Connie.'

'We'd better not *all* go,' said Joe, looking round at the little company.

'I must go to show you the way,' said Saucepan, who loved making a journey.

'And I must go, of course,' said Moon-Face.

'And I shall come with you to look after you,' said Silky, firmly. 'You always get into such silly scrapes if I'm not there to see to you.'

'And I shall certainly come, because I was really in charge of Connie,' said Joe.

'And *we're* not going to be left out of an adventure like this!' said Beth at once. 'Are we Frannie?'

'Well – it looks as if we're all going then,' said Moon-Face. 'All right, let's go. But don't let's get caught by any giants, for goodness' sake. *Must* we go

432

through Giantland to get to the Land of Marvels, Saucepan?'

'Must,' said Saucepan, cheerfully. 'The giants won't hurt you. They're quite harmless nowadays. Well, come on! Down the Tree we go, and then to the other end of the Wood.'

So down the Tree they went, and the red squirrel bounded with them to the bottom. They wished they could skip down as he did – it didn't take him more than half a minute to get up or down!

They reached the bottom, and then thought how silly they were not to have gone down the slippery-slip!

'It shows how worried we are, not to have thought of that!' said Beth. 'Which way now, Saucepan?'

Saucepan set off down a narrow, winding path. 'This way, look – under this bush, and across this field. We"ve got to get to the station,' he said.

'Station? What station?' said Joe, in astonishment.

'To get the train for Jack-and-the-Bean-Stalk's castle,' said Saucepan. 'How stupid you are, all of a sudden, Joe!'

They suddenly came to a small station set under a row of tall trees. A steam train came puffing in, looking very like an old wooden toy one that the children had at home. They got in, and it went off, puffing hard as if it was out of breath.

They passed through many mysterious little stations, but didn't stop. 'I said "Bean-Stalk Castle" to the engine, so it will go straight there,' said Saucepan.

The other passengers didn't seem to mind going to Bean-Stalk Castle at all. They sat and talked or read, and took no notice of the new little group of friends.

The train suddenly stopped and hooted. 'Here we are,' said Saucepan. 'Come on, everyone.'

They got out. The engine gave another hoot and went rattling off.

'There's Jack! Hi there, Jack!' yelled Saucepan, and rushed towards a sturdy young man in the distance. They shook hands, all Saucepan's kettles and pans rattling excitedly.

'What a pleasure, what a pleasure!' cried Jack. 'Who are all these people? Have they come to stay with me? I'll go and tell the princess to make up extra beds at once.'

'No, don't do that,' said Moon-Face. 'We haven't come to stay. We just want to know – can we please use your Bean-Stalk, Jack?'

'It hasn't grown this year yet,' said Jack. 'I forgot to plant any beans, you see. And, the giants were a bit of a nuisance last year, always shouting rude things down the Bean-Stalk to me.'

'Oh!' said Joe, staring at Jack in dismay. 'What a pity! We particularly wanted to go up your Bean-Stalk.'

'Well – I can plant the beans now, and they'll grow,' said Jack. 'They're magic ones, you know. They grow as you watch them.'

'Oh, good!' said Moon-Face. 'Could you plant some, do you think? We'd be very grateful to you.'

'Certainly,' said Jack, and he felt about in his pocket. 'I'd do anything to help old Saucepan. His kettles and saucepans are still going strong in my kitchen – never wear out at all. Now – wherever did I put those beans?'

The others watched anxiously as he turned an odd collection of things out of his pockets. At last came three or four mouldy-looking beans.

'Here we are,' said Jack. 'I'll just press them into the ground – like this – and now we'll watch them grow. Stand back, please, because they sometimes shoot up very fast!'

VI. TO THE LAND OF GIANTS

Everyone watched the ground where Jack had buried the beans. At first nothing happened. Then a sort of little hill came, as if a mole was working there. The hill split and up came some Bean-Stalks, putting out two bean-leaves. Then other leaves sprang from the centre of the stalk, and pointed upwards. Then others came, and the Bean-Stalks grew higher and higher.

'Incredible!' said Beth, watching them grow up and up. 'They don't even need a pole to climb up, Jack. Is that how they grew when you first planted them, years ago, to climb up to Giantland?'

'Just the same,' said Jack. 'Look – you can't even see the tops of them now! It's amazing how they spring up, isn't it? Look how thick and strong the stems have grown, too!'

So they had. They were like the trunks of young trees.

'Have they reached Giantland yet?' asked Moon-Face squinting up.

'Can't tell till you climb up,' said Jack. 'I'd come with you, but I've got visitors coming – and the princess isn't pleased if I'm not there to greet them. So I'd better go now.'

He shook hands politely all round, and was very pleased when the Saucepan Man presented him with an extra large kettle in return for his kindness. Beth was glad to see him taking the kettle.

Up the Bean-Stalk they all went. It was not at all difficult, for there were plenty of strong leaf-stalks to tread on and to haul themselves up by. But it did seem a very, very long way to the top!

'I think we're going to the moon!' said Joe, panting. 'We'll see the Man in the Moon peeping at us over the top!'

But they didn't go to the Moon. They went to Giantland, of course, because the beans never grew up to anywhere else. The topmost shoots waved over Giantland, and the children and the others rolled off them and lay panting on the ground to rest.

'Phew! I couldn't have climbed any further!' said Beth, trying to get her breath. 'Oh my, what ever is that, Joe?'

'It's an earthquake!' cried Frannie. 'Can't you feel the earth trembling and quaking?'

'Here's a mountain coming on top of us!' shouted Joe, and pulled Beth and Frannie down a nearby hole.

Saucepan peered down, laughing. 'No earthquake and no mountain!' he said. 'Just an ordinary giant coming along, whose footsteps shake the ground.'

The noise and the earthquake grew worse and then passed. The giant had gone by. Everyone breathed again and crept out of the hole.

'I suppose that's a rabbit hole we were in, where giant rabbits live,' said Beth.

'No – a worm hole, where giant worms live,' said Moon-Face. 'I saw one down at the bottom, like an enormous snake.'

'Oh dear – I won't go down a hole like that again!'

said Frannie. But she did, when another earthquake and walking mountain appeared! It was another giant, tall as the sky, his great feet shaking the earth below.

'Come on!' said Moon-Face, when the second giant had gone safely by. 'We must hurry. And for goodness' sake get out of the way if another giant comes by, because we don't want to be squashed like raisins under his feet.'

The third giant stopped when he came near them. He bent down, and the children saw that he wore glasses on his enormous nose. They looked as large as shop windows!

'Ha! What are these little creatures?' said the giant, in a voice that boomed like a thunder storm. 'Beetles, I should think – or ants! Most extraordinary, I have never seen any like them before!'

There was no hole to slip down. The children saw that the giant was trying to pick one of them up! An enormous hand, with fingers as thick as young tree trunks came down near them.

Everyone was too scared to move, and there was nowhere to hide, except for a large dandelion growing as tall as a tree, nearby. But Saucepan had a bright idea. He undid his biggest saucepan, and clapped it on top of the giant's thumb; it fitted it exactly, and stuck there.

The giant gave a loud cry of surprise, and lifted up his hand. He stood up to see this funny thing that had suddenly appeared on his thumb, and Saucepan yelled to everyone.

'To the dandelion, quick! Hurry!'

They rushed to the tall dandelion plant. One of

the heads floated high above them, a beautiful ripe dandelion 'clock', full of seeds ready to fly off in the wind.

Saucepan shook the stalk violently, and some of the seeds flew off, floating in the air on their parachute of hairs.

'Catch the stalks of the seeds, catch them, and let the wind float you away!' yelled Saucepan. 'The giant won't guess we're flying off with the dandelion seeds.'

So each of them caught hold of a dandelion seed. Frannie got two, and held on tightly! Then the wind blew, and the plumy seeds floated high in the air, taking everyone with them. They saw the giant kneel down on the ground to look for the funny creatures that had put the saucepan on his thumb – but then they were off and away, floating high in the breeze.

'Keep together, keep together!' called Moon-Face, grabbing Silky's hand. 'We don't want to be blown apart, all over Giantland. We'd never meet again! Hold hands when you get near.'

Frannie was nearly lost, because she had hold of two seeds instead of one, and was blown higher than the others. But Joe managed to grab her feet and pulled her down beside him. He made her leave go of one of her dandelion seeds, and took hold of her hand firmly.

Now they were all linking hands in pairs, and kept together well. They floated high over Giantland, marvelling at the enormous castles there, the great gardens and tall trees.

'Even the Faraway Tree would look small here!' said Beth.

'Look – there's the boundary between the Land of Marvels and Giantland!' cried Saucepan suddenly, almost letting go of his dandelion seed in his excitement. 'I'd no idea we would get there so soon. What a wall!'

It was indeed a marvellous wall. It rose steadily up, so high that it seemed to have no end, and it shimmered and shook as if it was made of water.

'It's a magic wall,' said Saucepan. 'I remember seeing it before. No giant can get in or out, over or under it, because it's painted with giant-proof paint.'

'What's that?' asked Joe, shouting.

'Giant-proof paint can only be bought in the Land of Marvels,' explained Saucepan. 'Anything painted with it keeps giants away, just like the smell of camphor keeps moths away. It's marvellous. No giant can come close to anything painted with that silvery magic paint. I only wish I had some!'

'Well – how are *we* to get over or under this wall?' said Moon-Face, as they floated near. 'It may be giant-proof, but it looks as if it's us-proof too!'

'Oh no – we can go right through it,' said Silky. 'You'll see that as soon as we get right up to it, it won't be there! It's only giant-proof.'

This sounded impossible, but Silky's words were quite true. When they reached the wall, it gave one last shimmer – and was gone! The children floated right down into the Land of Marvels, where everything was the right size. It was a great relief to see things properly again, and not to have to crane your neck to see if a flower was a daisy or a pimpernel!

They floated to the ground, let go of their dandelion seeds, which gradually became the right size, once they were away from Giantland, and looked round them.

'There's the ladder-without-a-top,' said Silky, pointing. 'No one has ever climbed beyond the three thousandth rung, because they get so tired. And there's the tree-that-sings. It's singing now.'

So it was – a whispery, beautiful song, all about the sun and the wind and rain. The children could understand it perfectly, although the tree did not use any words they knew. It just stood there and poured out its song in tree language.

'I could listen to that for ages,' said Joe. 'But we really must get on. Now – we must all hunt for Connie. Let's shout for her, shall we? Now – altogether – shout!'

They shouted. 'CON-NEE! CON-NEE! CON-NEE!'

An old woman nearby looked angrily at them. 'Be quiet!' she said. 'Making such a noise! I've a good mind to change you all into a thunder storm. Then you can make as much noise as you like! It's bad enough to have *one* child here, making a fuss and yelling and screaming, without having a whole crowd!'

'Oh – have you seen a child here?' said Joe, at once. 'Where is she, please? We are looking for her.'

'She went up the ladder-that-has-no-top,' said the old woman. 'And she hasn't come down. I hope she

441

stays up there for ever!'

'Oh – bother Connie!' groaned Joe. 'Now we'll have to do a bit more climbing, and see how far up the ladder she's gone! Come on!'

So off they all went to the shining ladder, that stretched from the ground up and up and up. No top could be seen.

'I'll go,' said Moon-Face. 'I'm not tired, and all of you are. I'll bring Connie down. I doubt if she's gone further than the hundredth rung!'

He went up the ladder, and the others sat down at the bottom waiting. They waited and they waited. Why didn't Moon-Face come back?

VII. UP THE LADDER-THAT-
HAS-NO-TOP

Joe and the others waited and waited, looking up the
ladder every now and again. Beth got impatient and
wandered off to look at some of the marvels. Joe called
her back.

'Beth! Don't go wandering off by yourself, for
goodness' sake! We don't want to lose *you*, as soon as
we find Connie. We'll have a look at the marvels when
Moon-Face brings Connie back.'

'Well, he's such a long time up the ladder,'
complained Beth. 'I did want to go and see the cat-
that-tells-fortunes. She might tell me how we can get
back home!'

'Back through Giantland, I suppose?' said Silky.

'I *wish* Moon-Face would come!' sighed Frannie,
looking up the ladder for the twentieth time. 'What *is*
he doing up there? Surely Connie can't have climbed
very far!'

Moon-Face had gone up a good way. He climbed
steadily, looking up every now and again, hoping to
see Connie. At last he saw a pair of feet, and he gave a
yell.

'Connie! I've come to rescue you! It's Moon-Face
coming up the ladder!'

The feet didn't move. They were big feet, and it
suddenly struck Moon-Face that they were too big to
be Connie's. He looked above the feet, and saw a

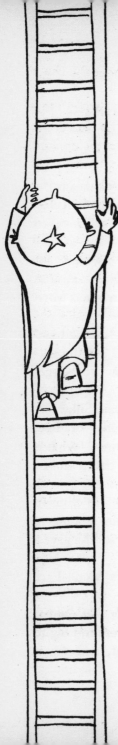

goblin looking down at him.

'Oh!' said Moon-Face. 'I thought you were Connie. Let me pass, please.'

'Can't think why there's so much traffic on this ladder today,' said the goblin, grumbling as he sat to one side. He had big feet, big hands, a big head, and a very small body, so he looked rather odd. On his knees he balanced a big can of paint, out of which stuck a paintbrush.

'What are *you* doing up here?' asked Moon-Face. 'Painting or something?'

'I'm the goblin painter who made that wall giant-proof,' said the goblin. He pointed to where the wall between Giantland and the Land of Marvels shimmered and quivered like a heat-haze. 'But I got into trouble with Witch Wily, who used to go and shop in Giantland. I splashed some of my paint over her, and that meant she was giant-proof too. No giant in Giantland could go near her, so she couldn't do any more shopping!'

'So she chased you, I suppose, to put a spell on you, and you rushed up the ladder-that-has-no-top!' said Moon-Face, sitting down beside him to peer at his paint. 'Bad luck! Why doesn't she chase you up here?'

'She doesn't like climbing,' said the goblin. 'But she's waiting down there at the bottom, I'm sure of it.'

'She isn't,' said Moon-Face. 'I've just come up, and there was no witch down there. You go on down now, and see. I'm sure you can slip off and escape.'

'She said she'd empty my giant-proof paint all over me if she caught me,' said the goblin, miserably.

'Well, leave it here with me,' said Moon-Face. 'I'll bring it down for you. Then, if the witch *is* at the bottom it won't matter, because you won't have your paint with you.'

'Right!' said the goblin, cheering up. He tied the handle of his paint can to a rung of the ladder, and began to go down. Moon-Face suddenly remembered Connie, and he called down to the goblin.

'Hey! Just a minute! Have you seen a little girl go up the ladder?'

'Oh yes,' said the goblin, stopping. 'A dirty little girl, very frightened. She was crying. She pushed past me very rudely indeed. I didn't like her.'

'Oh, that's Connie all right,' said Moon-Face, and he began to climb up again. 'I hope she hasn't gone too far up. She really is a nuisance.'

He lost sight of the goblin. He went on climbing up and up, and at last he heard a miserable voice above him. It was Connie's.

'I can't climb any further! This ladder doesn't lead anywhere. I can't climb down because that goblin will scold me. I shall have to stay here for the rest of my life. Boo-hoo, boo-hoo!'

445

Connie sobbed, and two or three tears splashed down on Moon-Face's head. He rubbed them off. Then he saw Connie's feet above him.

'Hey, Connie!' he called.

Connie gave a shriek and almost fell off the ladder. Moon-Face felt it wobbling. 'Oh! Oh! Who is it?' cried Connie, and began to climb hurriedly up the ladder again, afraid that the goblin was after her.

This was too much for Moon-Face. Here he was, having gone all the way to the Land of Marvels, through Giantland, and up goodness knows how many rungs of the ladder – and just as he had found Connie she began climbing up and up again. He caught firmly hold of one of her ankles. She screamed.

'Let go! I'll pinch you! Let go!'

'You come down,' commanded Moon-Face. 'I've come to take you back home, you silly girl. You've caused us all a lot of trouble. Come on down! I'm Moon-Face.'

Connie sat down on the ladder with great relief. She put her arms round Moon-Face as he came up beside her, and hugged him.

'Moon-Face! I was never so pleased to see anyone. Tell me how you got here.'

'No,' said Moon-Face, wriggling away. 'There's no time. The others are waiting at the foot of the ladder. Come on down, you silly girl!'

'But there's a gob . . .' began Connie.

'No, there isn't,' said Moon-Face, beginning to wonder how many other people there were sitting on the ladder, afraid to go down because they thought someone was watching for them at the bottom.

'There's no goblin and no witch and no nothing. Only Joe, Beth, Frannie, Silky and Saucepan. Come on, please!'

He made Connie climb down below him. 'Now, if you don't climb down pretty fast, I shall be treading on your fingers!' he said, and that made Connie climb down much more quickly than she had meant to. Down and down they went, down and down. And, at last, there they were on the ground!

The others crowded round them. 'Moon-Face! We thought you were never coming!'

'Connie! Are you all right?'

'A goblin came hurrying down, but he wouldn't stop to tell us anything!'

'Moon-Face, what have you got in that can?'

Moon-Face showed them the can of giant-proof paint he had brought down with him. He had untied it from the ladder when he came to it. He told them about the goblin.

Connie was longing to tell her adventures, too. She told them at last.

'When I got here, into this land, I wandered about a bit,' she said. 'And I came to the cat that could tell fortunes, so I asked her to tell me mine. And she told me all kinds of nasty things that would happen to me, so I scolded her, and she hissed and ran away.'

'You naughty girl!' said Silky.

'Well, she shouldn't have said nasty things to me,' said Connie. 'Then a goblin, whose cat it was, chased me and said he would lock me up. Horrid creature!'

The others laughed. They thought Connie deserved all she got. 'So I suppose you shot up the ladder to escape and didn't dare to come down?' said Joe.

'Yes,' said Connie. 'And I was so pleased to see Moon-Face. I don't like this land. And I don't like the Faraway Tree either, or the Enchanted Wood.'

'Or me, or Beth, or Frannie, or Silky, or Moon-Face, or Saucepan, I suppose?' said Joe. 'Pleasant child, aren't you? I think if I was a goblin I would certainly chase you away. Well, what about going home? It's getting late.'

'Oh dear – have we got to go through Giantland again?' said Silky. 'I didn't like those enormous giants. I'm afraid of their great big feet.'

'Yes, we've got to go through Giantland,' said Moon-Face. 'But I've got an idea. I'll splash you all with a few drops of giant-proof paint! Then no giant can come near us. We'll be like that wall – giant-proof!'

'Oh, what a good idea!' said Beth. So Moon-Face quickly dabbed a few drops of paint on each of them. The places he dabbed shone and shimmered strangely, like the wall. The children laughed.

'We look peculiar. Never mind – if it keeps the giants away from us, it will be worth it.'

They made their way to the shining wall, which disappeared as they walked through it, and re-appeared again as soon as they were on the other side. Then they began to walk cautiously through Giantland, to find the top of the Bean-Stalk.

Many giants were out, taking an evening walk. Some of them saw the children and pointed in surprise. They knelt down to pick them up.

But they couldn't touch them! The giant-proof

paint prevented any giant from getting too near, and no matter how they tried they couldn't get hold of any of the little group of friends.

'This is jolly good stuff, this paint,' said Joe, pleased. 'It was a good idea of yours, Moon-Face.'

'Look – there's the top of the Bean-Stalk,' said Silky, happily. 'Now we won't be long!'

The giants followed them to the Bean-Stalk. The children and the others climbed down as quickly as they could, half afraid that the giants might shake the Bean-Stalk so that they would fall off. But they didn't. They just called rudely down after them.

They got to the ground and sighed with relief. 'My goodness, we're late!' said Joe, looking at his watch. 'We must head for home at once. Where's that train?'

Soon they were in the funny little train. They got out at the Enchanted Wood, said goodbye to Moon-Face, Silky and Saucepan, and made their way home. Connie was very tired.

'Well – I guess you didn't enjoy the party very much?' said Joe to Connie. 'And what about the Faraway Tree and the people there? Do you believe in them now?'

'I suppose I'll have to,' said Connie. 'But I didn't like any of them much, except Moon-Face. I can't bear Saucepan.'

'He doesn't seem to like you, either,' said Beth. 'Well, Connie – you don't need to come with us again if you don't want to. We can leave you behind.'

But that didn't please Connie! No – she meant to go where the others went. *She* wasn't going to be left out!

VIII. THE FARAWAY TREE AGAIN

Mother wasn't very pleased to see how dirty, ink-stained and ragged Connie's clothes were when she came back with the others.

'I won't let you go with the others to the Faraway Tree again if you can't keep youself cleaner than this,' she said, crossly. Connie was not used to being talked to like this, and she burst into tears.

The children's mother popped Connie's clothes into the washtub and said, 'Tomorrow you will iron and mend these clothes, Connie. Stop that noise, or I will send you to bed straight away.'

All the children were tired, and fell asleep as soon as their heads touched the pillow. When Connie woke up, she remembered all that had happened the day before, and wondered if she could possibly have dreamt it. It seemed so amazing when she thought about it.

'Are we going to the Faraway Tree today again?' she asked Joe, when they were all having breakfast.

Joe shook his head.

'No, We've got lots of work to do. And anyway you didn't like it, or the people there, so we'll go alone.'

Connie looked as if she was going to burst into tears. Then she remembered that tears didn't seem to bother anyone here, so she blinked them away. 'What land will be at the top of the tree this week?' she asked.

'Don't know,' said Joe. 'Anyway, we're not going, Connie. We've had enough travelling this week!'

For the next two days it rained so hard that Mother wouldn't let the children go out. They heard nothing from their friends in the Faraway Tree.

The next day was sunny and the sky was a lovely blue. 'As if it had been washed clean by all the rain,' said Frannie. 'Let's go to the Enchanted Wood. Can we, Mother?'

'Well, yes, I should think so,' said Mother. 'I badly want a new saucepan, a nice little one for boiling milk. You could go and ask the Saucepan Man to sell me one. Here's some money.'

'Oh, lovely!' said Beth, overjoyed at the thought of visiting the Faraway Tree folk again. 'We'll go this morning.'

'I'm going too,' said Connie.

'You're not,' said Joe. 'You're going to stay at home like a good girl, and help Mother. You'll like that.'

'Indeed I won't!' said Connie. 'Don't be mean. Take me with you.'

'Well, it's no fun taking you anywhere,' said Joe. 'You've got bad manners, and you don't do what you're told, and people don't like you. You'll be far better at home. Anyway, you don't believe in anything in the Enchanted Wood, so why do you want to come?'

'Because I don't want to be left out,' wailed Connie. 'Let me come. I'll be good. I'll have nice manners. I'll like everyone.'

'Well, you won't go in that nice

451

dress,' said Mother, firmly. 'I'm not going to let you spoil another one. If you go, you must borrow some old clothes of Frannie's. They're a bit patched, but that won't matter.'

Connie didn't want to wear Frannie's old clothes, but she went to put them on. She couldn't bear being left out, and if the others were going off to the Wood she really must go too. She came back wearing Frannie's old washed-out clothes.

'You look sensible now,' said Joe. 'Very sensible. It won't even matter if you go down the slippery-slip without a cushion again. That material won't wear out in a hurry. Come on, everybody!'

They set off, Joe jingling the money for the saucepan in his pocket. They jumped over the ditch and landed in the Enchanted Wood. At once everything seemed magic and different. Connie felt excited again. She was longing to see Moon-Face who, since he had rescued her from the Land of Marvels, had become her hero.

They came to the Faraway Tree. It was so hot that the children didn't feel like climbing up. 'We'll go up on cushions,' said Joe. 'We'll send the red squirrel up to tell Moon-Face to send some down on the ropes.'

He whistled a little tune and the red squirrel popped out of his hole. 'Your sweater is getting so holey you won't be able to keep it on soon!' said Beth.

'I know,' said the squirrel. 'But I don't know how to mend it.'

'I'll do it for you one day,' said Beth. 'I'm good at needlework. Now, squirrel, please go up to Moon-Face and ask him to send down four cushions on ropes. It's really too hot to climb up today.'

The red squirrel bounded up the Tree as light as a feather, his plumy tail waving behind him. The children sat down and waited, watching the funny little folk that trotted up and down the big Tree, going about their business.

There soon came a rustling of leaves, and down through the branches came four fat cushions, tied firmly to ropes. 'Here we are,' said Joe, jumping up. 'Moon-Face has been jolly quick. Choose a cushion, Connie, and sit on it. Hold the rope tightly, give it three tugs, and up you'll go!'

It was exciting. Connie sat on the big, soft cushion, held on to the rope, and gave it three tugs. The rope was hauled up from above, and Connie went swinging upwards between the branches. She saw that the Tree was growing apricots that day. She wondered if they were ripe.

She picked one and it was deliciously sweet and juicy. She thought she would pick another one, but by that time the Tree was growing acorns, which was disappointing.

Soon everyone was on the broad branch outside Moon-Face's house. He was there with Mister Watzisname, pulling hard at the ropes.

'Hello!' said Mister Watzisname, beaming at the children. 'Haven't seen you for a long time.'

'You've always been asleep when we've come here,' said Joe. 'Watzisname, this is Connie.'

'Ah – how do you do?' said Watzisname. 'Is this the little girl Saucepan was telling me about? She doesn't look so dirty and ragged as he said.'

'*Well*!' began Connie, indignantly. 'Fancy Saucepan saying . . .'

'Now, don't lose your temper,' said Joe. 'After all, you *did* look dirty and ragged the other day. Where *is* Saucepan, Moon-Face? I want to buy something from him.'

'He's gone up into the land at the top of the Tree,' said Moon-Face. 'He heard that there was an old friend of his there, Little Miss Muffet, and he wanted to go and see her. She once gave him some curds and whey when he was very hungry, and he has never forgotten it. It was the only time in his life he ever tasted curds and whey.'

'Oh!' said Joe. 'Well, what land is up there this week, then?'

'The Land of Nursery Rhyme,' said Moon-Face. 'So Watzisname says, anyway. You went up, didn't you Watzisname, and saw Little Tommy Tucker, and Little Jack Horner?'

'Yes,' said Watzisname. 'Quite an interesting land. All sorts of friendly people there.'

'Let's go up and find Saucepan!' said Beth. 'It will be fun. It's quite a harmless land, that's obvious. Goodness knows how long Saucepan will be up there with Little Miss Muffet. Maybe he's feasting on curds and whey again, and won't be back for days!'

'Oh – please let's go!' said Connie. 'And Moon-Face, dear Moon-Face, you come too.'

'Don't call me "Dear Moon-Face",' said Moon-Face. 'You're not my best friend yet.'

'Oh!' said Connie, who was so used to being fussed and spoilt by everyone that she couldn't understand anybody not liking her.

'I think it would be fun to go up and see the Nursery Rhyme people,' said Joe. 'Come on – let's go now. We could get a saucepan from the Old Saucepan Man while we're there, and take it back with us.'

'Well, come along, then,' said Moon-Face, and he led the way up the topmost branch of the Tree. One by one they climbed it, came to the little ladder that led through the cloud, and found themselves in yet another land.

'The Land of Nursery Rhyme!' said Beth, looking round. 'Well – we should know most of the people here, though they won't know us! I wonder where Saucepan is. He could introduce us to everyone.'

'We'll ask where Little Miss Muffet lives,' said Moon-Face. 'Look – that must be Jack Horner, over there, carrying a pie!'

'Ask him where Miss Muffet is,' said Frannie.

So they went over to where a plump little boy was just about to make a hole in his pie with his thumb.

'Please, where is Miss Muffet?' asked Joe.

'Over the other side of the hill,' said Jack Horner, pointing with a juicy thumb. 'Look out for her spider – he's pretty fierce today!'

IX. NURSERY RHYME LAND

'What did he mean – look out for the spider?' asked Connie, looking round worriedly.

'Well, you know that a spider keeps coming and sitting down beside Miss Muffet whenever she eats her curds and whey, don't you?' said Joe 'We've just got to look out for it.'

'I'm scared of spiders,' said Connie, looking as if she was going to cry.

'You would be!' said Joe. 'You're just the kind of person who's afraid of bats and moths and spiders and everything. Don't be silly. Go back if you'd rather not come with us.'

'All the same – it may be quite a *big* spider,' said Frannie.

Connie looked even more alarmed.

The children, Moon-Face and Watzisname walked to the hill, went up it, and stood at the top. Nursery Rhyme Land was nice. Its houses and cottages had thatched roofs, and the little gardens were full of flowers. The children felt that they knew everyone they met.

'Here's Tommy Tucker!' whispered Frannie, as a little boy hurried by, singing loudly in a clear, sweet voice. He heard her whisper and turned.

'Do you know me?' he asked in surprise. 'I don't know you.'

'*Are* you Tommy Tucker?' asked Beth. 'Were you going to sing for your supper?'

'Of course not. It's morning,' said Tommy. 'I sing for my supper at night. I was just practising a bit then. Do you sing for *your* supper?'

'No, We just have it, without singing,' said Joe.

'You're lucky,' said Tommy. 'Nobody will give me any if I don't sing. It's a good thing I've got a nice voice!'

He went off singing like a blackbird again. The others watched him, and then saw someone else coming along crying bitterly. A small boy was walking along, while a bigger boy was giving him a scolding. Behind the two came a thin cat, its fur wet and draggled.

'Hey! Stop scolding that little boy!' cried Joe, who didn't like to see a small boy being bullied by a bigger one. 'Pick someone your own size!'

'Mind your own business,' said the big boy. 'Johnny Thin deserves all he gets. You don't know what a bad boy he is!'

'Johnny Thin! Oh, isn't he the boy who put the cat down the well?' cried Frannie. 'Then you must be Johnny Stout, who pulled her out!'

'Yes – and there's the cat, poor thing,' said Johnny Stout. '*Now* don't you think that bad boy deserves a good scolding?'

'Oh *yes*,' said Beth. 'He does. Poor cat. I'll dry it a bit.'

She got out her handkerchief and tried to dry the cat. But it was too wet.

'Don't bother,' said Johnny Stout, giving Johnny Thin a final scolding that sent him off howling loudly.

'I'll take the cat to Polly Flinders. She's always sitting by a fire, warming her toes!'

He picked up the cat and went into a nearby cottage. The children went and peeped in at the open door. They saw a little girl in the room inside, sitting close to a roaring fire, her toes wriggling in the heat.

Johnny Stout gave the cat to the little girl. 'Here you are, Polly!' he said. 'Dry her a bit, will you? She got put down the well again. But I've given Johnny Thin a good scolding, so maybe he won't do it any more.'

Polly Flinders took the cat on her lap, which made her pretty dress all wet. Johnny Stout was just going out of the door when somebody else came in. It was Polly Flinders' mother. When she saw Polly sitting among the cinders, warming her toes and nursing the wet cat, she gave an angry cry.

'You naughty little girl! How many times have I told you not to sit so close to the fire? What's the good of dressing you up in nice clothes if you make them so dirty? I'll teach you to be good!'

The children, Moon-Face and Watzisname felt rather scared of the angry mother. Johnny Stout ran away and the others thought it would be better to go too.

They went down the other side of the hill.

'Hello – who are these two coming up the hill?' said Moon-Face.

'Jack and Jill, of course!' said Beth. And so it was, carrying a pail between them. They filled it at the well that stood at the top of the hill, and then began to go carefully down the hill.

458

'Oh – I do hope they don't fall down,' said Frannie, anxiously. 'They always do in the rhyme!'

Jack and Jill began to quarrel as they went down the hill. 'Don't go so fast, Jack!' shouted Jill.

'You're always so slow!' grumbled Jack. 'Do hurry up!'

'The pail's so heavy!' cried Jill, and began to lag behind just as they came to a steep bit.

'They'll fall down – and Jack will break his crown again – he'll hurt his head badly!' said Beth. 'I'm going to stop them!'

She ran to the two children, who stopped, surprised. 'Don't quarrel, Jack and Jill,' begged Beth. 'You know you'll only fall down and hurt yourselves. Jill, let me take the handle of the pail. I can go as fast as Jack likes. Then for once you will get to the bottom of the hill safely, without falling down.'

Jill let go of the pail handle. Beth took it. Jack smiled at her. 'Thank you,' he said. 'Jill's always so slow. Come along with me, and I'll give you one of my toffees. I've got a whole bag full at home.'

Beth liked toffees. 'Oh, thank you,' she said. 'I'd like one.' She turned to the others. 'You go on to Miss Muffet's,' she said. 'I'll join you later.'

So off went the others, while Jack, Jill and Beth went down the hill together.

The others came to a gate with a name painted on it. 'LITTLE MISS MUFFET'.

'This is the place,' said Joe, pleased. 'Now we'll find old Saucepan. Hey, Saucepan, are you anywhere about?'

The door was shut. No one came. Joe banged on

459

the knocker. Rat-a-tat-tat! Still no one came.

'There's someone peeping out of the window,' said Moon-Face, suddenly. 'It looks like Miss Muffet.'

A little bit of blind had been pushed to one side, and a frightened eye, a little nose, and a curl could be seen. That was all.

'It *is* Miss Muffet!' said Watzisname. 'Miss Muffet, what's the matter? Why don't you open the door? Where is Saucepan?'

The blind fell back. There came a scamper of feet, and then the door opened a tiny bit. 'Come in, quickly, all of you – quick, quick, quick!'

Her voice was so scared that everyone felt frightened. They crowded into the cottage quickly.

'What's the matter?' asked Moon-Face. 'Has anything happened? Where's Saucepan? Didn't he come?'

'Yes, he came. But he was rude to my spider,' said Miss Muffet. 'He danced all round it, clashing his kettles and saucepans, and he sang a rude song, that began, "Two snaps for a spider . . ."'

'Just like Saucepan!' groaned Moon-Face. 'Well, what's happened?'

'The spider pounced on him and carried him off,' wept Miss Muffet. 'I brought him all the curds and whey in the house, but it didn't make any difference. He took no notice, and carried Saucepan away to his home. It's a sort of cave in the ground, with a web door. No one can get through it except the spider.'

'*Well*!' said Moon-Face, sitting down hard on a little chair. 'How very annoying! How are we going to get him out? Why must he go and annoy the spider like that?'

'Well, the spider came and suddenly sat down beside me, and made me jump,' said Miss Muffet. 'He's always doing that. It made me run away, and Saucepan said he would give the spider a fright to pay him back.'

'So he made up one of his silly songs, and did his crashing, clanging dance!' said Joe. 'What are we going to do? Do you think the spider will let Saucepan go?'

'Oh no – not till the Land of Nursery Rhyme moves on,' said Miss Muffet. 'He means to punish him well. I don't know if Saucepan will mind living here. He doesn't really belong, of course.'

'He'd hate to live here always and never see any of us except when the Land of Nursery Rhyme happened to come to the top of the Faraway Tree,' said Moon-Face. 'We must go and talk to that spider. Come on, all of you!'

'Oh – must I come?' asked Connie.

'Yes – the more of us that go, the better,' said Watzisname. 'The spider may feel afraid when he sees so many people marching up! You come too, Miss Muffet.'

So they all went, to face the spider in his webby cave. Connie and Miss Muffet walked hand in hand behind, ready to run! Neither of them was very brave.

'Beth will wonder where we are,' said Joe, remembering that she had gone off with Jack and Jill. 'Never mind – we'll find her when we've rescued Saucepan.'

They came to a cave in the ground. It had a thick,

grey web door. From inside came a mournful voice:

> *Two snaps for a spider,*
> *Two taps on his nose.*
> *Two claps on his ankles,*
> *Hi-tiddley-toze!*

'That's Saucepan, singing his rude spider song again,' whispered Miss Muffet. 'Oh – look out! There's the spider!'

X. MISS MUFFET'S SPIDER

'There's the spider! Here he comes!' cried everyone.

And the spider certainly was there. He was very large, had eight eyes to see with, and eight hairy legs to walk with. He wore a blue and red scarf round his neck, and he sneezed as he came.

'Wish-oo! Wish-oo! Bother this cold! No sooner do I lose one cold than I get another!'

He suddenly saw the little group of six people, and he stared with all his eight eyes. 'What do *you* want?' he said.

Moon-Face went forward boldly, looking far braver than he felt.

'We've come to tell you to set our friend free,' he said. 'Open that webby door at once and let him out. We know he's down there, because we can hear him singing.'

Out floated Saucepan's voice. 'Two snaps for a spider . . .'

'There! He's singing that rude song again!' said the spider, looking annoyed. 'No, I certainly won't let him go. He needs a lesson.'

'You *must* let him go!' said Moon-Face. 'He doesn't belong to your land. He belongs to ours. He'll be very unhappy here.'

'Serves him right,' said the spider. 'A wish-oo! A wish-oo! Bother this cold.'

'I hope you get hundreds of colds!' said Moon-Face, angrily. 'Are you going to let Saucepan free, or do we slash that door to bits?'

'Try if you like!' said the spider, taking out a big red handkerchief from somewhere. 'You'll be sorry, that's all I can say.'

'Anyone got a stick?' asked Moon-Face. Nobody had. So Moon-Face marched to a nearby bush and cut out two or three strong sticks. He gave one to Joe, one to Watzisname, and another to Frannie. He could see that Connie and Miss Muffet wouldn't be much use, so he didn't give them one.

'Now – slash down the door!' cried Moon-Face. The spider didn't say anything, but a horrid smile came on its face. It sat down and watched.

Moon-Face ran to the webby door and slashed at it with his stick. Joe and Watzisname slashed too, and Frannie followed.

But the webby door stuck to their sticks, and wound itself all round them. They tried to get it off, but the web stuck to them too. Soon it was floating about in long threads fastening itself round their legs and arms.

The spider got up. Connie and Miss Muffet were frightened and ran off as fast as they could. They hid under a bush and watched. They saw the spider push Joe, Moon-Face, Frannie and Watzisname into a heap together, and then roll them up in grey web so that they were caught like flies.

Then he bundled them all into his cave, and sat down to spin another webby door.

'A wish-oo!' sneezed the spider, suddenly. Then he

464

coughed. He certainly had a terrible cold. He spied
Connie and Miss Muffet under the bush and called to
them.

'You come over here, too, and I'll wrap you up nice
and cosy in my web!'

Both Connie and Miss Muffet squealed and ran
back to Miss Muffet's cottage as fast as they could.
When they got there they saw Beth coming along with
Jack and Jill.

'Hello, Miss Muffet!' called Jack. 'Guess what,
because of Beth's help, I got down the hill for the first
time without falling over and hurting my head.
Mother was very pleased, and she said we can have
the whole day to play. So we thought we'd come and
spend it with the other children, and Moon-Face.
Where are they?'

'Oh, they've been taken prisoner by Miss Muffet's
spider!' said Connie. She told them all about it, and

465

Beth stared in horror. What! Joe and Frannie being kept prisoner by a horrid old spider! Whatever could be done?

'And he had an awful cold,' finished Connie. 'I never knew spiders could catch colds before. He was coughing and sneezing just like we do.'

'Sounds as if he ought to be in bed,' said Jill. 'Look out – here he comes!'

'A wish-oo!' said the spider, as he came by. 'A wish-oo! Bother this cold!'

'Why don't you do something for it?' said Jill, stepping boldly forward. She knew the spider quite well, and was not afraid of him.

'Well, I've put a scarf on, haven't I?' said the spider, sniffing. 'What more can I do?'

'You'd better put your feet in a mustard bath,' said Jack. 'That's what Mother makes us do if we have a bad cold. And we have to go to bed too, and drink hot lemon.'

'That does sound nice and comforting,' said the spider. 'But I've got no bed, and no one to look after me – and no lemon.'

'If Miss Muffet will lend you a bed, and squeeze you a lemon, Jack and I will look after you,' said Jill. Miss Muffet stared at her in horror, but Jill gave her a nudge. She had a reason for saying all this. Miss Muffet swallowed hard and then nodded.

'All right! He can have my spare bed – but he is not to wander about my house and eat my curds and whey.'

'I won't, I promise I won't,' said the spider, gratefully. 'I'll be very good indeed. Thank you, Miss

Muffet. Perhaps I won't frighten you any more after this.'

'What about a bath to put his feet in?' said Jill. 'You haven't got a big enough one, Miss Muffet. You see, a spider has eight feet, not two.'

'I've got a big bath in my cave,' said the spider. 'I'll go and get it.'

'Certainly not,' said Jack. 'You mustn't go about in the open air any more, with that dreadful cold. You get into bed at once. *I'll* fetch your bath.'

'But – but – there's a webby door over my cave – and you can't possibly get through it – and besides, there are prisoners there,' said the spider.

'Well, tell me how to undo the door without getting caught up in that nasty webby stuff,' said Jack. 'Then I can get your bath and bring it here.'

'Have you got a nice big cotton reel, Miss Muffet?' asked the spider. 'You have? Good! Give it to Jack and he can take it with him. You'll find the end thread of the webby door just by the handle, Jack. Take hold of it and pull. Wind it round the reel and the web will unravel nicely. You will be able to pull the door undone just like people pull a woollen sweater undone!'

'Well, I never!' said Jill, in surprise. 'That's something to know, anyway. Is that the reel, Miss Muffet? Right! We'll go. We'll leave you to see the spider into bed, and squeeze him a lemon, and put a kettle on to boil. Then, when we come back with the bath, we can put mustard and hot water into it, and make the spider put his feet in. Then his cold will soon be better.'

The spider looked very happy at being cared for like

this. He looked gratefully at the children out of his eight eyes.

Connie, Jack and Jill and Beth set off. The spider called after them. 'Hey! What about my prisoners? I don't want them to escape. You'll find them all bound up in web. Leave them like that, and put a stone or something over the opening of my cave, will you?'

'We'll find a nice big stone,' promised Jack. 'Now hurry up and get into bed.'

Soon the four of them got to the spider's cave and saw the webby door. Behind it they could hear Moon-Face groaning and grumbling, and Saucepan humming one of his songs.

'Look – there's the end of the web, sticking out just there!' said Connie, pointing to the middle of the door.

'Who's there?' called Joe, from below.

'Me, Connie,' said Connie, 'and Beth too, and Jack and Jill, come to rescue you. We're going to undo the door.'

Jack pulled at the end of the web, and a thread unravelled. He wound it round and round the reel. Soon the door began to fall to pieces as all the thread was wound round the big cotton reel. Then the children could see inside the cave. They saw Moon-Face, Watzisname, Saucepan, Joe and Frannie all in a heap together, bound tightly, but Joe called out to them in warning: 'Don't come near us or you'll be all messed up in this horrid sticky web.'

'I'm just going to find the end of the web that is binding you so tightly, and unravel it,' said Jack. 'Then you'll be free.'

He found the end of the thread, and soon he was unravelling it like wool, and the four prisoners rolled over and over on the floor as their bonds were pulled away. And at last they were free!

'Oooh! Thank you,' said Joe, sitting up. 'I feel better now that sticky stuff is off. What a lot you've got on that cotton reel, Jack!'

'Perhaps you would like to take it home and give it to Silky, as a little present,' said Jack. 'I know she often makes dresses, doesn't she?'

'Oh yes, she'd love it,' said Joe, taking it. 'Come on – let's get out of here and go home. I'm tired of Nursery Rhyme Land.'

'We promised the spider we'd block up the door of his cave so that you couldn't escape,' said Jack, with a grin. 'You get out first, and we'll put a stone here after!'

So they did. Then, taking the spider's big bath on his shoulder, Jack led the way back. 'Don't go near the window in case the spider sees you,' he said to Moon-Face and the others. 'I'll just bring little Miss Muffet out to say goodbye to you, then you can go.'

He went in with the bath. Miss Muffet had the kettle boiling and poured the water into it, adding some yellow mustard. She stirred it up and called to the spider:

'Come along – it's ready!'

He got out of the bed and put his feet into it, all eight of them. Then he suddenly looked up. 'I can hear my prisoners whispering together!' he said. 'They must have escaped. I must go after them!'

XI. BACK AT MOON-FACE'S

Miss Muffet rushed to the door to warn the others to go. 'He's heard you whispering together!' she said. 'Go quickly!'

The children and the others all fled, Jack and Jill too. The spider took his feet out of the hot mustard bath and looked round for a towel to dry them.

'I won't give you a towel,' said Miss Muffet, severely. 'You can go after them with wet feet, and get an even worse cold, and be dreadfully ill. But I won't nurse you then.'

The spider sneezed. 'A wish-oo, a-wish-oo! Oh dear, this is such a dreadful cold. I don't want to make it any worse. I'll be good and put my feet back. I'll have to let my prisoners escape.'

'There's a good spider,' said Miss Muffet.

He was pleased. 'I wish I could have a hot-water bottle, Miss Muffet. I've never had one.'

'Well, as you've let your prisoners go, I'll lend you my hot-water bottle,' said Miss Muffet, and went to get it.

Joe, Moon-Face, Saucepan and the others had by this time got to the top of the hill and down the other side. They looked back but could see no sign of the spider.

'He's not coming after us, after all,' said Beth thankfully. 'Where's the hole through the cloud?'

'We'll show you,' said Jack and Jill. 'We'd like to come down it with you, and see the Faraway Tree.'

'Oh *do*!' said everyone. 'Come and have some dinner with us.'

'I'll send a message down to Silky and get her to come up and help to make some sandwiches,' said Moon-Face.

When they came to the hole in the cloud they all slid down the ladder and branch, and went to Moon-Face's house. Jack and Jill were amused to see his curved furniture.

They sent the red squirrel down to fetch Silky. She had been out shopping all morning, and came up delighted to know that Joe and the others were up the Tree. She was pleased to see Jack and Jill too.

'Hello!' she cried. 'It's ages since I saw you two. Do you still fall down the hill? Jack, you haven't got your head done up in vinegar and brown paper, for a change!'

'No – because Beth kindly helped me carry the pail of water down the hill today,' said Jack. 'And she goes faster than Jill, so we didn't fall over by getting out of step. We've had a lot of adventures today, Silky.'

'Oh, Silky, here's a present for you,' said Joe, remembering, and he gave the pretty little fairy the cotton reel with the spider thread wound onto it.

'Oh, thank you, Joe!' cried Silky. 'Just what I want! I couldn't get any fine thread at all this morning. This will do beautifully.'

'Will you help to make some sandwiches, Silky?' said Moon-Face. 'We thought we'd have a picnic dinner up here. Let me see – how many of us are there?'

'Six children – and four others,' counted Joe. 'Ten. You'll have to make about a hundred sandwiches!'

'It's a pity the Land of Goodies isn't here,' said Moon-Face. 'We could go up and take what food we wanted then and bring it down. Got any Google Buns or Pop Cakes, Silky dear?'

'I've got some Pop Cakes in my basket somewhere,' said Silky. 'Do Jack and Jill know them?'

They didn't, and they did enjoy them. They went pop as soon as they were put into the mouth, and honey flowed out from the middle of each cake!

'Delicious!' said Jack. 'I could do with a big box of these cakes.'

Soon they were all sitting on the broad branch outside Moon-Face's house, eating sandwiches and cakes and drinking lemonade.

There was as much lemonade as anyone wanted, because, in a friendly manner, the Faraway Tree suddenly began to grow ripe yellow lemons on the branches round about. All Moon-Face had to do was pick them, cut them in half, and squeeze them into a jug. Then he added water and sugar, and the children drank the lemonade!

'This is a marvellous tree,' said Connie, leaning back happily. 'Absolutely marvellous. You *are* clever, Moon-Face, to make such lovely lemonade.'

'Goodness me. Connie seems to be believing in the Tree at last,' said Joe. 'Do you, Connie?'

'Yes, I do,' said Connie. 'I can't help it. I didn't like that spider adventure – but this is lovely, sitting here and eating these delicious sandwiches and Pop Cakes, and drinking lemonade from lemons growing on the Tree.'

She shook the branch she was leaning on, and some ripe lemons fell off. They went bumping down the Tree.

There came a yell from below.

'Now then! Who's throwing ripe lemons at me, I should like to know. One's got in my washtub. Any more of that and I'll come up and punish the thrower.'

'There!' said Moon-Face to Connie. 'See what you've done! Shaken down heaps of juicy lemons on to Dame Washalot. She'll be after you if you're not careful.'

'Oooh!' said Connie, in alarm. She called down the Tree. 'I'm sorry, Dame Washalot. It was an accident.'

'Connie's getting some manners,' said Joe to Beth. 'Any more Pop Cakes? Have another, Saucepan?'

'Mother's very well, thank you,' said Saucepan.

'I said, "Have ANOTHER?"' said Joe.

'You haven't asked him to sell you a saucepan,' said Beth. 'Ask him about a saucepan to boil milk.'

'Oiled silk?' said Saucepan. 'No, my mother doesn't wear oiled silk. Why should she? She wears black, with a red shawl and a red bag and a bonnet with . . .'

'Can't we get away from Saucepan's mother?' groaned Joe. 'I never even knew he had one. I wonder where she lives.'

Saucepan unexpectedly heard this. 'She lives in the Land of Dame Snap,' he said. 'She's works for her. She needs lots of saucepans because she has to cook meals for all the children at her school.'

'Gosh!' said Beth, remembering. 'We've been to Dame Snap's Land! We flew there once in a 'plane.

We had an awful time because Dame Snap put us into her school!'

'Does your mother really live there?' said Joe. 'Do you ever go to see her?'

'Oh yes, when I can,' said Saucepan. 'I believe Dame Snap's land is coming next week. I'd like you all to meet my dear old mother. She will give you a wonderful dinner.'

There was a silence. No one wanted to be mixed up with Dame Snap again. She was a most unpleasant person.

'*Well*?' said Saucepan, looking round. 'I didn't hear anyone say "Thank you very much, we'd love to know your mother".'

'Well, you see – er – er – it's a bit awkward,' said Moon-Face. 'You see, your mother working for Dame Snap – er . . .'

'I suppose you are trying to say that my dear old mother isn't good enough for you to meet!' said Saucepan, unexpectedly, and looked terribly hurt and upset. 'All right. If you won't know my mother, you shan't know *me*!'

And to everyone's alarm he got up and walked straight up the branch into the cloud, and disappeared into the Land of Nursery Rhyme. Everyone yelled after him.

'Saucepan, we'd love to meet your mother, but we don't like Dame Snap!'

'Saucepan, come BACK!'

But Saucepan either didn't or

wouldn't hear. 'You go and fetch him back,' said Joe to Jack and Jill. So up they went after him. But they soon came back.

'Can't see him anywhere,' they said. 'He isn't anywhere to be found. I expect he is hiding himself away in a temper. He'll soon be back again.'

But Saucepan didn't come back.

'We'll have to go home,' said Joe, at last. 'Let us know when Saucepan comes back, Moon-Face. Tell him we would love to meet his old mother, and it's all a mistake. All the same – I hope he *won't* want us to go to Dame Snap's Land – I wouldn't like that at all.'

'Go down the slippery-slip,' said Moon-Face, throwing the children cushions. 'Yes, I feel upset about Saucepan too. He isn't usually so touchy. You go first, Joe.'

Joe sat on his cushion, gave himself a push and down he went, whizzing round and round the slippery-slip right to the bottom of the Tree.

He shot out of the trapdoor and landed on the tuft of moss. He got up hurriedly, knowing that Connie was coming down just behind him.

Soon all four were at the foot of the Tree. The squirrel collected the cushions and disappeared with them. Joe linked arms with the girls, and they turned towards home.

'Well, that was quite an adventure,' Joe said. 'I guess you don't want to meet Miss Muffet's spider again, Connie?'

'No, I don't,' said Connie. 'But I'd like to please old Saucepan, and meet his mother, even if he hasn't been very nice to me so far.'

'You're getting quite a nice little girl, Connie!' said Joe, in surprise. 'Well – maybe we'll all have to go and meet his mother next week. We'll see!'

XII. SAUCEPAN IS VERY CROSS

For a few days the children did not hear anything from their friends in the Faraway Tree.

'I wonder if the Old Saucepan Man calmed down a bit and went back to Moon-Face's,' said Joe.

On the fifth or sixth day there came a knock at the door. Joe opened it. Outside was the red squirrel and he had a note in his paw.

'For you all,' he said, and gave it to Joe. 'I need an answer, please.'

Joe slit the envelope and read the note out loud.

> *Dear Everybody,*
> *When are you coming to see us again? Old Saucepan came back yesterday from the Land of Nursery Rhyme. He had been staying with Polly-Put-The-Kettle-On. He gave her a new kettle, and she said he could stay with her in return. He is still upset because he says we don't want to meet his dear old mother. He won't speak to any of us. He is living with the Owl, and he has made up a lot of rude songs about us. Will you come and see if you can put things right? He might listen to you. He won't take any notice of me or Silky or Watzisname. So do come.*
> *Love from,*
> *Moon-face.*

'Well!' said Joe, putting the note back into its envelope. 'Funny old Saucepan! Who would have thought he would be so touchy? Why, I'd love to meet his mother. She must be a dear old thing.'

'It's only that she works in Dame Snap's school and if we go and see her, Dame Snap might catch us again,' said Beth. 'We had an awful time with her last time.'

'We'd better go up the Tree tomorrow, and tell Saucepan exactly what we think, and make sure he hears and understands us,' said Frannie. 'Let's do that.'

'Is that the answer then?' asked the red squirrel, politely.

'Yes, that's the answer,' said Joe. 'We'll be up the Tree tomorrow – and we'll try and put things right. Tell Moon-Face that.'

The squirrel bounded off. The children watched him. 'What a dependable little fellow that squirrel is,' said Joe. 'Well – we must go up the Tree tomorrow, no doubt about that. Coming, Connie?'

'Oh yes,' said Connie, beginning to feel excited again. 'Of course. I'd love to, Joe.'

So the next day, the four children went off to the Faraway Tree. 'We'll climb up,' said Joe. 'Because if Saucepan is living in the Owl's home, it's only just a little way past the Angry Pixie's, and we can call for him there.'

So, when they came to the Tree, they didn't send for cushions to go up on, but began to climb. The Tree was growing blackberries, ripe and juicy. It was fun to pick them, and bite into them, feeling the rich, sweet juice squirt out.

All of them had blackberry stained mouths as they climbed. They came to the Angry Pixie's and Connie kept well away from the window this time. But his door was open, and he was out. A small fieldmouse was busy scrubbing the floor, and another one was shaking the mats.

'Bit of spring cleaning going on,' said Joe, as they passed. 'I suppose the Angry Pixie's gone out for the day, to get away from it!'

Soon they came to the Owl's home. They peeped cautiously in at the window. Saucepan was there, polishing his kettles at top speed, making them shine brightly. He was singing one of his silly songs, very loudly:

> *Two scoldings for Connie,*
> *Two shakings for Joe,*
> *Two snarlings for Beth,*
> *Hi-Tiddley-ho!*

> *Two drubbings for Moon-Face,*
> *Two snubbings for Fran,*
> *Two snappings for Silky,*
> *From the old Saucepan Man!*

'Gosh! He must still be in a very bad temper,' said Beth, quite hurt. 'And imagine talking about snapping at Silky. He's always been so fond of her.'

'Do you think we'd better stop and talk to him now or not?' said Joe.

'Not,' said Frannie at once. 'He'll only be rude and

horrid. Let's go up to Moon-Face and Silky, and see what they suggest.'

So up the Tree they went, leaving behind the cross old Saucepan Man, still polishing his kettles. They just dodged Dame Washalot's water in time. They heard it coming and darted to the other side of the Tree. They waited till it had all gone down, then climbed up again.

They came to Silky's house and knocked at the door. Moon-Face opened it, and smiled.

'Hello! So you've come all right! Come in. I was just having a cup of hot chocolate with Silky.'

They all crowded into Silky's dear little tree house and sat down. Silky poured them out cups of hot chocolate, and handed round some new Pop Cakes. How Connie loved the pop they made, and the honey that flowed out from the middle! She sat enjoying her lunch and listened to the others talking.

'Saucepan is really awful,' said Silky. 'He sings rude songs about us all day long, and all the Tree folk laugh!'

'Yes, We heard the songs,' said Joe. 'Not very kind of him, is it? What can we do about it? Will he listen to us, do you think, if we go back and talk nicely to him?'

'I don't know,' said Moon-Face, doubtfully. 'When Silky and I went down to fetch him last night to beg him to be sensible and to be friends, he sang his songs at us, and did his clashing, clanging dance. He frightened everyone in the Tree, and Dame Washalot sent a message to say that if the noise went on she would empty twenty washtubs down at once, and drown us all!'

'We can't let Saucepan go on like this,' said Beth. 'How can we make him feel better, and ashamed of his rude behaviour?'

'I know!' said Connie, unexpectedly. 'Let's go down and take presents for his mother. Then he will be so pleased he will be nice again.'

Everyone stared at Connie. 'Well, isn't that a splendid idea!' said Silky. 'Why didn't we think of it before? Saucepan will be thrilled!'

'Yes, really, Connie, that's a great idea!' said Beth, and Connie went red with pleasure. The others ticked her off so much that it was very pleasant to be praised for a change.

'Connie's getting quite nice,' Frannie said to Silky and Moon-Face. 'Now she has to live with us, she's different – not so silly and selfish. You'll get to like her soon.'

'It's a good idea to take presents to Saucepan for his mother,' said Moon-Face. 'We'll do that. It's the one thing that will make him smile. What shall we take?'

'I'll look in my treasure bag,' said Silky, 'and you go up to your house and see if you've got anything that would please an old lady, Moon-Face.'

Moon-Face went off. The others watched as Silky turned out what she called her 'treasure bag.' It had lots of pretty things in it.

'Here's a lovely set of buttons,' said Silky, picking up a set of red buttons, made like poppies. 'She'd like those.'

'And what about this pink rose for a bonnet?' said Beth, picking up a rose that looked so real she was

481

sure it must have a smell. It had! 'This would do beautifully for an old lady.'

'And here's a hat pin with a little rabbit sitting at one end,' said Frannie. 'She'd like that.'

Just then Moon-Face came back. He brought with him three things – a tiny vase for flowers, a brooch with 'M' on it for Mother, and a shoehorn made of silver. The others thought they would be lovely for the old lady.

'We can take one thing each and give it to Saucepan for his mother,' said Moon-Face. 'Come on! We'll let Silky do the talking. Saucepan likes her best. Don't let him see you at first, Connie. He doesn't like you very much.'

They all went down to the Owl's home. They peeped inside. Saucepan had finished polishing his kettles, and was sitting silently, looking gloomy.

'Go on, Silky!' whispered Moon-Face. So Silky went in first, holding out the pink rose.

'Dear Saucepan, I've brought you a present to give to your mother from me, when you see her,' she said, in her very loudest voice. Incredibly, Saucepan heard every word. He looked at Silky, and said nothing at first. Then he said:

'For my old mother? Oh, how kind of you, Silky! She'll love this pink rose.'

'Quick, come on!' whispered Moon-Face to the others. So they all crowded in, holding out their gifts nervously, and saying, 'For your mother, Saucepan.'

Saucepan put each gift solemnly into one of his kettles or saucepans. He seemed very touched.

'Thank you,' he said. 'Thank you very much. My

482

mother will be delighted. It's her birthday soon. I will take her these presents from you. I expect she will invite you to her birthday party.'

'That would be very nice,' said Joe, in a loud voice. 'But Saucepan, we don't like Dame Snap, and you said your mother worked for her. If we go to see her, will you promise we don't get put into Dame Snap's school again? We went there once and she was horrid to us.'

'Oh, of course I'll see to that,' said the old Saucepan Man, who looked quite his old cheery self again. 'I'm sorry I sang rude songs about you. It was all a mistake. I'll go up into Dame Snap's Land tomorrow and see my dear old mother, and take your gifts and messages. Then you can come and join us for her birthday party.'

'All right!' said Joe. 'We'd like to do that – but mind, Saucepan, we don't want to see Dame Snap even in the distance.'

'You won't,' said Saucepan.

But oh dear – they did!

XIII. IN THE LAND OF DAME SNAP

It wasn't very long before a message came from Moon-Face. 'I have heard from Saucepan. He says we must go up to Dame Snap's land tomorrow, and meet his mother. If we go to the back door of the school, she will be there.'

So the next day, the four children set off. They went up the Faraway Tree, and called for Silky first. She was wearing a pretty party dress, and had washed her hair, which looked more like a golden mist than ever.

'I'm just ready,' she said, giving her hair a last brush. 'I hope Moon-Face won't keep us waiting. He lost his hat this morning, and he's been rushing up and down the Tree all day, asking everyone if they've seen it.'

When they got to Moon-Face's he was quite ready, beaming as usual, a floppy hat on his head.

'Oh, you found your hat then?' said Silky.

'Yes – it had fallen down the slippery-slip,' said Moon-Face. 'And when I went down there, I shot out of the trapdoor at the bottom, and there was my hat on my feet! So that was all right. Are we all ready?'

'Yes,' said Joe. 'But for goodness' sake do look out for Dame Snap. I feel very nervous of her.'

'Saucepan will be looking out for us, don't worry,' said Moon-Face. 'I expect he will be at the top of the

484

ladder, waiting. We're sure to have a lovely meal. His mother is a wonderful cook.'

They climbed up the topmost branch of the Tree, and came to the ladder. They all went up it and found themselves in Dame Snap's Land. There wasn't much to see – only, in the distance, a large green house set in the middle of a great garden.

'That's Dame Snap's School,' said Joe to Connie.

'Who goes to it?' asked Connie, curiously.

'All the bad pixies and fairies and elves,' said Beth. 'We saw some once when we were there. Dame Snap has to be very strict or she wouldn't be able to teach them. They are very naughty.'

'Where's the back door?' said Connie, looking nervously around. 'Let's go there, quick. I do wish Saucepan had waited for us at the top of the ladder.'

'Yes, I don't know why he didn't,' said Moon-Face, puzzled. 'Shall we call him?'

'No, of course not, silly!' said Joe. 'We'll have Dame Snap after us at once! Come on – we'll find the back door. We really can't wait about any longer.'

So they went round the large garden, keeping carefully outside the high wall, until they came to two gates. One opened on to the drive that led to the front door. The other opened on to a path that clearly led to the back door.

'This is where we go,' said Beth, and they went quietly through the back gate. They came to the back door. It was shut. No one seemed to be about.

'I suppose Saucepan and his mother *are* expecting us?' said Joe, puzzled. He knocked on the door. There was no answer. He knocked again.

'Let's open the door and go in,' said Beth, impatiently. 'We must find Saucepan. I expect he's forgotten he asked us to come today.'

They pushed the door open and went into a big and very tidy kitchen. There was no one there. It was very strange. Connie opened another door and peered into what seemed to be a big hall.

'I think I can hear someone,' she said. 'I'll go and see if it's Saucepan.'

Before the others could stop her she had opened the door and gone. No one felt like following. They sat down in the kitchen and waited.

Connie went into the big hall. There was no one there. She went into another room, that looked like a living room. Connie peered round it in curiosity. Then, through a door opposite came a tall, old woman, with large spectacles on her long nose and a big white bonnet on her head.

'Oh!' said Connie, beaming. 'Happy birthday! Where's Saucepan? We've all come to meet you!'

The old woman stopped in surprise. 'Indeed!' she said. 'You have, have you? And who are the rest of you?'

'Oh – didn't Saucepan tell you?' asked Connie. 'There's Joe and Beth and Frannie and Moon-Face and Silky. We did hope that Saucepan would meet us by the ladder, because we were so afraid of meeting that awful Dame Snap.'

'Oh, really?' said the old woman, and her eyes gleamed behind her big spectacles. 'You think she's awful, do you?'

'Well, Joe and the others told me all about her,' said Connie. 'They were all here once, you know, and they escaped. They were very afraid of meeting her again.'

'Where are they?' said the old woman.

'In the kitchen,' said Connie. 'I'll go and tell them I've found you.'

She ran ahead of the old woman, who followed her at once. Connie flung open the kitchen door.

'I've found Saucepan's mother!' she said. 'Here she is!'

The old lady came into the kitchen – and Joe and the others gave a gasp of horror. It wasn't Saucepan's mother. It was Dame Snap herself, looking absolutely furious.

'Dame Snap!' yelled Joe. 'Run, everyone!'

But it was too late. Dame Snap turned the key in the kitchen door and put it into her pocket.

'So you escaped from me before, did you?' she said. 'Well, you won't escape again. Bad children who are sent to me to be good don't usually escape before they are taught things they ought to know!'

'Look here!' began Moon-Face, putting a bold face on. 'Look here, Dame Snap, we didn't come to see you; we came to see Saucepan's mother.'

'I've never in my life heard of Saucepan,' said Dame Snap. 'Never. It's a naughty story. You're making it up. I punish people for telling stories. You wicked man!' she snapped at Moon-Face.

'Saucepan's mother works for you!' he shouted, dodging round the kitchen. 'She cooks for your school! Where is she?'

'Oh – the lady who cooks,' said Dame Snap. 'Well, she walked out yesterday, along with a dreadful creature who had kettles and pans hung all round him.'

'That was Saucepan,' groaned Joe. 'Where did they go?'

'I don't know and I certainly don't care,' said Dame Snap. 'The lady was rude to me, and I shouted at her. So she went off. Can any of you cook?'

'I can,' said Beth. 'But if you think I'm going to cook for you, you're mistaken. I'm going home.'

'You can stay here and cook meals for the school till I get someone else,' said Dame Snap. 'And this girl can help you.' She pointed to Frannie. 'The others can come into my school and learn to work hard, to get good manners and to be well behaved. Go along now!'

To Joe's horror, she pushed everyone but Beth and Frannie into the hall, and up the stairs to a big classroom, where lots of noisy little elves, fairies and pixies were playing and pushing and fighting together.

Dame Snap dealt a few scoldings and sent them to their seats, yelling.

Connie was very afraid. She stayed close to Joe and Moon-Face. Dame Snap made them all sit down at the back of the room.

'Silence!' she snapped. 'You will now do your homework. The new pupils will please find pencils and paper in their desks. Everyone must answer the

488

questions on the blackboard. If anyone gets them wrong, they will have to be punished.'

'Oh dear!' groaned Silky. Connie whispered to her:

'Don't worry! I'm very good at lessons. I will know all the answers, and I'll tell you them too.'

'Who is whispering?' shouted Dame Snap, and everyone jumped. 'You, new girl, come out here.'

Connie came out, trembling. Dame Snap gave her a sharp scolding.

'Stop crying!' she snapped. And Connie stopped. She gave a gulp, and stopped at once.

'Go back to your seat and do your homework,' ordered the old Dame. So back Connie went.

'Now, no talking and no playing,' said Dame Snap. 'Just hard work. I am going to talk to my new kitchen staff about a nice syrup pudding. If I hear anyone talking or playing when I come back, or if anyone hasn't done the homework, there will be no nice syrup pudding for any of you.'

With this threat Dame Snap walked out of the room. She left the door wide open so that she could hear any noise.

The pixie in front of Connie turned round and shook his pen on her book. A big blot came out! The goblin next to him pulled Silky's hair. A bright-eyed pixie threw a pencil at Moon-Face and hit him on the nose. Dame Snap's pupils were a really naughty lot!

'We *must* do our homework!' whispered Silky to the others. 'Connie, read the questions on the blackboard, and tell us the answers, quick!'

So Connie read them – but, oh dear, how could she answer questions like that? She never could. They

would all go without syrup pudding, and be scolded
and sent to bed! Oh dear, oh dear!

XIV. DAME SNAP'S SCHOOL

The more the children looked at the three questions on the blackboard, the more they felt certain they could never answer them. Moon-Face turned to Connie. 'Quick! Tell us the right answers. You said you were good at lessons.'

Connie read the first question. 'Three blackbirds sat on a cherry tree. They ate one hundred and twenty three of the cherries. How many were left?'

'Well, how can we say, unless we know how many there were in the beginning?' said Connie, out loud. 'What a silly question!'

Joe read the next one out loud. 'If there are a hundred pages in a book, how many books would there be on the shelf?'

'The questions are just nonsense,' said Moon-Face, gloomily.

'They were before, when we were here,' said Joe.

The third question was very short. Joe read it out. 'Why is a blackboard?'

'Why is a blackboard!' repeated Silky. 'There is no sense in that question either.'

'Well – the questions are nonsense, so we'll put down answers that are nonsense,' said Joe.

So they put down 'none' about how many cherries were left on the tree. Then they read the book question again. And again they put down 'none'.

'We are not told that the shelf was a bookshelf,' said Joe. 'It might be a shelf for ornaments, or a bathroom shelf for glasses and tooth brushes and things. There wouldn't be any books there.'

The third question was really puzzling. 'Why is a blackboard?'

Joe ran out of his place and rubbed out the two last words. He wrote them again – and then the question read 'Why is a board black?'

'We can easily answer that,' said Joe, with a grin. 'Why is a board black? So that we can write on it with white chalk!'

So, when Dame Snap came back, the only people who had answered all the questions were Joe, Silky, Moon-Face and Connie! Dame Snap smiled at them.

'Dear me, I have some clever children at last!' she said. 'You have written answers to all the questions.'

'Are they right then?' asked Silky, in surprise.

'I don't know,' said Dame Snap. 'But that doesn't matter. It's the answers I want. I don't care what's in them, so long as you have written answers. I don't know the answers myself, so it's no good me reading them.'

Then Moon-Face undid all the good they had done by giving an extremely rude snort. 'Pooh! What a silly school this is! Fancy giving people questions if you don't know the answers! Pooh!'

'Don't 'pooh' at me like that!' said Dame Snap, getting angry all of a sudden. 'Go to bed! Off to bed with you for the rest of the day!'

'But – but,' began poor Moon-Face, in alarm, wishing he had not spoken, 'but . . .'

'You'll turn into a goat in a minute, if you are so full of 'buts',' said Dame Snap, and she pushed Moon-Face out of the door. She drove the others out too, and took them to a small bedroom, with four tiny beds, very hard and narrow.

'Now, into bed you get, and nothing but bread and water for you all day long. I will not have rudeness in my school!'

She shut the door and locked it. Moon-Face looked at the others in dismay. 'I'm sorry I made her do this,' he said. 'Very sorry. But really, she did make me feel so angry. Do you think we'd better go to bed? She might punish us if we don't.'

Connie leapt into bed at once, fully dressed. She wasn't going to risk Dame Snap coming back and punishing her! The others did the same. They drew the quilts up to their chins and lay there gloomily. This was a horrid adventure – just when they had looked forward so much to coming out to the birthday party.

493

'I wonder what Beth and Frannie are doing,' said Moon-Face. 'Hard work, I suppose. I do think Saucepan might have warned us that his mother had gone. It's too bad.'

Just then there came the sound of a song floating up from outside.

> *Two worms for a sparrow,*
> *Two slugs for a duck,*
> *Two snails for a blackbird,*
> *Two hens for a cluck!*

'Saucepan! It must be Saucepan!' cried everyone, and jumped out of bed and ran to the window. Outside, far below, stood Saucepan, and with him were Beth and Frannie, giggling.

'Hi, Saucepan! Here we are!' cried Joe. 'We're locked in.'

'Oh – we wondered where you were,' said Saucepan, grinning. 'Dame Snap's locked in, too – locked into the storeroom by young Beth here. She was just doing it when I came along to see if you had arrived.'

'Arrived! We've been here ages,' said Joe, indignantly. 'Why didn't you come to warn us?'

'My watch must be wrong again,' said Saucepan. He usually kept it in one of his kettles, but as it shook about there every day, it wasn't a very good time keeper. 'Never mind. I'll rescue you now.'

A terrific banging noise came from somewhere downstairs. 'That's Dame Snap in the storeroom,' said Saucepan. 'She's in a dreadful temper.'

'Well, for goodness' sake, help us out of here,' said Connie, alarmed. 'How can we get out? The door's locked, and I heard Dame Snap taking the key out the other side.'

Crash! Bang! Clatter!

'Sounds as if Dame Snap is throwing a few pies and things about,' said Joe. 'Saucepan, how can we get out of here?'

'I'll just undo the rope that hangs my things round me,' said Saucepan, and he began to untie the rope round his waist. He undid it, and then, to the children's surprise, his kettles and saucepans began to peel off him. They were each tied firmly to the rope.

'Saucepan does look funny without his kettles and pans round him,' said Connie in surprise. 'I hardly know him!'

Saucepan took the end of the rope and tied a stone to it. He threw it up to the window. Joe caught the stone and pulled on the rope. It came up, laden here and there with kettles and saucepans.

'Tie the rope end to a bed,' called Saucepan. 'Then come down the rope. You can use the kettles and saucepans as steps. They are tied on tightly.'

So, very cautiously, Moon-Face, Joe, Silky and a very nervous Connie climbed down the rope, using the saucepans and kettles as steps. They were very glad to stand on firm ground again!

'Well, there we are,' said Saucepan, pleased. 'Wasn't that a good idea?'

'Yes – but how are we to get your kettles and saucepans back for you?' said Joe.

'It doesn't matter at all,' said Saucepan. 'I can take

as many as I can carry out of the kitchen here. They are what I gave my mother each birthday, you know, so they are hers.'

He went into the kitchen and collected a great selection of kettles and saucepans. He tied them all to the rope used for a washing line, and then once more became the Old Saucepan Man they knew so well, with pans of all shapes and sizes hung all round him!

Crash! Smash! Clang! Dame Snap was getting angrier and angrier in the storeroom. She kicked and she stamped.

'Dame Snap!' cried Joe, suddenly, and he stood outside the locked storeroom door. 'I will ask you a question, and if you can tell me the answer, I will set you free. Now, be quiet and listen.'

There was a silence in the storeroom. Joe asked his question.

'If Saucepan takes twelve kettles from your kitchen, how long does it take to boil a cup of hot chocolate on a Friday?'

The others giggled. There came an angry cry from the storeroom. 'It's a silly question, and there's no answer. Let me out at once!'

'It's the same kind of question you asked *us*!' said Joe. 'I'm sorry you can't answer it. I can't either. So you must stay where you are, till one of your school children is kind enough to let you out. Goodbye, dear Dame Snap!'

The children and the others went out giggling into the garden. 'Where are we going now?' asked Beth. 'Where's your mother, Saucepan?'

'She's in the Land of Tea Parties,' said Saucepan.

'It's not very far. I took her there because it's her birthday, you know, and I thought she'd like to have a party without going to any trouble. Shall we go?'

So, hearing Dame Snap's furious cries and bangs gradually fading behind them, the little group set off together, very glad to have escaped from Dame Snap in safety.

'Come on – here's the boundary between this land and the next. Jump!' said Saucepan.

They jumped – and over they went into the Land of Tea Parties! What a fine time they meant to have there!

XV. THE LAND OF TEA PARTIES

The Land of Tea Parties was peculiar. It seemed to be made up of nothing but white-covered tables laden with all kinds of good things to eat!

'Gosh!' said Joe, looking round. 'What a lot of tables – big and small, round and square – and all filled with the most gorgeous things to eat!'

'They've got chairs set round them too,' said Frannie. 'All ready for people to sit on.'

'And look at the little waiters!' said Connie, in delight. 'They are rabbits!'

So they were – rabbits dressed neatly in aprons, and little black coats, hurrying here and there, carrying jugs of lemonade and all kinds of other drinks.

It was lovely to watch them; they were so very busy and so very serious.

'There are some people choosing tables already!' said Joe, pointing. 'Look – that must be a pixie's birthday party, sitting over there. Aren't they sweet?'

'And oh, look! – there's a squirrel's party,' said Frannie. 'Mother and Father Squirrel, and all the baby squirrels. I expect it's one of the baby squirrels' birthdays!'

It was fun to see the little parties. But soon the children began to feel very hungry. There were such nice things on the tables! There were sandwiches of all kinds, with little labels showing what they were.

Frannie read some of them out loud.

'Dewdrop and honey sandwiches – ooh! And here are some tunafish and strawberry sandwiches – what a funny mixture! But I dare say it would be nice. And here are oranges and lemon sandwiches – I've never heard of those. And pineapple and cucumber! Really, what an exciting lot of things!'

'Look at the cakes!' said Connie. 'I've never seen such beauties.'

Nor had anyone else. There were pink cakes, yellow cakes, chocolate cakes, ginger cakes, cakes with fruit and silver balls all over them, cakes with frosting, cakes with flowers made from sugar, cakes as big as could be, and tiny ones only enough for two people.

There were desserts and fruit salads and ice-creams too. Which table should they choose? There were different things at every table!

'Here's one with chocolate ice-cream,' said Connie. 'Let's have this one.'

'No – I'd like this one – it's got blue cakes, and I've never seen those before,' said Silky.

'Well, shouldn't we find Saucepan's mother before we do anything?' said Moon-Face.

'Gosh, of course we should!' said Beth. 'Seeing all those gorgeous things made me forget we had come to celebrate Saucepan's mother's birthday. SAUCEPAN, WHERE IS YOUR MOTHER?'

'Over there,' said Saucepan, and he pointed to where the dearest little old woman stood waiting, her apple cheeks rosy red, and her bright eyes twinkling as brightly as Saucepan's. 'She's waiting. She's got the pink rose in her bonnet, look! – and the hat pin – and

she's sewn the red poppy buttons on her dress, and she's pinned the M for Mother brooch in front. The only thing she can't wear are the shoehorn and the vase, and I think she's got them in her pocket. She was really pleased with everything.'

'Let's go and wish her a happy birthday,' said Beth, so they all went over to the little old lady, and wished her a very happy birthday. She was delighted to see them all, and she kissed them, each one, even Moon-Face.

'Well, I *am* glad you've come,' she said. 'I began to think something had happened to you.'

'It had,' said Joe, and he began to tell her about Dame Snap. But old Mrs Saucepan was just as deaf as Saucepan was himself.

'Here you are at last,' said Mrs Saucepan to Saucepan.

'Yes, we did come fast,' agreed Saucepan. 'We locked up Dame Snap.'

'Locked up the cat?' said Mrs Saucepan. 'Why?'

The children giggled. Joe went up to Mrs Saucepan and spoke very clearly.

'Let's have some food! The tables are getting filled up!'

Mrs Saucepan heard. 'Yes, we will,' she said.

'I'd like the table with blue cakes,' said Silky.

'I'd like the one with pineapple and cucumber

sandwiches,' said Connie.

'Well – as it's Saucepan's mother's birthday, don't you think we should let *her* choose the table?' said Beth. 'She should have the things *she* likes best today.'

'Yes, of course,' said the others, rather ashamed not to have thought of that. 'MRS SAUCEPAN, PLEASE CHOOSE YOUR OWN TABLE.'

Well, Mrs Saucepan went straight to the big round table, set with eight chairs, and sat down at the head of it – and wasn't it strange, there were blue cakes there for Silky, pineapple and cucumber sandwiches for Connie, a big fat chocolate cake for Moon-Face, and all the things the others wanted too!

'This is fantastic,' said Connie, beginning on the sandwiches. 'Oh – I never tasted such beautiful sandwiches in my life, never!'

The little rabbit waiters ran up, and smiled at old Mrs Saucepan. 'What will you have to drink?' they asked.

'Hot chocolate for me,' said Mrs Saucepan. 'What for you others?'

'Lemonade! Soda! Orange juice!' called the children and the others. The rabbits ran off, and came back with bottles of everything asked for, and a big jug of hot chocolate for Mrs Saucepan.

What fun they all had! There were squeals of laughter from everyone, and from every table there came happy chattering. The Land of Tea Parties was a great success.

The children finished up with ice-cream. Then the rabbits brought round big boxes of presents and they shared them all out. There were brooches, and rings, and little toys, and everyone had a funny paper hat to wear.

'Well, we've had a fabulous time,' said Joe, at last; 'but I think we should go now, Mrs Saucepan. Thank you very much for asking us here. I hope you get another job somewhere soon.'

'Oh, I think I shall go and live in the Faraway Tree with Dame Washalot,' said Mrs Saucepan. 'She's always so busy with her washing, she hasn't much time to do anything else. I could do the cooking for her. I could make cakes to sell too, and have a little shop there.'

'Oh – that would be lovely!' cried Beth. 'I'll often come and buy some from you.'

'We'd better go back through the Land of Dame Snap very cautiously indeed,' said Moon-Face. 'We can't get back to the Tree from this land because it's not over the Tree. We'll have to creep back through Dame Snap's Land and rush to the ladder quickly.'

So they said goodbye to the busy little rabbit waiters, and jumped over the boundary line again, back into Dame Snap's Land. They had to pass near the school, of course, and they listened carefully to find out what was going on.

There was a terrific commotion of shouting, laughing and squealing. The grounds of the school were full of the school children, and what a time they were having!

'Old Dame Snap must still be in the storeroom,' said Moon-Face. 'Yes, listen – I believe I can still hear her hammering away!'

Sure enough, over all the noise made by the school

children, there came the sound of hammering!

'Shouldn't we set her free?' said Frannie, rather alarmed. 'She might stay there for ages and starve to death!'

'Don't be silly! How can she starve when she is surrounded by food of all kinds?' said Moon-Face. 'It will be the children who will go hungry! I guess when they are hungry enough they will open the door and let Dame Snap out all right! Gosh, what a bad temper she will be in.'

They all hurried through the land at top speed, half afraid that Dame Snap might be let out before they were safe, and come after them. Still, they had Mrs Saucepan with them, and if anyone had to stand up to Dame Snap, she certainly would.

At last they came to the ladder sticking up into the land from the cloud below. 'You go first, Moon-Face, and help Mrs Saucepan down,' said Joe. So down went Moon-Face, and politely and carefully helped the old lady down the little yellow ladder, through the cloud and on to the topmost branch of the Tree.

Everyone followed, breathing sighs of relief to be safely away from Dame Snap once more. Nobody ever wanted to visit *her* land again!

'We really must say goodbye now,' said Joe to the Tree folk. 'Shall we just take Mrs Saucepan down to Dame Washalot for you, Saucepan?'

'I'll come too,' said Saucepan, hearing what was said. So down they went, and when Dame Washalot saw old Mrs Saucepan, she was very excited. She threw her soapy arms round the old lady's neck and hugged her.

'I hope you've come to stay!' she said. 'I've always wanted you to live in the Faraway Tree.'

'Goodbye, Mrs Saucepan,' said Beth. 'I shall come and buy your cakes the very first day you put them on sale. I do hope you've had a happy birthday.'

'The nicest one I've ever had!' said the old lady, smiling. 'Goodbye my dears, and hurry home!'

XVI. IN THE LAND OF SECRETS

Connie could not forget the exciting Faraway Tree, and the different lands that came at the top. She asked the others about all the different lands they had been to, and begged and begged them to take her to the next one.

'We'll see what Moon-Face says,' said Joe at last. 'We don't go to every land, Connie. You wouldn't like to go to the Land of Whizz-About, for instance, would you? Moon-Face once went there, and he said he couldn't bear it – everything went at such a pace, and he was out of breath the whole time.'

'Well, I think it sounds rather exciting,' said Connie, who was intensely curious about everything to do with the different lands. 'Oh, Joe, let's find out what land is there next. I really must go.'

'All right,' said Joe. 'We'll ask Mother if we can have a day out tomorrow, and we'll go up the Tree if you like. But mind – if there is a horrid land, we're not going. We've had too many narrow escapes now, to risk getting caught somewhere nasty.'

Mother said they could go up the Tree the next day. 'I'll give you sandwiches, if you like, and you can have lunch in the Wood or up the Tree, whichever you like,' she told them.

'Oh, up the Tree!' cried Connie. So, when the next day came, she wore old clothes without even being told! She was learning to be sensible at last.

They set off soon after breakfast. They hadn't let Silky or Moon-Face know they were coming, but they felt sure they would be in the Tree.

They jumped over the ditch and made their way through the whispering Wood till they came to the Faraway Tree. Joe whistled for the red squirrel to tell him to go up and ask Moon-Face to send cushions down. But the red squirrel didn't come.

'Bother!' said Beth. 'Now we'll have to climb up, and it's so hot!'

So up they climbed. The Angry Pixie was sitting at his window, which was wide open. He waved to them, and Connie was glad to see he had no ink or water to throw at her.

'Going up to the Land of Secrets?' he shouted to them.

'Oh – is the Land of Secrets there?' cried Joe. 'It sounds exciting. What's it like?'

'Oh – just secrets!' said the Angry Pixie. 'You can usually find out anything you badly want to know. I believe Watzisname wanted to try and find out exactly what his real name is, so maybe he'll visit it too.'

'I'd like to know some secrets too,' said Connie.

'What secrets do you want to know?' asked Joe.

'Oh – I'd like to know how much money the old man who lives next door to us at home has got,' said Connie. 'And I'd like to know what Mrs Toms at home has done to make people not speak to her – and . . .'

'What an awful girl you are!' said Beth. 'Those are *other* people's secrets, not yours. Fancy wanting to find out other people's secrets!'

'Yes, it's not nice of you, Connie,' said Frannie. 'Joe, don't let Connie go into the Land of Secrets if that's the kind of thing she wants to find out. She's gone all curious and prying again, like she used to be.'

Connie was angry. She went red and glared at the others. 'Well, don't *you* want to know secrets too?' she said. 'You said you did!'

'Yes, but not other people's,' said Joe at once. 'I'd like to know where to find the very first violets for instance, so that I could surprise Mother on her birthday with a great big bunch. They are her favourite flowers.'

'And I'd like to know the secret of curly hair, so that I could use it on all my dolls,' said Beth.

'And I'd like to know the secret of growing lettuces with big hearts,' said Frannie. 'Mine never grow nice ones.'

'What silly secrets!' said Connie.

'Better to want to know a silly secret than a horrid one, or one that doesn't belong to you,' said Joe. 'All you want to do is to poke your nose into other people's affairs, Connie, and that's a horrid thing to do.'

Connie climbed the Tree, not speaking a word to the others. She was very angry with them. She was so angry that she didn't look out for Dame Washalot's water coming down the Tree, and it suddenly swished all round her and soaked her.

That made her angrier still, especially when the others laughed at her. 'All right!' said Connie, in a nasty voice. 'I'll find out *your* secrets too – where you've put your new book so that I can't borrow it, Joe – and where you've put your paints, Beth – and I'll find out which of your dolls you like the best, Frannie, and hide her!'

'You really are a nasty child,' said Joe. 'You won't go up into the Land of Secrets, so don't worry yourself about all these things!'

They climbed up to Silky's house, but the door was shut. They went up to Moon-Face's, but his door was shut too. The Old Saucepan Man was not about and neither was Watzisname. Nobody seemed to be about at all.

'Perhaps Saucepan's mother would know,' said Beth. So they climbed down to Dame Washalot, and found old Mrs Saucepan there.

'Saucepan and Watzisname have both gone up into the Land of Secrets,' she told them, 'but I don't know about Silky and Moon-Face – I expect they have gone with them, though Saucepan didn't tell me they were going. Have a cake?'

Old Mrs Saucepan was already busy making all kinds of delicious cakes and pies, ready to open her shop on Dame Washalot's broad branch. Two goblins were busy making a stall for her. She meant to open her little shop the next day.

The children took their cakes with thanks. They were really delicious.

They climbed up the Tree again to Moon-Face's house. Joe turned the handle. The door opened, but the curved room inside was empty.

'What a nuisance!' said Joe. 'Now what shall we do?'

'We might as well go up into the Land of Secrets, and find the others, and have our picnic with them,' said Frannie.

'Yes,' said Connie, who was dying to go up into this new land.

'Well, but we didn't want Connie to go,' said Joe. 'She'll only go prying into other people's secrets, and we can't have that.'

'I won't try and find out your secrets,' said Connie. 'I promise I won't.'

'I don't know if I trust you,' said Joe. 'But still, we can't go without you. So, if you do come, Connie, just be careful – and remember that you might get into trouble if you're not careful.'

'I wonder if old Watzisname has found out what his real name is,' said Beth, beginning to climb up the topmost branch. 'I'd love to know it. It would be nice to call him something else. Watzisname is a silly name.'

They all went up the topmost branch, and up the yellow ladder through the hole in the cloud, and then into the Land of Secrets.

It was a curious land, quiet, perfectly still, and a sort of twilight hung over it. There was no sun to be seen at all.

'It feels secret and solemn!' said Joe, with a little shiver. 'I'm not sure if I like it.'

'Come on!' said Beth. 'Let's go and find the others and see how we get to know secrets.'

They came to a hill, with several coloured doors in it, set with sparkling stones that glittered in the curious twilight.

'They must be the doors of caves,' said Joe. 'Look! – there are names on the doors.'

The children read them. They were peculiar names. 'Witch Know-a-Lot.' 'The Enchanter Wise-Man.' 'Dame Tell-You-All.' 'Mrs Hidden.' 'The Wizard Tall-Hat.'

'They all sound really clever and wise and informed,' said Joe. 'Hello! Here's somebody coming.'

A tall fairy was coming along, carrying a pair of wings. She stopped and spoke to the children.

'Do you know where Dame Tell-You-All lives, please? I want to know how to fasten on these wings and fly with them.'

'She lives in that cave,' said Beth, pointing to where a door had 'Dame Tell-You-All' painted on it in big letters.

'Thank you,' said the fairy, and rapped sharply on the door. It opened and she went inside. It shut. In about half a minute it opened again, and out came the fairy, this time with the wings on her back. She rose into the air and flew off, waving to the children.

'The Dame's really clever!' she cried. 'I can fly now. Look!'

'This is an exciting place,' said Beth. 'Goodness, the things we could learn! I wish *I* had a pair of wings. I've a good mind to go and ask Dame Tell-you-All how to get some, and then how to fly with them.'

'Look – isn't that old Watzisname coming along?' said Joe, suddenly. They looked in the dim distance, and saw that it was indeed

Watzisname, looking rather proud. Saucepan was with him, his pans clashing as usual.

'Hi, Watzisname!' called Joe, loudly.

Watzisname came up. 'My name is not Watzisname,' he said a little haughtily. 'I've at last found out what it is. It is an absolutely marvellous name.'

'What is it?' said Beth.

'It is Kollamoolitoomarellipawkyrollo,' said Watzisname, very proudly indeed. 'In future please call me by my real name.'

'Oh dear – I shall never remember that,' said Frannie, and she tried to say it. But she didn't get any further than 'Kollamooli.' Nor did the others.

'No wonder everyone called him 'Watzisname,' said Beth to Frannie. 'Watzisname, where are Silky and Moon-Face?'

'My name is not Watzisname,' said Watzisname, patiently. 'I have told you what it is. Please address me correctly in future.'

'He's gone all high-and-mighty,' said Joe. 'Saucepan, WHERE ARE SILKY AND MOON-FACE?'

'Don't know,' said Saucepan, 'and don't shout at me like that. I haven't seen Silky or Moon-Face today.'

'Let's have our picnic here, and then go and see if Silky and Moon-Face have come home,' said Joe. 'Somehow I don't think we'll go about finding out secrets. This land is a bit too mysterious for me!'

But Connie made up her mind *she* would find a few secrets! She would have a bit of fun on her own.

XVII. CONNIE IN TROUBLE

They all sat down on a flowery bank. It was still twilight, which seemed very odd, as Joe's watch said the time was half past twelve in the middle of the day. As they ate, they watched the different visitors coming and going to the cave on the hillside.

There was an old woman who wanted to ask Witch Know-a-Lot the secret of youth, so that she could become young again, and there was a tiny goblin who had once done a wicked thing, and couldn't forget it. He wanted to know the secret of forgetting, and that is one of the most difficult secrets in the world if you have done something really bad.

The children talked to everyone who passed. It was peculiar, the different secrets that people wanted to know. One grumpy looking pixie wanted to know the secret of laughter.

'I've never laughed in my life,' he told Joe. 'And I'd like to. But nothing ever seems funny to me. Perhaps the Enchanter Wise-Man can tell me. He's very, very clever.'

The Enchanter plainly knew the secret of laughter because, when the grumpy looking pixie came out of the cave he was smiling. He roared with laughter as he passed the picnicking party.

'Such a joke!' he said to them. 'Such a joke!'

'What was the secret?' asked Connie.

'Ah, that's nothing to do with you!' said the pixie. 'That's *my* secret, not yours!'

The tiny goblin who had once done a wicked thing came up to the children. 'Did you find out the secret of forgetting?' asked Beth.

The goblin nodded.

'I'll tell it to you, because then if you do a wrong thing, maybe you can get right with yourself afterwards,' he said. 'It's so dreadful if you can't. Well, the Wizard Tall-Hat told me that if I can do one hundred really kind deeds to make up for the one very bad one I did, maybe I'll be able to forget a little, and think better of myself. So I'm off to do my first kind deed.'

'Gosh! It'll take him a long time to make up for his one wicked deed,' said Joe. 'Poor little goblin! It must be awful to do something wicked and not be able to forget it. No wonder he looked unhappy.

A very grand fairy came flying down to the hillside. She looked rich and powerful and very beautiful. Connie wondered what secret she had come to find out. It must be a very grand secret indeed. The fairy did not tell the children what she wanted to know. She smiled at them and went to knock on Mrs Hidden's door.

'Ah! Did you see that fairy?' said Watzisname. 'It would be interesting to know what secret *she* is after! She has beauty and wealth and power – whatever secret can she want now?'

'What do you think she wants to know, Watzisname?' asked Connie.

'Call me by my proper name and I might tell you,' said Watzisname, haughtily. But Connie couldn't remember it. Nor could the others.

'Well, it isn't going to be much use finding out my real name, if nobody is going to bother to remember it,' said Watzisname, in a huff. 'Saucepan, do *you* remember my name?'

'Shame? Yes, it is a shame,' said Saucepan.

In the middle of all the explanations to Saucepan as to what Watzisname had really said, Connie slipped away unseen. She was longing to know what secret the beautiful fairy wanted to find out. It must be a very powerful secret. If only she could hear it! Perhaps if she listened outside Mrs Hidden's door, she might catch a few words.

She went off very quietly without being seen, and climbed a little way up the hillside to where she had noticed Mrs Hidden's door.

There it was – a pale green one, striped with red lines and a curious pattern. It was open!

Connie crept up to it. She could hear voices inside.

She stood in the doorway and peeped inside. There was a winding passage leading into the hill from the doorway. She crept down it. She turned a corner and found herself looking into a very curious room. It was small, and yet it looked very, very big because when Connie looked at the corners they faded away and weren't there.

It was the same with the ceiling, which Connie felt sure was very low. But when she looked up at it it wasn't there either! There didn't seem to be any end or beginning to the room at all, and yet Connie knew that it was small.

It gave her an uncomfortable feeling, as if she was

in a dream. She tried to see Mrs Hidden. She could see the beautiful fairy quite well, and she could hear Mrs Hidden, whoever she was, speaking in a low, deep voice.

But she couldn't see her!

'Oh well, I suppose she's called Mrs Hidden because she is hidden from our sight,' thought Connie. 'I will just hear what she says to the fairy, and then slip away.'

Connie heard the secret that the beautiful fairy wanted to know, and she heard Mrs Hidden give her the answer. Connie shivered with delight. It was a very wonderful and powerful secret. Connie meant to use it herself! She began to creep out of the cave.

But her foot caught against a loose stone in the passage and it made a noise. At once Mrs Hidden called out in a sharp voice: 'Who's there? Who's prying and peeping? Who's listening? I'll put a spell on you, I will! If you have heard any secrets, you will not be able to speak again!'

Connie fled, afraid of having a spell put on her. She came rushing down the hillside, very frightened. The others heard her and frowned.

'Connie! Surely you haven't been after secrets when we said you were not to try and find out anything?' began Joe.

Connie opened her mouth to answer – but not a word came out! Not a single word!

'She can't speak,' said Watzisname. 'She's been listening at doors and hearing things not meant for her ears. I guess old Mrs Hidden has put a spell on her. Serve her right.'

516

Connie opened her mouth and
tried to speak again, pointing back
to the cave she had come from.
Saucepan got up in a hurry.

'I can see what she means to say,' he
said to the others. 'She's been caught
prying and peeping, and she's afraid Mrs
Hidden will come after her. She probably will as soon
as she has finished with that beautiful fairy who went
into her cave. We'd better go. Mrs Hidden is not a
nice person to deal with when she is angry.'

They all ran to the hole, and got down it as quickly
as possible. Connie was so anxious to get away from
Mrs Hidden that she almost fell off the topmost
branch. Joe caught her just in time.

'Look out!' he said. 'You nearly went headlong
down the Tree. Let me go first.'

Connie couldn't answer. Mrs Hidden's spell was
clearly very strong. She simply couldn't say a word. It
was very unpleasant.

'Hey – do you think Silky and Moon-Face are still
up there in the Land of Secrets?' asked Beth. But they
weren't, because as they came down the branch to
Moon-Face's house, they heard voices, and saw Silky
and Moon-Face undoing shopping parcels.

'Oh – so you went shopping, did you?' said Joe. 'We
wondered where you were.'

'Yes, we took the little red squirrel shopping and
bought him a new sweater,' said Moon-Face. 'He's
very pleased. Well, did you go up into the Land of
Secrets? Did you find out anything?'

'Yes, we found out Watzisname's real name,' said Joe.

'Oh, *good*!' said Silky. 'I've always wanted to know it. What is it, Joe?'

Joe wrinkled up his forehead. 'I can't remember,' he said.

'What's the good of a name nobody remembers?' said Watzisname, gloomily. 'It's just stupid.'

'You tell me it, and I'll promise to remember,' said Silky. 'I'll write it down and learn it by heart, Watzisname really I will.'

Watzisname said nothing. Silky gave him a little nudge. 'Go on, Watzisname. Tell me your name – slowly, now, so that I can say it after you.'

Watzisname shook his head, and suddenly looked miserable. 'I – I can't tell you my name,' he said at last. 'I've forgotten it myself! It was such a fine name too. You'll have to call me Watzisname just the same as before. I expect that's why people *did* begin to call me Watzisname, because nobody could ever remember my real name.'

'Well, it's a pity to think that the only secret we found out has been forgotten already!' said Joe. 'Though I suppose Connie found out a secret she wasn't supposed to know and got punished for it. Moon-Face, Connie can't speak. Isn't it dreadful?'

'Good thing,' said Saucepan, hearing unexpectedly. 'Never says anything really sensible.'

Connie glared at him and opened her mouth to say something back. But no words came.

Silky looked at her in sympathy.

'Poor Connie! Whatever can we do about it? We'll have to wait till the Land of Enchantments comes, and then go up and find someone who can take the

518

spell away. *I* don't know how to make you better.'

'Why bother?' said Saucepan, annoying Connie even more, when she was already angry at being unable to answer him back. 'Why bother? She'll be much nicer if she can't say a word. We won't know she's there!'

'Never mind, Connie,' said Beth, seeing that Connie looked really upset. 'As soon as the Land of Enchantments comes, we'll take you there and have you put right!'

XVIII. OFF TO FIND CONNIE'S LOST VOICE

Mother was surprised and very concerned, to find that Connie couldn't speak.

'We'd better take her to the doctor,' she said.

'Oh no, Mother, that's no use,' said Joe. 'It's a spell that Mrs Hidden put on Connie for hearing something she shouldn't have listened to. Only another spell can put her right.'

'When the Land of Enchantments comes we will take Connie there, and see if we can find someone who will give her her voice back again,' said Beth.

'She'll have to be patient till then,' said Frannie.

But Connie wasn't patient. She kept opening her mouth to try and speak, but she couldn't say a word.

'Connie shouldn't be so curious,' said Joe. 'It's her own fault she's like this. Perhaps it will teach her a lesson.'

Three days went by, and no news came from the Tree folk. Then old Mrs Saucepan arrived, with a basket full of lovely new-made cakes for them.

'I have heard so much about you,' she said to their mother, smiling all over her rosy-cheeked face. 'I felt I must come and call on you, and bring you a few of my cakes. I have started a shop up the Tree, near Dame Washalot, and I'd be so pleased if you'd try some of my cakes.'

'Stop and have a drink with us, and we'll try your cakes,' said Mother at once. She like the little old lady very much. So Mrs Saucepan stopped and had a drink. She shook her head when she saw that Connie still couldn't speak.

'A pity,' she said. 'A great pity. It just doesn't do to poke your nose into other people's affairs. I hope the poor child will be put right soon. The Land of Enchantments will be at the top of the Tree tomorrow.'

Everyone sat up. 'What, so soon?' said Joe. 'That's a bit of luck for Connie.'

'It is,' said old Mrs Saucepan. 'Still, there are plenty of lands where she might get her voice put right. You'll have to be a bit careful in the Land of Enchantments, though. It's so easy to get enchanted there, without knowing it.'

'Whatever do you mean?' said Mother, in alarm. 'I don't think I want the children to go there, if there is any danger.'

'I'll send Saucepan with them,' said the old lady. 'I'll give him a powerful spell, which will get anyone out of an enchantment if they get into it by mistake. You needn't worry.'

'Oh, that's all right then,' said Joe. 'I didn't want to get enchanted, and have to stay up there for the rest of my life!'

'You must remember one or two things,' said Mrs Saucepan. '*Don't* step into a ring drawn on the ground in chalk. Don't stroke any black cats with green eyes. And don't be rude to anyone at all.'

'We'll remember,' said Joe. 'Thank you very much.

521

Will you tell Saucepan we'll be up the Tree tomorrow, please?'

Old Mrs Saucepan left after they had all had a drink and eaten some of her delicious cakes. She had made firm friends with Mother, who promised to send the children once a week to buy her cakes.

'We'll go to the Land of Enchantments tomorrow,' said Joe. 'Cheer up, Connie – you'll soon get your voice back!'

The next day it was raining, and Mother didn't want the children to go up the Tree. But Connie's eyes filled with tears, and Mother saw how badly she wanted to go.

'Well, put on your raincoats,' she said, 'and take umbrellas. Then you'll be all right. It may not be raining in the Land of Enchantments. And do remember what Mrs Saucepan said, Joe, and be very careful.'

'We'll be careful,' said Joe, putting on his old raincoat. 'No treading in chalk rings – no stroking of black cats with green eyes – and no rudeness from anyone!'

Off they went. The Tree was very slippery to climb, because it was so wet. Somebody had run a thick rope all the way down it, and the children were glad to hold on to it as they went up the Tree. The Angry Pixie was in a bad temper that morning because the rain had come in at his window and made puddles on the floor. He was scooping up the water and throwing it out of the window.

'Look out!' said Joe. 'Go round the other side of the Tree. The Angry Pixie's in a bad mood.'

Silky was not at home. Dame Washalot, for a change, was not doing any washing, because it really was too wet to dry it. So she was helping Mrs Saucepan to bake cakes on her little stove inside the Tree. The children got a fresh cake each.

Saucepan and Silky were at Moon-Face's house waiting for the children to come. 'Where's Watzisname?' said Joe.

'Gone to sleep,' said Moon-Face. 'Didn't you see him on the way up? Oh no – he would be indoors on a day like this, of course. He sat up half the night trying to remember his real name and write it down so that he wouldn't forget it again. So he was very sleepy this morning. And he didn't remember his name of course.'

'Is the Land of Enchantments up there?' said Joe, nodding his head towards the top of the Tree.'

'It must be,' said Silky. 'I've met two witches and two enchanters coming down the Tree today. They don't live here, so they must have come down from the Land of Enchantments.'

'They come down to get the scarlet-spotted toadstools that grow in the Enchanted Wood,' said Saucepan. 'They are very magic, you know, and can be used in hundreds of spells.'

'There goes an old wizard or enchanter now,' said Silky, as someone in a tall pointed hat went down past Moon-Face's door. 'Shall we go now? I'm sure Connie will be glad to get her voice back.'

Connie nodded. But she suddenly remembered what Mrs Saucepan had said – that she would give Saucepan a very powerful spell, so that if any of them got caught in an enchantment, Saucepan could set them free by using his spell.

But she couldn't say all this, of course. So she pulled out the notebook she had been using for messages and scribbled something on one of the pages. She showed it to Joe.

'What about the spell that Saucepan was going to take with him?'

'Oh, goodness, yes,' said Joe, and he turned to Saucepan. 'Did your mother give you a powerful spell to take with you, Saucepan, in case we get caught in an enchantment?'

'Uh-oh!' groaned Saucepan, beginning to look all round him in a hurry. 'Where did I put it? Silky, have you seen it? What did I do with it?'

'You really are a silly, Saucepan,' said Silky, looking everywhere. 'You know it's a spell that can move about. It's no use putting it down for a minute, because it will only move off somewhere.'

The spell was found at last. It was a funny round red spell, with little things that stuck out all round it rather like spiders' legs. It could move about with these, and had walked off Moon-Face's shelf, and settled itself down at the edge of the slippery-slip.

'Look at that!' said Saucepan, snatching it up quickly. 'Another inch and it would have been down the slippery-slip and gone for ever. Where shall I put it for safety?'

'In a kettle and put the lid on,' said Joe. So into a kettle went the spell, and the lid was put on as tightly as could be.

'It's safe now,' said Saucepan. 'Come on, up we go,

and be careful, everyone!'

They all left their umbrellas and raincoats behind, and went up into the Land of Enchantments. It wasn't a twilight land like the Land of Secrets; it was a land of strange colours and lights and shadows. Everything shone and shimmered and moved. Nothing stayed the same for more than a moment. It was beautiful and strange.

There were curious little shops everywhere where witches, enchanters and goblins cried their wares. There was a shining palace that looked as if it was made of glass, and towered up into the sky. The Enchanter Mighty-One lived there. He was head of the whole land.

There were magic cloaks for sale, that could make anyone invisible at once. How Joe longed to buy one!

There were silver wands full of magic. There were enchantments for everything!

'Spell to turn your enemy into a spider,' cried a goblin. 'Spell to enchant a bird to your hand! Spell to understand the whispering of the trees!'

The spells and enchantments were very expensive. Nobody could possibly buy them, for no one in their little group had more than a few coins in their pockets. Even the cheapest spell cost a sack of gold!

'Oh, look at all those fairies dancing in a ring and singing as they dance!' said Beth, turning her head as she saw a party of bright-winged fairies dancing in a ring together.

She went over to watch them, and they smiled at her and held out their hands. 'Come and dance too, little girl!' they cried.

Beth didn't see that they were all dancing inside a ring drawn on the ground in white chalk! In no time she was in the ring too, linking hands with the fairies and dancing round and round!

The others watched, smiling. Then Joe gave a cry of horror, and pointed to the ground.

'Beth's gone into a ring! Beth, come out, quick!'

Beth looked alarmed. She dropped the hands of the fairies, and came to the edge of the ring. But oh dear, poor Beth couldn't jump over it! She was a prisoner in the magic ring.

'Saucepan, get out the spell at once, the one your mother gave you!' cried Joe. 'Quick, quick! Before anything happens to Beth. She may be getting enchanted.'

Saucepan took the lid off the kettle where he had put the spell. He put in his hand and groped around. He groped and he groped, a worried look coming on his face.

'Saucepan, be *quick*!' said Joe.

'The spell has gone!' said Saucepan miserably. 'Look in the kettle, Joe – the spell isn't there. I can't get Beth out of the magic ring!'

XIX. THE LAND OF ENCHANTMENTS

Everyone stared at Saucepan in horror.

'Saucepan! The spell can't be gone! Why, you put the lid on as tightly as can be,' said Silky. 'Let *me* look!'

Everyone looked, but it was quite plain to see that the kettle was empty. There was no spell there.

'Well, maybe you didn't put it into that kettle, but into another one,' said Joe. 'You've got so many hanging round you. Look in another kettle, Saucepan.'

So Saucepan looked into every one of his kettles, big and small, and even into his saucepans too – but that spell was not to be found.

'It's really most peculiar,' said Moon-Face, puzzled. 'I don't see how it could possibly have got out! Oh dear, why didn't one of us keep the spell instead of Saucepan? We might have know he would lose it!'

'We're in real danger in this strange land, without a spell to protect us,' said Silky. 'But we can't run off home because we mustn't leave Beth in a magic ring, and we have to try and get Connie put right. Oh dear!'

'We'll have to find someone who will get Beth out of the ring,' said Joe anxiously. 'Let's go round the Land of Enchantments and see if anyone will help us.'

So they started off, leaving poor Beth looking sadly after them. But the fairies took her hands and made her dance once again.

The children came to a small shop where a goblin with green ears and eyes sat at the back. In front of him were piled boxes and bottles of all sorts, some with such strange spells in them that they shimmered as if they were alive.

'Could you help us?' said Joe, politely. 'Our sister has got into a magic ring by mistake, and we want to get her out.'

The goblin grinned. 'Oh, no, I'm not helping you to get her out!' he said. 'Magic rings are one of our little traps to keep people here.'

'You're a very nasty person then,' said Moon-Face, who was upset because he was very fond of Beth.

The goblin glared at him and moved his big green ears backwards and forwards like a dog.

'How dare you call me names?' he said. 'I'll turn you into a voice that can do nothing but call rude names, if you're not careful.'

'Indeed you won't,' said Moon-Face, getting angry. 'What, a silly little goblin like you daring to put a spell on *me*, Moon-Face! You think too much of yourself, little green goblin. Go and bury yourself in the garden!'

'Moon-Face!' said Frannie, suddenly. 'Don't be rude. Remember what Mrs Saucepan said.'

But it was too late. Moon-Face had been rude and now he was in the goblin's power. When the little green goblin beckoned to him, poor Moon-Face found that his legs took him to the goblin, no matter how he tried not to go.

'You will work for me now, Moon-Face!' said the goblin. 'Now, just sort out those boxes into their right sizes for me. And remember, no more rudeness.'

Frannie burst into tears. She couldn't bear to see Moon-Face having to work for the nasty little goblin. 'Oh, Saucepan, why did you lose that spell?' she wailed. 'Why did you?'

'Here's a powerful looking enchanter,' said Joe, as a tall man in a great flowing cloak swept by. 'Maybe he could help us.'

He stopped the enchanter and spoke to him. A black cat came out from the tall man's shimmering cloak, and strolled over to Silky, blinking its green eyes at her.

'Can you help us, please?' asked Joe, politely. 'Some of our friends are in difficulties here.'

He was just going on to explain, when he suddenly stopped and ran at Silky who was stroking the black cat and saying sweet things to it! She was very fond of cats, and stroked every one she saw. But she mustn't – she mustn't do that in the Land of Enchantments!

It was too late. She had done it. Now she had to follow the enchanter, who smiled at them. 'A nice little fairy!' he said to them. 'I shall like having her around with the black cat. She will be company for him. She can take care of him.'

To the great dismay of the others, the enchanter swept off, taking poor Silky, his cloak flowing out, covering her and the cat.

'Oh, now Silky's gone!' sobbed Frannie. 'First it

was Beth, then Moon-Face, and now Silky. Whatever are we going to do?'

'Look!' said Saucepan, suddenly, and he pointed to a little shop nearby. On it was painted a sentence in yellow paint:

'COME HERE TO GET THINGS YOU HAVE LOST!'

'What about trying to get Connie's voice there,' said Saucepan. 'Not that *I* want her to have her voice back; I think she's much nicer without it – but we might be able to get it back if we go to that shop.'

They went over to it, Frannie still wiping her eyes. The shop was kept by the same beautiful fairy who had flown to Mrs Hidden's cave, and whose secret Connie had overheard! Connie was afraid of going to her, but Saucepan pulled her over to the shop.

The beautiful fairy knew Saucepan, and was delighted to see him. When he told her about Connie, she looked grave. 'Yes, I know all about it,' she said. 'It was *my* secret she heard, and a very wonderful secret it was. Has she written it down to tell any of you?'

Connie shook her head. She took out her little notebook and wrote in it. She tore out the page and gave it to the fairy.

'I am very sorry for what I did,' the fairy read. 'Please forgive me. I haven't told the secret, and I never will. If you will give me back my lost voice, I promise never to peep and pry again, or to try and overhear things not meant for me.'

'I will forgive you,' said the fairy, gravely. 'But,

Connie, if you ever to tell the secret, I am afraid your voice will be lost again and will never come back. Look! I will give it back to you now – but remember to be careful in future.'

She handed Connie a little bottle of blue and yellow liquid, and a small red glass. 'Drink what is in the bottle,' she said. 'Your voice is there. It's a good thing I didn't sell it to anyone.'

Connie poured out the curious liquid and drank it. It tasted bitter, and she pulled a face.

'Oh, how horrid!' she cried, and then clapped her hands in delight. 'I can speak! My voice is back! Oh, I can talk!'

'It's a pity!' said Saucepan. 'I like you better when you don't talk. Still, I needn't listen.'

Connie was so excited at having her voice back again that she talked and talked without stopping. The others were very silent. Both Joe and Saucepan were worried, and Frannie was still crying.

'Be quiet, Connie!' said Joe at last. 'Saucepan, WHAT SHALL WE DO?'

'Go back and ask my mother for another spell,' said Saucepan. 'That's the best thing I can think of.'

So they all went back to the hole in the cloud. But they couldn't get down it because there were so many people coming up!

'The Land of Enchantments must be moving away again soon,' said Saucepan, in dismay. 'Look! Everyone is hurrying back to it, with their toadstools and things!'

'We can't risk going down to your mother then,' said Joe, more worried than ever. 'If the land moves on it will take Moon-Face, Beth and Silky with it, and we shall never see them again.'

They sat down at the edge of the hole, and looked worried and upset. What ever were they going to do?

Then Frannie gave such a loud cry that everyone jumped. 'What's that? What's that sticking out of the spout of that kettle, Saucepan? Something red, waving about – look!'

Everyone looked – and Saucepan gave a shout. 'It's the spell! It must have crawled up the spout, and that's why we didn't see it when we looked in the kettle! It couldn't get out because the spout is too small. Those are its leg-things waving about, trying to get out of the spout!'

'Quick! Get it out, Saucepan,' said Joe.

'Bad spell, naughty spell,' said Saucepan severely, and poked his finger into the spout, pushing the spell right back. It fell with a little thud into the inside of the kettle. At once, Saucepan took off the lid, put in his hand and grabbed the spell. He jumped to his feet.

'Come on! Maybe we've just got time to rescue the others, Beth first!'

They rushed to the magic ring, and Saucepan stepped into it with the spell held firmly in his hand. At once the chalk ring faded away, the fairies ran off and Beth was free. How she hugged Saucepan!

'No time to waste, no time to waste,' said Saucepan, and ran off to find Silky. He saw the enchanter in his floating cloak, talking to a witch, and rushed up to him.

'Silky, Silky, where are you? I've a spell to set you free!' cried Saucepan.

The enchanter looked down and saw the wriggling red spell in Saucepan's hand. He shook out his cloak and Silky appeared. Saucepan took her by the hand.

'Come on! You're free. You don't need to follow him any more. He's afraid of this spell.'

The enchanter certainly was. He ran off with his black cat without a word.

'Now for Moon-Face,' said Saucepan. 'Gosh, can I hear the humming noise that means this land will soon be on the move?'

He could, and so could the others. With beating hearts, they rushed to the green goblin's shop. There was no time to waste. Saucepan threw the red spell at the goblin, and it went down the back of his neck.

'You're free, Moon-Face. Come quickly!' cried Saucepan. 'The land is on the move!'

Moon-Face rushed after the others, leaving the goblin to try and grab the wriggling spell. Everyone rushed to the hole that led down through the cloud. The land was shaking a little already, as if it was just going to move.

Beth and Frannie were pushed down quickly. Then Silky and Connie followed, almost falling down in their hurry. Then came Moon-Face and Joe, and last of all Saucepan, who nearly got stuck in the hole with his saucepans and kettles. He got free and fell down with a bump.

'The land's just off!' he cried, as a creaking sound came down the ladder. 'We only just escaped this time! Gosh, look how I've dented my kettles!'

XX. WHAT IS WRONG WITH THE FARAWAY TREE?

Connie was very talkative for a few days after they had been to the Land of Enchantments. It seemed as if she had to keep on making sure she had her voice back.

'Well, I half wish you'd lose it again,' said Joe, when Connie had talked for about ten minutes. 'Do let someone else get a word in, Connie!'

'We'll have to take her to the Land of Silence!' said Beth. 'Then she'd be quiet for a bit.'

'What's the Land of Silence?' said Connie, who really loved to hear of all the different lands that came to the top of the Tree.

'I don't know. I only just thought of it,' said Beth, laughing. 'It may not be a land at the top of the Tree for all I know!'

'I wonder what land is there now,' said Connie. 'When are we going to see, Joe?'

'There's no hurry,' said Joe. 'You know Silky and Moon-Face have gone away on holiday for a bit, so they aren't in the Tree. We'll wait till they come back.'

'They'll be back on Thursday,' said Frannie. 'We'll go and see them then. We'll stop and buy some of Mrs Saucepan's cakes, and take them up to Moon-Face's. Mother, can we go on Thursday?'

'Yes,' said Mother. 'I'll bake some new bread for you to take, too.'

Connie could hardly wait till Thursday came. Joe

laughed at her. 'Well, considering that you jeered at the Enchanted Wood, and didn't believe in the Faraway Tree or any of the folk in it, to say nothing of the lands at the top, it's funny that you're keener than any of us to visit there now!' said Joe.

Thursday came. After their dinner the children packed up Mother's lovely new bread, and set off to the Enchanted Wood. They jumped over the ditch and landed in the quiet Wood. The trees were whispering together loudly.

'They seem to be louder than usual,' said Joe. 'They seem sort of excited today. I wonder if anything has happened!'

'Wisha, wisha, wisha,' whispered the trees together, and waved their branches up and down. 'Wisha, wisha, wisha, wisha!'

The children walked to the Faraway Tree. There it was, enormous, its great trunk towering upwards, and its wide-spreading branches waving in the wind.

Joe gave a little cry of surprise.

'What's happening to the Tree? Look, some of its leaves are curling up – sort of withering. Surely it isn't going to shed its leaves yet.'

'Well, it's only summer time,' said Beth, feeling the leaves. 'Don't they feel dry and dead? I wonder what has happened to make them go like this.'

'Perhaps the leaves will be all right a bit higher up,' said Connie. 'It's not growing any sort of fruit down here, is it? That's unusual.'

It certainly was. The Faraway Tree as a rule grew all kinds of different fruits all the way up. It might begin with lemons, go on to pears, load itself a bit

higher up with peaches, and end up with acorns. You never knew what it would grow, but it certainly grew something.

Now today there was no fruit to be seen, only withering leaves. Joe leapt up on to the first branch. Up he went to the next and the next, but all the way up the leaves seemed to be withering and dying. It was curious and rather alarming. The Faraway Tree was magic – something very serious must be the matter if the leaves were dying.

'That's the first sign that a tree itself is dying, if the leaves wither,' said Joe. The others looked upset. They loved the Faraway Tree, and all its little Tree folk. It wasn't only a tree, it was a home for lots of little people – and the path to strange adventures far above.

The Angry Pixie was in his room. Joe rapped on the window, and the Pixie picked up a jug of water to throw. But he put it down again when he saw it was Joe.

'Hello!' he said. 'Are you on your way to Moon-Face's? He's just back.'

'Hey, what's the matter with the Faraway Tree?' asked Joe.

The Angry Pixie shook his head gloomily.

'Don't know,' he said. 'Nobody knows. Nobody at all. It's a very serious thing. Why, the Faraway Tree should live to be a thousand years old – and it's only five hundred and fifty three so far.'

The Owl was asleep in his bed. No water came down from Dame Washalot. When the children got up as far as her branch, they saw her talking seriously to old Mrs Saucepan, who was busy arranging stacks of new-made cakes on her stall.

'Can't think what's the matter,' Dame Washalot was saying. 'I've been here on this branch for nearly a hundred years, and never – no, never – have I known one single leaf wither. Why, the tree grows new ones each day, and fruit, too. Many's the time I've stripped this branch of fruit, and before I've cooked it, it has been full again of some other kind of fruit. Now there's none to be seen.'

'What do you think is the matter?' asked Joe, climbing up. But neither of the old women knew. Mister Watzisname was looking carefully at every curled up, withering leaf, to see if caterpillars were the cause of the trouble.

'I thought if it was caterpillars I'd send a call to all the birds in the Enchanted Wood,' he said. 'They would soon put things right by eating the grubs.

But it isn't caterpillars.'

The children went on to Moon-Face's. He was in his curved room with Silky. But he didn't beam at them as usual as he opened his door. He looked anxious and sad.

'Hello!' he said. 'How nice to see you! We've just got back – and what a shock we got when we saw the Tree! I believe it's dying.'

'Oh *no*!' said Joe, quite shocked. 'It's a magic tree, surely?'

'Yes, but even magic trees die if something goes wrong with them,' said Moon-Face. 'The thing is – no one knows what's wrong, you see. We might put it right, if we knew.'

'Do you think the roots want water?' asked Beth. Moon-Face shook his head.

'No – it's been a wet summer, and besides the Tree's roots go down very, very, deep – right into some old caves deep down below. Jewels were once found there, but I don't think there are any now.'

'You know,' said Joe, looking serious, 'my father once had a lovely apple tree that suddenly went like this, all its leaves curling up. I remember quite well.'

'What was the matter with it?' said Silky.

'There was something wrong with its roots,' said Joe. 'I don't know what. But I know my father said that when a tree's roots go wrong, the tree dies unless you can put the trouble right.'

'But what could go wrong with the Faraway Tree's roots?' said Moon-Face, puzzled.

'Could there be anyone down there, interfering with them?' said Joe.

Moon-Face shook his head. 'I shouldn't think so. No one is allowed at the roots, you know. Those old jewel caves were closed up as soon as the Tree's roots reached to them.'

'Still – it would be a good idea to find out if anything is damaging the roots,' said Joe. 'Could you send a rabbit down, do you think? He could tell you, couldn't he?'

'Yes. That's quite a good idea,' said Moon-Face. He went to the door and whistled for the red squirrel. When the little squirrel came, Moon-Face told him to fetch one of the rabbits that lived in the wood.

One soon came bounding up the Tree like the squirrel! It was odd to watch him. He was pleased to help Moon-Face.

'Listen, Woffles!' said Moon-Face, who knew every single rabbit in the Enchanted Wood. 'Do you know your way down to the jewel caves at the roots of the Faraway Tree?'

'Of course,' said Woffles. 'But the caves are closed, Moon-Face. They have been for years.'

'Well, we think something may be damaging the roots of the Tree,' said Moon-Face. 'We want you to go down as far as you can, and see if there is anything to find out. Come back and tell us as soon as you can.'

'Could I please go down the slippery-slip, just once?' said the rabbit, shyly.

'Of course,' said Moon-Face, and threw him a cushion. 'There you are. Give it back to the red squirrel at the foot of the Tree.'

The rabbit shot off down the slippery-slip, squealing with excitement and delight.

'Isn't he sweet?' said Frannie. 'I wish he was mine! I hope it won't be long before he's back. Shall we have lunch, Moon-Face? We've brought some new bread from Mother, and some cakes from Mrs Saucepan.'

They began their meal. Before they had finished the rabbit was back, looking very scared.

'Moon-Face! Oh, Moon-Face! Look at my bobtail! Half the hairs are gone!'

'What's happened to it?' asked Moon-Face.

'Well, I went down to the old jewel caves, and I heard a hammering and banging noise,' said the rabbit. 'I burrowed a hole to see what the noise was – and guess what, all the caves are filled with little people! I don't know who they are. They saw me and one caught hold of my tail and nearly pulled all the hairs out.'

Everyone sat silent, staring from one to the other. People in the old jewel caves – hammering and crashing round the roots of the Faraway Tree! No wonder it was dying. Maybe the roots were badly damaged!

'We'll have to look into this,' said Moon-Face at last. 'Thank you, Woffles. Your hairs will grow again. Red Squirrel, go down the Tree and tell everyone to come up here. We must hold a meeting. Something has got to be done!'

XXI. DOWN TO THE JEWEL CAVES

The red squirrel bounded off down the Tree to call everyone to a meeting. 'Go up to Moon-Face's,' he told everyone. 'There is to be an important meeting about the Faraway Tree. Most important.'

Soon everyone was on their way up the Tree to Moon-Face's house at the top. Dame Washalot arrived, panting. Behind her came old Mrs Saucepan. Mister Watzisname came, and Saucepan too. The Owl came with two friends. The woodpecker came, and two or three squirrels, with a good many baby squirrels to join in the excitement. The Angry Pixie came too, of course.

It was too much of a squash in Moon-Face's curved room, so everyone sat outside on the broad branch. Moon-Face addressed the meeting.

'Something very serious is happening,' he said. 'The Faraway Tree is dying, as you can all see for yourselves. Even in the last hour or two its leaves have curled up even more. And not a single fruit or berry of any kind is to be found from top to bottom, a thing that has never happened before.'

'That's true,' said Dame Washalot. 'I've always depended on the Tree for my pies. But now there isn't any fruit, not even a raisin.'

'We have discovered that there are people in the jewel caves at the roots of the Tree,' said Moon-Face, solemnly.

'Oooooh-ooooh!' said everyone, in amazement.

'Woffles went down and saw them,' said Moon-Face. The little rabbit almost fell off the branch with pride when his name was mentioned.

'But – the jewel caves have been closed for many years!' said Dame Washalot in surprise.

'Yes – because the roots of the Tree went deep into them,' said Moon-Face. 'Anyway, I don't think there were any more jewels to be found. But certainly, there are robbers who think there may be some left, and they have come after them, forced open the caves, and are damaging the roots of the Tree in their hunt for jewels. Unless we can stop them quickly, I am afraid the Faraway Tree will die.'

'Oh dear, would it have to be chopped down?' said Beth in dismay. She couldn't bear to think of such a thing. It would be dreadful. All the children were as fond of the friendly Faraway Tree as the Tree folk were themselves.

'What are we going to do about it?' said the Angry Pixie. 'I wish I could get at those robbers!'

'We'd better find out who they are first. And how many of them,' said Silky. 'Then we could send a message round the Enchanted Wood and get lots of people to come and help us to force the robbers out of the caves. Maybe if we could stop them damaging the roots any more the Tree would recover.'

'I will go down to the jewel caves myself and speak with the robbers,' said Moon-Face, his round face looking sad. 'Saucepan, will you come with me?'

'Oh yes. Of course. Without a doubt,' said old Saucepan at once.

'I'm coming too,' said Watzisname.

'And all of us are,' said the children at once, and Silky nodded as well. This looked like a very unpleasant kind of adventure, but they meant to share it as usual.

'Well, I think we should go right away,' said Moon-Face, getting up. 'No time like the present. Coming, all of you?'

'Yes,' said everyone, and stood up. Connie was thrilled. What adventures she had had since she came to stay with Joe, Beth and Frannie!

'Where's Woffles?' said Moon-Face, looking round. 'Ah, there you are! Woffles, please lead the way.'

Woffles proudly ran down the Tree in front of the others. Everyone followed. When they came to the ground Woffles ran to a big rabbit hole.

'Down here,' he said. So down went the children and the four Tree folk, down down into the darkness. It was a good thing the rabbit hole was so big. Rabbit burrows in the Enchanted Wood were always on the large side because the goblins, gnomes, pixies and elves liked to use the underground tunnels when it rained.

'I've never been down a rabbit hole before,' said Connie. 'Never! It's like a dream! I hope I won't wake up and find it isn't real. I like this sort of thing.'

So did the others. It was peculiar down the rabbit hole, rather dark, and a bit musty. Woffles knew the way very well, of course. He knew every burrow in the Wood!

Here and there were strange lanterns hanging from the roof where it was a bit higher than usual, usually at sharp corners. It was a bit of a squash when anyone else came along in the opposite direction, for then everyone had to flatten themselves against the wall of the tunnel.

Quite a lot of people met them. Rabbits, of course, and elves and goblins seemed to be hurrying about by the hundred.

'Woffles, are you sure this is the way?' said Moon-Face at last, when it seemed as if they had been wandering along dark tunnels for miles and miles. 'Are you sure you are not lost?'

Woffles made rather a rude snort. 'Lost! As if any rabbit is ever lost underground!' he said. 'No, Moon-Face, you can trust me. I never get lost here. I am taking you the shortest way.'

They went on again, feeling their way along the tunnels, glad of an unexpected ray of light from a lantern now and again. And then they heard something!

'Listen!' said Moon-Face, stopping so suddenly that Joe bumped right into him. 'Listen! What is that?'

Everyone stood and held their breath – and they heard strange muffled noises coming from the depths of the earth.

'Boom, boom, boom! Boom, boom, boom!'

'That's the people I told you about,' said Woffles importantly. 'We're getting near the jewel caves.'

Connie felt a bit strange. She held Watzisname's hand tightly.

'Boom, boom, boom!'

'It's the robbers all right,'

545

said Moon-Face, and his voice echoed strangely down the tunnel. 'Can't you hear their choppers?'

'Is it safe to go on?' said Silky, doubtfully. 'You don't think they'd take us prisoners or anything, do you?'

'I'll go first with Joe,' said Moon-Face, 'and you others can keep back in the shadows, if you like. I don't think the robbers would try to capture us. They would know that a whole army of people would come down from the Enchanted Wood after them, if they did!'

They went forward again, making as little noise as they could. Even old Saucepan hardly made a clank or a clang with his saucepans and kettles.

'Boom, boom, boom!' The sound came nearer still. 'BOOM, BOOM, BOOM!'

'They are certainly working very hard,' said Joe, in a whisper. 'They are using choppers to break down the caves to see if any more precious stones are hidden there. No wonder the Tree is dying. They must be striking the roots every time.'

'There's a root, look!' said Silky, and she pointed to a thick rope-like thing that jutted out into the tunnel, right across their path. It shone strangely in the light of an old lantern that swung from the roof just there.

'Yes, that's a root,' said Moon-Face, climbing over it. 'Be careful of it, all of you!'

So they were very careful, because they didn't want to hurt the Faraway Tree at all. It was being hurt quite enough, as it was, by the robbers.

'Now, here are the caves,' said Woffles, excitedly, as they turned a corner, and came to a great door, studded with iron and brass. 'You can't get through that door. It's locked.'

'How did you get into the caves?' said Moon-Face. 'Oh yes, I remember, you made a burrow. Where is it?'

Woffles pointed to it with his paw. But gosh, out of it pointed something sharp and glittering! Whatever could it be?

Moon-Face stepped up to see. He came back and whispered gravely. 'It's a sharp spear! The robbers certainly don't want anyone to get into the caves again. There are three of these doors, I know, but the robbers will have locked them all – and any rabbit hole will be guarded by them too – with spears!'

'There must be someone holding the spear,' said Joe. 'Let's go and talk to him! Come on, Moon-Face. We'll tell him what we think of robbers who hurt the roots of the dear old Faraway Tree!'

XXII. THE RABBITS COME TO HELP

Joe and Moon-Face walked boldly up to the rabbit hole. It was the one Woffles had made that day, when he had gone down to inquire into things. It was clear that the robbers had discovered it and were guarding it.

The shining spear moved a little, and a harsh voice cried out sharply:

'Who goes there?'

'This is Joe and Moon-Face,' said Moon-Face. 'We have come to tell you that you are making the Faraway Tree die, because you are damaging its roots.'

'Pooh!' said the voice, rudely.

Moon-Face felt angry. 'Don't you care whether or not you kill a tree?' he asked. 'And the Faraway Tree, too, the finest tree in the world!'

'We don't care a bit,' said the voice. 'Why should we? We don't live in the Tree. We are Trolls, who live underground. We don't care about trees.'

'Trolls!' said Moon-Face. 'Of course, I might have guessed it. You live under the ground and work the soil there to find gold and precious stones, don't you?'

'How clever you are!' said the mocking voice. 'Now go away, please. You can't get into the caves, nor can you stop us doing what we want to. There are plenty of precious stones here still, and until we have found them all, we shall hold these caves against any enemy.'

'You can have all the jewels you like if only you won't hurt the roots of the Tree,' said Moon-Face, desperately.

'We can't help it,' said the voice. 'The roots grow through the walls, and are always getting in our way. We chop them off!'

'Good heavens! No wonder the poor Tree is dying,' said Joe. 'Moon-Face, whatever are we going to do?'

Moon-Face went a little nearer the rabbit hole. Would it be possible to bring a whole army of Wood Folk and force a way down the hole – or even get the rabbits to make more holes? No, it certainly wasn't possible to get down *this* hole, in any case. Another spear had now appeared, horribly sharp and pointed.

'How did you get into the caves?' shouted Moon-Face, moving back a little. 'The doors were always

kept locked, and Pixie Long-Beard had the key.'

'Oh, we stole it from him and got in easily!' said the voice, with a laugh. 'Then we locked the doors on this side, so that no one else could get in. We've been here a week now, and nobody knew till that interfering rabbit came along. Wait till we get him! We'll deal with him all right.'

Woffles fled to the back of the listening party, terrified. 'It's all right,' said Silky, 'we won't let them get you, Woffles. Don't be afraid.'

Moon-Face and Joe went back to the others. 'I don't see what we can do,' whispered Moon-Face. 'All the doors are locked, and we certainly can't get keys to unlock them, for the one Pixie Long-Beard had was the only one that could unlock those cave doors. And the Trolls are guarding that rabbit hole too well for us to get down it. Even at night there will be someone there to guard it.'

'Do you think we could get the rabbits to tunnel silently somewhere else?' said Joe. 'If only they could make a way for us somewhere, we could all pour in and surprise the Trolls.'

'It's about the only thing to do,' said Moon-Face. 'What do you think, Watzisname?'

'I think the same,' said Watzisname. 'If we can get the rabbits to make a really big hole, we could do something to surprise the Trolls. It's the only way we can get into the caves, isn't it?'

'Yes,' said Moon-Face, thoughtfully. 'Well, we'd better get to work at once. Where's Woffles?'

'Here, Moon-Face!' said the rabbit eagerly. 'Here I am. What can I do? I daren't go down that hole I made, so don't ask me to!'

'I won't,' said Moon-Face. 'It was brave of you to go the first time. What I want you to do, Woffles, is to go and round up all the biggest and strongest rabbits in the Wood and get them here. Then we'll set them to work quickly on a burrow that must come up right in the very centre of the jewel caves. Maybe the robbers won't expect us to force a way there. They will expect us to come through the walls, not under the floor of the caves.'

'Right, Moon-Face!' said the rabbit, and sped off, his white bobtail bobbing up and down as he went down the tunnel.

It was rather dull, waiting for the rabbits to come. The lantern nearby gave only a faint light. Moon-Face told everyone to speak in the lowest of whispers.

'I'm hungry!' whispered Connie.

Watzisname gave a little giggle. 'I've got some Toffee Shocks,' he said. 'Do you like toffees, Connie?'

'Oh *yes*,' said Connie, pleased. 'What's a Toffee Shock? I've never heard of one before.'

Watzisname was holding out a paper bag to Connie. The others watched. They knew Toffee Shocks, which were very peculiar. As soon as you began to suck a Toffee Shock it grew bigger. It grew and it grew and it grew, till it completely filled your mouth and you couldn't say a word! Then, very suddenly, it burst into nothing, and your mouth was empty.

Connie took *two!* Gosh, what would happen? One was bad enough, but *two* Toffee Shocks would give her something to remember!

She popped the toffees into her mouth. Everyone

watched her. Beth began to giggle.

Connie sucked hard. 'It's funny,' she thought. 'The more I suck, the bigger they seem to be. Gosh, they're getting enormous!'

They were! They swelled up, as they always did, and filled Connie's mouth completely, so that she couldn't speak or chew! She stared at the others in horror.

'Gug-gug-gug,' said Connie, in fright, her eyes almost falling out of her head. Her cheeks were puffed out with the swollen toffees, and her tongue was squashed at the bottom of her mouth.

Just as she thought she really couldn't bear it for one moment more, the Toffee Shocks exploded, and went to nothing! Connie stood in the greatest surprise. Her mouth was empty. Where had the toffees gone? She hadn't swallowed them.

The others burst into giggles. Connie was really cross. 'What a nasty trick to play on me!' she said to Watzisname, glaring at him.

'Well, you should only have taken one, not two,' said Watzisname, wiping the tears of laughter from his eyes. 'One Toffee Shock is fun, but two must be awful!'

'Sh! Sh!' said Moon-Face. 'Don't let the Trolls know we are still here. They will be on the watch if they think we are.'

'Well, *I* think it would be a very good thing to stay here and make a noise,' whispered Silky. 'Then the Trolls will guard this hole, and keep their attention on us, which will give the rabbits a chance to burrow unheard.'

'Silky's right,' said Joe. 'We'll talk loudly and make a noise. Then perhaps when the rabbits do their burrowing under the floor of the caves, the Trolls won't notice it.'

So they all began to talk and laugh loudly. A third spear appeared at the entrance of the hole, and a voice said: 'If you are thinking of getting down here, think again!'

'Your spears won't stop us when we charge down that hole!' yelled Moon-Face, which made a fourth spear appear, shining brightly.

In a little while a whole army of rabbits appeared at the back of the passage, jostling one another, headed by Woffles, who was bursting with pride again. 'I've brought them,' he said. 'Here they all are, the biggest and strongest.'

Moon-Face told them what he wanted them to do. 'We want you to make a passage right *under* the caves,' he said, 'so that it comes up in the floor. The Trolls won't be expecting that. Whilst you're doing it, I'll send a message to the pixies in the Wood to come, and help us to burst through the tunnel you make as soon as it is finished.'

As the rabbits began to burrow rapidly downwards, Moon-Face decided to send Silky, Frannie, Beth and Connie back up the Tree, so they could send out the message to the pixies in the Wood.

'Oh, but we want to see what happens!' said Beth.

'We'll tell you what happens as soon as we know,' promised Joe. 'Silky, can you send a message to the pixies when you get above ground?'

'I will,' said Silky, and she and the three girls made their way back up the burrow and into the Wood. They met a pixie and gave him the message to get a small army together.

The rabbits burrowed quickly and silently down into the earth, down and down and down. When they knew they were right underneath the centre of the jewel caves, they began to burrow up again, up and up and up. They meant to come up just in the middle of the floor of the centre cave.

Pixies poured down into the tunnel. Everyone followed the rabbits closely, meaning to rush the caves as soon as the tunnel broke through the floor.

But it was not to be! When the rabbits had burrowed upwards to the caves, they came to a stop. Something hard and solid was above them. They couldn't burrow into it.

'What is it?' whispered Moon-Face anxiously. 'Let me feel.' He felt. 'It's heavy blocks of stone!' he groaned. 'Of course, the floor of the caves is paved with stone. I had forgotten that. We can't possibly get through. I'm so sorry, rabbits – all your work has been for nothing!'

'Ha, ha, ho, ho!' suddenly came the distant sound

of laughter. '*We* heard you burrowing! You didn't know the floors were made of stone! Ha ha, ho ho!'

'Horrid Trolls!' said Moon-Face, as they all made their way back down the tunnel. 'What can we do now?'

XXIII. THE LAND OF KNOW-ALLS

'We'd better get back up the Tree, and tell Silky and the others we've failed,' said Moon-Face, gloomily. 'It looks to me as if the poor old Faraway Tree is done for. It's very, very sad.'

They all went back up the Tree, and the pixies returned to their homes in the Wood. Silky and the girls were very upset to hear that the rabbits hadn't been able to get through the floors of the caves.

'Heavy stone there,' said Joe. 'No one could burrow through that, or even move it. It's bad luck. There's no other way of getting down to the caves at all.'

Everyone sat and thought. Nobody could think of any plan at all. 'It isn't that we're stupid,' said Moon-Face. 'It's just that it's impossible.'

'I suppose we couldn't ask anyone in the Land of Know-Alls for help, could we?' said Dame Washalot, at last.

'The Land of Know-Alls! Is that up at the top of the Tree now?' said Moon-Face, looking excited.

'Yes. Didn't you know?' said Dame Washalot. 'I went up there this morning to find out how to do my washing in cold water, when I can't get enough hot. I found out all right, too. There's nothing they don't know up there!'

'Goodness! Perhaps they know how to get down into the caves then!' said Moon-Face. 'Or maybe they could give us a key to open the doors.'

'That wouldn't be much use,' said Joe. 'You can be sure the Trolls have put guards at the doors in case we thought of that. They are well armed too. It is only by taking them completely by surprise that we could defeat them.'

'That's true,' said Moon-Face. 'Well, what about going up into the Land of Know-Alls? We might get some good advice. There are only five Know-Alls, and between them they know everything.'

'Oh, do let's go now, this very minute!' said Connie, impatiently.

'All right, we will,' said Joe, and he got up.

'I'll go and finish my washing,' said Dame Washalot. 'And you had better see if your cakes are burning, Mrs Saucepan. You left some in the oven.'

'My goodness, so I did,' said old Mrs Saucepan, and climbed quickly down the Tree.

The rest of them wanted to go into the Land of Know-Alls, even the Angry Pixie, who didn't often go into any of the strange lands.

They all went up the topmost branch and climbed up the yellow ladder through the cloud. They came out into the Land of Know-Alls.

It was a small land, so small that it looked as if anyone could fall off the edge quite easily here and there. In the very middle of it, on a steep hill, rose a magnificent glittering palace, with so many thousands of windows that it looked like one big shining diamond. From the middle of the palace rose a tremendously tall tower.

The children and the others went up two hundred steps to the great front door. Then they saw about a thousand attendants lining the hall inside, all dressed in blue and silver. They all bowed to the little company at once, looking like a blue and silver cornfield blown by the wind, so gracefully did they bow at the same moment together.

'What is your wish?' said the thousand attendants, sounding like the wind whispering.

'We want to see the Know-Alls,' said Moon-Face.

'They are in the Tall Tower,' said the attendants. Then a hundred of them took the little party to what looked like a small room, but which was really a lift. Ninety-nine attendants bowed them in. One got in with them and pulled a silver rope. The children and the others gasped as the lift shot up the tower. It went so fast. Up and up and up it went, till the children thought they would land on the moon!

At last the lift slowed down and stopped. The door slid open. The children saw that they had come to the top of the Tall Tower. It was surrounded on all sides by wide windows, and the children gasped again as they looked out. It looked as if they could see the whole world from those windows! Oceans, seas, lands spread out on each side of them, and lay glittering in the brightest sunlight they had ever known.

Then they saw the five Know-Alls. They were strange, wonderful and peculiar folk, so old that they had forgotten their youth, so wise that they knew everything.

Only their calm, mysterious eyes moved in their old, old faces. One of them spoke, and his voice came from very far away – or so it seemed.

'You have come to ask for advice. You want to know how to get into the jewel caves?'

'How does he know?' whispered Connie to Joe in amazement.

'Well, he is a Know-All,' said Joe. 'Sh! Don't talk now. Listen!'

Moon-Face stood before the wise Know-All, and spoke to him. 'The Faraway Tree is dying. It is because there are Trolls in the jewel caves underground, cutting the roots that give the great Tree its life. How, please Know-All, can we get down to the caves and stop them?'

The wise Know-All shut his gleaming, mysterious eyes as if he was thinking or remembering something. He opened them again and looked at Moon-Face.

'There is only one way. Your slippery-slip goes to the foot of the Tree, down its centre. Bore down still further, from your slippery-slip, and you will come out at last right under the tree, in the centre of its tangled roots. Then you can surprise the Trolls and overcome them.'

Everyone looked thrilled. Of course! If only they could make the slippery-slip go deeper down and down and down, they would come out in the middle of the roots! It was a marvellous idea.

'Thank you so much, wise Know-All,' said Moon-Face. 'Thank you! We will go straight away and follow your advice!'

The little group of friends bowed to the five strange

Know-Alls, with their calm, mysterious eyes. Then they stepped into the lift, and the little attendant pulled on the silver rope.

'Oh!' gasped everyone as the lift moved swiftly downwards. It really seemed as if it was falling! It slowed down at last, and the children and everyone else walked out into the vast hall.

Down the steps they went, and back to the hole in the cloud, feeling excited and a little strange. The five Know-Alls always made people feel strange.

'Well,' said Moon-Face, when they were safely in his curved room, and were beginning to feel a little more ordinary. 'Well, now we know what to do. The next thing is – how do we bore a hole down through the rest of the Tree to its roots? I haven't any tools big enough to do that.'

'You know,' said Silky, suddenly, 'you know, Moon-Face, there is a caterpillar belonging to a goat-moth, that bores tunnels in the trunks of trees. I know, because I've seen one. It had made quite a burrow in the wood of the tree, and it lived there by itself till it was time to come out and turn into a chrysalis. Then, of course, it changed into a big goat-moth.'

'Surely you don't think that a little caterpillar could burrow down this big tree!' said Joe.

'Well, if Moon-Face could get about twelve of these goat-moth caterpillars, and could make them ever so much bigger, they could easily eat their way down, and make way for us,' said Silky.

Moon-Face slapped his knee hard and made everyone jump. 'Silky's got the right idea!' he said. 'That's just what we will do! We can easily make the caterpillars large. Then they can burrow down fast. Silky, you're really very clever.'

Silky blushed. It wasn't often she had better ideas than Moon-Face, but this time she really had thought of something good.

'Now we'll have to find out where any goat-moth caterpillars are,' said Moon-Face. 'What tree do they usually burrow in, Silky?'

'There is one in the big elm tree, and two or three in the willows by the stream, and some in the poplars at the other side of the wood,' said Silky. 'I'll go and get them, if you like. They smell a bit horrid, you know.'

'Yes, like goats, don't they?' said Watzisname. 'They're funny creatures. They live for three years in the trunks of trees, eating the wood! Funny taste, some creatures have. Go and get some, Silky. Take a box with you.'

Silky sped off on her errand, taking a big box from Moon-Face's curved cupboard. Joe looked at the time.

'I really think we should go, Moon-Face,' he said. 'It's getting very late. I suppose Silky will bring back the caterpillars soon, and you'll make them enormous and set them to work tonight? We'll come back tomorrow morning and see how you are getting on.'

'I shall rub the caterpillars with growing magic when Silky brings them,' said Moon-Face, 'but it will take them all night to grow to the right size. I shall probably set them to work after breakfast, Joe; so come then.'

Joe and the girls slid down the slippery-slip, shot out of the trapdoor and made their way home. They

561

were tired, but very thrilled. How they hoped they could defeat those Trolls, and perhaps save the dear old Faraway Tree!

'We'll go back tomorrow, first thing after breakfast,' said Joe. 'I expect old Moon-Face will have worked out some brilliant plan by then. I only hope we punish those bad Trolls properly. Fancy not caring if they killed the Faraway Tree or not!'

'I can hardly wait for tomorrow,' sighed Connie. 'I really don't think I can.' But she had to, of course – and tomorrow came at last, as it always does. What was going to happen then?

XXIV. A SURPRISE FOR THE TROLLS

Next morning, immediately after an early breakfast, the four children set off to the Faraway Tree. They felt sad when they got near it and saw how much more withered the leaves were.

'It looks almost dead already,' said Joe, miserably. 'I don't believe we can save it, even if we defeat the Trolls today.'

They climbed up. Moon-Face and Silky were waiting for them in the curved room. With them, in the room, were some very peculiar looking creatures – eleven goat-moth caterpillars.

They were great pinkish-coloured caterpillars with black heads. A broad band of chocolate brown ran down their long backs. They were really enormous, like long, fat snakes!

'Hello!' said Moon-Face, beaming round. 'The caterpillars are nearly ready. I rubbed them with the growing magic last night, and they have grown steadily ever since. They are almost ready to go down the slippery-slip now and start eating the wood away at the bottom, to go right down into the roots of the Tree.'

The caterpillars didn't say a word. They just looked at the children with big solemn eyes, and twitched their many legs.

'I think they're ready,' said Moon-Face. 'Now, Joe,

listen! The caterpillars are going to burrow a way for us right through the bottom part of the trunk of the Tree, into the heart of its roots. They are going to crawl out and frighten the Trolls, who will probably run away. Then our job is to rush after them and capture them. All the pixies are ready at the foot of the Tree. They are going to climb in through the trapdoor, as soon as the caterpillars have gone down into the roots.'

Everyone listened to this long speech, and thought the plan was excellent. Moon-Face gave a cushion to the biggest goat-moth caterpillar, who curled himself up on it. Then off it whizzed down to the foot of the Tree, followed by all the others, one after another.

The children gave the caterpillars a little time to burrow, and then followed them down the slippery-slip. When they got to the trapdoor they shot out and saw lots of pixies waiting there. Moon-Face climbed back in through the trapdoor and looked by the light of a lamp to see what had become of the caterpillars.

All he could see was a tunnel eaten out, going down and down into the roots!

'They're going fast!' he said, looking out of the trapdoor. 'Out of sight already! My word, fancy being able to eat wood like that.'

Soon Moon-Face reported that he thought they might all follow down the way the caterpillars had made. Their strong jaws made easy work of the wood of the Tree, and they were now almost at the bottom, among the roots. It was time to follow them, and help to surprise the Trolls.

Moon-Face, Saucepan, Mister Watzisname, the Angry Pixie, Joe and all the other pixies from the Wood, crept down the hole. Sometimes it was as steep as the slippery-slip, and they slid. It was dark, but everyone was too excited to mind. Silky, Frannie, Beth, Connie and Silky waited impatiently by the trapdoor. The caterpillars came to the end of the enormous trunk, and found themselves in a tangle of great rope-like roots, going down and down. They crawled among them, with Moon-Face holding on to the tail end of the last one, so as not to lose the way.

They came out into the very middle of the biggest cave. There was no one there, though the sound of distant hammering or digging could be heard.

'No Trolls to be seen!' whispered Moon-Face to the others. 'Sh! I can hear some coming now!'

Moon-Face and the others slipped back into the tangle of roots, but the great snake-like caterpillars went crawling on. Just as they came to the entrance of the cave, two Trolls came in, almost falling over the caterpillars. They gave a yell.

'Oooh! Snakes! Run, run! Snakes!'

They ran off, screaming. The caterpillars solemnly followed, all eleven of them in a line. They met more Trolls, and every one of them ran away shrieking, for they were really afraid of snakes, and they certainly thought these enormous caterpillars were some dreadful kind of snake!

'After them!' cried Moon-Face, and waving a strong stick in the air he led the way into the jewel caves. In one corner was a great pile of glittering jewels. The Trolls had found a fortune down there!

The Trolls were shouting to one another. 'The caves are full of snakes! Hide! Hide!'

The robbers crowded into a cave, put a great stone at the entrance, and pressed against it to prevent the caterpillars from entering. When Moon-Face came up, he lowered his big stick and grinned round at the others.

'Our work is easy! They've shut themselves in, and we can easily make them prisoners!'

'Who's there?' called a Troll, hearing Moon-Face's voice.

'The enemy!' said Moon-Face. 'You are our prisoners. Come out now, and we will keep off the snakes. If you don't give yourselves up, we will push away the stone and let the snakes in!'

Joe giggled. It was funny to think that anyone

should be so afraid of caterpillars. The creatures were quite enjoying themselves, crawling round and about, getting in everyone's way.

'We'll come out,' said the Troll's leader, after talking to his men. 'But keep off those snakes!'

'Hold the caterpillars, you others,' whispered Moon-Face. 'Now, all together – heave away the stone!'

The Trolls came out, looking very scared. They were glad to see that the 'snakes' were being held back by Joe and the others. The pixies at once surrounded them, and bound their hands behind their backs.

'We'll keep them in prison till next week, when the Land of Punishment comes back again,' said the head pixie with a grin. 'Then we'll push them all up the ladder, and see that they don't come down. They can move off with the Land of Punishment – it will do them good to live there for the rest of their lives!'

Moon-Face stayed down in the caves whilst the pixies found the key, unlocked the doors and marched out the frightened Trolls. They were strange looking folk, with large heads, small bodies and large limbs.

'Let's have a look round and see what damage has been done to the Tree,' said Moon-Face. 'Just look – see how they've chopped that root in half, and cut this one, and spoilt that one. The poor Tree! No wonder it began to wither and die.'

'What can we do for it?' said Joe, anxiously.

'Well, I've got some wonderful ointment,' said Moon-Face. 'I'm going to rub the damaged roots with it – you can all help – and we'll see if it does any good. It's very magic. I got it out of the Land of Medicines, years ago, and I've still got some left. I hope it's still got magic in it.'

Moon-Face took a little blue pot out of his pocket and removed the lid. It was full of strange green ointment.

'Better send up for the others and let them help too,' said Joe. But just at that moment the girls and Silky came rushing up, led by Woffles. The pixies had told them all that had happened, and they had come down in great delight.

'We're going to rub the damaged roots with magic ointment,' said Moon-Face, and he held out the blue pot. 'Dip your fingers in it, everyone, and hurry up. We can't afford to waste a single moment now, because the poor old Tree is almost dead!'

The children and the others kept dipping their fingers into the pot of ointment, which, in a most magical way, never seemed to get empty. Then, with the green ointment on their fingers, everyone rushed about to find damaged roots. They rubbed the ointment well into the roots, and came back for more.

'Well,' said Moon-Face, after two hours' very hard work, 'shall we take a rest, and go up to see if the Tree is looking any better? I could do with some hot chocolate or something. Let's go and see if old Mrs Saucepan has got some cakes and will make us something to drink.'

So they walked up through the rabbit burrows and then climbed the Tree to Dame Washalot's. To their great disappointment all the leaves were still curled up and withered, and the Faraway Tree looked just as dead as before.

'I suppose the magic ointment isn't any use now,' said Silky, sadly. 'Poor, poor Tree. Moon-Face, will we have to leave it if it dies? Will it be chopped down?'

'Oh, don't talk about such horrid things,' said Moon-Face.

Suddenly Joe gave a shout that made them all jump.

'Look! The leaves are uncurling! The Tree is looking better. It really is!'

It was quite true. One by one the withered leaves were straightening out, uncurling themselves, waving happily in the breeze once more. And then, to everyone's delight, the Tree began to grow its fruits as usual!

Large and juicy oranges appeared on all the nearby branches, and shone in the golden sun. The children put out their hands and picked some. They had never tasted such lovely oranges in their life!

'There are some pineapples just above us, and some raisins just below!' said Connie, in surprise. 'The Tree is doing well, isn't it? I've never seen such a lovely lot of fruit before!'

'The magic ointment has begun its work,' said Silky, happily. 'Now the Faraway Tree will be all right. Thank goodness we found out how to capture those horrid Trolls, and how to cure the poor old Tree!'

Everyone in the Tree rejoiced that day. The folk of the Enchanted Wood came up and down to pick the fruit. Woffles the rabbit came, his eyes shining with pleasure to think he had helped to save the Tree. He was dressed in the red squirrel's old sweater, and was very proud of it.

'He gave it to me as a reward,' said Woffles,

proudly. 'Isn't it lovely?'

'Yes, and you look really nice!' said Silky. 'Come and have a drink, you funny little rabbit!'

XXV. THE LAND OF TREATS

Everyone was very, very glad that the dear old Faraway Tree was all right again. It had been dreadful to think that it was dying, and might have to be chopped down. Now it seemed to be better than ever.

The children visited it every morning to pick the fruit to take home for their mother to make into pies and desserts. Everyone in the Tree was doing the same, and old Mrs Saucepan made quite a lot of money by selling fruit pies to the people who went up and down the Tree.

The bad Trolls, who had damaged the Tree's roots, had all been taken up to the Land of Punishments, which was now at the top of the Tree.

'You should just hear the shouts and yells that those bad Trolls make up there,' said Moon-Face with a grin, to the children. 'They're having a bad time. They keep on trying to escape, and get down the ladder, but they can't.'

'Why can't they?' asked Joe.

'Look and see,' said Moon-Face, with a wider grin than before.

So Joe climbed up the topmost bough, and got on to the bottom rung of the ladder. He couldn't go any further because on the other rungs were the goat-moth caterpillars, still enormous! There they were curled, like enormous snakes, waiting for the Trolls to try and escape.

'The Trolls are very scared of them,' called up Moon-Face, 'and as soon as they see them, they rush back into the Land of Punishment. They don't know which is worse, snakes or punishment!'

The others giggled. 'What are you going to do with the caterpillars when the Land of Punishment has moved on?' asked Beth.

'Oh, change them back to their right size again and take them to the trees we got them from,' said Silky. 'Right now, they are having pies and cakes to eat, instead of the wood they like, but we'd need to give them trees to gnaw if we fed them properly, they're big now! Still, they seem to like the pies.'

'How long is this land going to stay?' asked Connie, suddenly. 'I hope it won't stay too long, because I've got to go home soon. Mother's better and she's coming back, so I've got to go too. I don't want to, because it's such fun here.'

'Well, you should be glad your mother is better and ready to take you home,' said Joe. 'You're a selfish little girl, Connie!'

'All the same, it *has* been such fun here,' said Connie. 'You'd hate to leave the Enchanted Wood and the Faraway Tree and Moon-Face and Silky and the rest of your friends, you know you would!'

'Yes, we would,' said Beth. 'Moon-Face, I wish a really nice land could come before Connie goes – just for a treat for her, you know. Something like the Land of Tea Parties, or the Land of Take-What-You-Please – or the Land of Goodies! That was lovely! Connie, some of the houses in the Land of Goodies were made of chocolate!'

'Oooh – how lovely!' said Connie. 'Moon-Face, what land is coming next?'

'Well, I think it's the Land of Treats, but I'm not quite sure,' said Moon-Face. 'I'll find out and let you know.'

'The Land of Treats! What's that like?' said Connie, thinking that it sounded fine.

'Well, it's full of treats,' said Moon-Face; '*you* know – donkey rides, presents, Christmas trees and ice-creams, and things like that.'

'And parties, and musicals and balloons and . . .' went on Silky.

'Gosh!' said Connie, her eyes shining. 'What a lovely land that would be to visit for my last one. Oh, I *do* hope it comes before I go!'

It did. Two or three days after that, the red squirrel, dressed in his new sweater, arrived at the children's cottage with a message.

He knocked on the window, and made Mother jump. But when she saw it was the squirrel, she opened the window and let him in. She was getting quite used to the children's strange friends now.

'Joe! Beth! Here's the red squirrel!' she called, and the children came running in.

'Good morning!' said the squirrel, politely. 'I've come with a message from Moon-Face, and Moon-Face says that the Land of Treats will be at the top of the Tree tomorrow, and are you coming?'

'Of course!' cried the children, in delight, 'Tell Moon-Face we'll be there.'

'I will,' said the squirrel and bounded off.

The next day the four children all went up the Tree in excitement. A rope had again been run down through the branches, for hundreds of the Wood folk were going up to the Land of Treats. Whenever a really nice land was at the top, the Tree had plenty of traffic up and down!

Moon-Face, Silky, Watzisname and Saucepan were waiting for them impatiently. 'There are elephants,' said Silky, 'They give you rides. I'm going on an elephant.'

'And you can go up in a balloon,' said Moon-Face. 'Can't you, Saucepan?'

'Moon? Go to the moon? Can you really?' said Saucepan, looking excited.

'UP IN A BALLOON!' yelled everyone, and Saucepan looked startled.

'All right, all right! No need to shout,' he said. 'Come on, let's go now. I want a treat.'

The Old Saucepan Man led the way up the topmost branch. The others followed. Soon they all stood in the Land of Treats.

It looked absolutely lovely. Near them was a large size roundabout, with animals to ride – and they were magic animals who sometimes came alive!

'Oh, let's go on the roundabout!' said Connie.

'No, let's get ice-creams first,' said Joe. '*Look* at these! Did you ever see such beauties?'

574

The ice-cream man was standing with his little van, handing out ice-creams for nothing. They were enormous, and you could have any flavour you liked.

'You've only got to say 'chocolate!' or 'lemon!' or 'pineapple!' and the man just dips his hand in and brings you out the right kind,' said Moon-Face, happily.

'He *can't* have got every flavour there,' said Connie. 'I'll ask for something he won't have and see what happens.'

So when her turn came she said solemnly, 'I want a fish ice-cream please.'

And hey presto! The ice-cream man just as solemnly handed her out a large ice-cream which was quite obviously made of fish because the others could see a few fish bones sticking out of it!

'Ha, ha, Connie! Serves you right!' said Joe.

Connie looked at the ice-cream and wrinkled up her nose. She handed it to the ice-cream man, and said 'I won't have this. I'll have a strawberry one, please.'

'Have to eat that one first, dear,' said the ice-cream man. So Connie had to go without her ice-cream, because she didn't like the taste of the fish one, and couldn't eat it. She gave it to a cat who came wandering by looking for *his* treat, which he hoped would be fish!

'Now let's go on the roundabout,' said Joe, when he had finished his ice-cream. 'Come on! I'm going on that giraffe.'

'I shall have a lion,' said Moon-Face, bravely. 'I'll have that one. It has such a wonderful mane.'

Connie didn't feel like a lion or a giraffe. She thought she would choose an animal who might be a pet. So she chose a nice tabby cat, who stood waiting for someone to climb on her back.

'Take your seats please!' called the roundabout man, a very amusing man who turned himself round and round and round all the time his roundabout was going, and only stopped when the roundabout stopped too.

Frannie chose a duck that had the softest back she had ever sat on! Beth liked the look of a brown bear. Silky chose a hen. Saucepan chose a large mouse, and Watzisname took a dog with a waggy tail.

The roundabout music began to play. The roundabout moved on its way, round and round and round, going faster and faster. The animals came alive and real, and Saucepan made his mouse move over to Connie, meaning to ask her how she was enjoying such a treat.

But this was a great mistake, because Connie was riding a cat. The roundabout man always put the mouse on the opposite side to the cat, and now here was the mouse almost under the cat's nose!

The cat gave an excited mew when it smelt the mouse. It shot out its paw, and the mouse squealed in fright. It leapt right off the roundabout, and Saucepan almost fell off. He clung to the large mouse, all his pans rattling and clanging.

The cat rushed off the roundabout after the mouse. The roundabout man gave a yell and stopped the roundabout. The children leapt off and stared at Connie and the cat chasing Saucepan and the mouse!

'Gosh! I hope the cat doesn't eat old Saucepan as well as the mouse!' groaned Moon-Face.

XXVI. GOODBYE TO THE
FARAWAY TREE

Everyone in the Land of Treats stood and watched Connie's cat chasing Saucepan's mouse. Round and round and in and out they went, knocking over stalls of fruit and upsetting all kinds of little folk.

The mouse ran into a hole in the ground, and Saucepan fell off with a crash. He stood in front of the hole and clashed a kettle and saucepan together, frightening the cat, who stopped so suddenly that Connie shot over its head.

'Now, now, now!' said the roundabout man, panting along, looking very angry. 'Puss, have you forgotten this is the Land of Treats? I shall have to stop you coming alive if you don't behave!'

The cat looked very sorry. 'We shall have to give the mouse a real treat all for himself,' said the roundabout man. 'Go back to the roundabout, Puss. Come out, Mouse, and you will have a treat to make up for your fright.'

The mouse came out, its nose twitching. The roundabout man beckoned to an old woman who was selling sandwiches at a nearby stall.

'Four cheese sandwiches, please,' he said. There you are, Mouse, that's a lovely treat for you!'

The mouse squealed his thanks and took the sandwiches down the hole, in case the cat came back again. The roundabout man frowned at Saucepan.

'You should have known better than to take your mouse over to the cat,' he said. 'I always keep them on opposite sides of my roundabout in case they come alive. Don't do it again, please.'

'Let's come and have a ride in a balloon,' said Moon-Face, seeing that Saucepan looked rather miserable. 'Look! We get into that basket-thing there, and they let the balloon go, and it carries us up in the basket below it.'

So they all got into the basket, and the balloon rose into the air and took them with it. They had a wonderful view of everything.

And then somebody cut the rope! Connie gave a squeal as the balloon rose high, and floated right across the Land of Treats!

'The balloon's flying away! What shall we do?'

'Don't be silly!' said Moon-Face. 'This is all part of the treat. We come down near the boating pool, and choose a boat to go on the water.'

He was quite right. It was all part of the treat. The balloon floated on gently, and came down beside a big blue boating pool, where there were many exciting boats, all in the shape of birds or animals.

'Now, Saucepan, for goodness' sake don't choose that mouse-boat and take it near the cat-boat,' said Moon-Face.

'Come on, Saucepan! We'll share a boat together, then you can't get into trouble,' said Silky.

They hustled him into a boat shaped like a grey-and-white seagull. Joe got into a boat like a goldfish, which sometimes put its head under the water and opened and shut its mouth to breathe. The others all chose boats too, and Connie's was the best, a magnificent peacock! It spread its tail to make a sail, and everyone stared at it in admiration.

Silky's seagull-boat gave her and Saucepan a great surprise, because it suddenly rose into the air, spread its wings and flew around the pool. It came to rest with a little splash, and Silky got out hurriedly. Saucepan stayed in. He liked boats that flew. He was so pleased with the seagull-boat that he presented it with a large-sized saucepan when he did at last get out. The seagull thought it was a hat and put it on proudly.

'Now, what next?' said Joe, when they had all had enough of the boats. 'What about something to eat. There's an exciting place over there, where you can get anything you like, just by pressing a button. Let's try it, shall we?'

So they went to the curious little counter, where a

smiling pixie stood. There were buttons all over the counter, which could be pressed. As you pressed them, you said what you wanted, and it came out of a little trapdoor in the side of the counter.

'I'll have chicken, sausages, and salad,' said Joe, who felt hungry. Moon-Face pressed a button for him, while Joe watched the trapdoor. It opened, and out came a plate with chicken, sausage and salad on it. Joe took it and went to sit at a nearby table, which was set with knives, forks and spoons.

'What will *you* have, Silky?' asked Saucepan, who was longing to press a button.

'Pears and cream,' said Silky.

Saucepan pressed a button and spoke loudly. 'Bears and cream!'

Immediately, a plate shot out of the trapdoor with a little jug of cream – but there were no pears on the plate, instead there were small teddy bears, arranged in rings.

'Oh, Saucepan, I said *pears* not *bears*!' cried Silky, and she gave the plate back to the pixie behind the counter. She pressed a button herself, and a plate of juicy pears came out of the trap door. Silky joined Joe at his table.

'I'll have a big chocolate pudding,' said Moon-Face as he pressed a button, and out came the biggest chocolate pudding he had ever seen.

Saucepan pressed a button and got a cherry pie and cucumber sandwiches. He went off to a table by himself to eat them.

Everyone got what they wanted. In fact, they had more than they wanted, because it was such fun to press the buttons and get something else. The buttons were marvellous and they produced anything that anyone asked for. Even when Connie asked for a strawberry cake, stuffed with sausage meat, iced with chocolate, and topped with syrup, the button she pressed made exactly what she wanted come out of the trapdoor. Connie said it tasted really lovely.

They went over to the circus after that, and had an exciting time, especially when anyone who wanted to could have a ride on a horse. It was lovely to ride around the circus ring, on the back of a beautiful horse.

Then they went into a magician's room and sat down on the floor to watch him do magic tricks. He was the best conjurer anyone had ever seen.

'Ask me what you want, and I will do it!' he cried, after every trick, and then somebody or other would call out something very difficult. But, the magician always managed to do it.

'Make roses come in my kettle!' said Saucepan, and he held out one of his kettles.

'Easy!' said the magician, and tapped the kettle with his wand. Immediately the smell of roses came into the room. Saucepan took off the lid, and put in his hand. He pulled out lots of deep red velvety roses. He gave one to everyone to wear.

'Make me fly round the room!' cried Connie, who had always longed to fly. The magician tapped her shoulders, and two long blue wings shot out from them. Connie stood looking over her shoulder at them. Then she flapped them – and to her great joy, she flew into the air as easily as a butterfly, hovering here and there as light as a feather.

'Oh, oh! This is the greatest treat I've ever had!' she cried, and flew round once again. Then, as she came to the ground, the magician tapped her once again and the wings disappeared. Connie was disappointed. She had hoped she would be able to keep them. She wouldn't have minded going back home, if only she could have taken her wings with her.

The magician took a couple of goldfish out of Joe's ears. 'What a place to keep goldfish!' he said. 'You should keep them in an aquarium.'

'But . . . but,' began Joe in surprise.

The magician took an empty aquarium from the top of Silky's head, made Joe lean over sideways, and filled the aquarium with water that seemed to come out of Joe's ear. He gave the goldfish to Joe.

'Now don't you keep those goldfish in your ears any more,' he said. 'You keep them in that!'

Everyone laughed at Joe's astonished face.

'I'll take them home to Mother,' he said. 'She's always wanted goldfish.'

Just then a bell rang loudly. 'Oh, what a pity! It's time to go,' said Moon-Face, getting up. 'They turn you out of the Land of Treats every evening, you know. No one is allowed to stay here for the night. It's too magic. Come on, we must go!'

Rather sadly they went to the hole in the cloud, with a crowd of other visitors. They went down to Moon-Face's, and there Connie said goodbye.

'I'm going home tomorrow,' she said, 'but I *have* had a wonderful time, I really have. Goodbye, Moon-Face, and thank you for rescuing me from the ladder-that-has-no-top. Goodbye, Watzisname, I hope you remember your real name some time. Goodbye, dear Silky; it has been lovely to know you. Goodbye, Saucepan! I'm sorry you thought I was a nasty little girl.'

Saucepan actually heard what she said. 'Oh, you're much nicer now,' he said, 'much, much nicer. Come back again. You may get nicer still then!'

'Goodbye everyone in the Faraway Tree!' said Connie.

They all went down the Tree. Connie said goodbye to the little red squirrel. 'You're the best little squirrel I ever knew! Goodbye!' she said.

They went through the Enchanted Wood, and the trees whispered to Connie. 'Wisha, wisha, wisha!'

'They're wishing me goodbye,' said Connie. 'Oh Joe, Beth, Frannie, how lucky you are to live near the Enchanted Wood, and to be able to go up the Faraway Tree whenever you like. I wish I did too!'

So do I, don't you.

THE END